DEAD UNION

OTHER BOOKS BY ANTHONY GIANGREGORIO

THE DEAD WATER SERIES

DEADWATER
DEADWATER: Expanded Edition
DEADRAIN
DEADCITY
DEADWAVE
DEAD HARVEST
DEAD UNION
DEAD VALLEY

ALSO BY THE AUTHOR

DEAD RECKONING: DAWNING OF THE DEAD
THE MONSTER UNDER THE BED
DEAD END: A ZOMBIE NOVEL
DEAD TALES: SHORT STORIES TO DIE FOR
DEAD MOURNING: A ZOMBIE HORROR STORY
ROAD KILL: A ZOMBIE TALE
DEADFREEZE
DEADFALL
DEADRAGE
SOUL-EATER
THE DARK
RISE OF THE DEAD
DARK PLACES

DEAD UNION

Anthony Giangregorio

DEAD UNION

ISBN   Softcover   ISBN 13: 978-1-935458-13-5
                          ISBN 10: 1-935458-13-2

www.livingdeadpress.com

ACKNOWLEDGMENTS

Thank you to my wife, Jody, and my son, Joseph, for their contribution to this work.
Without their tireless efforts to help and support me, none of these stories may have ever come to fruition.

AUTHOR'S NOTE

This book was self-edited, and though I tried my absolute best to correct all grammar mistakes; there may be a few here and there. Please accept my sincerest apology for any errors you may find.

This is the second edition of this book.

Visit my web site at undeadpress.com

WHAT HAS COME BEFORE

ONE YEAR AGO, a deadly bacterial outbreak escaped a lab to infect the lower atmosphere across America, unleashing an undead plague on the world.

With rain clouds now filled with a killer virus, to venture outside in the rain was tantamount to suicide.

To get caught in the rain and exposed to the bacteria would be an instant death. But that wasn't the end. Once dead, the host body would rise again, becoming an undead ghoul, wanting nothing more than to feed on the flesh of the living.

The United States was torn asunder, civilization collapsing like a house of cards in weeks.

But mankind survived, eking out a dreary existence, always keeping one eye on the sky for the next rainstorm.

Only one year after the zombie apocalypse, the world has become a very different place from what it once was. Gone are cell phones, the internet, restaurants and shopping malls; now all lost relics of a culture slowly fading into history.

In this new world, the dead walk and a man follows the rules of the gun, where the strong are always right and the weak are usually dead. Major cities are nothing but blackened husks, nothing but giant tombs filled with walking corpses. Across America, though, smaller towns have become small municipalities with makeshift walls protecting them from both live and dead attackers. Strangers are not welcome and are either shot on sight or made to move on, that is, if they are not exploited by the rulers of the towns.

Through the destruction of what once was walks a man, crushing death beneath his steel-tipped boots. Before he was an ordinary man, living a quiet life with a wife and a career, but the rules have changed and so to, has he adapted, becoming a warrior of death who wields a gun with an iron hand, but shows mercy and wisdom when it is needed.

His name is Henry Watson, and with his fellow companions, Mary, Jimmy and Cindy, by his side, he travels across a blighted landscape searching for someplace where the undead haven't corrupted every-hing they touch, and where he can lay his head down in safety.

Though life is fleeting, each breath means the possibility of life, and a better future for all.

PROLOGUE

TERRANCE JORGENSEN WALKED the perimeter wall surrounding the small town of Cumberland, Kentucky, just three miles north of Lake Cumberland. He was scratching his bright red hair and rubbing the freckles on his face as he enjoyed the bright sunshine of the day. Some folks called him Rusty for his bright red hair, but he tried not to answer to it, not liking the name one bit.

The wall surrounding the town consisted of nothing more than bags of dirt piled six feet high, some sand mixed in wherever it was needed.

Wooden planks had been laid out on the rim of the dirt wall so men could walk it easily when on watch.

It didn't happen too often, but every now and then one of the men would lose his balance and fall over to the grass below on the opposite side of the barricade.

Usually, the man would just climb back up, only his pride hurt, but once every so often, a man would fall into a crowd of zombies milling below and be torn to pieces.

There weren't as many of the dead folks around as a year and a half ago when the outbreak first began, but as the town of Cumberland was only ten miles or so from the Frankfort city line, there were still plenty of fresh dead ones to keep the guards of the town occupied.

Terrance looked up at the bright yellow orb overhead; squinting his eyes while he wiped sweat from his brow. His shift was almost over and he was looking forward to a good meal and some fun in the sack with his girlfriend, Wendy. He grinned as images of her tight ass and pert breasts fluttered across his mind, causing him to become hornier, if that was humanly possible.

Suddenly he didn't feel that tired as he thought about the pleasure that was only a few hours away.

The sound of multiple engines filled the air and he looked up and down the two lane highway that led away from town. Where the highway crossed the dirt wall, there was a chain link gate. The main posts for the gate had been sunk deep into the pavement, then filled in with cement. The fence allowed the men of the town to come and go easily when they left on raids on the surrounding countryside for food. It was becoming harder and harder to find supplies and the town had taken to growing their own, knowing if they didn't, they would end up starving come winter.

Still, supplies from the surrounding towns and cities were very much needed to make up for what couldn't be grown.

Terrance gazed down the empty highway and watched as what looked like a convoy of four vehicles approached. Without hesitation, he sent out an alarm over the two-way radio, informing everyone inside the perimeter wall they were about to have guests.

This was the first time the guests appeared to be alive.

Since the fall of humanity, only a few sporadic vehicles had arrived seeking shelter from the zombie scourge. Sometimes the town elders would let the refugees in, other times they were sent away with a threat of being shot.

Terrance wondered what would happen this time as the first vehicle in the convoy began to grow closer. Heat lines obscured the convoy from view until the trucks were no more than a half mile away. Terrance let out a gasp when he saw they were definitely military vehicles.

Each truck was covered in gray and green camouflage, the canvas over the truck beds flapping in the hot wind as they made their way across the empty highway.

Terrance turned at the sound of footsteps and a few cars pulled up along the inside of the wall. Men jumped out, all armed with an assortment of weapons to run towards Terrance.

"What you got? More dead ones?" A man asked. He was bald and carried a sub-machine gun and his face was brutally serious.

Terrance shook his head, no. "Got four vehicles headed our way. Look military, too."

"Do ya think it's the Army? Maybe the government finally got their act together and are here to help," another man said while he climbed onto the wall. He held a pump-action shotgun in his hand and a sidearm rode his left hip.

Terrance shrugged, wiping sweat from his brow. Damn, if it wasn't a hot one today.

"Don't know, but I figured I should get you guys over here. Does the mayor know?"

The bald man with the sub-gun nodded. "Yeah, he's being informed as we speak."

The convoy was only a thousand feet away and the change in pitch of the engines signaled they were beginning to slow down.

"Maybe they came from Fort Knox. I heard there were people there," a man said, climbing onto the hood of an old Honda to look over the wall.

"That's over fifty miles from here. I doubt they're from there," Terrance spit, watching the convoy move ever closer. Damn, now he wouldn't be getting off in time to see Wendy. It figured. Something always happened when he was on watch. Still, maybe these trucks carried men and women who were here to help them.

Many a discussion had been had over a drink of homebrew about whether the government would ever get back on its feet.

Since the zombie outbreak more than a year ago, civilization had collapsed, sending America into a downward spiral. Now America was similar to the Old West, where each town was a law unto itself, and once outside the walls of a town, only the law of the gun ruled the land.

Some hadn't been able to handle the change and were either dead or worse, had become food for the ghouls and then become the walking dead themselves. In some parts of the country, rumors of gangs of humans becoming cannibals had become the new stories, replacing the old tales of boogiemen. It was said when the supply lines had collapsed and food wasn't shipped to cities and states, those that couldn't find food had to resort to whatever they could to survive. It was said there were now large gangs of humans who fed solely on other humans.

As far as Terrance was concerned, it was all bullshit. Merely stories to make people scared in the wee hours of the night. As if the walking dead wasn't enough of a horror to keep people up at night.

It was amazing what people could become accustomed to if they were exposed to it long enough.

After more than a year, the dead, shambling corpses were almost nothing but a nuisance. As long as they didn't surround the town in large numbers, it was easy to dispose and burn them. He knew some towns weren't so lucky, but he also knew that his people had to take care of themselves; the rest of the world was on its own.

Terrance looked up from his thoughts when the first truck in line applied its brakes, and with a squealing of metal pads on metal drums, slowed to a halt in front of the chain-link gate. Next to Terrance, the five other men stood strong, their weapons ready as they watched the trucks impassively.

A few zombies which had been milling about the gate moved towards the trucks, but were quickly dispatched with shots to the head by the soldiers as the men climbed out from the rear of the vehicles. Terrance swallowed hard when he lost count of the soldiers spilling onto the highway. More than twenty-five men, all carrying what looked like brand new M-16A's, climbed onto the road, weapons ready; their faces hard and stern. Some of the soldiers looked young. Really young, like fifteen or sixteen years old. But Terrance assumed after all the men that had been lost fighting the walking dead, the reserves were dry and the statute of age had dropped for enlistment.

Hey, children as young as eleven knew how to shoot a weapon over in Iraq and other Middle Eastern countries, so why not here in America? Or what was left of America.

Next to him, the men of Cumberland stood quietly, watching the tableau fold out in front of them. No one knew what to make of the convoy, but already hope was brewing inside chests. They had to be here to help, after all, why else would they have come?

A soldier ran over to the first truck and called up to the driver, informing the occupant that all the zombies had been taken down in the general vicinity and that it was safe to disembark the vehicle. The passenger door of the first truck opened and a man climbed out, dropping to the ground with ease.

Terrance knew immediately that this man was in charge. First, the other soldiers saluted him and moved to the side as he crossed the highway on his way to the chain-link gate. The second was the stars on his khaki shirt collar that reflected the sun like tiny spotlights. The man wore two large side arms on his hips, and though Terrance wasn't sure, he believed they were .357 Colt Magnum Pythons. A modest, six and a quarter inch polished SOG Desert Dagger rode his left hip. The weapon was made of 440A stainless steel and had a double-edged blade with a blood gutter and a steel pommel with kraton grips.

The man was average height and build, with dark brown hair under his military cap, but he walked like he was six feet tall. He carried himself like a man who was used to being obeyed and for that not to happen was unthinkable. His face was grim, and there were no laugh lines near his clean-shaven mouth to even suggest he ever laughed or smiled. His military boots were shined a glossed black that caught the reflection of the sun like a mirror. His uniform was impeccable, the jib line perfectly straight and every crease ironed to razor sharpness.

With two soldiers at his back, as escort, the man crossed the highway on his way to the gate and the guards standing watch.

A zombie appeared from the side, it had once been male and its face was almost gone from rot and decay, only shallow holes where the eyes and mouth were even told the story of a pre-existing face. Before the soldiers could shoot it, the man with the stars drew one of his side arms and shot the zombie in the head. The brains of the ghoul exploded backwards, riding on a piece of scalp. The putrid corpse dropped to the road and remained still, the brains spread out on the highway like road kill. The man holstered his weapon and continued strolling towards the gate as if nothing had transpired. A few of the guards on the wall began to murmur to one another, impressed with the man's calmness.

The man stopped when he was in front of the gate, and raised a hand to his forehead to shield the sun from his eyes as he looked up at Terrance and the others.

"Good afternoon, gentlemen. My name is Colonel George T. Miller and I've come to liberate your town from the zombie epidemic. Those of you that are fit to work and fight will become a part of my army. My goal is to take back America from the dead bastards that now infest the earth and rebuild this land of ours better than it was before. In fact, with the rebirth of America, I felt it deserved a new name so I want to welcome you all into the United Unions of America or the U.U.S. In this new union I'm forming, we will become strong again and will take back what is ours." He lowered his hand and gazed up into the eyes of Terrance and the others. "So, what do you say? Are you with me?"

The bald man with the sub-gun spit onto the highway and looked at his brothers, then back down at the colonel.

"Is this some kind of joke? Aren't you here to help us? I mean, you're the army for Christ sakes. We've been waiting for you to arrive for more than a year, and when you do finally show up, you're spitting bullshit about taking back America from the dead ones? And changing the name to boot? I don't know about anyone else here, but if that's what you're sellin', then we ain't buyin'. Am I right men?"

A murmur of agreement carried through the other men and Terrance nodded with them. He knew the mayor would need to be informed about what was happening, but he also knew the old man would never go for whatever this colonel was spouting.

The colonel shook his head and turned back to his soldiers. All twenty-five men were lined up, rifles held at ease as they watched their colonel and the surrounding area. Other men were on the rear side of the convoy, watching for ghouls in that direction.

"That's a damn shame, gentlemen, it really is. I was hoping to do this the easy way. But if you're minds are made up..." Colonel Miller said.

"They are," Terrance said and checked the other men's faces to make sure. All eyes told him they were in agreement. This man was crazy.

"Okay, Colonel, we gave you you're answer, so if that's all you came for then why don't you just turn around and move on," Baldie said, raising his weapon in a threatening gesture.

Terrance didn't like what Baldie was doing. There was three times the amount of soldiers on the highway than there were guards for the town, and though Terrance and the others had the high ground, they were still woefully outnumbered.

But his warning seemed to work, because the colonel turned around and began walking back to the convoy.

"Okay, gentlemen, you can't say I didn't try," Colonel Miller added while he strolled away.

"Whatever, just get the fuck out of here and don't come back. We need help. We need food and supplies. Not some bullshit about taking back America." Baldie tossed these last words to the back of the colonel, but the man didn't seem to mind. Terrance didn't like it at all. If the man was leaving so easily, then why did he bring so many soldiers with him?

Colonel Miller climbed back into the cab of his truck and Terrance saw him speaking into a two-way, hand radio.

It all seemed to be too easy to turn the convoy away, Terrance thought as he heard truck engines surge to life and begin to turn around on the two-lane road; the soldiers waiting to climb back aboard. The right side of the trucks were now facing the chain-link gate and wall of the town, and it was at that precise instant that Terrance realized it had been too easy and that things were about to become downright hard.

The trucks lined up on the road so that the two vehicles in back of the others had enough space to see the wall and gate.

The canvas on the sides of the trucks was pulled up and all the men on the dirt wall of the town came face to face with four .50 caliber machine guns.

"Oh, shit, it's an ambush!" Baldie screamed as he fired his sub-gun at the trucks and soldiers who were seeking cover near the vehicles.

The machine guns began to bark, sending steel-jacketed rounds into the dirt wall. But once the gunners got their range, the bullets began creeping up until the guards on the wall were shot into chunks of steaming flesh and bloody clothing.

Terrance was saved by a barrage of metal death by an act of fate or dumb luck. Just as he was about to fire his weapon, his foot slipped and he tumbled over the wall and onto the road. He tucked his head under his arm and hit the road with a jarring slam that had him seeing stars. Above him, his friends and fellow guards were shredded like hamburger meat, their lifeless bodies falling inside the wall to remain still.

Terrance lay perfectly still on the road. He was about fifteen feet to the right of the gate and he was all but ignored by the soldiers. From their vantage point, he was just another corpse lying under the sun.

Colonel Miller spoke into his radio and the first truck in the convoy swung forward, and then without preamble, drove into the gate and onto the road that would lead to the town. The gate was smashed open, the sides swinging wide to bounce off the support poles. Only the chain securing it had been damaged and the gate was still useable, not that the colonel cared. His vehicle continued through the portal and continued on towards the town.

He was followed by two other trucks, and the last one in line pulled up and parked so that the vehicle was now blocking the gate. By doing this, the soldiers who now clambered around its tires could prevent either entry or exit from the exposed egress.

The convoy of three trucks continued on and did not stop until the first vehicle had pulled into the middle of the town. It was a quaint street, with small storefronts and well dressed townspeople who now stared in awe at the convoy of three military trucks that had come out of nowhere into their midst. Children hugged their mothers in fright and fathers stood with hands clenched, wondering what was going on. Those that had weapons held them warily, not knowing what to do yet.

When the last truck had turned off its engine and more than twenty armed soldiers climbed out and surrounded the street on both sides, Colonel Miller climbed down from the cab once again.

"Where's the leader of this town? I want him here in five minutes or there's going to be hell to pay!" He called out, pulling a cigar from his shirt pocket. In a casual movement, he lit it with a gold-plated lighter, then puffed a small gray cloud of smoke into the air.

He didn't have long to wait. Less than three minutes had passed since he lit his cigar and a small man no more than five-five waddled over to him. The man was in his sixties and he was vastly overweight. His jowls seemed to have a life of their own as he moved up next to the colonel. Despite his weight and age, his eyes had a kindness to them that bespoke of a man who had led his people fairly.

"Hello, hello, I am the leader of this town. Welcome and may I ask what is the meaning of this? I must say it's a pleasure to see a man in uniform again. I haven't heard from my men on watch at the main gate, I hope there were no problems."

Colonel Miller smiled and glanced at some of his men. "Nothing that couldn't be handled, Mr...?"

"Mayor Lansdale, sir, and who might you be?"

"My name is Colonel George T. Miller and I've come here to liberate your town from the zombie infestation. I need you to gather all the residents and have them in front of me in a half hour or you won't like what happens next."

The Mayor took a step backwards at the hard face Miller gave him. The Mayor gazed at the .50 cals and the soldiers with their rifles and realized he really didn't have much of a pedestal to argue over the request, so he waved a man over to him.

"Yes, Mayor?"

"Spread the word. You have a half hour to get everyone over here. And hurry," he whispered the last part.

The man nodded and began moving off, pausing at other people to solicit their help. In seconds people were running off in all directions, calling out to get the attention of others. Not that they needed to. Like wildfire, the news was spreading there were soldiers inside the town's perimeter on Main Street.

To the minute, a half hour later, the entire town was gathered ten deep on Main Street. Old and young, men and women were all gathered to hear what the colonel had to say.

Colonel Miller climbed onto the hood of the first truck and gazed down on the townspeople below him. He took out another cigar, lit it, and blew a smoke cloud into the air, then opened his arms wide like a preacher welcoming his flock to service.

"My friends, I have come here to liberate you from the zombie scourge and to give you the opportunity to join me in rebuilding America. With your help, every man, woman and child that is able to work and fight will come back with me to my base at Fort Knox, and once there, will help to rebuild this great country of ours. Only together can we overcome the walking dead and take back what we lost more than a year ago." He studied the faces of many of the people before he spoke again. "So, what do you say? Are you with me?"

There was a murmur of dissent in the crowd, epitaphs were yelled and a general sense of negativity and dissent ran through the people. Colonel Miller smiled. He had expected this. It had happened before in the other towns he had liberated in the past months.

Finally, the Mayor moved up to the cab and waved his hands in the air. Near him, other men began shouting, trying to quell the residents. It took almost five minutes, but eventually everyone became silent so the Mayor could speak.

"Colonel Miller, what you ask is not possible," the Mayor said while looking up at the colonel. "As you can see, we're fine here. We're safe. We've built a wall around our town and have managed to survive and will continue to survive. If you aren't here to help us, then I must kindly ask you to leave us in peace."

Colonel Miller lowered a hand for the Mayor to take. "Mayor, will you come up here with me for a moment?"

"Why I hardly see the reason…"

"Please, Mayor, humor me before I leave."

The Mayor decided what would be the harm and let the colonel help him onto the hood of the truck. He was unsteady on his feet and felt dizzy as he stared down at the residents of his town.

"So, I can't change your mind? Are you sure that is your final decision?" Miller asked with a slight scowl as he gazed down at the townspeople below.

Mayor Lansdale nodded and gazed down at the upturned eyes of his people.

"Yes, Colonel, my decision is final, and as you can see, my people all agree with me." Heads nodded below, joining in their leader's decision.

"Very well, you made your decision." Without hesitation, Colonel Miller drew his right Colt Magnum from its holster, and before the mayor could so much as blink, Miller shot him point-blank in the chest.

The old man's back exploded outward and the crowd immediately below him became baptized with his blood and gore. The Mayor's eyes seemed to go wide and his face took on a look of wonder as he tumbled off the hood of the truck to fall to the ground; dead before he landed on the warm asphalt.

That was the cue for every soldier to go into action.

Before the Mayor's body settled on the ground, soldiers were moving into the crowd while two .50 cals sprayed round after round over the townspeople's heads. Storefronts were destroyed, glass shattering as the barrage of death chewed into buildings. A few unlucky people were caught in the blasts, and they were promptly torn to pieces.

The crowd began to scream, a few trying to bring up weapons to retaliate, but before they could so much as get off a shot, they were stopped in their tracks by the barrels of M-16's aimed at their chests.

Weapons were gathered from the angry townspeople and soon the entire town was being herded back to the main gate where troop loaders had arrived, their engines ticking softly under the warm sun.

One at a time, the townspeople were loaded onto the vehicles, and when one was full, it was driven away, always under armed guard by sour-faced soldiers who watched the frightened men, women and children with eyes of ice.

Three men tried to make a run for it and were immediately gunned down, their bodies left where they fell. That helped to control the rest of the townspeople who realized there was no hope for escape at the present time.

Colonel Miller stood in the center of the turmoil, sending men, women and children to the trucks according to age and health. He would size each person up, his eyes creasing as he studied their frames, their faces, and then with a nod, he would send them to the left or right. If they went to the right, stone-faced soldiers waited to lead the able-bodied conscripts toward the waiting trucks and if sent to the left side, they were lined up against the brick face of a building, its use in the past irrelevant.

Any child under seven was sent to the left side, as were all men and women over seventy and the sick and ill. Miller had found after seventy years of age, there simply wasn't enough energy left in the bodies to perform the tasks needed.

When the entire town was loaded into the trucks and the last one had pulled out of the gate, he studied the faces of the men, women and children still left before him. Small, doe-eyed faces of the children, all with tears in their eyes, gazed up at him, watching. The old had more defiant faces and held onto the children, despite the fact some didn't know who the child they held was.

"All you people have been deemed too old or too young to help in the rebuilding of our great country. While it saddens me to leave you here, I simply cannot take anyone who is not fit enough to take care of themselves and do what is needed. I only have so many resources to feed and clothe you so I can only take the fittest. Unfortunately, I can't just leave you here alone. It wouldn't be long before the undead arrived and turned you into one of them. Once that happens, you will all add to the undead scourge and that I cannot allow. The same goes for your town. If it stays standing, then the undead will fill its buildings. Crawl into its dark places and attics and holes and will only wait until an unwary soldier walks by. So like in any good war, I have to destroy my back trail so the insurgents cannot take up residence behind me."

"So what does that mean for us? Why can't you just leave us in peace? You've taken everyone else, at least let the children go, for God's sake," an old man pleaded. He was on crutches and could hardly walk, which was why he hadn't been taken with the others.

"God? There is no God, old man. Now there is only me." He snapped his fingers and a soldier ran up to him with a freshly loaded M-16. The colonel would never ask one of his men to do what he was about to do. He felt if he wasn't man enough to do it, then no one else should have to, and though it left a foul taste in his mouth, he did what he had to do to rebuild the country he loved so much.

Screams went up in the crowd and men and women both fell to their knees in terror, some begging for their lives. Children began crying anew and the old man who had spoken before took a step forward.

"I was but a small child when Hitler took me and my parents and placed us in a concentration camp. I lived through that and told the tale countless times. What you are doing now is nothing more than a replay of what Hitler did to millions of Jews. How can you live with yourself? You're a monster."

Colonel Miller nodded slightly, his eyes locked with the old man. On both sides of him, his soldiers guarded the prisoners, threatening to shoot any who tried to run.

"Perhaps you're right, sir, but what I do now, I do for America. I take no pleasure in this, but it has to be this way. All of you are simply too weak to do what needs to be done and so you are useless to me. Better this than a bite by a walking corpse.

The old man stood taller, balancing on his crutches.

"At least a zombie knows not what it does. It's an animal, a force of nature. You, Colonel, are a devil in human form and I will be waiting for you in Hell because sooner or later that is where you'll end up."

Colonel Miller blinked. This was the first time he had let one of the condemned talk for so long. Usually, he would just kill them and be done with it, but this man, he had courage, despite his coming death.

"I salute you, sir, you are a man of courage and I tell you what. When you get to hell, wait for me. I believe you. I'll be going there someday. But not before I take my country and bring it back to its greatness once again. You see, sir, I am on a mission, and on this mission, distasteful things will be done, but in the end it will be worth it. You do not give up your life in vain. It's for a greater cause."

"The ends justify the means?" The old man spit. "You are truly full of shit, Colonel, and you are mad to boot."

Colonel Miller decided he was done debating his reasons for what he was doing with this old fool and before the old man could say another word, he opened fire, spraying the crowd of old, young and sick. The bullets ripped into bodies, blood spraying in all directions. Heads were blown apart, organs were destroyed and in less than a minute, every person was dead.

Miller turned to the closest soldier near him.

"Private, make sure there are no survivors. We don't need them getting bit and coming back later as one of the undead," Miller ordered. "Sergeant, front and center!"

A soldier ran up and saluted.

"Colonel, yes, sir."

"Set the town aflame. I want it razed before we leave."

"Yes, sir," the sergeant said and moved off to get the napalm out of the nearest truck. He gathered six soldiers to him, and after a jeep pulled up, they climbed into it and the vehicle drove off into the town.

That was another of his protocols. Once he'd liberated a town, he made sure to burn it to the ground, and by doing so, would make sure the undead could not take up residence in the abandoned buildings later. With the help of the incendiaries, the entire town would be nothing but a blazing fireball in less than an hour.

The sounds of rifles firing caused him to look back at the slaughtered townspeople. Two of his men were finishing up, shooting any survivors. It was distasteful business, especially the children, but in this new world there was no room for mercy.

If he wanted to rebuild America, he had to be hard. He needed to do what had to be done and he would let history sort out what was right or wrong.

In his heart, he knew he was doing the right thing.

With the fires set, his men loaded up into the last of the trucks and vehicles and pulled out of the town of Cumberland. The buildings were already ablaze, the wind fanning the flames so that by morning, the town would be nothing but a smoking crater.

When the last truck passed through the gate and was lost in the distance, Terrance Jorgenson pulled himself to his feet on shaky legs and walked back to the perimeter of his town. For the moment there were no zombies in the area. Miller's soldiers had seen to that. Terrance had heard the gunshots but had stayed still, knowing if he moved, the soldiers would have seen him and he would have been shot or captured. So he'd lain in the hot sun for hours, waiting for the soldiers on guard at the gate and Miller to leave.

As he stumbled through the gate, he saw the pile of bodies off to the right, and when he made his way there, he was numbed with shock at the carnage that greeted him.

Young and old alike had been slaughtered like animals. Blood covered the ground, an inch thick in places and already flies were everywhere. Off in the distance, the fires were growing and Terrance could see the town was lost.

Wearily, with tears in his eyes, he turned and began walking out of the gate which hung wide open.

He was in shock, the sight of seeing family and friends now dead and rotting in the sun threatening to drive him mad. But he didn't go crazy, because underneath the horror and sorrow was something else.

Anger and hatred.

Hatred for the man who had come into his peaceful town and kidnapped most and slaughtered the rest.

With the smoke billowing into the sky behind him, Terrance walked down the lonely highway.

Colonel Miller had said something about Fort Knox. That was where the man was holed up. And if that was where he was, then that was where Terrance would be going.

He didn't know how he would do it, but he was going to find Colonel Miller and kill him.

Or die trying.

CHAPTER ONE

HENRY WATSON SQUINTED through the PV-4 scope of his Steyr SSG-70 sniper rifle, waiting for the exact moment to squeeze the trigger and end the life of the deer grazing in the meadow a hundred and fifty feet away. The 44.5 inches of rifle weighed easily in his hands, the walnut stock smooth near his chin.

The deer was standing motionless, quietly chewing the Kentucky bluegrass that grew untamed below its hooves. The glade once belonged to a ranch, and by the half dozen corrals, it probably raised thoroughbreds.

Now it was nothing but scrub, the grass and trees growing so wild the shape of the corrals were barely noticeable. Off to the right, a quarter mile or so stood the main house that once resided over the ranch. Now it was nothing but a blackened shell with a few supports that had resisted the high temperature of the fire, and the stone foundation, which was already beginning to crumble as weeds grew between the mortar holding the bricks together.

Henry's belly growled again, letting him know how hungry he was. He grunted in answer, not wanting to take his eye away from the deer. It had been almost a full day since either he or his three friends had eaten and he was looking forward to enjoying some slow roasted venison.

Suddenly, a click and a snap sounded next to him. It was the sound of a soda can being opened. In the emptiness of the glade, the subtle sound carried across the land to the deer's sensitive ears.

Just before Henry could fire the rifle and send the deer to the afterlife, it pricked up its ears, looked around for danger, and jumped out of his gun sights, running into the overgrown brush behind it.

Henry fired anyway, the round missing the animal by inches. But an inch or a mile, a miss was a miss.

"Dammit, I missed," Henry spit as he took his eye away from the scope and turned to glare at the young man sitting next to him.

Jimmy Cooper held the warm can of soda an inch from his mouth, preparing to take a sip, and looked at Henry with an innocence that reminded the older man of the deer.

"Nice going, Henry, now we're gonna starve," Jimmy said with a disapproving tone.

Henry opened his mouth to speak, ready to yell at his friend, and to chastise him for cracking the soda, when another gunshot echoed across the glade.

Both men turned to look in the same direction and waited quietly, watching the area. Both were confident they knew where the gunshot came from, but only a fool assumed anything in the new world where the dead walked.

"Do you think that was...?" Jimmy asked but wasn't able to finish.

"You better hope it was or so help me we'll be eating you for lunch," Henry snapped back at Jimmy as he stood up and moved towards the copse of trees lining the glade.

Oblivious to what was eating Henry, and just assuming he was upset that he'd missed the shot; Jimmy picked up his Remington pump action shotgun and followed his friend.

If another person had been watching the two men, they would have seen two hardened warriors who had eyes looking into every shadow they came upon.

After over a year of traveling across the United States, nicknamed the deadlands by many, the two had become warriors in their own right. They were now men who knew how to fight and would shoot a man dead if given cause; no questions asked or excuses given.

Henry was the older of the two, a man in his late forties with a hard, muscular body and graying hair. A year ago his hair had been mostly brown and he'd been out of shape, but after a hard year of survival traveling the deadlands, his body had become strong, hard and unforgiving. Much like the land he now traveled.

His arms were thick and muscular, and his jaw was square underneath the light beard he brandished with pride.

Whenever he had the chance, he would shave it off, but like now, on the road, there was no chance and so he embraced the wild look.

His beard was full of gray, as well, giving him an air of wisdom. All he needed to add to the picture of a wise, older man was a pair of glasses. His skin was tanned a deep brown from the sun, blending in easily with the green BDU's he wore.

On his right hip was a large, sixteen inch panga. The long blade was more like a machete than a blade and had saved his life more times than he could count. On his hip in a leather holster was a Police Glock 9mm. The seventeen round clip was half full and he only used the side arm when he had no choice until he could find more ammunition for it.

On his back was slung a Steyr SSG-70 sniper rifle. He had picked it up in a small town in Ohio a few weeks ago and after using the weapon countless times, he couldn't imagine living without it.

He now had the opportunity to take out a target long before it was close enough to become a threat, something he and his companions had been sorely lacking in for the past year and a half.

Behind him, moving at a good clip, Jimmy kept pace with him. Where Henry was an older, wiser man, Jimmy was in his early twenties, with a quick mouth and a quicker gun hand. Along with his Remington pump, Jimmy wore a .38 Smith and Wesson strapped to his hip and a small Bowie knife, used mostly for cleaning kills when hunting and cutting ropes and vines. But the blade had seen its fair share of blood, the tip anointed with many a dead man's fluids.

Jimmy was adorned in BDU's as well. After finding a stash of military gear near the Ohio, Kentucky border, all the companions had availed themselves of the new clothes, their old ones ripe and ready for the trash heap.

Jimmy was wiry, and skinny, but not weak. Under his skinny frame was nothing but muscle and the young man could hold his own in a fight. Over the past year, both he and Henry had sparred repeatedly, honing their skills in battle. While the undead threat was always around the next corner, usually it was other humans that were the most dangerous. With the fall of the government and local law enforcement, an opportunistic few had taken to carving out a piece of the American dream, not hesitating if a few or a hundred men and women needed to be crushed on their way to the top.

Jimmy's eyes were wide and intelligent as he studied the overgrown brush surrounding them. Every now and then he slowed and took a swig from the can of soda. It was the last one in his backpack and he'd be dammed if he would waste it.

Moving through the brush, Henry came out into an open glade where horses would once graze. Now the grass was three feet high and he had to move slowly through the waving stalks, not wanting to find a snake in its midst. The other threat was the possibility of a zombie hiding out in the tall grass. Many times the ghouls would lie in wait, patient for its food to come to them.

Henry moved across the glade, Jimmy at his back, and when both men were halfway through the grass, a woman called out from their left.

Both men swiveled at the same time, but when the long blonde hair of a twenty year old woman caught the sun, they both relaxed.

"Was that shot from you?" Henry called to the woman, though he was fairly confident it was.

She nodded, "Yup, got the bastard as he tried to run away. You missed, huh?"

Henry frowned deeply, but deigned to reply, and when Jimmy snickered he turned to glare at him.

"What, you have something you want to say?"

Jimmy shook his head no. "No, Henry, I'm good, better luck next time. Least my woman got it for you."

Henry growled in his throat, but decided not to take the bait Jimmy was dangling. Jimmy loved to tease Henry, using every opportunity to try and anger the man. It was all in fun, but sometimes Henry just wasn't in the mood.

Like now for instance.

The two men moved closer to the woman and Jimmy ran up beside her. Her name was Cindy Jansen and she had been traveling with Jimmy and Henry for more than a year. She was also Jimmy's girlfriend. The statuesque blond tossed her golden tresses over her shoulder and moved into Jimmy's waiting arms. They kissed briefly, not wanting to make a spectacle of themselves in front of Henry. Cindy was five foot seven and had a body that would make the average male drool. Her deep blue eyes flashed intelligence and her skin was flawless. An M-16 was slung over her shoulder and she was wearing matching BDU's. Even in the unflattering attire her shapely form peeked through. On her hip she wore a .32 caliber Ruger, its dull grip made for easy handling even in wet weather. Unfortunately, Cindy wasn't that good with handguns. She liked rifles better.

Altogether, Jimmy could have done worse.

"Where's the kill?" Henry asked as he studied the terrain. Cindy pointed to a slight incline to the land off to the left.

"Over there. It went down on that hill somewhere," she told him while Jimmy kissed her cheek.

"Where's Mary?" Henry asked, looking around for the last of their party.

"I'm here," came a voice from behind him.

Henry turned to see another beautiful woman in her late twenties move up next to him. Her name was Mary Roberts. Her brown, shoulder length hair fluttered in the breeze and her eyes twinkled with amusement. On her hip she wore a .38 Police Special and on her belt was a small hunting knife. As were the others, she was also in the green attire of a soldier.

"So you missed, huh?" She asked jovially. "It's a good thing us women are around or we'd be going hungry tonight."

"Hey, now wait a minute. I would have had that deer if Jimmy could have held off on drinking a damn soda."

Jimmy's eyes went wide with innocence.

"Me? What did I do?"

"You cracked the damn soda can and scared away the deer, that's what," Henry snapped back, his anger returning at the remembrance of losing the kill.

"All right, now stop it, the both of you. It doesn't matter who got it. All that does matter is its down. Now shall we go fetch it or what?" Mary asked, taking a step into the tall grass towards the hill.

No sooner did she finish her statement than a rotten hand wrapped itself around her leg. She yelped in alarm, her eyes going down to see a putrid, bloated body trying to crawl up her leg. The ghoul's legs dangled behind it, useless, the limbs shattered in multiple places.

Henry, Jimmy and Cindy all stopped what they were doing and turned as one, seeing Mary standing in the tall grass. With the grass in the way, none of them could see her predicament.

"Mary, what's wrong?" Henry barked, searching for danger.

She didn't answer him, her eyes on the dead thing climbing up her leg. Her right hand moved towards her gun, her eyes never leaving the pale-white eyes of the ghoul. While her hand crept to her side arm, her eyes studied the pitiful creature below her. It had once been a man, she was sure of it, though with the skin peeling and melting in places it was hard to discern what the man might have once looked like. Even the color of its skin was up for grabs.

The mouth opened and closed, a pus-like ichor seeping out of the corners of its dried lips to fall to the grass below it. Mary held her breath and wrapped her hand around the butt of her gun. The ghoul was about to bite, its mouth opening wide to sink into her leg. In one fluid motion, Mary pulled the gun from its holster, flicked off the safety, and shot the ghoul in the forehead.

The sound of the gunshot echoed off the land, causing a few birds to take flight in nearby trees. The ghoul's head exploded, the rotting skull almost disappearing with the force of the round. The bluegrass below the head was splattered with gray matter and a dull maroon liquid that once must have been blood. The slaughtered corpse dropped to the grass, lifeless forever.

Mary swallowed hard, her gulp almost a tangible thing, and then the others were by her side, all with weapons drawn, scanning the surrounding ranch.

"Oh shit, will you look at that? And I thought snakes were the problem," Jimmy said as he stared at the dead humanoid on the grass.

"You all right?" Henry asked, placing a hand on Mary's shoulder. The woman was like a daughter to him and he would die for her if necessary. The feelings were mutual and the two were closer than most father and daughters could ever hope to be.

She nodded, breathing heavily. "Yeah, I'm fine. Just took me by surprise." She struggled to clear her face of worry. "Now what do you say we find that deer?"

Henry nodded, and with his three companions by his side, they moved off deeper into the grass, searching for the deer while the dead corpse lay rotting in the waving bluegrass. More fertilizer for the already lush vegetation.

An hour later the glade was filled with the rich aroma of cooking venison. The four companions were all sitting by the fire, watching the meat cook. They had set up on the top of the incline, only a few yards from where Cindy had shot the deer. Henry had reasoned that way, they didn't have to carry the dead animal far, and by being on the incline, they had a grand view of the surrounding terrain, and could keep watch for trouble, either living or undead.

The fire crackled softly, the meat from the venison causing it to hiss when a particularly juicy piece of fat slid from the carcass. Henry had cleaned the animal, and though he had killed more men than he could count over the past year, he still felt something as he gutted the innocent creature. But he needed to eat and there was no avoiding it.

If he had to kill an animal, at least it was for sustenance, not for fun like so many big game hunters of the past were fond of doing. He idly wondered where all those big, brave men were now.

Probably either dead or had ended up in the belly of an even more dangerous animal, man.

With Jimmy and the women watching the meat, he wandered a few yards away from the smoke and the campsite. His eyes scanned the austere countryside, on the lookout for anything amiss. The empty shell of the ranch house sat silent, a monument to the past. Ever since the rains fell and had changed the world into a walking tomb, he'd been moving, never staying in one place for too long. True, he had made some friends along the way, good people who were only trying to survive like himself, but he had also made enemies.

But as far as he knew, they were all under the ground or walking around as shambling corpses. Henry had learned early in his odyssey not to leave an enemy alive to come back and bite him in the ass later.

If someone was unfortunate enough to cross him, then he would send them to hell, postage paid.

Despite this mentality, Henry was still a merciful man. He would never kill another human if said person wasn't trying to hurt him. He was a kind man who hadn't forgotten what it was like to live in a civilized world.

It was a difficult balance to uphold, but so far he'd managed to tread that fine line and would continue to do so for as long as he was able.

He sighed heavily, his mind racing with thoughts of the past. He didn't think about the future that much anymore. Truth was, for all he knew; tomorrow would be his last day on earth. Instead he tried to focus on the past, as the past was the only solid landmark he had left to hold onto.

The world was a very different place than it was a little more than a year ago. When the dead began to walk it hadn't taken that long for civilization to crumble. He had always known civilization was a delicate balance. A house of cards just waiting for the right breeze to topple it. And that was what had happened.

He turned at the sound of footsteps behind him. His hand reached for his Glock, despite the fact he knew it was Mary. He could tell by the way her steps echoed in the glade. She was light on her feet, usually only her toes touching the ground.

"Hey," she said as she moved next to him and sat down.

"Hey," he replied, not really in a talking mood.

"The meat's almost ready. Jimmy says another five minutes or so."

He nodded curtly for an answer.

Mary sensed his hesitation to talk and began to get up, figuring she'd go back to the others.

"All right then. Just thought I'd tell you. I'll go now," she said brusquely.

Henry reached out like a snake attacking its prey and grabbed her gently by the left wrist.

"No, wait, Mary. I'm sorry. I was just thinking, that's all. I didn't mean to be antisocial. Sit down again, please."

She paused for a moment, weighing his words and did as he requested.

"Look, Henry, we don't have to talk if you don't want to. In fact, why don't we just sit here and enjoy the weather. It's beautiful out here isn't it?"

"Yeah, it is. It'll be dark in a few hours. What do you say we just make camp and stay here for the night? It looks about as safe as anywhere else."

She smiled. "Okay, sounds good. Maybe tomorrow we can check out the ranch house. Maybe there's still something salvageable in there."

"Hey, you guys want to eat or what?" Jimmy called from the fire. He had his Bowie knife out and he was cutting strips of meat off the carcass, the grease and fat sizzling in the fire like rain drops.

"What do you say, Henry? Want to eat?" Mary asked with a grin.

He let out a heavy breath and then climbed to his feet, pulling Mary up, as well.

"Yeah, let's eat. I could go for some fresh meat for a change."

"Even if you didn't kill it?"

He grinned broadly at her tender jab. "Yes, Mary, even if I didn't kill it."

The two friends walked hand in hand across the few yards until they'd joined the others. Cindy handed each of them a piece of venison and under the golden sun they enjoyed their meal.

Across the glade, behind the ranch house, a dirty, disheveled man lowered a pair of broken binoculars from his eyes. He was wearing a pair of blue jeans that were once blue, but were now black from dirt and blood. Next to him was another man. This man wore a beard filled with twigs and residue from past meals. He wore an old three piece suit, minus the tie, and the white shirt was now a multicolored assortment of dried blood and other unnamable fluids. None of the blood was his.

Both men's stomachs were growling and the odor of cooked venison didn't help any.

"What do you think, Simon?" The bearded man asked.

Simon held the binoculars in his left hand as he wiped his nose with the back of his right hand, the snot sticking to his hand like glue. He hawked up a large phlegm ball and spit it onto the dusty ground.

"I say we wait till dawn and then hit 'em hard and fast while they're all out cold. That's what."

"Did you see the women? They look pretty good," Beardface said.

Simon nodded. "Yeah, they are. When we kill the men I get the blonde. You and the others can have the other one."

Though the arrangement didn't seem fair, Beardface knew better then to argue. Simon was their leader and he'd killed two men to get there, both once part of the clan.

"Whatever, Simon, I don't care. As long as it's warm and wet, oh yeah, as long as it's warm."

Simon turned to stare at his partner. He saw the same madness reflected in his partner's eyes that was in his own. After months of surviving, always keeping on the move, running from every dead man and woman who tried to eat them, their sanity had snapped. In a court of law, both men would be considered legally insane. Unfortunately, there were no courts of law anymore. Both men had nothing but knives in which to make their attack. They had firearms once, but after running out of ammunition they had never been able to replenish their supplies.

Simon turned around and glanced at the two other men and one woman who traveled with him. They were all waiting quietly in the debris of the old ranch house. Simon had told them to stay quiet and to wait for him to recce the situation, and they all knew better then to argue with their leader. Like Beardface, they all knew their place.

Both of the men were weak, skinny specimens of human males and the woman looked like an anorexic victim on crack. She heard the men talking and was glad there would soon be two other women to join her. For the past three months she'd been servicing all four men by herself and her pussy was so raw it felt like she'd dragged a cheese grater through it. While she wasn't wishing to put the two women sitting across the glade in the same predicament as her, it wasn't her call to make, so she might as well enjoy the reprieve for a while.

The two men watching in front of her pulled their blades and waved them in the shadows of the ranch house as they watched the fire across the glade. Simon had seen the firearms the four companions carried and he was eager to get them for himself and his men. With those weapons in his possession, he would no longer have to skulk around like a dog. If a ghoul came his way he could simply blast it to pieces without risk of being bitten.

A scattered thought crossed his mind that with only blades to attack the unknowing people he was foolish, and in fact could be committing suicide for himself and his small group.

He shook the notion away as foolish. The two men and two women had no way of knowing danger was so close to them. They didn't know Simon was coming to kill them and would be easy prey for his team's blades. All they had to do was wait for nightfall and attack once the companions were asleep.

Then the fun could begin.

CHAPTER TWO

DARKNESS FELL QUICKLY across the land, and before any of the companions realized what time it was, it was time to bed down for the night.

Cindy volunteered to take the first watch, followed by Mary, Henry and then Jimmy. With one last glance around the shadow enshrouded glade, Henry stretched out by the fire and closed his eyes. Mary was nearby, rolled up in a sleeping bag, and Jimmy and Cindy sat together just outside the glare of the fire.

Henry knew why the young couple was there. It was so Cindy wouldn't hamper her night vision being too close to the fire.

Whenever the companions were outside in the elements, exposed to whatever dangers may be nearby, they would always have one of their own on watch.

"Now don't you stay up too late, Jimmy, we've got a long day in front of us and we all need to be sharp as possible," Henry told the young warrior.

Jimmy waved the comment away. "Don't you worry about me, old man. We're not all a hundred years old, you know. Some of us can stay up past eight and still function the next day."

Mary chuckled at Jimmy's jibe and Henry frowned. Ever since they'd met it had been a running joke that Jimmy thought Henry was old. Henry couldn't wait for Jimmy to reach his forties so he could see how full of shit he'd been all the years he'd teased Henry. He could only hope the young man would live that long, and in the new America, a man's lifespan was sometimes measured in minutes, not years.

"Yeah, yeah, you keep flappin' your mouth, but remember what I said. You've got the last watch so you'll be getting the rest of us up."

"I'll do it, old man, you just get your beauty rest and let us youngin's have some fun," Jimmy retorted, not one to back down and always wanting the last word.

With his belly full of venison, Henry decided he wasn't up to the usual banter, so with a flip of his middle finger towards Jimmy, he rolled over and closed his eyes. His Glock was by his head, ready if he needed it.

Jimmy grinned from ear to ear as he curled up next to Cindy on a two foot wide boulder.

"Why do you always tease him like that?" She asked.

Jimmy shrugged. "He loves it, I know he does. Makes him feel young. That's why he hangs out with us."

Cindy shook her head as she turned her body to study the tree line a few hundred feet away. Off to her left was the ranch house, its skeletal timbers only barely perceived in the falling darkness. A wolf howled from somewhere to the east and she flicked her eyes in that direction.

It was dangerous to be out in the open like they were, but as far as they could tell, the undead population was low, as there were few homesteads nearby. As long as one of them stood watch, they should be fine for the night.

Jimmy reached a hand around her waist and cupped her left breast, kneading the soft flesh beneath her shirt. She wore a jacket as well, but the heat of the day was still trapped in the ground and so it was barely needed.

The zipper was open and her firm breasts were easy access for a determined Jimmy.

She slapped his hand like a mousetrap, Jimmy pulling it back like a wounded cat going for a fish in an aquarium.

"Quit it, will you? I'm on watch. I don't have time for that right now."

"But I'm horny," Jimmy said softly, nuzzling her throat.

"Will you stop it, please? How can you even think of sex while we're out here. We could be fooling around and a deader could come right up and bite you in the ass while we're screwing. How would that feel?"

Jimmy gave her question a moment's thought.

"Well, I don't know. Would the deader be a man or a woman? I mean, if it was a woman and she wasn't too rotted, well then maybe I could see…"

Cindy's mouth fell open as she studied her boyfriend.

"Jimmy Cooper, you are one sick man, do you know that?"

He grinned again, his teeth flashing in the darkness. "I know that. And I thought that's why you fell in love with me."

She pushed him off the boulder and he tumbled to the grass.

"Why don't you just go back to the fire and play with yourself. Better yet, why don't you find that deader and have fun with her!" She spun around then, arms crossed, ignoring him.

"Hey, Cindy, baby, come on, I was only joking. You know I'd never do it with one of them."

She sniffed and turned her head away farther.

With a sigh Jimmy climbed to his feet. He leaned over and kissed her on top of the head, smelling the odor of the trees and grass in her hair from when they'd made love that morning in the bushes a few yards from where they'd made camp. Henry and Mary had been polite enough to go for a walk for ten minutes and give them some privacy.

"Fine, I'm going. I'm sorry if I got you mad. I'll see you in the morning." He walked away from her and plopped down by the fire. Mary was stretched out, her head on her arms and she opened her eyes when he settled next to her.

"Didn't go so well, ay' Romeo?"

"Why, you heard us?"

She nodded, her face looking like it was moving sideways with her head horizontal on her arms.

"'Fraid so. Sound travels out here and you weren't that far away. Don't give up, there's always tomorrow."

Jimmy grunted. "Yeah, I suppose so, but still…"

Mary reached out and touched his arm.

"Jimmy, you should know how we women are by now. Haven't you learned anything yet?"

Henry chuckled next to Mary.

"Mary, the day Jimmy learns anything I bet we'll find a deader that can sing and dance and play the violin."

"You shut up, old man. If I want advice about women from you, then I know I'm in real trouble."

Henry chuckled but stayed silent, not wanting to go into a debate with his friend. Instead, he rolled over and gave Jimmy his back.

Jimmy huffed softly and turned over, now giving Mary his back.

Mary rolled onto her back, in-between the two men and smiled softly.

Much like the heavens, both men should know by now that understanding women was like understanding why the dead walked.

Some things would forever remain a mystery.

The night passed uneventfully, each person taking his watch. Jimmy was now on watch and he gazed out at the shadows of shifting darkness. The sky was slowly beginning to lighten, but just a tinge of light could be perceived. It would be more than an hour before dawn broke over the countryside.

It was that precious time before dawn when armies would attack their enemies. It was the time when a guard was most vulnerable, and he anxiously looked forward to the coming dawn.

Jimmy was in that condition as he leaned against a nearby tree, his eyes weary and tired. The campfire was a few yards behind him, the fire now only a few flickering flames. It would be dead soon, and by the time the fire was completely out, the four companions would have gathered their gear and moved out.

But until then, Jimmy was still on watch.

He had stayed awake after laying down last night, angry that Cindy had snubbed him. But later, when she had been relieved, she'd crawled into his sleeping bag and had curled up next to him in the classic spoon position.

While Mary stood watch over them a few feet away, Cindy reached down his body and cupped his already growing member in-between her hand.

Without saying a word she began stroking him, slowly at first, but soon she had a good rhythm going as she worked his throbbing member like a woman who knew what her man liked.

Only two feet away, Henry snored loudly, and Jimmy had to keep his mouth closed or risk waking his friend.

Cindy then used her hand to massage the tip of his penis and before Jimmy could stop himself he felt himself exploding all over her hand. She nuzzled the back of his neck and with a quick kiss goodnight, promptly rolled over and fell asleep.

Jimmy laid perfectly still, his underpants now sticky. But he also felt a warm glow after climaxing, and with the soft body of Cindy pressed against him tightly, he drifted off to sleep.

But now he was on watch and the time he'd spent laying awake earlier in the evening was coming back to bite him in the ass. His eyes were heavy and he wanted desperately to return to sleep. With nothing to do but walk around to stay awake, and no other form of stimulation, he pushed off from the tree and began walking in a circle around the campsite.

His eyes looked out on the slowly lightening sky and he mentally willed the sun to hurry the hell up so the others would wake up and they could all move on. Only physical exertion would be enough to wake his ass up.

Jimmy moved around the campsite, his friends sleeping softly, and as he moved to the west, five shadows moved across the glade behind him, coming from the ranch house.

In the darkness, the five shadows blended in easily with the terrain, and only a man with night vision goggles would have been able to spot them.

One at a time, in a skirmish line, the four men and one woman skulked towards the campsite.

They were hungry, horny and wanted the firearms the companions possessed. And in moments they would have them.

Each person in the group carried a sharpened blade, rubbed with ash to deflect the wan moonlight from the crescent moon in the sky. Simon was in the lead, and as he slowly moved closer to the sleeping bodies, he licked his lips and rubbed his crotch with his free hand in expectation of the blonde woman.

Behind him, the last in line, Marion followed. She was a used up skank and Simon only banged her because there was no one else. It would be nice to have a change of pussy for a while. At least until he wore that one out. But by then, if there was luck, he would have found another, or maybe two, or hell, if he was wishing, why not three?

Crossing the grassy glade, he stayed low so his body was hidden by the tall grass. Beardface was behind him and the others with him, all ready to attack the campsite.

It had been a long wait until this exact moment in time, but he knew whoever was on watch would be at their worst after spending hours staring at the darkness.

When he was no more than ten yards from the flickering fire, he ducked down in the grass. Behind him, the rest of his attack party followed suit, and with all five hidden in the waist high grass, they watched as Jimmy walked by them.

Simon was just able to see the man's face in the gloom and he saw a tired countenance.

Simon counted under his breath while Jimmy moved passed him and the others, never aware danger was only a few steps away.

Simon waited until Jimmy had rounded the campsite and was on the other side, for the moment out of sight, and waved his people on.

One at a time they raised their blades and crossed the remaining few feet to the dying fire where they would slaughter the men and capture the women. And if that failed, well then they would just slaughter them all. He could still get a few good screws in before the bodies of the females cooled to the point he wouldn't want to do them anymore.

Henry stirred in his sleep. He was dreaming about his wife again.

Though more than a year had passed since her death by his own hands, he still felt a heavy weight on his heart. His wife had been one of the first infected and when he had returned home to check on her, she had promptly attacked him. He had defended himself and when there was no other option, had caved her head in with a cast iron skillet.

He replayed the gruesome scene in his mind now, flinching every time the skillet connected with her head. He remembered the blood and brains that had splattered on the cabinet behind her and how like bloody snails, gravity had pulled the detritus down to the linoleum floor.

It was usually at that moment when he would wake up, covered in sweat and breathing heavily. Only this time he didn't get to that point. Instead he was pulled awake by the snap of a twig just outside the perimeter of the campsite.

Opening his eyes, but not moving his head or body, he waited for another heartbeat, assuming it must have been Jimmy. He debated if he should call out, asking Jimmy if all was well.

Next to him, Mary and Cindy were fast asleep, Mary snoring softly. He would have to tease her about that in the morning. She had adamantly admitted over and over that she did not snore. Never had and never will.

Knowing better to assume anything, Henry slowly reached down for his panga strapped to his hip. As they were sleeping outside, everyone was dressed, shoes on as well, and only side arms were unholstered for easy access.

Ever so slowly, Henry pulled the panga out of the sleeping bag and slid his legs out, as well. He still didn't know if he was making a big thing out of nothing, but he'd learned a lot in the year since the world caved in on itself and only a dead man guessed all was well without absolutely knowing it for fact.

The fire was almost out, and when he shifted his head to see around himself better, he caught an aroma over the dying fire that wasn't there when he had bedded down for the night. It was of body odor and filth, mixed in with what smelled like wet ash, as if whoever or whatever was out there had bathed in charcoal from a fire. At least it wasn't the smell of death and rot, so he was fairly confident it wasn't a group of ghouls that had found them in the night.

No, whatever was out there was human, no doubt about that. But despite this knowledge it only told him the prowlers would be even more deadly, if that were possible.

His eyes darted back and forth and he felt his pulse quickening. Something was definitely not right.

And where the hell was Jimmy?

Was he okay? Was he hurt, lying somewhere out in the glade after being attacked?

His grip tightened on the panga, and just as he looked to his right, a shadow appeared against the lightening sky. It was a man, and behind him were others. Henry didn't move, not wanting to let his attackers know he was awake and aware of their presence. Inside he wanted to yell out, warn Mary and Cindy they were under attack, but he knew the instant he opened his mouth, the attackers would be on him and the others before they could pull their weapons free.

So he waited, his adrenalin pumping so fast he felt like he could simply jump up without touching the ground. He felt as if he could merely push off with his fingers and his body would bolt upright, much like a jack-in-the-box after its spring had been tripped.

His eyes were creased into slits as he watched the first attacker move closer to him. The man was only three feet away, Henry was fairly confident it was a man by the width of the shoulders and the length of the arms which one held something to the side of his body, something in the hand.

Henry waited, counting the seconds, knowing he had to attack at the precise moment so he could do the most damage in the shortest amount of time.

The attacker was only two feet away and now Henry saw other figures behind the first, all moving into the campsite, all holding what must be weapons in their outstretched hands.

Henry waited for when the man was leaning over him. The attacker's arm went high, and Henry spotted the slight gleam of a darkened blade rise into the air above his head.

Just as the man brought his blade down, Henry swiped across his body with the panga.

Before the dulled blade could touch Henry's chest, the panga sliced into the man's arm, severing it just behind the wrist. The bone slowed the blade, but such was the razor honed sharpness, that even a man's wrist bone was no match for the keen blade of the panga. Blood shot out of the arm, spraying the fire and almost extinguishing the last of the flames, the odor of burning blood filling the air.

Simon let out a scream that filled the glade like a piercing siren warning an attacking enemy. Behind the flailing man, the other attackers seemed to hesitate for a brief moment, not understanding what was happening.

Simon held his arm, now minus the lower half, and spun in a circle in agony; the stump still spraying blood like a fire hose. Warm blood bathed Henry's face and splattered on Simon's friends. Beardface's jaw fell open and whatever he had planned in his mind seemed to fall apart as he watched his leader screaming in pain.

By now Henry had rolled to his feet and was inside the three men and one woman attacker, his panga dancing like a living thing. Beardface felt something cold glide across his stomach, and an instant later felt his intestines slide out of the jagged wound. He let out a bark of pain and terror and reached down to try and scoop his insides back into the emptying cavity. He fell to his knees, tears in his eyes as he shoved bloody intestines, inch by inch, back into his abdomen. Only this time there was bits of rock, twigs and grass added to the mix. Even if he lived the next ten minutes he would die by sepsis within a day.

Henry's blade never slowed as he slashed and cut again and again. A man with long hair and a droopy right eye never saw the blade that severed his jugular and had him drowning in his blood, his mouth opening and closing like a landed flounder. Next to him, the fourth man tried to fight back, his instincts slightly sharper than the others. He managed to deflect Henry's first blow, but he wasn't able to stop Henry's boot connecting with his testicles with bruising force. The fourth man doubled over in pain and Henry followed the kick up with a knee to the man's face.

That left the woman and she danced away from Henry. She was about to throw her knife at Henry's attacking body when a gunshot sounded and a neat hole blossomed on her forehead like a black flower. The woman's eyes seemed to slide up, as if she was trying to see the hole that had magically appeared on her forehead.

Then she slumped to the ground, dead.

The man who'd been kicked in the groin and then a knee to the face had gathered himself together and was turning around. He was preparing to run at Henry, his blade ready to thrust when another booming gunshot rang out. The man's chest seemed to explode with blood and gore as the blast from Jimmy's shotgun struck him dead on. The man was thrown off his feet to land in the dying flames of the fire. No sooner did he touch down then his clothing began to smolder and burn. With screams of pain and anguish, the man rolled out of the fire, his arms banging against the ground as he began to burn alive.

Cindy racked her M-16 and shot the man three times in the chest. This time he stopped moving, one of the rounds slicing through his heart and exiting out his back to bury itself in the ash of the flames.

Henry spun around to see the man who'd lost his arm running off into the glade. He was screaming to the lightening sky as he wobbled back and forth; in his blind panic to escape he was moving at a good clip, too.

Cindy raised her rifle to shoot the man in the back and Henry moved over to her. He placed his hand on the barrel of the weapon and gently pushed it down.

"No, let him go. If he doesn't get that arm checked and in a tourniquet in the next few minutes he's dead anyway and I highly doubt if there's a hospital nearby. Save the bullet for when we really need it."

Cindy acquiesced, lowering the rifle. The eviscerated man was on his knees, his arms trying to hold his insides together. The blade he'd carried was forgotten, lying on the ground by his knees.

"What about him?" Mary asked; her .38 aimed at the man's chest. Jimmy came up out of the gloom, his smoking shotgun leveled at the man also.

Henry turned and walked over the whimpering man, stopping in front of him so it appeared the dying man was praying to Henry to save him.

"Please, help me...my insides...oh God...what do I do now?" The man pleaded through blood-frothed lips, red spittle dripping from his mouth.

"Simple. You die," Henry stated coldly. Before the man could reply, Henry swiped the blade horizontally; cutting the man's head off like it was a chicken's. Blood geysered straight up and seemed to dance as it spun in the air, then it stopped and gravity pulled it back down to earth. Blood rained on the decapitated corpse and soaked its clothing. The man's hands, slack in death, let go of his abdomen and his intestines spilled out onto the dusty ground, the blood and slime soaking into the dry earth and turning it to mud.

"Goddamn, Henry. Was that really necessary?" Jimmy asked while he moved up next to him.

"Yeah, Jimmy it was. Shit. I did the son-of-a-bitch a favor. With that wound he would have died hard. And this way we save another bullet for when we need it." He spun around at Jimmy and gazed into his friend's eyes. "And where the fuck were you when they came at us? If I hadn't heard one of them coming, I don't even want to think about what could have happened!"

Jimmy's eyes went down and he shook his head. "Jesus, Henry, I don't know what to say. I was tired. I couldn't see straight so I started walking around the fire in circles to stay awake. If it helps, I saw them just before you jumped up and got the first guy. I was about to put a few rounds into them when you jumped into their midst like Conan the fuckin' Barbarian."

Henry stared at his friend for another ten seconds, but when Jimmy held his gaze, he looked away.

"All right then, whatever. Looks like you probably would have gotten them before they got us, but still. Shit, Jimmy, I thought you might have been dead when I saw them coming at me."

Jimmy slapped Henry on the arm as Mary and Cindy moved next to them.

"Hell, Henry. It'll take a lot more than that to take me out. You know me, I'm goddamn immortal."

Henry smiled, but only slightly. "King of the world, right?"

"Fuckin' A, Henry. King of the goddamn world."

"Uhm, excuse me, you two, but if it's all right with you, I think I'd like to get out of here. It's a little too crowded for my tastes now," Mary said as she looked from dead body to dead body.

Henry followed her gaze and nodded, then wiped the blood from his face with his shirt sleeve. It was already congealing and becoming sticky. He studied the lightening skyline, realizing it was only an hour till dawn, maybe less.

"She's right. Let's gather what we can and get out of here. Jimmy, you still got that map?"

Jimmy reached into his back pocket and pulled it out. "Yeah, what do you need?"

"Are there any lakes or rivers nearby? I know I need a bath bad."

Jimmy searched the map. There was black spot scratched out where they were, which had been placed there the previous night. All he had to do was go off from there to find what Henry wanted and he did, using the tip of his Index finger.

"Here we go. There's what looks like a stream about five miles from where we are. It looks like there's a lake near there. A lake Burkley, I guess. The stream must go into it."

"Great, good job, Jimmy. If it's all right with you guys, I'd like to head over there and wash up, not to mention we can see what's around there."

Both Mary and Cindy glanced at each other and then back to Henry.

"One place is as good as another, Henry, its fine with us," Mary said, the voice of the two. "Sides, I wouldn't mind taking a bath either."

Jimmy's eyes lit up as he stared at Cindy and Mary and imagined them both naked and frolicking in the water together.

"Hey, if either of you lovely ladies needs someone to wash your back, I'm your man."

Cindy walked over to Jimmy and grabbed him by the left earlobe, yanking gently.

"That'll be enough of that, right now, Jimmy. The only back you'll be scrubbing is your own."

Jimmy frowned and pulled himself away from Cindy, rubbing his ear and wincing.

"Sheesh, all right, all right, ease off. It was just a suggestion," he whined.

"Well, here's another one. Let's get the bedrolls packed up and move out. Its already beginning to stink here and in another hour it'll only be worse. And look over there. It doesn't take long for the cleanup crew to come out."

All eyes followed his pointing arm and each of them spotted the outlines of three wolves on the horizon.

"It doesn't take them long to sniff out a free lunch either, huh?" Jimmy asked while he watched the motionless animals.

"No, it doesn't and where there's three there'll be more, so let's get going. I want us moving in fifteen minutes. But before that there's something I gotta do."

All eyes were on him as he turned, walked a few feet away, and began to urinate in the tall grass. When he returned two minutes later, he still had three sets of eyes on him.

"What? I had to go since I got up, but I was a little busy before."

No one said anything, and with a chuckle from Jimmy, they got to work packing up their gear. While they worked, the wolves were slowly moving closer, though hesitant about getting too close. But they could smell the dead bodies and blood and they were hungry.

When the companions were packed and began moving out, the wolves were only fifty feet away, waiting anxiously with hungry eyes. Henry was last in line as they exited the site and he paused in the tall grass, looking back at the wolves. He waved to the animals and then pointed to the five corpses, one still smoldering slightly near the dead fire.

"They're all your boys. We're finished. Bon apetit!"

Then he turned and began walking away, the trampled grass an easy trail to follow as he and the others made their way out of the glade and onto the nearby dirt road next to the burnt ranch house.

Just as Henry and the others stepped onto the dirt road, the wolves reached the bodies, and a moment before Henry turned a corner in the road and the campsite was lost from sight, he spotted one of the wolves with a large piece of intestine in its mouth, chewing happily.

Then the animals were out of sight, and as far as Henry was concerned, the five attackers were receiving their proper funeral. They had tried to kill the companions for no other reason than because they could. Perhaps if luck had fallen their way, then it would be Henry and the others scattered around the campsite, their bodies being devoured by hungry wolves. But fate had decreed a different outcome; for the companions to live another day.

With the sun rising in the sky, signifying the scorcher that was to come, Henry moved along the dirt road, pleased it was he who was still breathing, as well as his friends.

Behind him in the incline, the wolves growled and tore apart the corpses, feeding on the dead bodies like it was their last supper. And who knows, perhaps by the end of their meal another predator would come and make it happen. But by then, Henry and the rest of his group of survivors would be far away and moving on to someplace better.

CHAPTER THREE

DESPITE THE SUN being ninety-three million miles away from earth, Henry felt like it was no more than a mile above his head.

It was coming on mid-afternoon and it felt like he was going to melt in the heat of the Kentucky day. The blood he'd been sprayed with earlier that morning had found its way into every crease and crevice in his face; even behind his ears. And with the sun beating down on him, the same blood was like glue, sticking with the sweat from his body to make him feel like he had molasses on his neck and in his hair.

"Hey, Jimmy, when the hell are we gonna get to this river? I'm dying for a bath," Henry asked his friend while he trudged along the gravel road. To the north of them was the interstate, but the companions had decided to stay on the smaller, less used road for the sake of safety.

Rusted and abandoned cars littered every highway in every state; debris from the first outbreak. If any of the vehicles ran, they wouldn't know as they had decided long ago to leave them be. More times than they could count, one of the companions had come upon a derelict car and found a ghoul waiting inside.

It usually wasn't a pretty picture. Sometimes the once human being was nothing but rotting pus and flayed skin, the inside of the vehicle incredibly hot, continually cooking the corpse like a chicken in an oven for months on end. Maggots usually filled the floorboards of the vehicles and flies were inside like a thousand black dots, zipping around for a way out. The tiny insects would live their entire lives inside the vehicle until they died, others taking its place in a revolving cycle of life and death.

None of the companions felt like dealing with a visceral scene like that and so they continued walking.

Jimmy held the map in his hands again, studying the skinny lines that indicated roads and highways, his brow furrowed in concentration while he read it.

"I don't know what to say, Henry. It says we should be there by now."

"You sure you didn't have the map upside down?" Mary asked.

Jimmy pursed his lips and frowned at her. "I'm not an idiot, Mary, of course not."

Mary was about to toss a rejoinder at him when Cindy shook her head and touched her arm. Her gesture was asking her not to say anything, despite the easy opening Jimmy had given her. Mary grinned slightly and nodded.

"I know you're not, Jimmy. I was just asking," Mary said instead of what she really wanted to. The two were like brother and sister, and Mary always took a chance to tease Jimmy if the opportunity arose. They had been together, along with Henry, when the first outbreak had reared its ugly head. Sometimes she would look back to that time a year ago and wonder how it was she was still alive. There had been so many adventures that had appeared to be her last, but like the proverbial phoenix rising out of the ashes, she and her friends had managed to survive, escape, or kill whatever was in their way.

She was pulled from her reverie by a low moaning coming from the highway. Though the guardrail was more than a thousand feet away, the four companions had been spotted by a crowd of roving ghouls, which had been shambling along like derelicts looking for food.

"Shit, looks like roamers," Henry growled with annoyance.

Turning, Mary watched as the ghouls tumbled over the knee-high guardrails and into the weeds. Once over the rails, they picked themselves up and began their descent to the shoulder of the highway, directly towards her and the others.

Henry stopped walking and turned to see Mary watching the ghouls' slow progress.

"Mary, come on. Let's keep moving. Either we'll outdistance them or we'll stop and take care of them later."

Mary's hand went to her .38. "Why don't we just take them out now and be done with it?" Her eyes were studying the ghouls while they made their slow but steady progress towards her. Three were men, one was a child of no more than seven or eight and the other two were once middle-aged women. She wondered if one of the women was the mother of the child. Sometimes, even after death and then revival, certain zombies would stay together by some unspoken bond that even they didn't understand. She had always wondered if there was truly any part of the person still inside the mind of a ghoul or was it nothing more than an autonomous eating and killing machine.

Henry shook his head. "No, just leave them be. We can't kill every deader or roamer we come across, you know that. 'Sides, we need to save our ammo for when we really need it. Let's just pick up pace and be done with 'em."

Mary hesitated for a brief moment, her hand caressing the grip of her .38. Then with a sigh, she turned and jogged to catch up with the others.

Henry smiled slightly when she caught up to the rest of them.

"Good girl. You'll see. In another mile or so we'll have them gone; and out of sight out of mind, right?"

"I guess so," she mumbled.

"All right, then. Okay, you guys, let's pick up the pace and see if we can outdistance those rotting piles of pus," Henry said, his way of a pep talk. "Besides, if I don't take a bath soon I'm gonna die."

"Yeah, yeah, you know, you're not the only one that hasn't bathed in a while," Jimmy said while he jogged behind Henry.

"That is stating the obvious," Cindy joked back by his side.

Jimmy looked at her but nodded in agreement. "I know, that's what I just said. Shit, I smell as bad as one of those dead bastards following us."

"Actually, Jimmy, I think the roamers might smell slightly better," Mary joked, her mouth turning up into a mischievous grin.

"Now wait a second there, missy. You don't smell like a rose yourself, you know."

"Yes, Jimmy, I'm, quite aware of my scent, thank you for pointing that out. My, you are such a gentleman. I have to tell you, Cindy, I'm so jealous you managed to snatch up this intelligent man all for yourself."

Cindy chuckled. "Ha, don't be too jealous Mary," Cindy told her with a grin of her own.

"Now just wait a damn second, you two. Since when did this turn into a pick on Jimmy subject?" Jimmy asked, his feelings hurt.

Cindy moved close to him and rubbed his arm. "Oh, relax, babe. We're just playing with you. Tell you what, when we rest for the night

I'll make it up to you, okay?" She said the last part low so only Jimmy could hear.

Jimmy's eyes lit up. "Really, you promise?"

"I promise, babe. When we make camp for the night I'm gonna rock your world."

Jimmy's face lightened and he began to step more lively.

"If you ladies are done chatting, can we pick up the pace, please?" Henry asked from the front of the line. His eyes were searching everywhere, but so far all was silent. It was one of the main reasons he preferred to stay away from the large cities and towns. More people meant more undead presence. Better to stay in the sticks, where the population was low. But as he passed a small sign that stated Richmond was eight miles away, he realized it might not stay quiet for long.

A warm breeze blew his way and his nose picked up the scent of water. He could feel the dampness on his face.

"Hey, I think we might be getting close to that river Jimmy was going on about," he said as he continued jogging.

Behind him the others were silent, now concentrating on jogging. Like a small military unit, they moved down the dirt road, crossed the highway and continued down into a small canal. In the bottom of the canal was the slightest trickle of water and Henry had high hopes they were moving in the right direction.

They stayed on this direction for another two miles and eventually came to an end to the canal. There was a large metal grate set into a stone wall and it was obvious to all who studied it that it led to an underground sewer system.

"Come on, let's get out of here and see what's up top," Henry said as he turned and began moving up the steep concrete. Mary checked behind them and the six ghouls were nowhere to be seen. She nodded to her herself. Henry had been right. All she would have done was wasted ammo on a few roamers who didn't matter at all.

Sometimes she forgot it was easier to walk away when there was no reason to fight. She smiled to herself as she began to climb the steep incline. There was a time when all she would have done was run and to fight would have been unheard of.

But like her friends, she'd changed over the past year. If she hadn't, then she was sure she would have been long dead.

The last one out of the canal, Mary stopped at the top and joined the others, who were admiring the vista below them.

The river, which was once no more than twenty feet across was now the size of a small lake. With no one to control the flood gates down stream, the river had grown until it had seeped into the surrounding land. Now there was a new lake where before, only a year ago, there would have been nothing but grassland.

Jimmy checked his map again, studying the lines like a historian in search of the fabled Holy Grail.

"That's not right. According to this map this lake shouldn't be here."

Henry took the map from Jimmy and studied it as well. He saw where the river began and ended and then nodded.

"This wasn't here before. Probably flooding or something. With no one around to man the dam or whatever is upstream, the river just kept growing until we have what's below us. I don't see the problem, actually. We needed water and here it is."

Jimmy took the map back and stuffed it into his shirt. "I guess." He gazed down at the serene lake. A few ducks and birds could be seen on the edges and every now and then a small bubble broke the surface of the water, signifying there was aquatic life in the new born lake.

"Well, then. If we're all in agreement it's a lake we're looking at, then why don't we go down there and take a bath?" Jimmy asked as he clapped his hands together.

"Jimmy, my boy, I couldn't have said it better myself," Henry added and then began moving down the small hillock the companions were on, as they continued towards the shoreline below. There was a small copse of trees near the eastern shore that looked inviting and he headed for them, the others right behind him.

"It's too bad we can't be alone, lover. Other wise I could rock your world right here," Cindy whispered seductively.

"Really? Then why can't we, I'm not shy."

"Because Cindy is thinking about the rest of us, Jimmy, that's why, and she doesn't want to subject me or Henry to your pale, white ass," Mary said, loud enough for everyone to hear.

Jimmy was about to reply, when Cindy placed her finger on his lips. She shook her head back and forth, telling Jimmy to let it go.

With a wary sigh, Jimmy obeyed her.

Mary chuckled as she passed him and with Cindy giggling softly, too, she wrapped her left hand around Jimmy's right hand and the two walked like young lovers on their first date to the edge of the lake.

By the time they reached the edge, Henry was already beginning to take off his boots, socks and weapons. He was planning on going swimming in his clothes as they were as filthy as he was and needed a good washing. The air was so warm he was confident his clothes would dry on his body once they set out again on their future path.

Mary agreed to wait and bathe after everyone else, knowing someone needed to stay on watch in case of trouble. With Henry, Cindy and Jimmy all jumping into the lake, Mary sat down on a rock and sighed, watching her friends play and wash themselves.

"Soon, Mary, soon. Just be patient," she told herself.

With a few birds fluttering in the trees. Annoyed that their roost was being disrupted, the companions laughed and splashed, enjoying a few stolen minutes of happiness.

Only a quarter mile away, the six zombies had been following the companions. They would not stop the chase until either they were once again dead for good or the companions had been torn apart and eaten, their warm flesh swallowed whole into the already bloated stomachs.

Meanwhile, a half mile away, on the opposite side of the lake, a dozen more ghouls had heard the echoes of laughter and were already on the move. This crowd of undead had originally been from Richmond, but had been traveling for months, wandering the highways looking for food. Now they'd found some, and as one large group, they moved out, unknown to them that they were actually providing a flanking maneuver to the half dozen ghouls coming from the opposite direction.

Oblivious to the approaching danger, the companions relaxed and enjoyed the warm summer day washing the sweat and blood of past battles from their bodies like a baptism.

CHAPTER FOUR

ALMOST AN HOUR had passed and the four companions were still relishing the cool water from the lake. Both Henry and Cindy were spread out on the dirt, using their sleeping bags for towels so they didn't get dust on their fresh washed clothing. Henry's face was scrubbed raw and cleanly shaven, both he and Jimmy taking the opportunity to shave with one of their last remaining disposable razors.

Mary had already taken her dip and had exited quickly, only staying in the lake long enough to bathe and shave in a few choice places, then she had stepped out of the water with a purpose, shaking her dark-brown hair like a shaggy dog.

Jimmy was still in the water, and had been for almost an hour. Though he'd climbed out for a few minutes every now and then, he couldn't get enough of the soothing water on his skin.

"You know, Jimmy, if you don't get out of there soon, you're gonna end up looking like a prune," Mary told him while she combed her hair with her fingers. She made a note to find a brush the next time they went by a store or something similar. Usually, items such as combs, mascara and other miscellaneous items could still be found on store shelves across America. It didn't take long for looters to realize only food and drinking water were the important things to go after and that plasma televisions and stereos were redundant.

"Maybe so, but what can I say? I love the water," Jimmy yelled back as he backstroked to the middle of the lake. He stopped and began treading water. Then he stared at his friends and a look of pleasure and a wide grin crossed his face.

"Hey, did the water just get warmer?"

Henry frowned, realizing what Jimmy meant. "Thanks a lot, Jimmy, you pig, I might have wanted to go back in."

Jimmy only chuckled and proceeded to swim around some more.

On the shore, everyone was relaxing, barely looking at him, deciding that with Jimmy, it was better to ignore him. Usually that was the only way to get him to stop. He needed an audience for his antics and was quick to tire if none existed.

Weapons were nearby all the companions, all within arm's reach, but no one was particularly watching their surroundings. Though Henry was always the first to post a watch, even he was becoming lazy in the beautiful paradise they had stumbled into.

With the exception of a few birds in the trees and a family of chipmunks, the area was devoid of activity, which was fine with him.

Jimmy swam a little further and stopped, treading water as he spit out a fountain of liquid from his mouth. His hair was plastered to his forehead and he looked like a ten-year-old who was getting his first chance to swim on his own.

So when he felt something brush his leg, he didn't give it much thought.

A few fish had been seen around the swimmers, but they would usually swim away the moment any of the companions got to close to them. Jimmy was about to swim back to the shore when he felt something else brush against his other foot.

Visions of sharks came to his mind and he almost expected to feel the cold searing pain of shark teeth on his exposed limbs. Of course, he didn't consider that he was in a fresh water lake and there could not be sharks nearby.

He stuck his face into the water, darting his head back and forth to peer into the murky depths, but could see nothing. The lake was only about fifteen feet deep in the deepest parts, but there were many small hills and gullies that would change the depths from six feet to twenty in others.

Henry noticed Jimmy searching the water and called out to him across the smooth surface of the lake.

"What's the matter, trying to find your wiener?"

Mary and Cindy chuckled, but Jimmy only shook his head, beads of water flying off his face to drop back into the lake.

"Ha, ha, very funny. No, I'm serious, man. I could have sworn I just felt something against my legs."

"Maybe it's the creature from the black lagoon, coming to eat you," Mary called in a lilting tone. She was laying down on a nearby rock and trying to sun herself dry.

"No, Mary, it's true. Something just brushed my legs."

Henry was about to tell Jimmy to just get out of the water, that he'd been in there long enough, when Jimmy's head disappeared from the surface like he'd been pulled down from below.

"What the hell?" Henry said as he studied the ripples that were the only remaining residue of Jimmy having been there at all.

Cindy was looking up at the sky, enjoying the day, and she turned her head to look at Henry and then the water.

"What's wrong, Henry? Hey, wait a minute. Where's Jimmy?" She asked her questions with concern on her face, though panic seemed to be hovering just out of sight.

"I don't know. He was there and now he's gone. He better not be screwing around."

Mary stood up, now joining Henry at the water's edge.

"That doesn't make sense. He wouldn't do that. Oh no, you don't think he went under, do you?"

"Oh my God, he's drowning! Henry, we have to save him!" Cindy yelled in panic, already ripping off her boots so she could jump back into the water. She carried a small hunting knife in her hand as she charged towards the lake.

Henry only grunted, but joined Cindy in removing his clothing and boots. They were almost dry and he wasn't about to get them wet again, especially if Jimmy was just screwing around.

"Mary, stay here and watch our backs, we'll go get Jimmy," Henry told her as he waded into the lake in his underwear. Cindy was right behind him, running passed him and diving into the cool water, her body slicing through the surface as she swam to where Jimmy was last seen.

But as they both began to swim to Jimmy's last known position, what they would find in the darkness of the lake would be something they couldn't have imagined in their worst nightmares.

*　*　*

At first, Jimmy didn't panic, assuming perhaps he'd caught his foot on a sunken tree limb or maybe a log. But as he was yanked down below the water and he tried to kick out, he quickly realized something was holding his leg in an iron grip.

He'd managed to take in a lungful of air before his head went under, so for the present moment he wasn't in danger of drowning. As he was pulled into the murky depths, his eyes tried to pierce the gloom to see what had grabbed him.

It was then that he came face to face with something out of one of his worst nightmares.

As he floated a few feet off the floor of the lake, he looked down at an upturned face of utter grotesquerie. A ghoul had been stumbling around the bottom of the lake and had come upon Jimmy's kicking legs. When Jimmy had swum over a slight rise of the lake floor, the bloated zombie had managed to reach up and grab his foot, pulling him down like plucking a floating balloon from the air.

Jimmy stifled a scream, not wanting to expel his air as he tried to free himself from the skeletal fingers of the demon beneath the water.

Its face was putrescently soft and yielding, as Jimmy found out when he tried to push off the head to escape its clutches. Whatever gender the ghoul had once been was unknown, the submersed zombie had been in the water for so long it resembled a giant blue slug, with a few tatters of clothing still attached to its skeletal frame. One eye was gone, the other, a dull white, with a milky haze covering it, stared up at Jimmy. The mouth opened wide, pale yellow teeth snapping in the water.

Did Jimmy actually hear the click when the teeth connected? Or was it only in his imagination.

He tired to kick away again, but the underwater ghoul only yanked down again, Jimmy sinking two more feet into the depths of the lake. In nothing but his underwear, he knew he had nothing to use as a weapon but his own hands. With his right hand free, he tried to punch the ghoul on the head, his hand sending out a ripple of pain when his fingers connected with skull. Though no match for a bullet, the skull was more than strong enough to handle Jimmy's attack.

With Jimmy struggling to free himself, his pulse pounding in his head as his oxygen ran out, his eyes went wide when more pale and blue faces appeared out of the gloom. More than a score of undead were moving across the bottom of the lake, their need to breathe not an option. They had been under water since the barrier a mile upriver had burst and they had been swallowed whole by the rising water table. Unable to reason, they had merely stayed where they were until they had been absorbed into the lake. Fish would pick at their decayed flesh, and sometimes if quick enough, a ghoul would manage to catch one of the fish for itself, tearing into the scales and fins like it was manna from Heaven.

But now they had live, human prey and they were hungry. Oh, so hungry. Jimmy tried valiantly to escape the ghoul's vise-like grip but as his vision began to dull, and the other shambling forms slowly moved through the darkness, stirring mud up with their footfalls, Jimmy began to fear for his life.

Henry kicked harder as he sliced through the water. Cindy was a few yards ahead of him, her younger, more agile body, easily out-distancing him.

He watched as she reached the spot where Jimmy was last seen and dived below the surface.

Her legs kicked hard and she dove deep until she was near the gravel floor. There was a small fence and a rusted out car to her right, reminding her the lake had been unnaturally made. Her eyes searched the muck, as she frantically tried to see Jimmy in the dull gloom.

Finally, her lungs fit to burst; she swam back to the surface, taking in great gasps of air while she treaded water.

"Did you see him?" Henry asked when he approached what looked like her floating head.

She shook her head no, but no sooner did she answer him then she dived again, this time moving off to the right a little more.

Her eyes darted left and right, not seeing anything resembling Jimmy and then she caught movement out of the corner of her eye. Turning in the water, her hair flying around her like a halo, she swam towards the shadowy object.

The closer she got to the forms, the more her heart began to beat when she realized she was seeing Jimmy.

But her excitement was short-lived when she saw what had him in its grip and what was approaching from behind. From her vantage point, she was able to see over the first ghoul's head, and she could see the slow moving army of the dead as they crossed the underwater terrain.

Placing the knife in her teeth, she swam towards Jimmy, and when she was no more than a few feet away, she plucked the knife from her teeth and began cutting at the wrist of the ghoul holding Jimmy captive.

For one brief instant, her eyes met Jimmy's and she saw the fear and terror within. Even under the water she could see his eyes were bloodshot, his face turning red as he tried to hold his last breath in his chest.

Then she was looking away, concentrating on hacking at the withered limb. The ghoul tried to grab her with its other hand, but failed miserably. Behind her, she sensed more than saw the other ghouls moving closer.

If she didn't free Jimmy fast, he would either be attacked by more of them or drown.

The blade was cutting through slimy flesh, but she wasn't powerful enough to cut through the wrist. She turned to look at Jimmy and his face seemed to be calming down as he realized she wasn't going to free him.

He seemed to nod to her, trying to tell her it was all right, when another shadow from above blocked out the wan light and came up next to her.

It was Henry, and in the second it took his eyes to see what was happening, he reached down, grabbed the wrist on both ends with each of his hands, and cracked the bone like he was snapping a tree branch for firewood.

Even underwater, the snap could be heard loud and clear and the ghoul was immediately without its lunch.

Jimmy was at the end of his ordeal, and without wanting to, his mouth opened and he tried to take in what could only be water, his body bucking as he began to drown.

Kicking away from the marching zombies, Henry and Cindy pushed Jimmy towards the surface of the water. With a mighty thrust, Henry forced Jimmy's head above the water and slapped his face hard to hopefully snap him out of whatever death spasm he was going through and breathe in the warm air.

Jimmy coughed loudly, puking water over his chest as he sucked in his first breath of air. A breath he was confident he would never have tasted while he had been trying in vain to free himself from the clutches of the undead under the surface of the lake.

Henry was next to him, and no sooner did his head break the surface then the sound of gunshots came to his ears.

Spinning in the water, he found Mary standing at the water's edge. Coming towards her from the left were the six roamers they had left alone, deciding to just leave them in their dust. Somehow the ghouls had managed to find the companions again. But that wasn't what froze him to the bone. To the right were at least fifteen more shambling bodies, all making their way towards Mary's position.

With the sun at their backs, it was hard for Mary to see the bodies clearly and the amount of head shots were few.

Henry said nothing; there was no time for talking. He left Jimmy with Cindy and began stroking for the shoreline. He needed to get to his weapons and help Mary or in a matter of minutes she would be overwhelmed. Behind him, Jimmy and Cindy were slowly following.

In no time, Henry was wading out of the water and was at his gear. Picking up his Glock, he checked the clip. He had brand-new hollow-point rounds in the clip and he was looking forward to testing them out.

They had been a rare find in an old gun shop. They'd been hiding under some old clothes in the back room of the shop and had been missed when looters had ransacked the place months before.

Dripping wet, with nothing but his underwear on, Henry moved next to Mary, firing a few shots at the closest ghouls.

"Stay calm, Mary, we're okay. If we have to, we can always retreat into the water and swim to the other side."

Cindy had reached the water's edge and she helped Jimmy limp onto dry land. Jimmy quickly inspected his ankle, and other than a black and blue bruise, his leg was undamaged. With a few more coughs as he sucked in air, he quickly ran over to his own gear and snatched up his shotgun, immediately firing a round and then cycling the weapon and firing again.

"You all right?" Henry called to him as he fired another shot with the Glock, his reward an exploding head.

"I'll live," Jimmy answered brusquely. "Thanks for the save."

"Happy to help," Henry answered back and then talk was finished as more of the living dead came at them.

But there were more ghouls to shoot than there were firearms and though a few went down, they slowly moved closer to the battling companions.

"Back up, get to the edge of the lake," Henry yelled, doing the same himself. He made sure to gather up his panga and rifle as he moved away from the attacking zombies.

Bullets went through bodies like cheesecloth, the hollow-points doing their jobs well. Dinner plate sized holes appeared in the ghoul's bodies, but without head shots, they still came on.

"Uhm, guys, I think our retreat just caught a snag," Cindy said while she fired at an old woman with half her face missing. The old woman dropped to the ground, the ones behind her merely stepping over her corpse.

"What are you talking about?" Henry asked, firing into two zombies that were too close for comfort. One got it in the head, half its skull blowing out onto the one behind it. The other was blind for a moment, the blood and brain matter covering its eyes. But then it wiped its eyes with rotting palms and continued on.

"Look behind you, Henry," was all she said as she fired again and again with her M-16. Though she was tempted to use full auto, she controlled herself, only using single shot, trying to make every round count.

When Henry had a chance, he glanced over his shoulder at the smooth surface of the lake and what he saw chilled his heart to the bone.

One at a time, the ghouls under the lake were walking out. Heads appeared, then shoulders, torsos and waists as each one slowly trudged out of the water towards the companions.

They were now surrounded on all sides with no hope of retreat.

"Shit, I don't believe it!" Henry yelled as he spun and began firing at the approaching, waterlogged ghouls. Their skin seemed to actually slide off their bones when they exited the water, their pale blue complexion even bluer now that they were out of the water and were being bathed by the sun.

The distinctive odor of drowned rat came to his nose when the wind shifted, blowing the redolence of the drenched dead directly at him.

Oh God, he thought, I was just swimming in that water only a few seconds ago.

"Spread out and try to find high ground!" Henry yelled as he fired again and again. When his clip went dry, he popped it out of the gun and popped in another. This was his last one. After the seventeen rounds left he would be down to his rifle and panga, and the rifle was really only good for long distance. He spun and concentrated his gun fire on the water ghouls, dropping one after another. But still more heads appeared from the surface of the lake as bodies with head shots slipped back into the water's depths.

The others did as they were told, and Jimmy continued firing again and again at the approaching horde. But there were more ghouls appearing behind the first wave and it was painfully clear they would be overrun in less than five minutes if the situation didn't drastically change in their favor.

For now, all they could do was to continue firing and hope for a miracle.

CHAPTER FIVE

"WHAT THE HELL are we gonna do!" Jimmy yelled as he blasted a ghoul with an already gaping chest wound. It looked like something had torn the zombie's chest open in the recent past, the ribcage sticking out like bizarre abstract art. Jimmy's barrage only added to the wound as pieces of bone flew off in all directions like shrapnel, peppering the other nearby ghouls.

"I don't know. Just keep firing and I'll try to think of something," Henry yelled back. But he could think of no way to escape the army of the undead. The lake was now full of bodies, some floating at odd angles. They were totally surrounded and he just didn't see how the hell they were going to get out of their present predicament without taking casualties on their side.

As if to prove that point, Mary let out a yell and tumbled to the ground when two female zombies attacked her. She managed to kick one away and shoot the other in the face, the dead woman's jaw disappearing in a spray of dried blood and teeth. She followed that shot with another, jamming the muzzle of her .38 into the jawless ghoul's open mouth. Closing her eyes to protect herself from blowback and falling debris, she squeezed the trigger, blowing the ghoul's head clean off. The blood red scalp flipped in the air, like it was dancing in the wind, then tumbled back to the ground, bouncing once before remaining still.

Then she rolled to her side, and with another kick to the face of the other she-ghoul, she fired into its left eye, putting the dead woman down for good. It was at this time that someone moving fast came up from her left side and cold-cocked her on the side of the head. She only had enough time to catch a few voices and realized it wasn't zombies that were attacking her before she fell partially unconscious, the blow to her head stunning her. Then she was struggling with pulling herself awake and away from her attackers. She knew something was very wrong, and if she lost coherency, she truly believed not waking up might mean her life.

Cindy was on her opposite side and saw nothing of what was happening to Mary as she fired again and again into the approaching army of the dead. Arms and legs were separated from their hosts as she attempted to end the rush of shambling corpses. A few acted like they were just old men, shambling on their morning walk, but she knew they were just as deadly as the more proactive ones and shot each one with precision.

Unfortunately, all their gunshots had attracted every ghoul in a half-mile radius and they were now all converging on the companion's position.

And with each ghoul shot, there was one less bullet for the rest.

Henry was starting to wonder if he should make sure he had at least one more bullet left for himself when the oddest thing happened.

The sound of motor vehicles could be heard, and a few seconds later, ten men and three women came charging into the area, all with some form of melee weapon. There were the standard ones like shovels, pitchforks and hoes, but a few had broadswords and katanas. But no one seemed to have any firearms.

With whooping yells that rivaled the moans of the dead, they charged into the backs of the ghouls, the living dead not ready for a rear guard attack.

These new arrivals swiped heads from shoulders and knocked bodies to the ground, only to decapitate the ghoul thereafter. Some kicked and punched, but most used some type of blade.

Henry and the others were now completely separated from one another and all were far to busy to fully take in what was happening. But they curbed their shots, not wanting to harm any of what they perceived to be their rescuers.

One after another, body after body was disposed of until the entire edge of the lake was nothing but a massive battlefield with dismembered corpses all around.

Henry dropped to his knees, swiveling on his right knee as he waved his weapon at the lake. There were two more ghouls coming out of the water, and with his left hand on his right for support, he shot each ghoul on the temple, taking them out for good. With a small splash, they sunk into the surface of the lake and were gone from sight. Henry nodded to himself, hoping that was the last of them and turned back around to see if there were any more targets that were in need of a bullet to the head.

But what he saw threw him for a loop. The rescuers were already pulling back, running and whooping up a storm as they charged back to their vehicles.

They didn't even bother to get a quick thank you from Henry or the others which was odd.

"Hey, where the hell are they going? You'd think they would want us to say thanks. Maybe pay them something for saving our asses," Jimmy said as he watched the last rescuer disappear over the top of the hill where their idling vehicles waited.

Henry nodded, not saying anything. It was then he realized Mary wasn't on the shore with the rest of them.

"Hey, where's Mary?"

Jimmy and Cindy looked around themselves and shrugged, their faces filled with concern.

"I have no idea. I lost track of her in all the shooting," Jimmy said as he spun in a circle.

Suddenly a scream of rage and anger filtered over the rise to Henry's ears and he distinctively knew it was Mary. Jimmy turned to him at the same time, his face recognizing her voice.

"Holy shit, that was Mary!" Jimmy screamed.

Henry pointed to the top of the incline that led to the highway and the dirt road they had traveled on to reach the lake.

"Come on, let's go, she needs us," Henry told Jimmy and Cindy. Then he was off, climbing up the small slope as fast as was humanly possible. He was still in his underwear, as were Cindy and Jimmy, but at the moment, modesty was the last thing on their minds.

Henry was the first over the rise and he spotted three vehicles as they finished loading their personnel. There was a pickup truck, a bread truck and an old work van. His eyes took in the area at a glance and he spotted Mary being dragged to the work van.

"Mary!" He yelled, taking a step towards her and the three vehicles. It was only when a shot rang out and bounced so close to his barefoot it had to be luck that stopped him from getting shot. He dove for cover, coming up behind a small mound of dirt, and returned fire as Jimmy and Cindy came up behind him.

"They got Mary. She's in the van, but be careful you don't shoot her by accident," he spit as he fired off another round at the work van. It was hard to know where to shoot as Mary could be anywhere inside the vehicle

Jimmy and Cindy concentrated their fire on the other two vehicles, not worrying about hitting Mary. The bread truck's windshield starred and cracked when Cindy shot two rounds through the middle of the glass, but whether she struck someone inside the cab was unknown.

There was a man trying to climb into the passenger side of the van and Henry lined up his shot, not pleased with the distance, and fired three times at the moving body. He succeeded in striking the man in the leg and thigh, the other round going wide. The van backed up, leaving the wounded man on the ground. Before Henry could do anything else, the van spun around in a spray of dust and began driving off. Cindy and Jimmy sent a few more shots at the other two vehicles but nothing seemed to do any damage. Jimmy managed to take out the small left side window of the bread truck, but then the vehicle was out of range and he stopped shooting, not wanting to waste ammunition.

Jimmy started running after the vehicles in nothing but his under-wear.

"Jimmy, get back here, you fool. It's not like you can catch them. Besides, you need your clothes.

"But they took Mary, the bastards. What the hell did they do that for? Christ, we were grateful for their help. What the hell is going on around here?"

Cindy gestured to the wounded man who was on the ground, moaning softly. He was already trying to crawl away into the scrub brush that lined the road.

"Why don't we ask him?" Cindy said as she pointed with the muzzle of her M-16 to the man.

Henry grunted as he popped out his clip to see how many rounds he had left. He wasn't pleased with the result. Only five more remained. He would need to find more ammo soon or the Glock would be nothing but a club.

"That was exactly what I was going to do. Look, I got this. Why don't you two go gather our things and bring them up here? And watch out for anything that ain't dead yet."

"I thought they were already dead?" Jimmy asked sarcastically. "Well, technically, anyway."

"Just go, dammit," Henry snarled, not in the mood for Jimmy's remarks. Mary was in trouble and they needed answers fast.

"All right, but don't do anything until we get back, I want to know what happened here," Jimmy told Henry.

"Fair enough, but hurry the hell up. The sooner we find out where they took Mary, the sooner we can get going," Henry said.

Jimmy and Cindy turned and jogged back down the small incline to gather their gear while Henry walked over to the wounded man. His weapon never waved as he watched the man for any signs of dangerous activity, but the closer he got to the wounded man he realized he was worried for nothing.

The man was bleeding pretty badly and Henry had a feeling he may have clipped the guy's femoral artery with one of his rounds. If that was true, then there was no time to waste.

Walking up to him, the prone man stopped trying to crawl away and rolled over onto his back.

Henry grinned down at him, but there was no joviality in his smile.

"You and me need to talk," Henry said as he leaned down closer to the grizzled face. "What's your name, pal."

"Cotter," the man said as he stared up into Henry's face.

Henry studied the man and his clothing. He wore average street clothes. A pair of jeans and a button down shirt, dirty but not absolutely filthy. Not much unusual there, but when the man talked, Henry noticed he seemed to have teeth that were pointier than they should be.

"Open your mouth," Henry ordered him.

Cotter did as he was told, wincing from the wounds in his leg and thigh. Henry studied the man's teeth and then gritted his own.

"Why are your teeth sharp like that, Cotter and where the hell is my friend?"

Cotter closed his mouth and stared at Henry again, his eyes saying he wasn't going to talk.

Henry leaned back and pressed his free hand on Cotter's thigh wound, causing him to scream in pain.

"Listen, pal. If I don't get a tourniquet on that leg real soon you're gonna be worm food. You hear me? Now talk. Where did your people take my friend and why."

Cotter laughed. "Screw you, buddy. If I'm gonna die anyway, then why the hell would I tell you anything?"

Henry leaned closer to Cotter as he studied the whites of his eyes. "Because you can go easy with blood loss or you can go hard. Now tell me what I want to know or it's gonna get real hard real fast. By the time I'm through with you, you'll be begging for death."

"Fuck you, asshole. But I'll tell you this. Where your friend is going is gonna be real fun for my pals. They're gonna have a good time with her before they…" he stopped talking, realizing he'd said too much.

"Go on, keep going. Before they what?"

Cotter turned his face away, not answering. His face was covered in a sheen of sweat and his eyes were becoming glassy from blood loss.

Henry sighed, studying the blood seeping out of the man's leg wound. He didn't have much time if he wanted an answer to his questions. He decided he needed to step it up a notch. He wished he had his panga with him, it would make the next phase of the questioning go more smoothly, but he decided he would just have to improvise.

"Tell me where they've gone or so help me…" Henry told him.

Cotter chuckled, bile and blood spilling out of the corner of his mouth. He had punctured something internal in his fall to the ground.

"Screw you. Go 'head and threaten me. You just said I'm too close to dyin' for it to matter."

"Fair enough, we'll do it the hard way." He reached over the man's head and picked up a stick that was lying in the road. It was about a finger's width and one end was sharp. Though not sharp enough to cut someone like a knife, it was more than pointy enough to do what Henry needed it for.

Setting the Glock down out of reach of Cotter's hands, and making sure the man had no weapons on him that Henry could see, the deadland's warrior pressed Cotter's head flat to the dirt and climbed on top of his chest.

"What the hell are you…?" Cotter gasped, but he never got the chance to finish his question.

Henry used the tip of the stick to lever Cotter's left eyeball out. It was harder than he would have thought. He had to force the tip into the edge of the socket and then press hard, angling down with the stick like he was trying to pry something out of a tight hole. The eye popped out like a hardboiled egg and Cotter screamed and yelped with pain as he struggled under Henry.

A clear liquid, tinted pink, dripped out of the raw, open socket and Henry yanked the eye away from the screaming man's face. Tendrils dripped from the orb like spittle as Cotter screamed and screamed and screamed some more underneath him. Behind Henry, Cotter's legs kicked a staccato of agony, the dirt pooling up near his heels.

Henry made sure to hold the slippery orb in his hand as he waved it in front of Cotter's remaining eye. Despite the shrieks of pain, Cotter was able to gaze on his expunged eye with his remaining one.

"Now, unless you want to go to hell blind, I suggest you tell me what I want to know," Henry growled as he squeezed the orb in his hand, the white mucus sliding between his fingers to drip onto Cotter's upturned face.

Cotter swallowed hard, his throat moving up and down, and with his remaining eye dripping tears of pain, the man began to talk.

Jimmy and Cindy reached the top of the rise with their hands full of gear and dropped all of it to the dirt. Henry was across the road, sitting on top of the wounded man. Both of them could see the man's legs kicking and spasming uncontrollably, and hear the man's screams, but before they could call out, the man's legs went motionless.

A silence descended over the area as Henry climbed to his feet, picking up his Glock as he stood. As he walked to Cindy and Jimmy, the young couple could see the wounded man was dead. His face was a bloody mess and both knew he hadn't looked like that when they had gone to retrieve their gear.

"What happened? We heard the yelling," Jimmy asked softly. "But when I didn't hear you or gunshots I figured you were fine." He glanced down at Henry's bloodied hands and already had a notion what had transpired while he and Cindy had been gone.

"His leg wound was bad, Jimmy. He would have bled out before you guys came back. We needed to know what he knew. I had to ask him where Mary was taken before he died."

With a sigh, Jimmy nodded. "Yeah, okay, so did he tell you?"

Henry nodded; his face grim. "Yeah he did. I had to ask real nice, but eventually he came around."

"So, Henry, tell us where she is so we can go get her," Cindy said anxiously.

Henry turned and pointed to the buildings a few miles in the distance. The city of Richmond was still standing tall, though it was now filled with the walking dead

"She's that way. That guy's people brought her to a hospital on the outskirts of the city. It's where they live. From there they raid the nearby areas gathering what they need to live."

"Okay, that doesn't sound so bad. So what's the deal, why did they take her?" Jimmy asked. Then his face took on a concerned look. "Oh shit, was it for mating and shit? Are they gonna rape her?"

Henry's face was hard and his voice was cold as he looked into the eyes of his two friends.

"It's pretty bad, Jimmy. Those bastards are cannibals. They took Mary so they could eat her for dinner."

Cindy gasped and Jimmy's jaw fell open. Henry ignored them both as he reached down, grabbed his clothing, and began getting dressed in the middle of the road.

"Come on, you two, get dressed, we need to move out now," Henry told them both.

There was no time to waste. As soon they were dressed they would be setting off. Unfortunately, the people they were pursuing had vehicles while the companions had to walk. That would definitely slow them down. But as Henry slid on his pants, he stared off at the distant buildings and his jaw went taut.

It didn't matter much. Even if he had to crawl the entire way, he would make sure he got to Mary in time to save her. He had to; the alternative was too much to bear.

He'd save her or he'd die trying. And he would kill anyone who got in his way.

"All right," he said pulling on his shirt, "let's move out. The sooner we get to that hospital the better. Who knows what those bastards are doing to her right now. Let's double time it for as long as we can. We're gonna find her and bring her home and God help who get's in our way."

Jimmy and Cindy nodded, agreeing wholeheartedly, and when Jimmy handed Henry his panga, the older man thanked him and strapped it on.

Shouldering their backpacks, the three companions set out to save their captured friend.

CHAPTER SIX

THE SURROUNDING COUNTRYSIDE was quiet as the three companions jogged down the dirt road and crossed onto the highway. No one spoke, all concentrating on placing one foot in front of the other, the steady rhythm almost hypnotizing each of them, only their steel willpower keeping their attention focused on their destination.

Henry was on point, followed by Cindy, and then Jimmy who took rear guard. As they jogged, all eyes were darting back and forth at each rusted and abandoned vehicle they passed, expecting something to jump out at them at any second.

Behind them in the distance, there was a flurry of activity in the sky as crows and other carrion feeders arrived to feast on the slaughtered dead ghouls lying by the shoreline of the lake.

It seemed like a large black cloud had materialized over the serene surface of the water and was even now dipping to the ground. Henry ignored it. It was the cycle of life. One creature died so another could live. That reasoning made the undead just one step closer to the ultimate abomination.

When a human died by infection it would rise again, thus breaking the cycle of life.

Henry slowed his jogging and raised his right hand for the others to slow down. They had been jogging at a steady pace for over an hour and the first of the outlying buildings for Richmond could now be seen easily. The details on the structures could be discerned without the use of binoculars and all three companions gazed at the burnt and destroyed edifices that were all that remained of the once beautiful buildings.

It was obvious to Henry that a fire had raged here in the past. Sniffing the air, only the most subtle odor of burnt wood and other flammable material came to him.

There was something else that he expected to see walking around on the garbage strewn streets and he wasn't disappointed.

The undead were there, as always, shambling around like a bunch of drunks sent home at closing time from their neighborhood bar. With no prey in sight, they merely moved about slowly, some staring at a particular object they were drawn to.

A few sat down on steps or against cars, their hands in their laps as they waited for something to happen.

Henry couldn't help but wonder if the ones that sat on the ground actually were able to think. Perhaps they were contemplating the fate of the universe, but as no one had ever asked a ghoul what it thought about, but merely shot it in the head on sight, no one would ever know.

"There's a lot of them around," Jimmy said as he studied the street with binoculars. "That's why I hate the cities."

Henry nodded in agreement. "Yeah, but they don't know we're coming and if we just run by them and don't stop, we'll be passed them before they even know we were here. Besides, it's not like we have a choice. If Mary's in there, then that's where we're going."

Cindy had the map and she was reading it, the corners fluttering in the gentle breeze. They were all hot and tired; the swim in the lake already forgotten like it had never happened. Henry hadn't even stopped to wash his hands after crushing Cotter's eyeball in it. He had merely wiped it on some stray weeds and had then finished cleaning his palm on his pant leg. There was no time for niceties. Every second Mary was with those animals was a second that could bring her closer to death.

The only chance she had was if Henry and the others could get to her quickly, before anything was done with, or to, her.

Cindy looked up from the map and pointed to the first intersection in sight.

"If that's Maple Avenue then we need to go that way for two blocks. Once we get to the second intersection we take a left and the hospital should be there."

"Does the place have a name?" Jimmy asked, wiping his brow with his sleeve.

"Yes it does, Jimmy. It's called the Richmond Community Hospital."

"All right then, enough talk," Henry said, "let's move out. Remember, it's not about shooting them down. If you can get around them then do it. Once we're passed the first corner we should be able to lose them fast enough."

"Maybe so, but you'll forgive me if I feel the need to take a few of their heads off," Jimmy exclaimed while racking his shotgun.

"Just keep your eye on the prize, Jimmy. Our goal is to get to the hospital and save Mary, not clean out the city."

Jimmy nodded and the three began moving towards the city limits.

They stayed to the middle of the highway, hoping to be able to get as much warning as possible if one of the ghouls got too close. It didn't take long for the first walking corpse to spot them, and as it sent up a wail that rendered the air, others turned to the sound.

It was the song of the dead.

Henry had heard it more times than he wanted to count. It was almost an instinct for one of the living dead to wail and moan when prey was spotted.

Like a dinner bell being rung, every ghoul in the area would now be coming towards Henry, Jimmy and Cindy.

All they could do was stay on their feet and keep moving.

The first wave of undead came at them from the right, and Henry had the companions immediately veer to the left. The guardrail was on their left and so Henry had them all jump over it. The knee-high barrier would slow the zombies minutely, but perhaps that would be the few seconds they needed to pass by unharmed.

No sooner were they running parallel with the highway, then three zombies popped their rotting heads up and tried to jump them. Henry was still in the front and he used his panga to lop off the hands of the first ghoul to come at him. Despite the loss of its limbs, it still charged forward, and Henry ducked under its arms and kicked it to the ground. Jimmy was on the second one, and as Henry had requested he saved his ammunition, merely whacking the ghoul on the forehead with the butt of the shotgun. A loud crack filled the air and the ghoul fell backwards, its skull fractured. But it wasn't down for the count and as the three companions rushed passed, the ghoul was already rolling to its feet to continue the chase.

Cindy was wielding her M-16 with the utmost precision. When the third ghoul tried for her, she raised the muzzle of the rifle and fired one round at the ghoul's forehead. The bullet took the top of the zombie's scalp off and the body dropped to the grass. She jumped over the body and continued forward.

Henry was using his Steyr, but sparingly, as he targeted any threat from a distance. He would stop running and line up a head in his scope, then after firing, would continue on, not even bothering to see if he had scored a hit.

There was no time. Even as they moved forward, dozens of ghouls were coming out of the woodwork, all wanting the three live humans for a feast.

Jimmy leveled the shotgun barrel at four ghouls that were coming from the right. They were climbing over the guardrail and in less than five seconds would be able to block their path. Moving in front of Henry for a clear shot, Jimmy fired from the hip, not particularly caring where his shots landed as long as they did land on something. The spray of buckshot peppered the ghoul's chests, exposing organs and ribcages. The barrage caused them to fall backwards, and while the dead floundered and tried to recover, the companions moved passed them.

Jimmy actually stepped on the face of one of them, crushing the poor dead man's nose under his combat boots.

"Sorry, fella," Jimmy said as he took his sole off the dead man's face. Then he was passed the ghoul and dealing with the next group of zombies in line.

Henry's plan was working, though. By continuing to keep moving, never slowing down to engage the undead, the three of them were making progress through the city. Already they had reached the first intersection, and after darting around a pile-up in the middle of the intersection, they dashed down the road, leaving the stumbling ghouls behind.

But they were still following and Henry realized he needed some form of a diversion to make sure their escape was complete.

"Jimmy, shoot at that blue car over there. Maybe there's something in the gas tank still left," he told his friend.

Jimmy shook his head. "I don't know, Henry. It's been like a year. What are the odds?"

"How the hell should I know, just do it already," he snapped while the horde grew steadily closer.

Jimmy lined up the shotgun and made sure he was far enough away, so if there was a blast, he wouldn't be caught in it. He fired two shots into the rear of the car, but nothing happened. He turned to look at Henry, an apologetic look on his face.

"Sorry, man, guess it's empty."

Cindy pushed passed him and aimed at the car with her M-16.

"Move away, babe, and let a woman handle this," she said with a slight smirk.

She leveled the M-16 and fired five rounds in quick succession. The first four rounds did nothing, but the fifth must have found the gas tank or fuel line, because one instant all was quiet in the intersection and then there was a loud explosion and a small eruption appeared out of the back of the car.

There was probably not much more than fumes in the gas tank of the old car, but it was more than sufficient to light up the street, catching dozens of ghouls in its blast radius and sending others for cover. A thick, oily smoke rose into the sky from the flattened tires, the caustic wind blowing the opposite way of the companions.

Zombies had quite a distaste for fire, as Henry and the others knew very well.

If he had been able to make a few Molotov cocktails, Henry would have used them happily. Bodies flailed around, waving burning arms and heads twisting back and forth as eyes boiled in their sockets. The smell of burning hair and clothing floated on the wind, the sweet odor of roasting flesh soon following. All the companions had to turn away and breathe through their mouths or risk retching in the street.

With the approaching ghouls now on fire, Henry slapped Jimmy on the shoulder and patted Cindy's arm gently.

"Great job, Cindy. Now come on, let's keep moving. That blast will wake up every friggin' deader in a five block radius."

With one last glance at the flames and the burning corpses, the three began moving again, following Cindy's directions. Multiple ghouls appeared in their path, but they were spread out and were easy to either avoid or take down.

Ten minutes later, they were staring at the hospital with more than fifty zombies following close behind.

Henry studied the building, trying to see how they were going to get inside. More than half of the second and third floor windows were broken, but the front doors and first floor windows were boarded up with heavy plywood, as were all the fire escapes. The sides of the hospital he could see were riddled with a thick layer of moss and a dense growth of thick ivy was covering most of the outside façade of the building. Someone had made the hospital a fortress and now Henry had to find out how to breach its portals.

He was able to see the sides of the hospital and he could see chain-link connecting to the walls and wrapping around the building.

"Uh, Henry, we need to decide what we're going to do quickly or we're gonna end up being zombie chow," Jimmy said as she spun around to watch their backsides. There was a wall of the dead coming straight for them and they had less than two minutes before the first ghouls would be upon them.

"I know that, quiet, I'm thinking," he said as he studied the façade of the hospital; trying to figure out just how the hell they were going to get in.

Cindy's arm suddenly shot across his face as she pointed at something.

"There, Henry, over there by the left corner! See that tree?"

"Uh-huh, what about it?"

"We can climb up it and from there we should be able to jump across to the third floor window."

"What? That's almost an eight foot jump and we'd have to do it while standing on a tree branch. No way, it's too risky," he said, shutting her idea down.

"Uhm, Henry, unless you got a better idea, I suggest we take it," Jimmy said and fired two blasts at the first wave of ghouls. Two went down and another spun in a circle like he was dancing. Then the zombie righted itself and continued forward, now somewhere in the middle of the crowd as others passed him by.

Henry turned around to see the zombie horde and realized Jimmy was right.

"Shit, I see your point. All right then, let's go. Jimmy, take the rear and keep them off our asses," Henry barked as they took off at a run for the tree.

The tree was an old birch that had to be at least thirty years old. Its branches were strong and thick, and the top of the tree was only slightly higher than the three-story hospital. As it was summer, the leaves were full and it was hard to see if there were any suitable branches for their purposes. But like Jimmy said, they were out of time at the moment.

Henry was the first one to the tree and just as he reached the trunk, a ghoul in a bloodied nursing uniform jumped out at him. She'd been hiding in the shade, evidently not wanting to go out in the sun and ruin her pale and blue complexion. Henry pulled his Glock and shot her in the face, the pale-blue face disappearing as the hollow-point round took her head off. He hated wasting a bullet, but time was of the essence right now and all the bullets in the world meant shit if you weren't alive to use them.

"Cindy, up, up, the tree, now, we'll watch your back," Henry told her brusquely. "Once you're up there you can pick off any that get too close."

She nodded, jumped up to the first branch and began climbing; her agile form no match for the tree limbs. In less than fifteen seconds she was six feet into the tree and still climbing.

"Okay, I'm up. Now you two get up here!" She called from inside the leafy canopy. She was so high Henry couldn't see her. But he heard her gunshots as she began dropping ghoul after ghoul moving towards them.

"Come on, Jimmy, pretend your ten again and hanging out in the park," Henry told him as Jimmy turned and began climbing the tree. He had a slow start and Henry pushed him up, his hands on his ass,

"Hey, watch your hands, old man, that ass ain't for you," he joked as he climbed up higher.

Cindy was still firing, every shot dropping a body.

"Just get up there and keep quiet for once, will you please?" Henry said and began climbing himself.

It was as he reached the first branch and was about to pull himself up that a zombie in a doctor's white lab coat came from around the tree and tried to sink his teeth in to his calf.

Henry looked down as the doctor wrapped rotting hands around his ankle and went in for the bite. Henry was able to study the face for one brief instant. Under a shock of black hair rolled two angry eyes that resembled black buttons. The doctor's teeth were a pale yellow with bits of brown in the crevices.

Before Henry could stop him, the doctor's teeth began to clamp down on his flesh. Henry gritted his teeth, expecting to feel the white hot feeling of pain from the bite, but an instant before the teeth connected with his leg, a shot rang out from above and the head exploded, splattering Henry's boots and leg with gore.

Without stopping for another ghoul to grab him, Henry kicked the dead doctor away from him and scurried higher into the tree. When he was few feet up, Jimmy reached down with his left hand. In his right was his still smoking .38.

"Thanks, Jimmy, I think you just saved my ass," Henry said while he was pulled into the tree branches just as the first line of ghouls arrived at the tree like a charging army. They clawed and moaned at the base of the trunk, but none had the dexterity to climb the tree. If a ladder had been there, then yes, perhaps a few would have figured it out. But to climb the tree, they would have to jump a foot into the air to grab the first branch and then haul themselves up. Those actions were far too advanced for the dead remnants of humanity.

Henry was breathing hard as he stared down at the mass of heads and upturned faces. His backpack was still hanging on his shoulder and he shifted it to the side. The packs would make climbing difficult, but they would make do.

Jimmy was next to him; his butt perched on the same branch. The limb was as thick as his thigh and was more than strong enough to hold them. Up above, Henry could hear Cindy shifting position. As soon as Henry made it into the tree she had stopped firing, not wanting to waste any more ammunition than necessary.

Jimmy hacked a load of phlegm and let it slide from his mouth. The green drop slid out of his lips, the strand of spittle stretching until it broke, then plummeted into the face of one of the undead below. The ghoul blinked the mucus away, but could have cared less. Already the odor of rotting bodies and a cloud of flies was surrounding the tree, threatening to gag the companions.

Henry decided it was time to keep moving. The sooner they were in the hospital the better.

"We're coming up," Henry called as he began climbing the tree. It wasn't hard. There were more than enough limbs shooting off at odd angles from the trunk of the tree, and much like a crooked ladder, he made his way upwards, with Jimmy following behind him.

Below them the wailing and moaning continued and Henry couldn't help but feel like the cat that had been chased up the tree by the neighborhood dog.

Cindy was waiting near the top and she moved to the side so Henry could climb up next to her. He stood on a lower branch and Jimmy waited below. There was only so much room and Jimmy didn't want to crowd them.

"Well, here we are, Cindy. So it's your idea, what's next?" Henry asked as he held on for dear life. A gentle breeze was blowing, and this high up in the tree, the top swayed back and forth gently, much like riding on a sail boat in gentle waters.

Cindy moved a few branches aside and cut a few of the smaller ones off with her knife. The young sapling branches wouldn't cut easily and she had to twist them again and again until only the bark was hanging on. Then she cut the remaining bark and tossed the branches away. Once she'd cleared a small opening, she was able to see the side of the hospital. She scooted out onto the nearest branch and only stopped when the branch began to dip under her weight, the end of the limb becoming thinner. The entire tree shifted slightly with her weight, but it was so minor it could hardly be felt over the movement from the wind.

She went as far as she could go. When she stared down at the swarming undead faces below and then at the hospital wall and windows, she felt her heart sink in her chest.

"Well, can we do it?" Jimmy called from below. From where he was, he couldn't see anything. He decided he needed to pee, and without any hesitation, he unzipped his pants and sprayed the warm stream onto the upturned faces of the dead, chuckling softly as he did it.

Henry chose to ignore his antics and focused on Cindy as she slid back to the tree trunk.

"Well? Which of the branches can we use?"

"Uhm, Henry, I, uh, don't quite know how to say this, but I think I may have spoken too soon about us climbing this tree."

"What was that?" Jimmy called as he zipped his pants back up.

"What are you talking about?" Henry asked, shifting his gaze from her face to the side of the hospital.

"Here, Henry, maybe you should just go out on the branch and look for yourself," she said, scooting out of the way.

Henry nodded and climbed higher, setting his boots on the branch Cindy had vacated. It was a strong and sturdy branch and he was confident it would hold him. Using a higher branch to hold onto, he slid out onto the limb, his feet swaying back and forth like he was crossing a tightrope connected to two buildings. It took him less than thirty seconds to reach where Cindy had been and when he was at the end of the branch; he looked down at the wailing bodies of the dead below.

Living dead people.

Every now and then he still was struck with the absolute absurdity of the situation. The dead walked and wanted to eat him, just like in a bad horror movie. He pulled his eyes away from the undead faces and looked up over his hands and into the top of the tree which was only another nine feet above him. As he was out on the limb, the tree angled slightly outward and he was able to see there were no tree limbs long enough to reach the window. Even if they tried to jump across, there would be no way to make it safely. At least they couldn't do it without ropes and climbing gear to swing across.

The reality slammed into him and he turned to look at Cindy who was watching him. Her eyes were wide and he could see the small tears welling up in the corners of her eyes. She knew the truth and had sent him out here so he could see it for himself.

They were trapped in a tree with a hundred zombies just waiting for them to either fall or die of starvation. They had a limited amount of ammunition and one of their own was captured and could even now either be dead or being tortured by sadistic cannibals.

He sat on the tree limb and glanced back down passed his boots at the wailing faces of the dead and shook his head.

He had no damn idea what they were going to do next.

"Hey, so what's the verdict? When do we go into the hospital? Guys? Hey, guys, hello up there?" Jimmy called from below.

Neither Henry nor Cindy answered him, both too numb to want to say anything; each lost in the hopelessness of their situation.

Meanwhile, below them, the song of the dead continued. A symphony that would have only one conclusion. And that would be when the three companions fell from the tree, their last breaths expelled from their bodies upon their deaths.

CHAPTER SEVEN

MARY BALANCED ON a tightrope of unconsciousness. Try as she might, she couldn't pull herself from her fugue state. She knew if she was going to survive whatever was happening to her, she would need to come to her senses, but her rattled brain refused to cooperate.

After being struck unconscious and dragged to the van, she'd lain prone on the floor as the vehicle jounced and bounced down the road.

A few times she struggled to wake, the light so close she thought she could touch it. In these times she felt rough hands caressing her body and could hear deep voices arguing. Then the hands were removed and she fell back into a pit of darkness.

It was when the van came to a halt, the brakes squeaking loudly, that she slowly regained some of her faculties. With her eyes creased partly, she played possum and tried to take in her surroundings. That she was inside a vehicle was obvious, and as she tried to peek out the front windshield, all she could see was sky.

But then the van moved closer to a building and she saw the distinct markings of a hospital or hospice center. She heard more than felt a loading dock door open and then the van was driving inside, like it had drove into a cave. The doors slammed shut behind her and as she shifted her head slightly so she was able to look through the small windows on the rear doors of the van. She saw the accordion doors close with a resounding crash and then the rear doors of the van were being tossed open and men with dirty faces and foul breathe were wrapping their hands around her and picking her up. She was thrown to the floor of the loading dock and was immediately tied up. Her arms were pulled behind her and she felt like a Christmas turkey when her ankles were secured, as well.

The room was full of people; women's voices could be heard alongside the gruff voices of men.

Someone picked her up and she was tossed across someone's shoulder like a sack of potatoes, she was then bounced and jumbled as the crowd began moving deeper into the building.

Her head was filling with blood and she began to feel queasy while she was carried upside down like an animal carcass. The foul fragrances penetrating her nose made her want to gag and she had to fight to keep her stomach quiet. Her nose was buried into the back of whoever carried her and the man's body odor was enough to knock her unconscious all by itself.

But she stayed silent, knowing her only chance was to try and gather as much information as possible on the hope she could try and break free later.

The man carrying her, it had to be a man as the figure was at least six-two, strolled through the hallway and up stairs and through fire doors, the rest of the crowd behind him. But slowly, as she moved deeper into the building, the crowd began to disperse until only a half dozen remained.

Sneaking peeks of her surroundings every now and then, through slit eyelids, it didn't take her long to realize she was inside a hospital, just as she'd assumed. The white walls and gurneys lining the hallway, plus the open doors where glimpses of hospital beds could be seen, more than told her where she'd been transported to. The hospital was in disarray, however, papers sprawled across the floor, the white walls marred every few feet by splashes of dried blood, like a mad artist had attempted his art and failed miserably. Beds in rooms were either stripped of their linen or the sheets were rolled into messy piles on the floor or the foot of the bed.

She was carried for another seven minutes, then the man slowed and she felt herself being whipped around and dropped onto a hospital bed. Her breath left her in a whoosh, and before she could do anything, her arms and legs were freed from their bonds only to be spread apart on the hospital bed, where they were quickly re-secured with straps used for mental patients.

A face leaned over and became so close she could feel breathing, the warm breath on her cheek.

"I know you're awake, darlin', so you might as well open your eyes and see your new home," a low voice said. It had a southern drawl to it and the miasma of his breath made her gag despite herself. "For the short time you'll be here, that is."

Deciding she had nothing to lose, she opened her eyes and gasped at her surroundings, a bright white light causing her to blink a few times, spots in front of her eyes, clouding her vision.

She was in what was once used for an operating room, the large room now missing most of the expensive machinery. Spotlights covered every wall, all pointed at different angles for maximum coverage. Her ears caught the faint sound of a generator purring nearby and she realized the white light was one of the spotlights aimed directly on her face.

The man shifted the light and she blinked away the spots.

When she gazed around the room again, her heart jumped in her throat. There were other beds in here with her, and two of them had people on them. Only the people weren't as whole as they once were. A man in his mid-thirties was missing the flesh of both his legs, only the gristle and tendons still remaining. His legs looked like turkey legs after a particularly hungry diner had finished gnawing on them. There was a leather belt secured around each of the man's legs near his crotch so he wouldn't bleed to death. The skin was purple and black around the belts. He was moaning softly, in and out of consciousness, and Mary tasted bile as she gazed on his pitiful form.

On the bed next to him, a woman around the same age was missing her right arm completely, another leather band protecting her from bleeding to death and both her breasts were cut away, leaving jagged and bloody scars that wept a clear red fluid like tears. Her eyes were wide with pain as she stared at the ceiling, her hair matted with sweat.

"See, you've got company while you're here," the man drawled as he spun her bed around so she could get a better look at her roommates.

"We're almost done with them, sugar, and when we are, we'll get started on you."

Both the man and woman had gags in their mouth, but their eyes spoke volumes. Both had orbs filled with utter agony and tears ran down the woman's cheeks in a steady trickle.

"Hey, Sterling, you comin' or what! We're starvin'," a voice called from the hallway. The man turned towards the voice and Mary now knew the man's name. It wasn't much, but at least it was something.

"Yeah, shut the fuck up, I'm comin'. Go on without me," Sterling yelled back into the hallway. "I'll be there in a minute."

An imprecation was tossed through the door and the hidden voice left. After receiving his answer, he turned around and lowered his face so he was less than an inch from Mary's.

His tongue slid out of his mouth and he licked her face from chin to forehead, his breathe smelling like something had died in there and he'd decided not to bother plucking it out afterward. His teeth appeared to be filed to small points. Nothing exaggerated, but simply enhancing what was in his mouth.

"Mmmm, you taste good," he said, exhaling onto her face, his tongue like a small pink snake exploring her features. "I'm looking forward to having some of you," he whispered into her ear. His right hand slid down her pants and he clutched her crotch from the outside. Mary cringed when she felt his hands on her, but she knew better than to show it. Instead, her eyes locked onto his and her face remained impassive, despite the fact she wanted to scream with anger and fear.

Sterling chuckled and pulled his hand away. His eyes roamed up and down her body one last time, then he turned and walked away from her. But he wasn't leaving yet.

Reaching out to a small table, he picked up a filthy scalpel and walked over to the wounded woman.

The woman began to squeal under her gag and tried to twist in her straps, but it was hopeless. She was trussed up like an animal for slaughter and as Mary watched, she saw that wasn't far from the truth. In fact, it was right on the money.

First, he picked up another leather belt and wrapped it around the woman's other arm, cinching it tightly. Then he got to work.

She could only watch helplessly while Sterling wielded the blade like a butcher, slowly slicing off a piece of the woman's remaining arm an inch at a time. He slid the scalpel in like she was a holiday ham and carved her skin until bone showed. The woman screamed behind her gag, thrusting her head back and forth in agony, while the man went wild on the next bed. It was then Mary realized they had to be together. She saw the angst on the man's face as he watched his mate being dissected like a worm in science class and he could do nothing to stop it.

Sterling continued his ministrations for almost ten minutes, his back to Mary most of the time. But she could see the blood dripping off the edge of the bed to pool on the floor, and the sounds of the tortured woman's screams through her gag.

Then Sterling grabbed the tourniquet and made sure it was tight enough so the woman wouldn't bleed out.

"There, that's good enough for now. I'll be back later for the rest of that arm," he grinned broadly while backing away from the shaking woman.

He had a stainless steel bowl in his hands and it was piled four inches high with the woman's flesh. The bloody meat looked like slices of pork being prepared for the grill and Mary stared in absolute shock when the man began licking his bloody hands clean like he'd just eaten a plateful of ribs and wasn't about to waste the barbecue sauce.

"Mmmm, that's good eatin'; especially when it's fresh. You want a taste?" He shoved a piece of human meat into Mary's face and she turned her head away, her stomach spasming inside her.

"You're sick, you know that? Get away from me, you prick."

Sterling giggled softly and dropped the meat back onto the plate, the blood glistening in the bright lights of the spotlights.

"Okay, darlin', I'll see you later. I've got to get this meat a grillin' before my mates kick my ass."

With a wave of a slightly less bloody hand after cleaning it with his tongue, Sterling left the room, leaving Mary alone with the suffering couple. As he passed the doorway, his hand reached out and he turned off the spotlights with the jury rigged on/off switch hanging from the ceiling, wires leading from it to the lights.

The room was immediately bathed in darkness, only the wan light from the hallway casting a few streaks of illumination into the room. Mary tried to see the man and woman but they were now only dim outlines.

The woman was crying and screaming in pain as her exposed left arm glistened dully in the shadows, the gristle and bone catching what little light and reflecting it back.

Mary couldn't even imagine how much pain the woman had to be in, but she had an inkling when the woman finally passed out and was silent. Now, only the man's weeping filled the room and Mary twisted her head so she could see him better. His eyes were glaring at her, tears in their corners.

"Hey, just hang on. I don't know if you believe me or not, but I have friends out there somewhere and I know they'll find me. We just have to hang on until they get here."

The man couldn't answer her, and didn't even try. Instead, he closed his eyes and continued weeping. He was beyond hope. With both his legs nothing but bone, how could he hope to survive, even if he did somehow manage to escape?

No, he already knew his fate and that of his wife.

Mary said nothing as the man turned away, his eyes squeezed closed in his anguish. There was nothing else to be said. Her eyes went back to the prone woman and the pieces missing from her.

Mary's heart began to pound faster. That was going to be her fate soon.

She could only pray she could find a way to escape this house of horrors or that Henry and the others would find her before she became the main course at a dinner in her honor, or end up on the dinner table next to the man and woman as a side dish.

Though she tried to keep her spirits up, tried to stay positive, there was a small part of her, deep down and growing with each passing minute that told her things were going to end badly.

CHAPTER EIGHT

MORE THAN TWO hours had passed when Henry spoke up; alerting the others he had something to say. Both Cindy and Jimmy were on a wide branch above him, sitting together with their arms wrapped around one another. Both had tired eyes and were only moments away from sleep.

"Enough of this, dammit, we need to find a way off this tree and into that hospital. It can't end like this. It's humiliating. After every-thing we've been through to get trapped in a goddamn tree. It's ridiculous."

"I hear ya, Henry," Jimmy said, "but we've tried to figure a way out of here and so far we've come up empty. All we'll end up doing is getting torn to pieces."

"One of us could drop down and try to draw the deaders away. Then while they go after one of us, the other two can try to get into the hospital," Cindy suggested.

"No, Cindy, that's not gonna happen. Whoever drops down from this tree is dead. No, there has to be another way. We just need to find it."

They all sat staring at one another again as the tree swayed softly in the wind. The sun was at its zenith and would be working its way down soon. None of them were looking forward to spending the night in the tree. Below them the undead continued scratching at the bark, trying to climb over one another to get at the companions. So far none had succeeded.

Henry wasn't willing to take that chance and had gone down a few branches, his panga ready at his side. If any of the ghouls actually made it to the first branch, all they would meet was the edge of his blade.

Henry was watching the dead again, studying their movements. It was hypnotizing, the way they swayed back and forth, arms and hands over their heads as they tried to grasp the prey out of reach. Above him, Jimmy sat quietly with Cindy, but the young man's mind was still working as he gazed at the hospital and its windows; so close yet so far. His eyes roamed up the tree trunk, to the top of the tree and he watched it sway gently in the wind.

Like a light bulb appearing over his head, Jimmy sat erect, his eyes staring at the top of the tree and then to the hospital window across the gap. He did some calculations in his head as he tried to guess if his idea would work, but he couldn't come up with any kind of certainty.

No, like most things in the dead world he now lived in, there was no certainty. Only assumptions and guesses.

Cindy noticed him looking at the tree and building and she realized something was happening in his head.

"What's wrong? Why are you looking around like that? Do you see something?"

Jimmy smiled widely as he pulled her closer and squeezed her arm. He hesitated, enjoying knowing something she didn't.

"Why yes, I did? I think I just figured out how we're gonna get into that hospital and out of this damn roost. I, my dear, have come up with a plan."

Henry heard him and he looked up at Jimmy's feet swinging above his head. He was in a foul mood and wasn't gonna get any happier anytime soon.

"Oh, you did? And what exactly is this great plan of yours? Are we gonna just fly over there?" Henry quipped.

Jimmy smiled even wider, his teeth flashing in the sun.

"Yeah, actually, that's exactly what we're gonna do."

"Are you crazy? That's ridiculous. It'll never work," Henry said while shaking his head vehemently.

Jimmy scowled at the older man, not pleased to have his idea shot down so fast.

"Well, I think it'll work and I'm gonna do it."

"Oh really. And are you willing to bet your life on it? Because that's what you'll be doing. If you miss and fall, you'll be torn to pieces by those dead bastards before me or Cindy can help you."

"He's got a point, Jimmy," Cindy said while placing a hand on his arm protectively.

"Oh great, now you're against me too?"

"No one's against you, Jimmy. Jesus Christ, we just don't want to see you get killed, that's all."

"And what happens if we stay here, Henry? We either die of starvation or try to run for it and end up being run down like dogs? But then we'll only be weaker from lack of food. No way, man; that's not for me. If I gotta go, then at least I can say I tried to get away. Besides, what about Mary? We're her only hope, right? If we die, so does she."

Henry didn't have an answer for him and thinking about Mary and what she may even now be suffering wouldn't help their present situation. They needed to get to her fast. Already too many hours had passed and it was very possible she was already beyond saving.

"Look, Henry, I'm gonna do it whether you help or not, so what do ya say you help me? It'll increase my odds."

Punching the tree with the side of his fist, Henry nodded.

"Dammit, Jimmy. I still don't like this, but fine, I'll help. But so help me if this doesn't work, I'll kill you myself before the first deader gets his teeth into you."

Jimmy flashed him a sly grin as he shrugged out of his backpack.

"Henry, I wouldn't want it any other way."

So the three of them got to work. Jimmy actually had the easy part, as did Cindy. It was Henry who had to do the physical labor.

Jimmy's plan was actually quite simple, though incredibly risky.

He would climb to the top of the tree and hold on for dear life while Henry would use his panga to begin hacking at the trunk about ten feet down from the top.

If all went as planned, Jimmy would topple over and the tip of the tree would fall directly near the closest hospital window. Jimmy would have to time it perfectly and jump into the opening, then once inside, could find some rope or something similar that could be used as climbing gear; then toss the gear across to the tree where Henry would secure it to the trunk. Once that was done, Henry and Cindy would simply slide over.

Piece of cake, right?

But there were a few problems. For one, the tree had to fall in just the right place or Jimmy would just end up plummeting to his death. And even if he survived the fall, the undead were waiting to catch him in their rotting embrace.

Jimmy handed Cindy his backpack, and with a soft kiss on her forehead, he scuttled up the tree. His stomach did flip-flops inside him as he hung on to the swaying tree top. He was only able to climb up to three feet from the top before the trunk became to thin to support him.

Once he was in place, he called down to Henry.

"Okay, old man. You better get this right or when I die I'm gonna come back and haunt you."

Henry didn't reply, deciding a comment wasn't necessary. He was pretty sure Jimmy was just talking trash, trying to psych himself up.

Henry nodded to Cindy. "Okay, honey, take out that window across from us and then I'll get started."

With her M-16 in hand, Cindy slid out onto the branch until she was only seven feet from the plate glass window, the limb bending dangerously to the point of breaking. Making sure she was secure, she cocked the weapon and fired three rounds at the glass. Bullet holes appeared, but the window didn't break.

"Dammit, Henry, it's safety glass. I'll need to waste a lot more ammo to get it open for Jimmy.

"Then do it. Ammo don't mean shit if we're dead."

She nodded and turned back to the window, spraying the glass with the weapon on full auto. With each round through the glass, another piece disappeared and soon the entire window was nothing but cracks and spider webs.

"Okay, that's about it. When he hits that glass it's gonna collapse easily."

"All right, then, good work. Now it's my turn." Henry looked up into the tree branches above his head and called up to Jimmy, despite the fact he couldn't see his friend.

"You ready, Jimmy?"

"Yeah, let's do this; I'm getting seasick up here!" He called down.

With butterflies in his stomach, Henry began chopping at the trunk while Cindy moved to a lower branch. Below them, the undead moaned louder, as if they sensed something was happening above them.

Henry used the panga like an ax, gouging an inch at a time out of the birch's trunk. It would take a while, but at the moment none of them had anywhere to go.

Fifteen minutes in, Henry was feeling confident his cuts were well placed. Hacking at an angle, the upper part of the tree would soon be ready to topple; with Jimmy on the tip like the star on a Christmas tree.

With another hearty, thwack, the tree trunk cracked softly and Henry realized one or two more blows would do the job.

"Okay, Jimmy, any second now! Get ready, 'cause you're going down at any moment!"

"I'm ready; just make sure I fall the right way, goddammit!"

Henry wiped the sweat from his brow, and with a glance from Cindy for support, he hacked at the trunk again.

This time the trunk cracked a little more and Henry knew the next one would do it. Cindy had her fingers crossed as she stared at the trunk and Henry drew back his arm and let the panga fly.

The last sinew of bark was severed and the tree began to fall towards the hospital. From inside the branches, Henry couldn't tell if the top was falling true, but he heard Jimmy yell as he went down towards the hospital window.

"Oh my God, Jimmy!" Cindy yelled and tried to climb higher. Henry stopped her, not wanting her or him to be caught in the falling trunk.

One second they were in the shade of the branches, and the next, the sun was shining brightly down on them as the top half of the tree became horizontal.

But there was no sign of Jimmy. Henry tried to see through the mess of leaves, and as he tried to climb through the debris of sticks and twigs, he already feared the worst for his friend.

Jimmy felt the tree tipping and let out a yowl of terror, his stomach remaining in the air while the rest of him plummeted to the ground.

It wasn't easy, but he stayed focused, understanding he was already at the point of no return.

He rode the tree down, and when he thought the window was at the right spot, he jumped from the tree, his body arcing through the air like an acrobat without a net.

For two brief seconds he was actually flying, like in one of his dreams when he was a young boy. He wanted to fly like Superman and now here he was doing it. Only he wasn't invulnerable, and if he didn't reach that window, he would be deader than dead.

The feeling of weightlessness was gone before he could even attempt to enjoy it and then he was crashing through the pockmarked window. But his timing was off and he ended up striking his right shoulder against the frame of the window. When his body hit, the left side of him spun in a circle and his legs struck the glass first. The weakened glass shattered into a thousand crystal shards and he tumbled into the hospital like a wet rag doll, his shotgun flying out of his hands to slide across the room.

Glass was everywhere and he cried out when something pierced his thigh just above his right knee. The air was knocked from his lungs as he landed hard on the floor of the room, his body rolling across the carpeting until he came up against a wooden door.

He could hear Henry and Cindy calling him, but he had no air to reply to their queries. All he could do was gaze up at the white painted ceiling and try to stay conscious. What seemed like minutes, but was in fact only seconds, passed by. He came to his senses and sucked in a lungful, of air.

Rolling over onto his side, he winced in pain. His leg was bloody and there was a sharp piece of glass sticking out of his pants. The glass was as thin as a pen and about as long. Careful not to cut himself, he yanked the shard free, howling when he did it.

White light flooded his vision as nerves overloaded, but after a minute everything reset in his brain and he could see again. He studied the wound, but the blood was minimal. It would need attention, yes, but at least he hadn't hit an artery. If he had, then their escape would have been over real quick.

Standing up, favoring the bad leg, he limped to the open window.

As he looked down at the ghouls below, some of them buried under the tree top, he couldn't help but start to laugh.

"Whoo-hoo, I did it! I fuckin' did it. I am a god!" He yelled out through the window at all who wanted to hear and to all who didn't. He was so pumped full of adrenalin he honestly thought if he jumped out the window he would just fly away.

"Jimmy? Are you all right? We can't see in here. You're in the window right? You've got to be, otherwise you wouldn't be talking to us," Henry said from inside the tree branches.

"Actually, Henry, you were right the second time. I didn't make it and now I'm a ghost. Like I said, I'm gonna haunt your ass till the day you die." He began moaning like a ghost, laughing all the while. God he felt good, alive.

"Very funny, ha, ha. Listen, stop screwing around. Are you all right or what?"

"Yeah, I'll live. I'm a little banged up, but hey, we're in the right place for that, right?"

"Uh, yeah, guess so. All right then. I'm glad your damn fool plan worked; congratulations. Now how about finding a way to get us across to join you," Henry called back.

"Okay, Henry, just hold on tight and I'll see what I can do." He turned from the window and began his search for something to use as a rope or wire.

Cindy was slightly below Henry and she called up, panic in her voice.

"Uhm, Henry, we've got a slight problem down here," she called and then Henry heard her fire the M-16.

He slid down the few feet until he was just over her head.

"What's wrong now?"

She gestured with the barrel of the rifle, then fired another shot at a ghoul's head. She missed the head, but the round caught it in the shoulder. The body tumbled back to the ground.

"That," she said coldly and fired again.

"Oh shit, you've got to be kidding me," Henry muttered as he looked down to the ground.

When the top of the tree had fallen to the ground, the large branches had landed against the tree trunk. Now the large branches were a perfect ladder for the undead to use to climb into the tree. One at a time, they were slowly climbing into the birch tree, their eyes locked onto Henry and Cindy.

"Come on, Cindy; get up higher in the tree. We can keep them back easier that way," Henry told her.

"But there's too many of them. We'll run out of ammo before long. Then we'll be down to knives."

"Yeah, I know, but hopefully Jimmy will be back before that happens. Now come on, get up while I cover you."

Cindy turned and began climbing higher; though minus the top half, the tree was much smaller now. Henry kicked the closest ghoul away from him. The body tumbled away to be lost in the tree branches. He could hear the snapping of branches even over the moaning of the dead and he knew that one would be down for the count for a while, if not for good. Then he began climbing into the top of the tree. When he reached the branch level with the open window, he hacked away a few of the limbs that were small and nothing but a nuisance.

"Cindy, get our packs together and put them near the window. That way we're ready to go when Jimmy gets back!"

"Got it," she said and got to work, shouldering her rifle so her hands were free. Henry reached up and plucked the Steyr from the branch he'd hung it on. He had made sure the strap was secure, not wanting to lose the new possession to his arsenal. Over the past year, he'd gone through many weapons, only the Glock and panga with him from the beginning. But he had to admit, he liked the long rifle. It made a tough job easier when he could pick off his targets from a distance.

Lowering the barrel of the rifle so it was pointing down, he slid the bolt-action and chambered a round. Then he took off the head of the next dead man in line. The ghouls head seemed to implode, then explode, blowing chunks of gore in every direction.

He fired one at a time at the approaching ghouls, but for every dead man or woman he put down, there were two more to replace them.

They were now fighting the clock.

Jimmy's escape had now closed the trap on Henry and Cindy and all they could do was try to hold on until he returned.

If he returned.

Henry had no idea what Jimmy would find in the hospital, and if he became wounded or killed before he could return with the rope, then Henry and Cindy would soon follow him into death.

Well, if that did happen and he died today, he thought, at least he'd have a lot of company in Hell.

CHAPTER NINE

JIMMY MOVED THROUGH the second floor wing of the hospital, a slight limp to his gait. His leg was throbbing, but he pushed it aside. He had already seen what was happening outside before going in search of some sort of climbing gear and he knew his time was short. Or rather, his friends' time was short.

Stepping into the hallway, he immediately detected the smell of decay.

The hall was littered with the trash one would expect to find in a hospital corridor. IV stands, gurneys and miscellaneous paraphernalia, such as needles and plastic gloves, were everywhere.

Ignoring it all as unnecessary for his needs, he moved further down the gloom filled hallway.

There was nothing so far that he could use. Poking his head into a few of the rooms off the hall, all he found were bloodstained sheets and empty rooms. More than one room had sprays of brown covering its walls, dried blood from more than a year ago.

He tried not to think what the hospital must have been like in those last days.

He imagined every person who was sick would have come here and then each one would have turned into a ghoul. One at a time the hospital staff would have been slaughtered until all that would have remained behind these hallowed walls would have been the living dead.

And if that was so, then where had all the bodies gone?

As he slowly walked down the corridor, stepping over stray debris, he idly noticed he had yet to see a single body or skeleton. Surely there would be some remnants of the slaughter that had taken place here all those months ago. And yet there were none.

He was at the end of the hallway when he looked down at his feet to see yet another dried blood stain. The stain was heavy in the middle, then spread out like a can of paint would do when spilt. Something or someone had been in the middle of that stain and had bled out.

But once again there was no body to be found.

With his shotgun leveled in his hands, he moved around the next corner, but still there was nothing. Just an empty hallway. Peeking into the first room, all that was there was another hospital bed with stained sheets and an empty room. Then he heard muffled sounds coming from the end of the corridor, and he slowly moved towards it, his finger on the trigger of his shotgun.

Step by step he crept to the double doors at the end of the hall, and when he tried to push them open they wouldn't budge. He was able to peek through the small four-inch window on the left-hand door. He immediately saw there was something blocking it. He was pretty confident one good kick would open it. While peeking through the glass panel, all he saw were shadows on the other side. Only a few splinters of light could be seen penetrating the darkened corridor, coming from partially opened doors that probably led to other rooms.

Were there darker shadows moving across the floor in there? He couldn't be sure, but he knew they were not large enough to be zombies as they appeared to only be about two feet in length, none more than a foot.

Another idea crossed his mind, but he quickly forced it down as implausible, and tried to think of something more rational.

Maybe the shadows were lost pets or something which had become trapped inside the wing? Or maybe a family of animals had taken up residence inside this part of the hospital.

It wouldn't be the first time the animal kingdom encroached on what had once belonged to mankind. Many times in the past year, wild animals had taken up residence in abandoned stores, old cars and empty apartment buildings. Jimmy wondered what the world would look like in another ten years with all the neglect in the world. He wondered if the dead cities that now littered America would even still be recognizable. Every day the trees and weeds and foliage seemed to take another inch back from mankind's world. Someday he figured it would all just be buried under a carpet of green.

And maybe by then, man would be gone, too. He figured it would be the animals who inherited the earth, with a few enclaves of humanity stretched far apart from one another. Instead of being the dominant animal, man would be relegated to just another hunted species.

In the end, it would be the living dead that would become the dominant life form on earth.

Jimmy didn't worry about it much, though. He figured sooner or later his luck would run out and he would end up long dead before any of his ideas would come to pass.

Then his eyes spotted a sign on the wall just a few feet past the double doors. Squinting to read the sign in the dim light, he mouthed the word softly.

If he had read the sign right, and he was pretty sure he did, then he thought he had an inkling to what was inside the closed off portion of the hospital wing.

Gunshots sounded from behind him, pulling him from his ruminations and telling him what he already knew.

He was running out of time to save his friends.

Deciding the shadows on the other side of the double doors could wait; his eyes scanned the empty rooms nearby again. What could he use as a rope?

Then an idea struck him.

Moving as fast as he could, he got to work gathering what he would need, while behind him gunshots continued to echo again and again, reminding him of fireworks on the Fourth of July.

Henry shot another two ghouls that were trying to reach him, sending both tumbling backwards into the undead crowd below.

With a half-second of breathing room, he popped the clip on his Glock to see how many remained.

Three rounds.

Three rounds and he'd be down to his Steyr again and he already knew he was low on ammo for the rifle, as well. He'd changed back to the Glock when the branches made it hard for him to aim, the twigs catching in the butt stock.

"I'm almost down to spitting at them, Cindy. How 'bout you?" He asked as he looked up at the blonde woman. She was perched a few feet above him, her M-16 aimed down at the shifting bodies.

"I don't know for sure. I'd have to say a few more bullets still in this clip and then I got one more left. My Ruger's dry, used it up a few minutes ago. After that I'm with you. If funny looks don't stop them, I guess that'll be it. But I know my boy. Jimmy will be here. We just have to give him time."

Henry kicked a ghoul in the face as the dead woman tried to reach for him.

"Yeah, but time is the one thing we don't have." As if to illustrate his point, five ghouls began trying to climb up the tree simultaneously, using the branches of the severed tree top.

"Okay, here they come again," Henry said and fired two rounds into the faces of the first two in line, the spent casings falling to the ground like silver hail. Cindy joined in and once again the air was filled with the moaning of the dead and the gunshots of the companions.

More minutes passed by and still no Jimmy.

Henry's Glock clicked on an empty chamber and he cursed, swinging the Steyr around to fire at the first ghoul coming for him.

"This is it, Cindy. A few more minutes and we're down to hands and feet."

"I'm ready, Henry, just say when," she answered back, her jaw taut.

Henry spared her an extra glance, admiring the beautiful woman's courage. Ever since she had joined the group, Cindy had been an asset. She was smart, fearless and not afraid to do something the hard way. She was a good influence on Jimmy and ever since she had met the wise-cracking younger man, Jimmy had slowly been changing into a new person.

He was not so quick to shoot without checking first, and he knew Cindy kept Jimmy on a tight leash, one where the young man wasn't allowed to wander to far. But despite all this, Jimmy was still Jimmy.

But Henry still couldn't imagine going into battle with another person besides her, with the exception of Mary and Jimmy. The four of them had become a family. Not all families had to be blood related. Some families were forged in battle and the blood of others that had been spilt.

That was what they were. Blood brothers that would live or die for one another. He had only wished he had been that close to someone in his own family like that.

Well, there was one. His wife, Emily. But she was worm food now, like millions of others, so she didn't count.

The next wave of zombies began coming at him, and with his Glock empty and not wanting to waste rounds for the Steyr unless he had to, he began to climb higher into the tree. Cindy followed and soon they were both at the new top, the jagged trunk where Henry had chopped it in two looking like a punk rocker's hair, all spiky and sprouting in different angles.

"We wait here until they come higher and then we use the rest of your ammo. After that it's kicking and punching. For however long we can last."

Cindy nodded in agreement and shifted position on the branch. Below them, the ghouls continued climbing. Thankfully they weren't the most athletic, and many of the clumsy ghouls would slip or miss a handhold, tumbling back down the tree, usually taking a few others with them. But still they came and Henry watched as the forerunner slowly climbed higher.

Then something white shot out of the hospital window where Jimmy had jumped into and Henry was hit in the face with a light material.

Grabbing on instinct, he immediately realized it was a sheet, though the whiteness was seriously discolored with multiple brown spots. He followed the end of the sheet to see it trail across the gap and into the window. Every seven feet or so there was a knot where two sheets had been tied together, making a makeshift rope. These knots appeared twice before until entering the window where Jimmy was waving, a smile creasing his lips.

"Hey, guys. This is the best I could do on short notice. Come on, I tied it off to the door frame!"

Henry didn't hesitate, knowing time was of the essence. Turning, he pushed Cindy to the end of the branch she was on, shoving the end of the sheet into her hand.

"Go, girl, now. Hurry, we don't have much time!"

She took the sheet and nodded, then began sliding out to the end of the tree, there was still over ten feet separating her from the window and she stared at the gap, not knowing how she was supposed to get across.

"Cindy, tie the end of the sheet to a branch and then you can crawl across!" Jimmy called to her.

Her face lit up with understanding and she quickly turned around, moving back until she was at the base of the trunk. As quickly as she could, she wrapped the end around the tree, pulling it taut. Then, with the sheet now like a thick clothesline, she moved back to the end, and with hands wrapped around the sheet, began to crawl across the gap hand over hand.

Her legs hung below her only a few feet from the tops of the undead and they reached up, wanting to pull her down with them. She tried not to look down, but instead concentrated on moving across the gap while her M-16 swung back and forth.

Inch by inch she made progress, her rifle slapping her back painfully and her backpack dragging her down from its weight. But she persevered and within a few minutes was within arms reach of Jimmy.

Jimmy leaned out the window, his right hand stretched out for her.

"Here, take my hand and I'll pull you up!" He screamed over the yells and moans of the dead below them. Henry waited impatiently while he watched Cindy pulled into the window.

He had been busy himself, as ghoul after ghoul tried to grab him from below. His boots had been busy, kicking heads in and pushing bodies away, but the tree was becoming full of bodies and he only had seconds before he would be surrounded from all sides.

Who knew zombies could climb trees? He thought as he pushed another away and reached out for the sheet.

Jimmy had finished pulling Cindy inside and waved for Henry to climb over. Henry punched a zombie in the face and grabbed the sheet, immediately swinging out.

His backpack felt like a leaden weight and the barrel of his Steyr kept whacking him on the top of the head, but he moved one hand across the other. He was halfway across when things went from bad to worse.

Two ambitious ghouls decided they weren't about to let their food get away and reached out with bent fingers. They began hanging from the sheet. The hands wrapped around the sheet, but because of the decayed muscles, they weren't able to move after they had secured themselves to the makeshift rope.

But their weight was still there and the middle knot in the sheet-rope began to slip. Whether it was because Jimmy had tied the knots in haste or the added weight was simply too much for the knots, either way the knots unraveled.

Henry felt the line go slack and he reached out and grabbed the sheet on the opposite side of the unraveling knot.

Behind him, the two hanging bodies tumbled to the ground; the snaps of their necks clear even over the wails of the dead. Henry managed to grab the sheet on Jimmy's side, but he still fell until the line went taut. His body slammed against the hospital wall, the wind knocked from him.

He was less than five inches from grabbing hands below, and he just hung there, too winded to try and climb. Already his arms were growing numb and his left knee ached from where he'd whacked it against the stone wall of the hospital. A small voice told him to just let go. Then the pain and numbness would end.

"Henry, hold on and I'll pull you up!" Jimmy called down and then Henry heard him talking to Cindy. "Give me a hand will ya? He's heavy."

A zombie managed to step on the head of another prone ghoul and its hand managed to reach Henry's right boot. The tug snapped Henry from his daze and he kicked away, the ghoul falling back to the ground. Then he felt himself being raised and the hands were out of reach. Slowly, an inch at a time, he was pulled up the hospital wall. Ivy slapped his face and he spit out the greenery that entered his mouth.

When he finally reached the window, Jimmy leaned out and grabbed him by his armpits.

"Come on, Henry, give me a hand here. You know I can't lift you on my own," Jimmy gasped as he tried to pull him in.

Henry reached up, his fingers now on the window ledge, and with a moan of exertion, began pulling himself up. Jimmy took one of his hands away from his armpit and wrapped it around the strap to the backpack. Now, with more leverage, he yanked as hard as he could. Henry was pulled through the window to land on the shards of glass on the floor. He lay there, staring at the ceiling for what seemed like hours and Jimmy lay right next to him, breathing heavily from exertion.

"Jesus, Henry, you need to go on a diet," he gasped as he sat up.

Henry did the same and turned his head to stare at his friend.

"Oh yeah?" Well, maybe you need to work out a little more, ever think of that?"

"Hey, where's my pack?" Jimmy asked.

"Sorry, pal, but there was no time. Hope you didn't have anything important in there," Henry told him.

Jimmy's face dropped. "No, not too much. I've got all the extra shells for my shotgun in my jacket. But shit, I did have a few rounds for my .38 in there."

"Yeah, well, I am sorry, but I wasn't about to risk falling for a few bullets. Sorry again. Guess you'll just have to make do with what you got left until we find more ammo."

Jimmy was about to send a quip back at Henry about what he could do about his lost ammo when Cindy slapped her hands together to get their attention.

"Quiet, both of you. You here that? I hear something. It sounds like scratching."

Jimmy climbed to his feet and walked to the door.

"Yeah, babe, I know what that is. Don't worry; we're safe here. They can't get to us."

With Jimmy's help, Henry was pulled to his feet.

"Why, Jimmy, what is it. Is it where Mary is?" Henry asked.

"Are there deaders in here with us?" Cindy asked, gripping her rifle harder.

"No, Cindy, 'fraid not. At least I haven't found any while I was searching for the sheets. Come on, it's a whole lot easier to just show you then to tell you. Actually, if I told you, you probably wouldn't believe me. Shit, I saw it and even I don't believe it's true."

He picked up his shotgun and walked out into the hallway with a casual gait, as if he'd spent years inside the hospital instead of just minutes. Henry looked at Cindy but she just shrugged.

"Christ, we don't even get a minute of a break do we," he said to her.

"Not in this job, Henry. Come on; let's go see what he's found before we go find Mary. You never know, it might even help us."

Henry nodded in agreement and gathered his gear, then they headed off into the hall, Jimmy waiting at the end of the hallway impatiently.

Once the three companions were reunited again, they moved off to see Jimmy's big secret.

CHAPTER TEN

THERE WAS WATER dripping somewhere and it was driving Mary crazy.

Drip, drip, drip. Again and again.

She tried to focus her attention elsewhere, but every time she thought she might succeed, the drip would invade her mind like the screech of sharpened nails on a chalkboard.

The man and woman had been awake for a while and Mary guessed she had been strapped to the hospital bed for at least two hours. She wasn't sure exactly as there were no working clocks in the room. With no windows to gauge the light outside she was lost in perpetual shadow, only the drip, drip, drip, and the moan of her two fellow captives to keep her company.

They couldn't talk to her even if they wanted to, their mouths still filled with gags. She idly wondered why her own mouth hadn't been gagged, but instead decided to thank whatever small favor had allowed her the use of her mouth.

She was thirsty now.

It was funny, actually, how when you knew you couldn't take a drink you always found yourself wanting one even if you didn't need one. The same could be said for the itchy nose she'd had for over an hour. With her hands secured, she couldn't scratch and it was driving her mad.

Each time she tried to console the man or woman neither had listened to her. If she was correct, then both were mad from pain and delirium. Not that she could blame them. Having your skin flayed off your body while you watched couldn't be an act that would keep the average person sane.

She looked up when she heard footsteps approaching.

Voices could be heard and a few seconds later, Sterling entered the room with a loud laugh, followed by two other men dressed in dirty clothes that resembled rags more than clothing. The sound of the generator nearby began to purr and Sterling turned on the spotlights.

Bright lights bathed the room and Mary turned her head to blink away the white spots criss-crossing her vision.

Sterling walked up to her and groped her left breast, licking his lips while he squeezed her like he was making bread.

"How ya doin', sugar? Miss me?"

"Fuck you, you asshole," Mary screamed, spitting into Sterling's face. She knew it was never good to aggravate your captors, but she honestly felt she had nothing to lose. If Henry and the others didn't find her soon, then she was in for a world of hurt when Sterling turned his attentions on her.

But he wasn't here for her at the moment and he grinned widely while wiping her spittle from his cheek.

"Oooh, we got us a little spitfire, here, boys. But don't worry, sugar, I'll blow that flame out soon enough." He finished his statement by twisting her breast hard. Mary gritted her teeth, not wanting to give the man the satisfaction of hearing her cry out. But she couldn't stop the tears that slipped from the corners of her eyes.

Sterling grinned broadly as he watched those tears roll down her face. He leaned over and licked the left cheek free of tears, moaning with ecstasy as he did it.

"Mmmm, you do taste good. I can't wait to find out how the rest of you tastes," he whispered into her ear.

She turned her face away so she wouldn't have to look at him.

Sterling growled and grabbed her chin with his powerful right hand.

"Look at me when I'm talking to you, bitch! You just might get to live another minute if you're nice to me."

Mary yanked her chin away from him, pulling something in her neck as she did.

"We'll see who's gonna live when my..." She stopped herself, realizing she'd said too much. But still, it felt good to say it out loud.

That Henry and Jimmy were coming for her, and soon it would be Sterling and his cronies who would be begging for their lives.

"Your what, sugar? Your friends? Well, I'm sorry to tell you but they're long gone. Even if they came after us they don't know where we are. It's a big world out there, ya know. No, sugar, I'm afraid you're here to stay. That is until dinner time." He laughed then, the two other men nearby chuckling, as well.

Sterling stepped away from Mary, but not before he spun her bed around so she was able to see the man and woman better.

"All right, boys. We need to harvest the man next. The Boss says to take it all and to bring him down to the kitchen when we're done." He leered at Mary as he said his next words. "We'll be eating good tonight. In celebration of finding more food, the Boss says we've got a little extra, so he wants to have a feast. 'Sides, if we don't eat it up, the damn meat will spoil anyway."

"Can I cut him up, Sterling?" One of the men asked by his side. The man had bone white hair and a harelip that gave the man a perpetual snarl.

"No fucking way, Adams. I'm the second so I get to do the fun shit. If you want to try and take my place then you can have a go at the carving." Sterling turned to face the man down. "Well, what's it gonna be?"

Adams backed down immediately, his eyes dropping to the floor. "No, Sterling, its okay, you do it, you're the second. I was just think…"

Sterling cut him off. "Yeah, well don't do that. You thinking is like a biter trying to play the piano. It'll just sound like shit."

The other man chuckled next to Adams so Adams turned and smacked the man hard across the arm.

"Shut the fuck up, Marvin. I can still kick your ass if I want to."

Marvin grew quiet, though a few snickers still left his closed mouth.

Mary watched the scene curiously. While Adams had been slapped down, Marvin was under Adams. Even in a world of the dead there was a hierarchy where the second and thirds would seek to slap down the ones that were still lower than them. In other words shit still rolled downhill.

"If you two pussies are done chatting, it's time to get to work," Sterling barked as he turned to stare at the wounded man with hunger in his eyes. "Get me my knives."

Marvin jumped, moving across the room until he came to a small stainless steel cart. Wheeling the cart next to Sterling, Mary was able to get a glimpse of the items lying face up on the top of the once gleaming cart.

But now the cart was covered in blood stains, the steel barely visible. It was like a child had tried to paint it and failed miserably.

The items appeared to be leftover surgical tools from the hospital. Though she had only seen some of the hardware in movies or television, she was pretty sure she saw a rib spreader, a bone saw and multiple sizes of scalpels. All were filthy and Mary realized if this was how her captors practiced good hygiene and food cleanliness, then they were all probably heading for the last train west sooner or later from contamination or a host of other bacterium.

"Hey, Sterling, can I have some fun with the woman while you carve up her man?" Adams asked with a gleam in his eye.

Sterling picked up a dull scalpel and turned to look at Adams and then the prone woman.

"You know what, Adams? Sure, go for it. I'm in a good mood anyway, so might as well share the love, right?"

"All-fucking-right! Thanks, man. You're a pal," Adams said and turned to move toward the trapped woman. Upon reaching her, he slapped her hard in the face, then undid her straps while she lay dazed from the blow. Once she was untied, he flipped her over so her face was in the mattress, then he climbed on top of her, already sliding his pants down to his filthy ankles.

Sterling watched for barely a moment, then got to work carving up the man.

The woman's eyes were wide open and filled with tears as she systematically watched her husband be killed and slaughtered while she was being raped.

With each thrust of Adams, she muffled a cry from around her gag.

Mary watched, jaw slack, eyes filled with tears of anger, rage and shock. If only she could get free, she'd get to one of those scalpels and slice Sterling's throat open.

But she was trapped and wouldn't be going anywhere anytime soon.

Sterling ignored Adams' sex play and got to work on the doomed man. First he slid the scalpel from the man's throat to the top of his groin; blood spilling from the wound like a leaking pool in a backyard on a warm summer's day.

Once the incision was made, Sterling picked up the rib splitter, and before the man could scream with terror, he watched his ribs cracked apart before his eyes. He shrieked around his gag, his head snapping back and forth in pain.

Mary sent the man a silent prayer that he would just pass out from the shock and just never wake up. But for some reason the man refused to go into the dark night and his eyes watched as he was slowly dissected like a worm on a tray.

Sterling started with the nonessentials first, taking out the man's spleen and appendix, then going for the liver. The entire time his wife watched her husband taken apart, she was raped from behind repeatedly.

When Sterling finished with every organ that wouldn't kill the man immediately, he decided the fun was over. Looking down on the man's still beating heart, he reached in with blood-slick hands and the scalpel, sliced the organ until it was free from its host and yanked it from the man's chest.

The man choked behind his gag and went still, the woman screaming for all she was worth. Adams seemed to get off even more as she screamed and fought against him.

Sterling held the still beating heart in his hand and watched as it slowed and stopped. Then he turned and set it down on the cart with the other organs, all dripping blood which pooled over the bowl and onto the floor.

"Oh yeah, gonna have some good stew tonight," he whispered as he licked his lips of plasma. Then he dived back in, continuing to hack and cut.

Mary was so preoccupied with watching the visceral scene she didn't notice when Marvin moved up against her. Before she could say a thing, he placed his hand over her mouth and began climbing on top of her, his other hand working at her fatigues while he lowered his pants.

With his face so close to hers, she could smell the fetid odor of a man who never bathed. His body odor was enough to make her gag and she fought it down, not wanting to choke on her own vomit.

Marvin was breathing hard as he raised himself over her. He was just about to plunge in to her when Sterling roared at the top of his voice in anger.

"Marvin, you no good piece of shit. What the hell do you think you're doing there!"

Marvin stopped in mid-thrust, the tip of his member only an inch from the most intimate spot between Mary's thighs. His face was frozen in fear, his mouth open slightly.

"She's mine, you half-wit. I'm gonna do her when I finish with this meat!" Sterling screamed as he ran towards Marvin.

Taking Marvin by the scruff of his filthy and ripped shirt, Sterling yanked the man away from Mary and dropped him hard to the floor. Unfortunately for Sterling, when Marvin was picked up, his left arm flailed wildly and he accidentally connected his fist with Sterling's balls. The leader of the pack wheezed softly and dropped Marvin, the smaller man forgotten as he bent over and tried to regain his breath.

Even Mary winced when Marvin made contact with Sterling's crotch, the blow was that hard. Sterling didn't move for almost a minute, while behind him, Adams kept right on screwing, the woman seeming unresponsive now. Mary had to assume she'd finally passed out from the shock of watching her husband butchered.

With each thrust by Adams, her head moved an inch and then returned to its previous spot. Adams hadn't noticed Sterling was in pain and so kept on pounding the suffering woman.

"Oh shit, Sterling, oh shit, I am so sorry. Please don't kill me. It was an accident. Adams was gettin' some and you was busy and she looked so pretty laying there all tied up. I just couldn't wait anymore," Marvin stammered, his eyes pleading for forgiveness.

Sterling's face slowly regained its composure and his visage seemed to change from pain induced anger to only anger.

"That's all right, Marvin. What say you just get all that meat to the kitchen and we'll call it water under the bridge, okay?"

Marvin nodded happily and picked himself off the ground.

Adams had stopped his thrusting to watch the scene with Marvin, but when he saw everything was all right, he continued pumping happily.

"Okay, Sterling, okay. Thanks man, really. I'll make it up to you, I promise," he said while moving away from Sterling, careful not to get too close to the larger man.

Sterling watched him go and Marvin quickly packed all the meat on the cart and with a brisk wave, pushed it out into the hallway and was soon gone, the sound of the cart's wheels slowly fading away.

Adams cried out as he climaxed and rolled off the woman, waving to Marvin just as he left the room. Checking her to see if she was still alive, his face sank when he realized she was dead. In his thrusts, he had accidentally forced her face too deep into the mattress and she'd suffocated. Later, when Mary had a chance to think on the events, she had to wonder if the woman hadn't done it on purpose to end her pain and suffering.

"Uhm, Sterling? I uhm, I think I screwed up. The bitch is dead. I don't know how it happened."

Sterling spun on his heels and slapped Adams in the face. The slap sent Adams tumbling backward where he caught himself by landing on the back of the dead woman.

"You are a bigger idiot than Marvin, you know that? You're just lucky we're gonna carve her up, too or I swear, it would've been you in the pot tonight instead of Marvin."

Adams blinked, not understanding what he'd just heard.

"But I thought you told him it was all right? Didn't you forgive him?"

"Fuck no," Sterling snorted. "I just didn't want to kill him here. Then I'd have to drag his dead ass down to the kitchen. No, better that I wait until he's done working, then I'll kill his ass good." Sterling glared at Adams. "Why, you got a problem with that?"

Adams shook his head immediately, agreeing with Sterling.

"No, Sterling, it's fine with me. Marvin is a dull-witted asshole anyway; serves him right for not listening to you."

"Damn straight," Sterling said, and while rubbing his crotch gingerly, he walked over to the dead woman.

"All right, let's get this bitch carved up and finished so we can get 'em a cookin'."

Adams nodded, quickly moving the cart full of scalpels to the next bed.

"Hey, Sterling, why don't we just slaughter 'em in the kitchen? Why do 'em up here at all?"

Sterling licked the blade of his scalpel clean as he prepared to begin slicing up the woman. He was turning her over as he spoke.

"Because by doing them up here we get to fuck 'em. Downstairs we'd have to share and probably wouldn't get to have some fun first. The Boss just wants to clean and eat 'em. He doesn't believe in screwin' 'em first."

"I heard the Boss can't get it up. That he's impotent and that's why he doesn't want us to have any fun."

Sterling slapped Adams across the face yet again and pointed a dripping, blood-soaked finger at his face.

"Better keep that shit to yourself, Adams. If the Boss hears you talk like that about him you're deader than dead, got me?"

Adams nodded, his head like a bobble-top.

"Yeah, yeah, I got it." He thought of something and moved closer to Sterling. "You won't say anything to him, will you? You won't tell the Boss what I said, right?"

Sterling smile widely. "Sure I'll keep it to myself." But inside he thought he'd keep it to himself until he needed Adams to disappear. Then he might let it slip.

The two men remained quiet then, with Adams sneaking a peek to Mary every now and then. Mary remained quiet, not wanting to call any more attention to herself then needed. Even with her hands secured to the bed she was just able to get her pants back up by bending her knees. She couldn't button them, but at least she wasn't exposed anymore.

The two men took the dead woman apart, carving her like a pig at the butcher shop. When they were finished, they wheeled the cart full of dripping body parts toward the door.

Sterling paused before leaving to talk to Mary. Probably without realizing it, he had his left hand touching his tender balls through his pants. He wasn't in the mood for sex anymore, and later he'd realize how close he came to never having it again when he inspected his black and blue testicles.

"I guess you don't get fucked tonight, sugar, but don't worry. By tomorrow morning I'll be all healed and ready to go. Sleep tight," he grinned while exiting the room. He flicked the spotlights off just before he left, bathing the room in darkness once more.

Mary was left all alone with her thoughts and everything she'd witnessed in the past hour flooded back to her even with her eyes closed. The smell of coppery death was in the room and she wanted to retch, but she parted her lips and slowly breathed through her mouth, trying to keep out the redolence of slaughtered human beings from entering her sinus cavity.

She tried not to think about what would happen to her next. To be cut up and eaten like cattle was almost as bad as becoming one of the walking dead.

She had to find a way out of her predicament and she realized at that moment she couldn't wait for Henry and the others to find her.

No, if she was going to escape to live another day she would have to do it on her own. The only question was, just how the hell was she going to make that happen?

CHAPTER ELEVEN

JIMMY STOPPED WHEN he reached the closed double doors.

"Well, here we are," he said almost cheerfully.

"What's on the other side of the doors, Jimmy?" Henry asked as he peeked through the left side window on the double doors.

"Don't really know for sure, but I have an idea, it's gonna be a little disgusting."

Henry's eyes roamed over the floor and walls, all wreathed in shadows, but when his eyes went up the side of the wall, he spotted the mounted sign hanging there.

"Pediatrics," he read, and there looks like there's an arrow pointing to deeper into the hospital. Then he saw a few shadows that seemed to glide across the floor. They were slow, but not so slow he could make out what they were. "What the hell was that?"

"Ah, did you see the shapes in the darkness?" Jimmy asked.

Henry pulled his head away from the door and nodded.

"Yeah, what the hell was that?"

Jimmy shrugged. "Don't know. Animals maybe…or something worse."

"Can we go around this part of the hospital?" Cindy asked, checking for herself. Unfortunately no shapes made themselves known. "Maybe we can just leave whatever's in there be."

Jimmy shook his head. "No go. I went through this section while I was looking for rope or something to help you guys out and I didn't find any fire doors or stairways. Even the elevators are down there. 'Fraid we need to go through there whether we like it or not."

"All right, fine; if we have to then let's get going. Time's wasting and Mary needs us," Henry said, then raised his right boot and kicked the right-hand door in with brutal force. The door swung inward loudly, the handle cracking against the plaster. Small speckles of plaster dust drifted to the floor like snow. But none of the companions noticed, and with Henry in the lead, they entered the pediatric wing of the hospital.

The smell of decay and rot assailed them immediately and everyone pulled bandanas from pockets and covered noses and mouths. The bandana had become an important item in their gear. With death and rotting corpses everywhere, something was needed to filter out the smell. Sometimes the sickly sweet smell of death was too much for even the companion's hardened stomachs.

Leading with his Steyr, the Glock now empty, Henry moved into the darkness. Suddenly a flash of light came from his left and he spun around, prepared to fire at an attacker. But it was just Jimmy standing in the first room they had passed. He'd opened the heavy curtains, finally allowing some natural light to penetrate the Stygian darkness. Henry noticed there was only one bed in the room with Jimmy.

"Let there be light," he said with a sly grin. Henry let out the breath he was holding and shook his head.

"Dammit, Jimmy, could you fill me in when you're gonna do something like that? I almost shot you."

"Sorry, Henry, I just thought we could use a little light on the subject."

Only grunting in reply, Henry turned back to the front to see Cindy standing very still. She was gazing into the shadows directly ahead of them and her hands were gripping her M-16 tightly.

"What is it, Cindy? You see something?" This from Henry as he moved up next to her.

She nodded slowly, her eyes never wavering. "Yeah, I think I did. Something small; on the floor. But I must be mistaken 'cause there were a lot of them."

Jimmy took a step in front of her and moved into the next room. They were about twenty feet from the double doors now and the shadows were deeper here.

"Here, let me get the curtains in this room, too," he said, but the instant he stepped into the room, something latched onto his boot.

"What the?" He said glancing down, but with the darkness all pervasive inside the room, he couldn't see what had gotten a hold of him.

"Jimmy, you all right!" Henry called out.

Jimmy was standing perfectly still, his .38 in his hand. When he first felt a pressure on his boot, his first instinct was too shoot, but with each passing second he realized there was nothing to fear. Whatever had a hold of him appeared to be harmless. He did feel a sucking and moist spot on his pants just above the top of his boot, but since it wasn't penetrating through the material, he relaxed slightly.

"Yeah, Henry, I'm fine. Just let me open the curtains and we can see what I found in here." He moved to the window and tossed the curtains aside, a years worth of dust and cobwebs flying around the room, floating on the sunlight like ash. Jimmy glanced down at his boot, expecting an animal, maybe a cat or something, but his jaw fell open as he stared at the one and a half foot monstrosity looking up at him with milky white eyes that were once baby blue.

"Ahhhh, holy shit!" He screamed and kicked his foot like he was punting a football. The object on his foot sailed away from him and into the hallway. It bounced off the far wall and landed with a soft thump.

Henry and Cindy both stared in shock and horror when the object turned over and began to move towards them again, only now its neck was slightly askew.

"Oh my God, it can't be," Cindy said while she stared at the small form moving towards them on hands and knees.

"Jesus Christ, yeah, Cindy, I'm afraid it is," Henry whispered, his eyes also staring at the small zombie baby as it crawled towards his boots.

As far as threats go, the small ghoul was hardly dangerous. It had no teeth and seems it hadn't been able to walk in life, it could not do so in death, but it was still a shakable sight. What a year ago had been a new life, filled with promise and hope, was now nothing but decaying death. The once pink skin was now a pale blue with streaks of white. The baby had once had a tuft of red hair, but now the hair was gone, leaving a rotting skull, with a soft spot in the middle. As the baby crawled to Henry, drool slid from its mouth and it seemed to moan like it was cooing.

Cindy aimed her rifle at the tiny ghoul, but she couldn't shoot the small creature.

"Jesus, Henry, I can't shoot it, it's only a baby for God's sake, even if it is dead!"

Jimmy entered the hallway and hovered over the small form. The baby's hands were trying to reach up and grab him, but Jimmy kept pushing them away.

Jimmy glanced to Henry. "What do we do with it?"

Henry stared at the small form and then gestured to the room Jimmy had just vacated. "Toss it into the room and close the door, will ya. There's no need to kill it. Dead or not, it's still a baby." He shook his head. "Christ, what the hell is this world coming to? What in God's name did we do to ourselves? The children were supposed to be our future. Not this...monstrosity." He gestured to the baby. "Jimmy, would you do the honors please?" Henry finished.

"Sure, Henry, I got it." He moved to the side of the baby and placed the front of his boot under the small ghoul's stomach.

"Alley oop!" Jimmy called out, and with a flip of his leg, sent the baby flying into the room.

"Jimmy, what the hell?" Cindy yelled, not pleased with the way he'd disposed of the small ghoul.

Jimmy just shrugged and looked at her apologetically as he walked to the room's door and closed it with a soft click. The baby was still near the window and wasn't even close to the door.

"Sorry, babe, I just figured whatever was easiest, you know?"

She just stared at him and Jimmy figured he probably wouldn't be getting any the next time they were safe. Cindy could hold a grudge for a long time if she wanted to.

"All right, you two, let's focus. We still need to find Mary. Come on," Henry said and began moving further into the hallway.

When he reached an intersection, he stopped cold. Jimmy and Cindy were only a few feet behind him and they each noticed Henry's back go stiff.

"What's up, you find some deaders?" Jimmy asked as he moved up next to Henry, his .38 tracking the shadows ahead.

"Oh shit, you've got to be kidding me," Jimmy whispered when he saw what was slowly heading for him and Henry. Cindy moved up next to the two men and she gasped in revulsion.

Coming from the end of the corridor, where there was a large glass wall which at one time would allow visitors to view the newborn babies, more than a score of living dead babies were crawling along the floor towards the three companions.

From a side room a window shade was open, or perhaps the window was shattered, because light spilled into the corridor, illuminating the dead faces of the newborns. Some still had umbilical cords hanging from belly buttons, the dried cords now fused to the babies' bodies.

A low gurgling sound seemed to fill the hallway, like a storm cloud in front of the approaching babies. The floor seemed to shift and roll with the small bodies as they crawled on hands and knees.

All were decomposing, with distended abdomens and pale-blue skin. A few seemed to be missing limbs, which only added to the macabre sight.

Henry was the first to shake free of his shock at the bizarre menagerie of tiny tots. In the course of their travels across dead America, the companions had come across children who had been turned and had even seen a few zombified babies. Henry remembered one time in particular. The companions had been staying in a town in Virginia. The same one in which Cindy had joined them. A library had caught fire and the town had used rainwater collected from the recent rainstorms to squelch the fire. Only the rainwater had been contaminated and the entire library of survivors trapped inside the burning building had become infected with the bacterium. Henry and the town's leader, along with Jimmy and a few security guards, had gone into the library to clean it out. It was there that Henry had seen the zombie baby and had actually become frozen with surprise. It had still been a child, though it was now one of the undead and Henry had found he couldn't destroy it. It had been Jimmy who had killed the small ghoul, and Henry had dreamed about the small baby for days until finally shaking off the image.

But now there were over twenty of the little demons and all were heading straight for him. Jimmy leveled his shotgun, but Henry placed his hand on the barrel of the weapon.

"No, wait a second. They should be harmless; we don't want to waste any ammo we might need later. They're newborns for God's sake. Let's just push our way through them and get to the other side and find the stairs to the next level." He turned to Cindy. "Cindy, you take the rear and let us clear out the worst of them. Don't fire unless you really have to."

She nodded and Henry turned to Jimmy, pulling his panga for defense. Jimmy saw his action and he turned and grabbed an IV stand from a few feet away.

"Okay, then let's do this thing," Jimmy said as he stared at the short wall of newborns only a few feet away.

With a deep breath, Henry took his first step into the charging babies, his boots kicking them to the side. For all their small mass, the small ghouls managed to grab onto him with iron-like grips and Henry soon found he had the small ghouls clinging to him like orphans at a carnival.

Inside himself he could feel his revulsion rising, but he forced it down. It was only in his mind. They were harmless, despite the distasteful little bodies. Next to him, weeding his way into their midst, Jimmy pushed and swept the small forms to the sides as he followed Henry.

One of the babies managed to begin climbing up Henry's leg, and for a few seconds, the man didn't realize the small ghoul was there. He only knew what was happening when he felt something sharp press against his pant leg. The cloth of his pants didn't rip, but he still felt the pressure of something and when he looked down, he saw the tiny bluish face staring up at him. It leaned back its tiny head to try and bite him again and that was when Henry spotted the small white tooth in the front of its mouth.

Not having children himself, Henry hadn't given much thought that some newborns were born with a few teeth in their mouths. This tiny ghoul was one of them and the little zombie was about to sink its tooth into his leg and possibly infect him.

Raising his panga, he swung it downward, barley missing his own leg with the swipe. The head of the tiny tot flew from its shoulders and a moment later the small fingers let go, the body tumbling back to the floor.

"Jesus Christ, they've got teeth! Some of them have teeth!" Henry yelled to Jimmy and Cindy. Both his friends knew what that meant. If they had teeth then they could possibly infect them with a bite and that made the small ghouls dangerous.

"Forget what I said, Jimmy. No more screwing around. Let's get through here and fast. Cindy, shoot us a path down the middle!"

Cindy flicked off the safety to the rifle and set the weapon to full auto. She fired three short bursts, and when she was finished, there were tiny, headless bodies strewn across the floor of the hallway.

"Okay, let's move, people," Henry ordered them as he jumped over two small bodies and almost slipped on the blood-slick floor. Regaining his balance, he charged down the corridor, Jimmy and Cindy right behind him.

Upon passing the last baby, the surviving ghouls immediately spun around and began crawling after them. Henry ignored them, concentrating on what was in front of him. He relied on Cindy who was in the rear to keep an eye on their backs.

Rounding another corner, Henry caught a glimpse of the emergency exit sign for the stairs hidden in the shadows.

With renewed strength filling him anew, he charged forward down the hallway, Jimmy right behind him. It was a long hallway that cut through the large building, but his goal was close. When the stairwell door was in sight, he let out a silent sigh, but then immediately had to stop. Jimmy halted, as well, actually running into Henry's back.

"What the fuck, Henry? Why'd you stop?"

"We got more company, that's why," Henry said, pointing in front of him with the muzzle of the Steyr.

Jimmy looked around Henry's shoulder to see a dozen ghouls coming out of rooms and from around the nurses station. Most wore hospital garb. White jackets and nursing scrubs were the norm, but a few wore the classic gowns of patients, right down to the opening in the back which exposed their pale-white asses to the air.

A moan went up, the first ghoul in line moving towards them. Cindy slowed and raised her M-16, prepared to fire at Henry's word.

"I'm getting pretty low, Henry. It would be real nice if we could just get around these bastards," she said as she moved the muzzle of the rifle from one target to the next, but refrained from firing.

Henry nodded, knowing she was right. They had already expended way more ammunition than they should have in a given day. It seemed like every damn ghoul in Kentucky was after them.

No, there had to be another way to take out these shambling corpses so they could get down the stairs and continue onward to find Mary.

They had already spent far too much time battling ghouls and not enough time searching for their lost friend. With the approaching adult zombies coming directly for them with gaping mouths and reaching hands, Henry knew he needed to come up with an idea quick, or when they finally found Mary, the companions would all just get slaughtered, because they would have no ammunition to defend themselves.

CHAPTER TWELVE

HENRY'S EYES DARTED back and forth as he tried to figure a way out of their dire predicament. While his mind tried to come up with a plan, he couldn't help but stare at the rotting bags of walking pus coming toward him, Jimmy, and Cindy.

One of the first ghouls in line was more than six feet in front of the others, and Henry realized the ghoul had been a doctor in his first life. His name tag was still prominently on his chest. He was literally falling apart from decomposing. His face was a visage of leprosy with skin that seemed to move on its own in the shadows of the corridor. But when the ghoul moved closer, Henry realized it was maggots under the doctor's flesh. The small worms twitched and moved about, feeding on the decaying tissue, making the skin undulate like a river. His right hand was nothing but withered flesh and his left was missing, the doctor having lost it somewhere in his travels. Tatters of hair draped over the sunken cheeks and a blackened tongue lolled out of the side of his mouth.

"Cindy, take that piece of shit out before he gets too close," Henry told her, pointing to the doctor.

She complied, the gunshot filling the hallway with its retort. The doctor's head blew apart and his brains splattered against the wall like a cherry pie, bits of gray matter sliding to the floor leaving snail trails of blood. The doctor slumped to the floor, immobile, but it was a small consolation as the ones behind it simply stepped over or around the slumped corpse.

Backing up, Cindy called out when she realized the zombie babies were still coming. They were now becoming trapped within the two undead forces with low ammo and a definite numerical disadvantage.

"Uhm, Henry, I think we're in more trouble, if that's possible," Jimmy stated as he swiveled his head back and forth.

Henry didn't answer, his mind still racing to find a solution to their problem. And it came like a sign from God a moment later. In the shadows of a hospital room they had just passed, just to the side of the doorway, he spotted four canisters standing a little over five feet tall near the doorframe. They had been left there at one time and had stayed there waiting patiently for him to come along and use them. The hand dolly used to move them was still there also, and in fact one of the cylinders was still sitting on it, the strap still holding it from falling.

"There, guys, in there. Get those canisters out into the hall fast," he snapped, moving to the first cylinder and trying to roll it into the hallway. Both Jimmy and Cindy complied, knowing there was no time to discuss whatever Henry was thinking. Working as a team, each of them grabbed a cylinder, Cindy wheeling the one still strapped to the hand dolly.

"Here, put them in the middle of the hall!" He yelled as he glanced over his shoulder at the approaching ghouls. He had less than twenty seconds before the first one would be able to reach out and attack him.

Jimmy and Cindy moved the cylinders into the hall and stood with hands on triggers, uneasy with the undead so close to them.

"Uh, Henry, this is getting pretty close," Jimmy said while watching the undead faces moving closer.

"I know, I know. Okay, we're good here," he said and studied the cylinders. It was easy to read the labels of each cylinder. They were all filled with liquid nitrogen.

"Okay, everyone get into the room across the hall, and Jimmy, I want you to be ready with your shotgun and you with your rifle, Cindy."

Nodding, Jimmy followed Cindy and when each of them was inside the room, Henry pointed to the cylinders.

"Okay, you need to wait until the last second and then shoot those canisters. The spread of your shotgun should take them out, but Cindy, you need to fire with your rifle, too, near the bottom of the tanks. One shot, right into the first tank, okay? The second you fire, fall back and I'm gonna close the door." He went to the hospital bed and picked up the mattress, bracing it against the door for added protection.

"Okay, get ready," he said as Jimmy moved to the partially opened door. Cindy got down on one knee, the barrel of Jimmy's shotgun above her head.

"Okay, guys, fire when ready," Henry said, his hand on the back of the door, ready to push it closed.

Jimmy gauged the shot, counting the seconds. He counted to six before the first ghoul was only inches from the tanks and then he fired, Cindy doing the same below him.

No sooner did they fire, then Henry pushed the door closed, both warriors barely having time to remove the barrels of their weapons from the shutting door before it slammed closed.

Jimmy was about to say something to Henry when his world became filled with a roaring blast and the door was knocked from its hinges. All three companions were knocked to the dusty floor, the mattress saving them from any serious harm. A white frost-like gas filled the hall and seeped into the room, and Jimmy could see his breath in the air when he exhaled.

Thirty seconds passed, but it seemed like an hour before Henry threw off the door and mattress, and gazed out into the hallway. His Steyr was leveled at the doorway, but as he took his first step back into the hallway, he realized there was no longer any danger.

His boots crunched on ice and his face turned red from the cold, the temperature in the hall dropping to below freezing in an instant. Moving away from the door, he stared at the ghouls in front of him, all still standing exactly where they had been when the canisters exploded, the liquid nitrogen enveloping everything in the hallway and crystallizing it in a heartbeat.

On the other end of the hall, the zombie babies were also frozen, their tiny bodies motionless. Henry noticed one of the small ghouls near the last of the line was only partially frozen and when the small ghoul tried to move, its right hand snapped off. It slipped to the floor where it lay on the ground like a turned over turtle, trying to roll back over.

Crunching from behind him caused him to spin, but he held his fire to see it was only Jimmy and Cindy.

"Goddamn it, Henry. You made zombie-sicles," Jimmy gasped as he stared at the frozen statues. Faces were frozen in their last expression, most with gaping mouths and vacant eyes.

"So that's it, we go find Mary now?" Cindy asked, askance of Jimmy.

Henry shook his head, then he slung the Steyr over his shoulder and pulled his panga free of its oiled sheath.

"Not quite. There's no way of knowing what will happen when these guys thaw out and I for one don't want to find them on my ass again." He stepped over to the closest ghoul, a nurse with blood-stained white scrubs on, and slashed at the undead ice statue with his panga.

The entire body shattered, the dense crystals falling to the floor of the hallway like hail. Henry turned to Cindy and Jimmy, nodding to the other frozen corpses.

"You guys gonna help or am I going to have to do this all by myself."

Jimmy and Cindy raised their weapons and began the task of shattering the bodies with the butts of their weapons. One at a time, they worked their way through the frozen crowd, each one smashing the humanoid ice sculptures.

Arms were knocked off to fall to the floor and shatter, leaving severed wounds that did not bleed. It was all weirdly satisfying in a macabre way. For once, the ghouls were absolutely helpless and the three companions could take out a year's worth of aggression on the zero degree bodies.

In no time at all, every adult zombie was nothing but frozen chunks lying on the floor. When Henry finished with the last one, he shifted his attention to the baby zombies. Striding across the hallway, careful not to slip on the thin layer of ice covering the floor, he reached the first tiny tot and stepped on its head. Like stepping on a snowball of ice, the head disintegrated, spreading frozen brains across the floor. He continued stomping, like a man making wine, and then he was at the last one; the small baby that had lost an arm and was now struggling to right itself.

Henry stared down at the small face for almost a minute, wondering how things could have gone so wrong. Small bits of moisture were dripping from the severed limb, the droplets pooling on the floor beneath the small body.

Deciding it was time to finish it, he used his panga to separate the small head from its shoulders. The head fell to the floor and lolled back and forth like a dropped plastic cup. Henry noticed the eyes still blinked at him and the small toothless mouth still moved up and down, but he ignored it. It was harmless and he assumed the head would remain active until the flesh and the brains inside the skull finally turned to dust.

"There," he said, walking back to the others. "Now we don't need to keep looking over our shoulders." His face, backpack and clothing were covered in a fine mist of ice with bits of red mixed in, as were all the companions. When it thawed, he would be covered in red dots of blood from the defunct ghouls. Cindy moved closer to him and began wiping him off, slapping at his clothing like a worried mother.

"There, that's better," she said, finishing up.

"Okay, so are we done here or what?" Jimmy inquired as he shifted from one foot to another. He was cold and wanted to vacate the frozen gravesite as soon as possible.

"Yeah, we're good here. All right, let's find the stairs and get the hell out of here. Mary needs us."

Nodding in agreement, Cindy and Jimmy repositioned their backpacks on their shoulders and all three companions moved out.

Somewhere in the vast hospital Mary was waiting for them.

That is, if they weren't already too late to save her.

CHAPTER THIRTEEN

MORE THAN AN hour had passed since Sterling had left Mary alone. She had spent the time in contemplation. She'd considered her mortality for yet another moment in her life. Since that fateful day she'd been driving home from work and had been attacked by a ghoul and had almost lost her life, it seemed her days had been filled with peril.

One event after another seemed to find her and every one of them seemed to have her life tied to a string. A string that was slowly unraveling. She couldn't help but wonder if this was the time the string would finally become undone and she would meet death in person.

Lord knows she had cheated the Grim Reaper more times than she could count. Mostly thanks to her friends. The companions had been a family. One she hadn't realized she'd been missing until becoming part of one again. Her parents lived in California and when she had moved to the Midwest, she'd basically severed ties with them. Oh sure, she could call them on the phone, but if you didn't see a person every so often, a phone call was just a disembodied voice on the phone. It wasn't a real connection. And email was even worse.

She thought of her parents now and then, but tried not to. She hadn't talked to them since the first rains came. They had said they were holed up in the house and were fine and that she shouldn't worry.

Three days later the phone lines were down and she'd never talked to them again. Henry had been with her that day, Jimmy in a nearby diner getting some food. They had just escaped from Henry's hometown and were now hiding out while they waited for the next shoe to drop.

Her first family was for all purposes dead and gone. Whether they had become zombies or had been killed by others was irrelevant.

But thanks to Henry, Jimmy and Cindy, she wasn't alone. She now had a new family. One that would fight and die for her...and kill for her if necessary.

And though she knew they would be coming for her, there was still a small well of doubt growing inside of her. What if they didn't know where she was? What if they had been killed when she'd been taken?

No, as she had realized more than an hour ago, she needed to find a way to escape by herself.

But how?

Pulling on her restraints, she felt almost no give to them. She was firmly strapped down. At one time the straps holding her would have been for unruly patients. Perhaps someone on LSD or some other mind-altering drug that needed to be secured for their own safety. Now those same restraints worked just fine to keep her from trying to escape.

Pulling on her left arm, she did feel a little more give by her wrist. Whether it was because the strap had stretched over time or simply because the person who had secured her hadn't paid enough attention, she thought she might have enough room to pull her wrist through, if only her thumb-knuckle could be shifted slightly.

Deciding she really didn't have a choice, she began working her wrist back and forth like a screw. It didn't take long for her skin to bleed from the cuts from the edge of the leather, but she ignored it, still twisting and pulling. Actually, the blood seemed to help. It was a natural lubricant and she was able to slide her hand down another quarter of an inch before it stopped again.

Her blood was staining the already dirty sheet by her head, but still she persevered, twisting and turning until her wrist felt like it was on fire.

Her face was a rictus of pain, but she gritted her teeth and continued, her wrist sliding out of the strap one centimeter at a time.

Her breathing became shallow as she tried to stay focused. Craning her neck to see how far she'd come, she let out a deep sigh to see she'd barely managed an inch in the past half hour. It was her damn knuckle to her thumb. Unless she could break it, she wouldn't be getting free anytime soon.

Slumping in the bed, she let her back go limp. She'd had it arced from the pain and she had to mentally force herself to relax. But she wasn't through yet. If she had to, she would rip the skin from her wrist and hand if that was what it took to set herself free.

Unfortunately, she would never get the chance to finish because she began to hear footsteps coming down the hallway. With her heart beating heavily, she waited to see who it was. Was it Sterling finally coming to take her to the slaughter?

She looked up when Marvin entered the room. He carried a small oil lamp with him and he moved across the room until he was standing over her. Somewhere in the shadows, another figure waited, watching the hallway.

Marvin licked his lips as he gazed down at her with lechery in his eyes.

"Hey baby, miss me? I thought I'd come back and pay you a visit. Seems we got some unfinished business together."

"I thought Sterling told you to leave me alone? If you try anything, I'll tell him when I see him."

Marvin grinned in the light of the flickering oil lamp, and in the blink of an eye, was waving a small knife below Mary's chin.

"I don't think you'll be saying anything to him or anyone else when I get through with you, bitch." He played the blade across her chin, slowly caressing her neck with the tip before he ran it down her body. He paused between her breasts, then continued until he stopped at her open belt buckle. She had managed to slide into her pants, but not to redo the buckle and buttons.

"You see? If you so much as utter a sob I'm gonna cut your tongue out. Even if you don't drown in your own blood you won't be able to talk."

Mary swallowed hard, her throat moving with a soft tremor as she tried to control herself. Despite her fear, she wondered if she could use what was happening to her advantage. She decided she had absolutely nothing to lose in trying.

She lowered her eyes seductively and pursed her lips, trying to keep the tremor of fear out of her voice.

"And what if I cooperate with you? What if I give you the screw of a lifetime? Would you promise to be gentle with me?"

Marvin chuckled, the sound resembling a grinding crankshaft in an old car.

"Honey, I don't do nothin' gentle, 'specially fuckin'."

She grinned slightly, trying another tactic.

"Well, then, would you ride me hard and fast like the whore that I am?"

Marvin grinned in the wan light of the oil lamp, his yellow teeth showing the slightly sharpened points.

"Baby, that I can do," he breathed as he began to unzip his pants and slide out of his clothing. He turned to the figure standing at the doorway. "Hey, shithead, make sure it stays clear over there. I want a heads up if someone's coming, especially if it's Sterling."

"Yeah, yeah, Marvin, I heard ya. Just make sure you save me some when you're through."

"Jesus Christ, I said I would, didn't I? Now shut the hell up and keep watch." Then he turned around and glared at Mary. "Okay, sweetcheeks, it's time for the best lay of your life."

Swallowing again, trying to keep the fear in her stomach from making her want to vomit, she smiled as sweetly as she could. "Bring it on handsome. If I gotta die, then at least I can have one last roll in the hay before I go, right?"

"Damn straight, missy, damn straight," Marvin said, his third leg already standing at attention. With a growl, he leaned forward and began pulling her pants down to her ankles to get down to business.

Mary could only lay there and wait for what would happen next, and though it wouldn't be the worst thing that could happen to her, getting raped was certainly in the top five.

Sterling walked through the empty corridors of the hospital when he felt a larger tremor as if something had exploded inside the hospital. It sounded like it had come from the part of the hospital that had been closed off.

He waited for a moment to see if the rumble would repeat itself, but when it didn't, he decided it didn't matter. As long as the building wasn't on fire, then who the hell cares. The west wing of the hospital had been boarded off when he had taken over the hospital, as it was easier to do that than to try and clean out the undead infestation. Almost all the ghouls had been herded to that part of the building, and for all Sterling cared they could rot till eternity in there. He made a mental note to send a scout outside to check on the exterior of the building. If no smoke was seen then he would forget about the bang. It was probably some of the tanks left behind that had finally burst. It had happened before and would probably happen again.

He was on the second floor and had just come from one of the half working bathrooms. Through a series of water cans, the new residents of the hospital were able to flush the toilets. Unfortunately, running water was a thing of the past.

He strolled down the hallway with purpose, his eyes always checking doorways as he past them. If someone tried to come at him, it wouldn't be the first time, or he assumed, the last.

He was the second-in-command of the ragtag group of cannibals and he had earned his position by killing all who tried to take it from him. All the losers had been tossed in the stew pot and he had feasted on their hearts.

Becoming a cannibal hadn't been a life choice, but instead had been a choice thrust upon him. Without weapons to hunt the sparse animals in the city, he and a few others had taken to cannibalizing one of their own out of necessity.

He and three men had been trapped inside an old shoe store more than half a year ago. After running out of ammunition, there was nothing else to be done but wait for help to arrive and pray the score of ghouls didn't break through their makeshift barrier. But help didn't come for almost a week and in that time he and his men would have starved if they hadn't taken to doing something rash, something so abhorrent it took all of his will to keep the sustenance down.

One of his men had been hurt in the escape to the store and had died after the third day. By the fourth day, with no food or water, it was either eat the man or follow him into the dark night.

Sterling had chosen the former and had found he actually had a taste for the meat that walked on two legs.

Once the taboos of the old world had been tossed aside like old bones, both he and the rest had quickly grown accustomed to the taste of human meat, or long pig as some of the others had begun saying.

And it was a lot easier to hunt the two-legged animals than it was the four legged ones. His stomach growled as he thought about eating, it had been hours since he'd put anything in his stomach. He found it amusing that not all humans tasted the same. Some would have an aftertaste while others did seem to taste like pork. He always assumed the aftertaste was from whatever those humans had been ingesting themselves, giving the old adage some credence that you are what you eat.

The smell of roasting meat came to his nose as he stepped out of the hallway and into a wide open area, the odor making his stomach rumble like storm clouds on a dark horizon. It was once the cafeteria, but now it was a large communal living place for most of the group. Altogether, they numbered twenty in all, though the entire tribe wasn't always in the same place at the same time. There was always at least one hunting party out looking for food at any given moment, and in another day it would be his turn again to go out and hunt.

But until then, he could relax, fill his face full of pink, juicy meat and enjoy the good life.

There was a large barbecue pit in the middle of the room, three metal barrels cut in half with cherry red coals burning brightly. A torso of what may have been a man or woman was turning over on one the grills, the meat covered in a rich, tangy barbecue sauce. Grey clouds rose up to play along the smoke-stained ceiling panels until it was sucked out of one of the dozen or so open or shattered windows lining the back wall.

Tammy was on duty and she was an excellent cook.

"Hey, Tammy, what time's chow, I'm starving," Sterling said to her while his eyes roamed up and down her stocky frame. She was a plump female with dark black hair and a large tattoo of a butterfly on the back of her neck. One time Sterling had asked her why she had placed the tattoo there and she said it was so men could have something pretty to look at as they fucked her from behind. After that, Sterling had decided to take her up on her suggestion and the two had rutted like dogs for more than a month before he grew tired of her and dumped her.

Sterling walked over to her and ran a finger down the middle of the cooking torso, then began to suck the rich juice clean from his finger.

She slapped at his hand as he went for another taste of the carcass and waved a paintbrush covered in sauce at him.

"Not for another hour or so, now you git, Sterling, and let me work. I promise to make sure you get the first slice of the roast when it's ready."

Sterling nodded. "Fair enough," he muttered as he turned to walk away. His balls were feeling better and he was beginning to grow horny again. He figured very soon he'd be in good enough shape to finish what he'd wanted to start with the fiery brunette.

Sterling moved through a few men and women, nodding to one another. On two tables nailed together there was a large chair, like a throne, and on that thrown sat an older man in his late sixties. He had graying hair and a large nose that gave the man the look of someone who had picked it far too much when he was younger. His complexion was pale and it was obvious the man was sick. Sterling knew it was only a matter of time before the man died and Sterling finally became the ruler for real.

This was the leader of the cannies, and though he was respected by all, everyone knew it was Sterling that was the true man in charge.

Sterling stopped when he was in front of the man, eyeing him with a cold eye.

"How's it going, Dad?" Sterling asked as he looked up at the man who had sired him.

The old man looked up towards the ceiling and then down at the voice of his son, coughing heavily as his eyes filled with tears. When his coughing fit was over, he wiped his eyes clear and glanced back down to Sterling.

"Ah, David, hello, my son. What news have you for me?"

David Sterling shrugged. "Not much. The hunters haven't reported back yet and all the meat is being cooked like you said."

His father glared down at him, knowing his son was holding something back.

"Oh really? All the meat has been cooked. Are you sure about that David?"

Unknown to Sterling, his father had been reported to only minutes ago by one of the men still loyal only to him. The man had told him about the couple and about Mary who was still alive.

"Uhm, well, there is still one more prisoner, but I plan on taking care of her personally. In fact, I was about to go do it in a few minutes, but first I wanted to find Marvin."

"Oh, and what did poor Marvin do that you need to find him with such urgency?"

Sterling's left hand went to his balls without realizing it. "Well, Dad, let's just say I owe the man some payback."

"Are you going to kill him? You know, son, if you keep on killing your men there won't be anyone left."

Sterling smiled slightly, his sharpened teeth showing. "Oh, I doubt that, Dad. Seems to me there's more than enough of us now. Actually, we could do to thin the herd a little bit, don't you think?"

The leader of the cannies shrugged, not really giving it any thought. He was old and dying and matters of the group didn't concern him much anymore. It was believed the man had pneumonia, and though they resided inside a hospital, all the medicine was long gone. Either smashed when the outbreak had first started more than a year ago or the rest having been stolen by looters.

"I leave those decisions to you now, son, you know that. All I'm asking is what your plans for the woman are."

"The woman?"

"Yes, David, the woman who was captured at the raiding party this morning. I hear she's still alive."

"Uhm, yeah she is. But we don't need to kill her yet. We got plenty of meat for a few days and then I'll take care of her."

The old man began to cough harder, his shoulders shaking with pain. When he was finally finished, he sat up straighter and looked down at his son.

"David, I don't know how much longer I have, but I want to go out with a bang, so I want that woman carved up and cooked so that I can give my followers one last feast before I go. So for me, go get her and kill her and bring her gutted corpse to Tammy so she can begin marinating the body." His eyes filled with emotion. "Call it my final request. For you see, at this feast I want to give you the reigns of leadership. It's time for me to step down, son. I know soon I will be going into the stew pot."

Sterling licked his lips. Finally. He had no idea this was coming, but he'd be damned if he wouldn't let it happen.

"Fine, Dad, I'll do it after I take care of Marvin, all right?"

The old man nodded. "Fine, David, fine." Then his head slumped down to his chest, the man falling into a light sleep. A woman climbed up onto the tables and placed a wet towel to the old man's head, wiping his face softly. She had the sole job of keeping the old man comfortable.

Sterling took a step back and wasn't at all surprised to see more than ten sets of eyes watching him. The others of the tribe had stopped their own conversations to listen to what was transpiring, and now, as Sterling began to walk out of the large room, he was greeted by pats on the back and congratulations.

A burly man in an old gray business suit, right down to the tie, moved next to Sterling to speak to him.

"Hey, Sterling, if you're looking for Marvin, I saw him heading towards the operating room where we keep the food until we're ready to carve it up."

Sterling's eyebrows went up in curiosity. "Oh yeah? How long ago?"

The man shrugged, his brow creasing in thought. "Shit, I don't know, almost fifteen minutes or so, why?"

Sterling squeezed his hands into fists, ignoring the man's question, and began pushing through the group of filthy men and women congratulating him. So Marvin had decided to finish what he'd started, even though he'd been ordered not to. The man was truly headed for the stew pots now, even if he hadn't been going there already.

Calling out to three other men to follow him, Sterling began running out of the cafeteria, back down the empty hallways on his way to the operating room.

Mary's .38 Police Special was nestled firmly in his belt and Sterling was already considering shooting Marvin to make a point of him so that all the others who would find out what happened would fear him even more than they already did now.

Or perhaps, Sterling considered, he would just use his bare hands and simply squeeze the life out of the little prick. As he dashed down the corridor, the three other men behind him, he decided he would just play it loose and do whatever came first to his mind when he found him. Either way, at the end of the meeting, Marvin would be dead.

Then he decided he would take the brunette once and for all and finally have his way with her...just before he cut her heart out.

Marvin had just finished puling Mary's pants down more than halfway and was climbing on top of her, prepared for some fun. His shirt was now off, lying in a ball on the floor next to the bed, and the knife he'd threatened her with was on top of the folds of clothing.

Her shirt was rolled up, her breasts exposed to the cool air of the operating room. After Marvin had kneaded them like dough for almost five minutes, he'd leaned over and began sucking each nipple. Despite her abhorrence to what was happening to her, her nipples reacted on their own accord, each one hardening.

Marvin grinned up at her, thinking he was doing a good job of arousing the trapped woman.

With his member hard between his legs, he was now lying on top of her, his tongue licking the back of her ear. She could feel his hardness pressing against her thigh and she had to use all of her willpower not to scream and kick to get him off her.

But her legs were still in restraints, and when Marvin tried to slide into her, he found her legs were still closed and her pants too high up near her crotch for his liking. With a mumbled curse, he rolled off her, now standing in the room with his pants down on his ankles. He reached down, and one at a time, undid her leg restraints.

He wasn't worried about her escaping, her hands were still secured.

With her legs now free, and her pants on the floor, he spread her feet apart, his eyes staring at her inner warmth like a child eyeing his first ice cream cone.

He said nothing, but merely climbed on top of her to begin raping her.

The entire time, Mary had said nothing, staying perfectly still. An idea had already come to her, and though it was risky, she decided she really didn't have much choice.

With a groan of expectation, Marvin positioned himself between her legs, his face hovering over hers. She could feel the tip of his penis at the folds of her most cherished place and knew she had less than a second before she was violated.

At the exact moment, Marvin arced his back, preparing to slam his shaft home inside of her; she leaned forward as far as she could go, Marvin's neck now within reach. With his Adam's apple brushing her lips, she opened her mouth as wide as it would go. Marvin barely noticed her actions, only assuming she was just getting into the fun and had finally come around to him. He figured she was going to caress his neck with her tongue, perhaps even give him a hickey.

But he was very wrong.

With his back arced and his thrust beginning, the tip of his penis only managed to penetrate inside her by less than an inch. Because then he was in far too much pain and shock to even consider the act of rape on his prisoner.

Mary had waited until he was ready to thrust and had used her teeth, sinking them into the folds of his neck. Marvin's Adam's apple was ripped from his throat, and before he could scream, Mary had spit out the torn chunk of flesh and had gone in for more, tearing into the man's jugular like a zombie feasting for the first time.

Warm blood filled her mouth, some sliding down her throat and gagging her, but she ignored it, holding back the coughs that wanted to spill from her lips.

Marvin went stock still, his back still arced. His mouth was opening and closing as if to scream, but nothing but a gargle came from his mouth. The blood began filling his throat so he was unable to utter anything louder than a gargle.

Mary's mouth was filled to the brim with the copper tasting plasma and it spilled out the sides of her lips to soak the pillow under her head.

The man on watch by the doorway peeked inside the room, but in the shadows, all he could see was Marvin's body moving around on top of the woman.

Jealous that he wasn't allowed to get any, he turned away from the sexual act to watch the hallway again.

Marvin was dying on top of Mary and he could do nothing to prevent it. Mary's face was buried in the flesh of his throat, worrying away muscle and tendon as she chewed and spit, and then went in for more. Her face, neck and upper chest were bathed in scarlet, the warm fluid still filling her mouth and making her want to retch.

But she continued to fight the reflex to vomit, knowing this was her only chance of escape. Two full minutes went by until Marvin finally collapsed on top of her, the gushing blood from his throat wound subsiding, the gash now only seeping crimson like a spent water hose.

Wiggling her head, Mary managed to allow herself some room to breathe and she sucked in her first breath since going in for the kill. Marvin was heavy on her and her chest was restricted, but she managed a few ragged breaths.

Blinking blood from her eyes, she heaved the body off her with a jolt of her hips, Marvin tumbling to the floor to land in a heap.

Sucking in gasps of air, Mary knew she had only seconds before Marvin's partner checked on them again.

With her legs and feet free, Mary quickly kicked off her boots and socks on her right foot, the latter increasingly difficult with only her toes. But she did it and when finished, she swung her legs off the bed and began fishing for the knife still lying on top of the shirt.

It took her almost a minute before her foot found the cold steel and then she had to carefully manage to stick the blade between her toes while not cutting herself.

On the third try she succeeded, and like a gymnastic contestant, she bent at her waist so her legs were perpendicular to the bed, and dropped the blade onto the mattress.

Once this task was completed, she used her toes to work the blade up the bed, but when this failed miserably, she grasped the knife in her toes again and bent her leg over her so her foot was almost next to her head.

By doing this she handed the knife to her right hand, and once done, she used the knife to begin cutting the restraints. It wasn't easy, the blade at an odd angle. She had to be careful too, because if the weapon slipped from her fingers it would make a noise on the floor, and once Marvin's partner was alerted to her machinations all would be lost.

But she continued cutting and after another tense minute passed she found her hand free. It was then easy to unbuckle the other hand, the wrist tender from her earlier escape. The skin around the left wrist was red and blotchy and she knew it would need medical attention before it could become infected and become life threatening.

With all her limbs free, she sat up, blood dripping from her torso to drip onto the floor. Though her shirt was soaked in blood, she still took an extra second to roll it back down, now covering her breasts, and grabbed her pants from the bed, quickly sliding into them. As for her boot, she left the other one off, not having the time it would take to put it on and tie it.

Feeling slightly better that she was dressed and armed, she moved across the room until she was at the doorway. The shadowy figure of the guard was easily seen, and with the knife in front of her, Mary stepped into the hall and smiled like a wild animal at the man on watch.

The man's mouth fell open as he stared at the blood drenched woman before him. She was like something out of a horror movie. Her brown hair was slicked back to her head, blood coating it so it glistened with any light that touched it. Her face and upper body was a bright red, her eyes peering through the mask of death like a banshee. When she smiled, her once white teeth were also coated in red, the globules of plasma in-between her teeth.

Before the man could so much as gasp, Mary sliced the blade across the man's throat, opening his carotid artery to the air. Blood geysered out of his wound like a faulty water fountain, the fluid spraying the nearby wall.

He raised his hands to his throat to try and staunch the flow of blood, but warm blood slipped through his fingers to soak his shirt a bright vermilion. The man slumped against the wall and slid to the floor, his eyes already glazing over in death.

Mary nodded, pleased with herself, then padded back to get her other boot. Behind her she left red footprints to stain the hospital floor.

She quickly slid into her boot, lacing it as fast as she was able, then with a quick look around; she dashed out of the room and down the hallway.

But no sooner did she round the first bend than she came face to face with Sterling and three other cannies who were armed with knives and clubs.

Mary became frozen for barely a moment as she gazed up at the unexpected face of Sterling, but the taller man went into action immediately. Before Mary could defend herself, Sterling's left hand snapped out and punched her in the side of the face with the power of a steel piston. Her head rocked back and she fell to the floor, unconscious, the blade falling from her hand, useless.

"What the fuck is going on around here? How the hell did this bitch get loose?" Sterling snapped to no one on particular.

"You, watch her," he said to one of the men and then proceeded to the operating room. Once inside the room, he took in everything that had happened in a glance, right down to the half-naked form of Marvin spread out in a heap of arms and legs.

Shaking his head, he turned to the other two men, his face filled with rage.

You two, get those bodies on a cart and take them to Tammy," he snapped.

"What about her?" the other man asked, gesturing to Mary.

Sterling moved back down the hallway until he was standing over Mary's prone form.

"Take her to the kitchens, too. I think this one's at the end of the line." He grinned while watching the man pick Mary up and toss her over his back like a sack of potatoes and begin to walk away. Sterling saw Mary's head sway back and forth with the rhythm of the man's gait and he smiled slightly; an evil, malevolent smile that would have sent a chill up Mary's spine if she had been awake to witness it.

"But don't kill her yet. As this will be my father's last day as leader, and my first official day, I want her to be something special. I think

I'm gonna start a new ritual. I always liked the idea of having a sacrifice and what better time than now."

The man paused to listen to Sterling and then began walking away. Sterling grinned as he thought about what was to come. Yes, he would sacrifice Mary in front of the entire tribe. Then he would eat her raw heart in front of everyone and seal the deal as leader of the cannies.

After that, no one would stand against him. If they did, they might just risk ending up as the next sacrifice.

With a quickening to his step, he left the hallway, following the drops of blood still sluicing off Mary's unconscious body while he already began imagining the fun to come.

CHAPTER FOURTEEN

MOVING THROUGH THE deserted hospital, the three companions were making lousy time. Each doorway had to be checked and rechecked or else risk a ghoul jumping out and attacking them. Not to mention the cannibals were around somewhere, also, and they were just as dangerous as the zombies, only in a different way.

More than an hour had passed and Henry was growing irritable. The hallways were riddled with open doors, as they appeared to be on a floor with nothing but patient's rooms. A few of the rooms still had occupants, though the bodies had been dead for a very long time. In hospital gowns and wearing oxygen masks, the bodies told the tale of what it must have been like in the last days before everything crumbled like a sandcastle in the rising surf.

Jimmy stopped at one of the doorways, and after making sure it was clear, he reached up and plucked a dusty clipboard from a plastic wall unit. Most of the rooms had one bolted near the doorframe, as the clipboards told of the patient's welfare and ailments for the doctor doing rounds and for the nurses to keep track of medications.

"Looks like this dude, had cancer," Jimmy said while scanning the clipboard. "Says here it was in remission."

Henry peered into the room of the cancer patient. The body was lying half-on, half-off the bed and the man's throat had been torn out, though as the body was nothing but a withered skeleton, it was hard to notice. But Henry had seen enough dead bodies over the past year to have a good eye for cause of death, and this man hadn't gone easy.

"Looks like the cancer might have left him alone, but a deader didn't," he said idly and turned away from the room. "Come on, let's keep moving."

Nodding in agreement, Jimmy and Cindy followed him further down the hall after Jimmy chucked the clipboard into the dead man's room. Spider webs draped from every crevice and while they walked, small dust balls were stirred around the floor like tiny tumbleweeds. Small dried up flies were everywhere, after feasting on the dead bodies, the small insects had tried to escape the hospital but had failed. In the short lifespan of a common housefly, the insects had lived their entire lives without ever leaving the confines of the building. Now they were just more debris littering the floor.

Moving to the end of the hall, Henry stopped at another set of double doors. But these doors were tightly secured, the tips of nails sticking out of the wood from the sheets of plywood securing the doors from the other side. He casually ran his hand over the splintered surface.

"Looks like this is the end of the line," Henry said as he touched a tip of a nail with his finger. He didn't press enough to draw blood, but he did leave a small indentation on the tip of his finger. "Someone had to board this door up and my guess is it's whoever is on the other side of these doors."

"Maybe they closed off this part of the hospital to keep the deaders out," Cindy suggested while she slid next to Henry. Her eyes studied the door, the nails like tiny needles of a porcupine. "So, how are we gonna get through? If we try to blow it up or something, whoever's on the other side is gonna hear us."

"Yeah, that's true, Cindy. But we need to get through fast. Every minute that passes could be Mary's last. God knows what's happening to her right now," Henry said, his forehead creasing in worry for his lost friend.

"Well, we can't just stand here, Henry, we need to do something now," Jimmy said as he waved his arms in the air. Henry already knew what Jimmy would prefer to do. Shoot the damn door apart and let the rest of the events after take care of themselves. Jimmy was one for action, and he never liked to talk about a problem too much. It had gotten him into more jams than he wanted to admit, but that was how God made him so there it was.

"Yeah, Jimmy, I know that. So why don't you come up with an idea instead of talking about what we can't do!"

Jimmy was about to toss back a harsh retort when Cindy moved between the two men. "All right, you two, that's enough. Come on, we have to work together, Mary needs us."

Jimmy looked down, embarrassed by her words. "Sorry, Cindy, but it's just, you know, talk, talk, and more talk. Let's just blow the damn hinges off and get moving already."

"Hey, wait a sec', Jimmy, that's not a bad idea. Better yet, I think I know how we can get through here without resorting to using our weapons." To make sure he was right, he pushed on the double doors. He nodded when the doors moved back and forth an inch or two, creaking softly. Yes, he was correct. The doors were boarded shut, but they weren't really reinforced too well. Oh sure, they would hold up fine against a half a dozen ghouls, but he doubted the barricade could take any real pressure.

And he was about to find out.

"Okay, guys, here's what we're gonna do," Henry said. First he laid out his idea, and then told each person what they would need for supplies to get the job done. Once finished, Jimmy nodded.

"Yeah, okay, that just might work," the younger man said, then took off to find his assigned items.

With a wink and a nod, Cindy was off, as well, leaving Henry alone for a brief moment before he, too, would go off to find what was needed to take out the barricade so they could move on.

As he passed back through the corridor, leaving footprints in the thick layer of dust, more dust bunnies were stirred up, moving across the floor like they had a life of their own.

Twenty minutes later, the sound of something rolling filled the empty corridor. In the shadows and gloom, if someone had been standing on the opposite side of the double doors, peeking into the dank hallway, they would have seen nothing. But slowly, gaining speed with every second, something in the middle of the shadows would begin to make itself seen.

The double doors were lined with wood, odd assortments of plywood, oak from a few office desks, and even a piece of Formica from one of the small nurse's stations on the third floor. All had been nailed sloppily to the doors and the frame, keeping the double doors from opening and thusly separating the wing of the hospital from the rest of the structure.

But all that changed in a heartbeat when the wood was shattered and thrown across the floor, the double doors snapping open like a hurricane had pushed them from the opposite side. Splinters littered the dusty floor and nails fell across the hallway like pieces of shrapnel, only a danger if a person was barefoot or very unlucky to step on one of the boards with nails still sticking up like steel grass.

The reason for the doors destruction was apparent a half-second after the explosion of wood. A hospital gurney, filled with anything that had weight to it, such as an office desk and an old oxygen tank, unfortunately long depleted, smashed through the doors like a battering ram, knocking the left door askew and the right so hard the handle was forced into the drywall.

With a whoop of excitement, Jimmy and Henry rammed the door and were through to the other side, the gurney tipping over when one of the front wheels struck a piece of wood. Both men had to balance themselves carefully or risk tumbling to the debris strewn floor, but managed to stay on their feet, Henry by luck and Jimmy by the dexterity of youth.

Right behind the two men was Cindy, her rifle up and ready for whatever might be waiting for them on the other side, but if she was expecting danger, she wasn't at all disappointed when there was nothing but more spider webs and dust balls to meet her gaze.

Breathing heavily from the excitement of the past minute, Jimmy stood up and fixed the strap of his shotgun, and with a smile creasing his lips, patted Henry on the back.

"Goddamn, Henry, that was awesome, I felt like I was storming the gates of Hell itself!"

Henry fixed his Steyr, making sure the weapon hadn't been damaged in the destruction of the barricade and nodded. "Well, get over it because we're a long way from where we need to be," he said as he gazed around the new hallway. There was nothing. This hallway was the same as the last one and the one before that. This damn hospital was like a maze and he was the mouse searching for cheese.

He was beginning to wonder if they would ever find their way out and to Mary.

Something caught the corner of his eye and he turned in that direction. Cindy noticed his movements and was immediately wary of danger.

"You see something, Henry?"

"Don't know, thought I saw something over in that corner," he told her and began moving in the same direction. With the need for stealth not an issue, as the noise they had just made would have attracted anyone within hearing, he still left his rifle slung on his shoulder and pulled his panga instead. With the closeness of the walls in the hallway, the panga was an excellent up-close weapon. Stepping around the few boards littering the floor, he moved down the dusty hall, the panga reflecting the smallest amount of illumination.

"What did you see?" Jimmy asked suddenly from Henry's side, causing the older man to jump.

"Jesus, Jimmy, sneak up on me why don't you," he gasped, his heart beating like a triphammer. "I don't know what I saw. It was just a shadow inside the darkness over there in the corner."

"Well, let's go then. No reason for you to go alone, right Cindy?" He asked her over his shoulder, and the woman nodded quietly, not wanting to speak.

With a sigh, Henry knew it wasn't worth discussing, so he nodded. "Fine, fine, let's go then," he said while shifting his backpack to make it more comfortable. One of the straps had loosened and the pack was slanting to the right, making him have to compensate.

With one step in front of the other, the three moved across the floor until Henry slowed at what looked like the nurse's station. Paper files were scattered everywhere, more than half on the floor behind the counter. Defunct monitors were sitting quiescent on the long desk, one or two with shattered screens and maroon stains on the edges of the glass.

Henry's eyes wandered around the area and then he swung the Steyr around, finger hovering on the trigger as the shadow he had spotted came into view. But when he saw the whiskers and beady eyes of a very large rat walk out onto the counter, he held his fire.

"It's a rat," Jimmy stated the obvious as he eyed the rodent.

"A big one," Cindy added.

The rat moved so it was only a few feet from Henry. If it had any fear of the human confronting it, the rodent hid it well. It sniffed the air, its nose twitching with a cuteness that belayed its ferocity when provoked. Henry noticed there appeared to be something in its mouth, and as he leaned closer to the rodent, he realized it was an ear, a human ear. Blood was still wet on the small morsel and Henry wondered where the rest of the person might be.

The rat studied the three people for another few seconds and then decided there was nothing here for it, so the rat spun around and waddled back to the end of the counter where it promptly disappeared inside a hole in the sheetrock without a backwards glance.

"Huh, must be hundreds of them inside the walls," Henry said while he eyed the hole. "Did you see what it was carrying in its mouth?" As an afterthought he picked up a binder of papers and tossed them across the counter to land in front of the hole in a spray of dust. He knew it wouldn't stop the furry rodents for long, but it would slow them down for a second or two as the companions made their way out of the hallway.

"Yeah, was that what I think it was?" Jimmy asked.

"It was an ear and it still looked fresh. That must mean we're getting close, Henry," Cindy said as she eyed the covered hole in the wall.

"Yeah, you're right. We must be. Okay, let's keep moving. At least this was a false alarm, but the next time might not be, so stay sharp," he told the others as he turned away from the counter to begin the trek once more. There was only another twenty feet until they would come to yet another set of double doors and Henry could only hope these weren't barricaded with wood.

With Jimmy to his right and Cindy to his left, the three companions made their way down the last leg of the hallway to the double doors. Using his boot, Henry shoved the left side open and was relieved to see it swing open a few inches, then swing back again. On creaking hinges it moved back and forth for another second and then remained still.

Henry glanced over his shoulder at Jimmy and Cindy, who both nodded for him to proceed. Letting out a deep breath, Henry pushed the doors open wide, his Steyr leading the way, and stepped into the gloom and shadows like he was wading underwater in a murky lake.

He didn't know if this next part of the hospital would be the one where Mary was being held captive, and wondered just how many more hallways they would have to traverse until the end of their hunt was finally in sight. But the second he entered the dusty, spider web infested hallway, he knew he was heading in the right direction.

A pungent, sickly sweet smell assailed his senses and he realized it was the odor of cooking meat. He recognized the redolence for what it was immediately. In his travels across an undead land, he had come across, and been a part of, many things he wished he could take back.

But one of the moist detestable things he had ever come across was the act of cannibalism. He still didn't know what would make a man or woman so unstable that they would want to feed on their own kind, especially when there were other food sources to be had. More than six months ago, the companions had found themselves in a shopping mall in New England where a group of survivors had set up an enclave. But what the companions didn't realize was that the man in charge was killing men and women and tossing their bodies into the cooking pot, disguising the human meat by making a rich stew that all the companions had partaken of before they had realized what was truly happening. And things had only gone from bad to worse when Henry and the others were next on the menu, the boss of the enclave wanting them dead and cut up for the next meal. The enclave was also the first place Henry had found love again after the loss of his wife. Her name had been Gwen and the woman had been kind and beautiful and about the same age as Henry. The two had hit it off immediately and had become friends which later had blossomed into love. But she had been killed by the boss of the enclave only moments before Henry had killed the man, sending him to his death amid a horde of zombies, who had torn him apart like a housewife shucking corn. His only regret was that he could only kill the man once. Henry sometimes wondered what his life might have been like if Gwen had lived. Would he still be living at the mall, doing his part to hunt and supply food for the enclave?

No, the time for thinking of what might have been was long gone, merely a waste of energy. The only thing that mattered was the here and now and saving Mary from a similar fate as Gwen.

Jimmy sniffed the air, curling his mouth in disgust. "Hey, guys, you smell that?"

"Yeah, smells like bacon a little, but off a little, too, like the meat is bad."

Henry turned slightly so he could see both of them in the gloom. "We're here," he said flatly. "If we can smell their cookfires, than they've got to be close, so get ready."

"What's the plan?" Jimmy inquired; already making sure his shotgun was fully loaded, as well as his sidearm. Cindy was doing the same by his side, fishing in her backpack for the last full clip for her rifle, her .32 Ruger already loaded with a few extra rounds of fresh lead. She had been in luck and had found some extra ammunition in the bottom of her backpack, but once she used what she had, that would be it for the foreseeable future.

Later, hopefully when they were safe, she could combine any half clips and loose bullets hiding in the bottom of her pack to make them at least partially full once again, but for now she didn't want to have to worry about changing clips in the middle of a firefight.

Henry's face was grim as his eyes flicked from Cindy to Jimmy.

"The plan is simple, we go in, get Mary, and kill every damn cannibal bastard we find."

Without waiting for an answer, he spun around and began moving off deeper into the building at a steady trot; Cindy and Jimmy close on his heels. The time for talk was over, now it was time for action.

CHAPTER FIFTEEN

HENRY WAS MOVING fast, his eyes darting back and forth at the doorways to his left and right, wary for any unseen dangers. He had already guessed this part of the hospital was zombie free, the boarded up double doors behind him the proof. He knew any attackers he now came across would be living, though still as dangerous as the dead, perhaps even more dangerous as human adversaries were more cunning.

The companion's boots echoed off the walls of the hospital, sounding like a parade of drummers was moving through the corridor, but Henry ignored it. He truly felt the time for stealth was over. Now they needed to find Mary, strike hard, and hopefully escape with their hides intact.

The first opposition came no more than five minutes after they had passed the last set of double doors. The companions almost blundered into the heavily tattooed man as they rounded a corner riddled with old wheelchairs and crutches. The tattooed man had been carrying a bucket of water, and he stopped like a deer caught in the headlights of an oncoming car, when he realized the three people charging towards him weren't from his tribe.

He opened his mouth to yell a warning to others in the area, but before he could even begin to unfurl his cry for help, Henry plowed into the man, the panga already coming down to carve into the side of the man's neck, then angle down into his sternum. Blood cascaded down the man's chest like a waterfall, the razor-sharp blade slicing clean through meat and bone.

The man's eyes rolled straight up into his head and bloody drool slid out of the corner of his mouth as Henry kicked him away with his boot to free the long blade.

Henry barely gave the man another look, knowing the cannibal was truly dead, and stepped over his cooling corpse to continue down the hall. The panga was in his left hand, dripping blood onto the stained linoleum like tiny raindrops, the droplets marring the dirty hospital floor with yet more fluids from days long past. He didn't sheath the blade, knowing there was more work to do with the razor-sharp weapon. Before the hour was finished, the panga would either drink deeply in blood or Henry and the others would be dead.

Jimmy and Cindy flanked either side of him as they charged down the hall, the pungent odor of cooking meat becoming almost overwhelming. A sign on the wall told of the cafeteria being only a few feet away, and as Henry approached the large doorway, the doors already propped wide open; he knew he was in the den of his enemies.

Multiple events happened almost simultaneously, all moving too fast to contemplate.

The first event was that the instant Henry entered the large room once designated as the hospital cafeteria, his eyes scanned to the left and then the right, trying to take in the position of every man and woman in the room, his friends doing the same by his side. He studied the hunks of meat hanging over large barbecue grills, the roiling smoke clouds rising to the ceiling where it seemed to hover like an approaching thunderstorm. He noticed the torches and car batteries with car headlights connected to their terminals, the bulbs facing at crisscrossing directions for maximum illumination. He saw an old man sitting on what appeared to be a makeshift throne, and the larger man standing next to him.

He also saw Mary.

She was hanging from a chain attached to the ceiling only a few feet from the throne, her toes barely touching the filthy floor, her boots missing. Her face, hair and shirt appeared to be slathered in blood, but from a quick glance, Henry couldn't tell if the blood was hers or not. Her head hung low on her chest and she was either unconscious or resting, something he would find out very soon. Two men bracketed her, holding her from swinging back and forth, while a woman was standing next to her with a large kitchen knife she was running over a sharpening stone. And it looked like she was about to use the knife on Mary while the score of men and women stood or sat around watching with glee. Some of the revelers had pieces of meat in their hands, munching happily on what Henry tried not to think about too deeply, while others were drinking from a bucket similar to the one the tattooed man had been carrying.

From a quick glance, it seemed like the cannibals were having some kind of party or celebration.

Well, the party was about to have some unexpected party crashers.

The second event to happen while Henry and the other companions were scanning the room, was that Sterling turned to see three strangers come charging into the cafeteria. His face immediately recognized them as intruders and his hand dropped down to his newly acquired revolver, courtesy of Mary.

He yelled at the top of his lungs, warning the rest of the tribe they had been invaded and like one tight military unit, the entire tribe dropped what they were doing and reached for weapons. Vastly outnumbered by more than five to one, the companions would have been doomed if the cannibals had possessed firearms, but with the exception of a few old rifles that had been poorly maintained and Sterling's newly acquired .38, the tribe had only blades and a few crossbows pilfered from the nearby city.

Just as Henry, Jimmy and Cindy moved into the room with their weapons prepared to fire, every man and woman swung around with weapons drawn, prepared to fight.

Henry said nothing, but aimed the muzzle of the Steyr at the first man he saw. The 7.62mm round struck the man in the neck and a gush of blood shot out to bathe the cannibal next to him in crimson warmth. While the first man died, the second man, now blinking his eyes clear of warm blood, never got the chance to try and attack the companions as Cindy shot the man in the chest, sending the body tumbling to the floor like a puppet with the strings cut. The second man ended up falling on top of the first, the two men looking like lovers sleeping softly. A woman cannie screamed bloody murder and charged at Cindy from her right, but before she could get within striking range, Cindy swiveled her waist and shot the woman in the stomach. The woman staggered back, her mouth still open in a silent scream as she looked down at her intestines now seeking to escape her body like oily snakes abandoning a ship of death. Falling into shock, the woman fell to her knees as she desperately tried to push her ropy insides back into her body where they belonged.

A short man with a large mole on his chin came at Jimmy from his left and Jimmy swung the Remington at the man, firing from the hip. The man received the delivery of buckshot postage due and the man's face and the back of his head disintegrated in a spray of blood and bone matter. Brains struck the floor, sounding like a wet mop slapping the tiles while the man fell over like a mighty oak cut down in its prime. Three more cannies who had been behind the man now had to jump over his cooling corpse as they did their best to take down the three intruders.

Flicking her M-16 from single shot to full auto, Cindy sprayed half a clip at the oncoming horde of cannies. Bodies were struck with hot lead and danced a jig of death as one at a time they fell back to the floor, either dead or moaning in pain.

A crossbow bolt shot passed Henry's head, missing him by inches, and he ducked instinctively, searching for the source of the projectile. He spotted it when he saw a woman with wild red hair and a filthy blouse trying to reload the crossbow in her hands. She was frail and was having trouble reloading the weapon, but Henry saved her the trouble by sending a round through her chest, the force of the impact throwing her across the room to strike the wall behind her. As she slid to the floor, a bloody streak was left in her wake to paint the wall scarlet.

A spear flew threw the air and all three companions dove for cover, Henry knocking over a cafeteria table to hide behind. With something strong enough to repel the primitive weapons, and perhaps even a few bullets, the companions got busy dealing death.

Tammy was ducking low, trying to stay out of the line of fire when Mary began to regain consciousness above her. Cursing the chained woman, Tammy decided she was going to finish Mary off quick, before her friends got to her. Tammy had recognized the companions from earlier in the day at the raid near the lake. She knew they were here for Mary and she'd be dammed if she would let the woman go free. Not after all the trouble it had taken to get her. Nearby, Sterling was roaring orders, trying to rally his diminishing men and women. Tammy noticed with a grin that though he was telling others to go into the breach of the thrice warrior's fire, he was hiding behind a stack of crates, keeping his head down.

The two men that had been bracketing Mary were gone, already joining in the attack, and with a glint in her eye, Tammy stood up to slice Mary's abdomen open.

But if she expected a scared woman who would beg for her life like so many before her, Tammy was very wrong. Knowing she was in mortal danger, Mary waited until Tammy was within reach and then raised her legs up and over Tammy's head, wrapping her thighs around the woman's neck and face before the cannie knew what was happening. Tammy found her nose and mouth being smothered by Mary's thighs and she began to fight to free herself. But Mary would not let go, despite the slices she received to her legs from the knife in Tammy's hand. After a full minute had passed, Tammy's movements began to slow as her body fought for oxygen. Still Mary squeezed, so hard she had to scream with all the rage and anger she felt. Tammy's face turned red, then blue and when her eyes rolled up into her sockets and her arms dropped limply, Mary released the limp body; Tammy falling to the floor in a heap of limbs.

With a mighty yell, Mary laughed. If she died today then at least she sent that bitch to Hell before her. Now all she had to do was get free, but as she jingled her chains, her wrists bleeding from the weight of holding her up, she knew she was trapped unless some outside intervention came to aid her. And when she turned her head to take in the chaos surrounding her, she spotted her friends hiding behind a turned over table. She smiled and her heart filled with joy. There were her friends, seeking to save her even now.

But first they had to fight off the dozen or so remaining cannies and do it all without a stray bullet or any other projectile hitting her by accident. Which was becoming almost impossibly hard as bullets whined about the room like a nest of angry bees.

Henry ducked when a bullet whined off the edge of the table, leaving splinters in its wake. His face was smeared with blood from a slight gash on his forehead he'd received from a stray round. Though the wound was minor, the blood still screwed with his vision as it dripped over his eyebrows and into his eyes.

Wiping his brow for the tenth time, he turned to look at Jimmy and Cindy.

"We need to end this quick. If some of them manage to flank us, we're screwed!"

"I hear that, but what do you suggest?" Jimmy replied as he shot another cannie in the chest and then pumped the shotgun to chamber more rounds.

"I've got an idea, but someone needs to get to Mary before I do it," Cindy said while spraying another burst with the M-16. She didn't know how many rounds remained in the clip, but she knew it wasn't that many. Her backpack was at her side, tossed there so she could move more freely.

"Whatever your idea is, go for it, 'cause I'm out of ideas at the moment," Henry called back as he shot a man trying to sneak around them to his right. The round caught the man in the arm, but the bullet continued into the side of the cannie's ribcage. The body dropped to the floor and was lost from sight behind a table and some chairs. With a grunt of satisfaction, Henry turned away to find his next target.

"I'll get her," Jimmy said. "But you two better cover my ass good!"

"Fair enough. Okay, on three," Henry yelled, and prepared to send enough ammo at the enemy to keep their heads down.

"One," Henry said.

"Two," Cindy added.

"Three!" Jimmy finished and dashed across the cafeteria as quarrels and bullets whined around him. Henry and Cindy began systematically peppering the cannies with gunfire, aiming to keep them down, not necessarily kill them.

It worked and Jimmy had the precious seconds he needed to charge across the room until he was standing next to Mary. With a wide smile on her face, she looked into Jimmy's haggard visage.

"What took you so long?" She asked.

"Sorry, Mar'. Traffic was a real bitch, now shut up and get ready to fall." Jimmy raised the Remington over his head and sent a blast at the chains bolted to the ceiling. Plaster rained down on the two companions, covering them in white dust, but the chain was severed, the links tumbling to the floor like metal hail.

Jimmy yanked Mary aside, preventing the links from striking her in the head. When both were clear, they began crawling back to the cover of the table, but not more than halfway there, Jimmy realized the road was blocked as five more cannies filled the gap, trying to catch them in a circle.

"I think we've got trouble," Jimmy said to Mary as he fired a blast that sent the cannies ducking for cover.

Mary didn't answer, but began searching around herself for a weapon. She found one in seconds on one of the dead bodies of a fallen cannibal. She pulled the machete clear from the dead hand and held the weapon aloft. Jimmy glanced at her and saw the machete in her hand. Nodding to her, he ducked as a few rounds went over his head.

"What do we do now?" Mary asked as she kept her head low.

"Just stay down. Cindy says she had an idea, but we needed to get you out of harm's way first. Now that you're safe, she should be..." He wasn't able to finish his sentence because a large explosion filled the cafeteria and a rolling fireball filled the room, inches from their heads, sucking the atmosphere from the room for a few precious seconds. So close to the blast, Jimmy felt his hair singe and the odor of burning hair came to his nose. Patting his head quickly, he put out the glowing embers as he tried to clear his ears of the ringing now filling them.

Next to him, Mary was doing the same, shaking her head to try to clear it. Bits of tables, body parts and miscellaneous detritus fell onto their backs, the storm of material only lasting for a few brief seconds. Then all went quiet.

After almost a minute, with silence reigning over the cafeteria, Jimmy poked his head up over the bodies and debris surrounding him and scanned the room.

And that was when the screaming began, filling the room with anguish.

No one was standing and when he looked for more targets to shoot, he saw none that would be any further danger. A few cannies were still alive, but all were wounded in one way or another. A wail of pain filled the air, rendering the survivors with a chill as they listened to the suffering men and women. Standing up behind the table that had fallen on top of him and Cindy, Henry raised the Steyr and shot a woman in the head that was no more than five feet away. Another man was rolling around on the floor, his clothing on fire. He had fallen into one of the barbecue grills and the hot coals had begun to burn him alive. His face was on fire and his eyes were gone as he screamed and choked from the smoke. Henry sent a round into the man's chest, mercifully putting him out of his abject misery and agony. Sometimes there were more important things than saving a bullet.

Fires were burning everywhere, the smoke filling the cafeteria to darken the already smoke-stained ceiling. With each passing second, more of the ceiling was catching fire, everything flammable beginning to burn and smolder. The rear of the cafeteria was a roiling fireball that was growing with every second.

"What the hell did you do?" Jimmy asked Cindy when he made his way back to Henry and Cindy's side, Mary right behind him.

"I shot a couple of tanks at the back of the room. I don't know what was in them, oxygen I guess, but wow, did you see that?" She was covered in ash and a sleeve was smoldering. She patted it out and she swung her rifle around at any opposing enemies. Even as Jimmy and Mary joined them, the surviving cannies that had just been knocked over by the blast were already regaining their feet. But more than half had been decimated by the explosion and their numbers were now very close to even, with the companions still having loaded firearms.

Mary stumbled next to Henry and he touched her arm and then her face, knowing there was no time for sentiment now.

"It's good to have you back safe and sound," he said simply, then turned to Jimmy and Cindy. The smoke was becoming heavy and it was already becoming difficult to breathe.

Stifling a coughing fit, Henry glanced around the room.

"We need to go before the whole hospital comes down on us."

"Fine, let's go," Jimmy said, then shot a cannie that was trying to attack them from their left. "Christ, these guys just don't quit," he gasped as he began loading more rounds into the shotgun.

"Which way?" Cindy asked.

Mary raised a weary arm, pointing to a set of doors located on the far side of the cafeteria. "That way. There's more rooms down there and I think the loading dock is down there, too. I'm not sure; I was out a lot of the time."

Henry nodded. "No, Mary, that's fine. We really don't have any choice anyway. We already know what's behind us and we can't get out that way. All right then, let's get moving. Take out anyone you see. We don't want to have to worry about what's behind us."

Both Jimmy and Cindy nodded, and with Henry in the lead, panga in his left hand, Steyr in his right, they began moving through the cafeteria. The remaining cannies came at them, though only in ones and twos, and it was an easy task to shoot them down. Mary used her new machete once, slashing a woman across the throat with the dull blade and taking a few of the woman's fingers off at the same time when the woman tried to use a knife, slashing back and forth like a maniac. But she missed Mary and the machete did its work well, severing the woman's jugular, spraying crimson across the room to squelch a few fires that flared on the floor. The gurgling woman's fingers shot blood also, her life's blood pumping from the jagged nubbins of flesh to join her severed jugular and pool onto the floor where it boiled and bubbled from the heat of the nearby flames. She slumped to the ground, bleeding to death, and was promptly forgotten by Mary. Cindy passed her Ruger to Mary, then, wanting the woman to be armed with more than a knife. Mary smiled thanks, feeling much better with a firearm in her hand.

"Don't thank me too much, there's only a few rounds in there," Cindy told her. Mary nodded, understanding.

Passing by the mock throne, none of the companions so much as glanced at the corpse of the dead old man sagging against the overturned chair, other than to make sure the body was truly immobile. Then they'd reached the opposite side of the cafeteria and were pushing through the shattered doors and into another long hallway. The air was slightly better here, and all of them sucked in the fresher air, trying to clear their lungs of smoke. More than one of them had mucus dripping from their noses and shirtsleeves were used as hasty handkerchiefs.

With Henry still in the lead, the companions moved away from the conflagration, the fire slowly spreading to the floor above and below as the flames began working their way into the ventilation shafts, seeking oxygen wherever it could find it.

Moving with urgency, they moved down the hallway until they came to another fire door. One at a time they entered the stairwell, the smoke from the cafeteria following them like a playful puppy. No one spoke, all concentrating on their environment. Halfway down the stairwell, they paused to regroup, checking their weapons and hastily patching any wounds sustained in battle. Cindy ripped a piece of her shirt off and used it as a loose bandage for Mary's wrist and Jimmy helped Henry clean his face of blood, wiping his forehead with a rag soaked in water from his canteen. Their water supply was finite and he hated wasting it on the bandage, but sometimes there was little choice. If Henry couldn't see what he was doing then the water wouldn't matter much if they were all dead.

Four minutes later, with weapons primed and ready, the companions finished moving down the stairs. At the bottom was another fire door and with utmost caution, Henry pulled the door open, expecting a barrage of gunfire to greet him. He waited for more than a minute for something to happen, but when all was quiet, he swallowed hard and took a chance, poking his head out of the doorway. Deep inside himself he was waiting for that bullet that would come out of the darkness and pierce his forehead, giving him a third eye as he slumped into death. But there was still nothing that appeared dangerous and he stepped out into the dark corridor with four exits in front of him. The corridor was like a cross with hallways moving off to all points on the compass. There were signs on the walls and arrows, telling patrons where they needed to go. The right passageway led to the loading dock, and with Henry still on point, the four reunited companions began the last leg of their trek.

"Hey, Henry; have you thought about what we're gonna do once we get to the dock? I mean, once we leave here there's a shitload of deaders outside."

"I know, Jimmy, but those cannibals had vehicles and where the hell else should they be but the loading dock? We should be able to hotwire one of their cars and drive it out of here."

"Where are we gonna go?" Mary asked from behind. She was last in line, only slightly behind Cindy. The Ruger waved back and forth in her hand as she walked, the muzzle dipping up and down

Henry shrugged. "Frankly, Mary, at the moment I really don't care. Anywhere is better than here." To illustrate his point, a far off explosion could be heard and the entire building shook slightly. The fire was spreading fast, finding any chemicals or tanks full of explosive gas. In a very short time, the entire building would be a raging inferno, so time was against them. If they ran into more opposition and were pinned down, they might find themselves having to deal with flames on their backs while they tried to escape their enemies from the front.

Henry slowed to a stop upon reaching another set of doors. The words, Loading Dock, Authorized Personnel Only was emblazoned on the door and overhead frame.

"Looks like we're here," Henry said. Reaching down to his Glock, he cursed to himself that the weapon was useless until he found more ammo for it. Until then he would have to settle for his Steyr. He had what was left in the clip in the rifle, and he had fifteen more loose rounds in his pockets. The rifle's circular clips held five bullets each, and once they were gone, he would have to load the remaining loose rounds one at a time. Not the best way to fight a gun battle.

"So, what's the plan?" Jimmy asked gruffly. They always had a plan. That was why they were all still alive. It was only when you ran into a situation like an idiot, taking it as it came that you ended up dead. No, the key to survival was preparation and planning. The more the better.

Henry turned to stare at the loading dock door and then back at his three friends. His face was grim as he shrugged hesitantly.

"I don't have one, Jimmy. If you have any ideas I'm all ears."

Cindy moved up until she was standing next to Henry. Holding her M-16 higher so all could see it, she gestured to the metal door.

"Look, I've got the most rounds left, so I should go in first. Once through the door, I'll go right. Jimmy, you go straight and Henry and Mary go left. Shoot first and let God sort 'em out. How's that for a plan?"

Jimmy smiled and leaned over to kiss Cindy on the cheek.

"Sounds good to me, babe. That's why I love you, there's a brain in that head of yours, too. You're not just a great pair of legs."

"Oh, Jimmy, you're such a hopeless romantic," Mary joked as she shifted the Ruger from one hand to the other, trading places with the machete. Her wrist throbbed with a dull agony and the weight of the machete was causing her added pain, but she didn't want to relinquish the weapon if she didn't have to.

"You all right, Mary?" Henry asked concern written on his face like a worried father.

She nodded. "Yeah, Henry, I'm fine. Believe me, I could be a lot worse. Once we're safe I'll tell you about it."

"Yeah, okay, but you're right, Mary. Once we're safe we can talk and we ain't there yet, people. All right, on three, Cindy will go first and then we go in after her. Take out anyone you see. We have no allies here, so everyone's a target. We don't know how many of them are left and there might be guards posted on the vehicles, so stay focused." He glanced at each of them. "Any questions?"

"Uh, yeah, is it too late to go to the bathroom?" Jimmy asked with a grin.

Henry frowned. Good old Jimmy, always a joke when none was needed.

"Hold it until we're done, all right?"

Jimmy nodded, raising his Remington in preparation for what was to come. Another explosion ripped through the building, shaking the structure to its very foundation. The acrid smell of burning material began to fill the hallway as the fire spread with every passing second.

Turning around, the companions saw thick rolling clouds of smoke heading towards them and there was more smoke coming from under the stairwell door. There would be no going back even if they wanted to. The only way of escape was through the loading dock and out into the falling dusk.

Cindy moved into position, already trying to hold back the coughing fit that was threatening to incapacitate her.

With a brief look to the others who nodded to her they were ready; Cindy pushed down on the latch and kicked the door in. She charged through the opening, rolling on the floor to throw off any sudden gunfire. Henry never hesitated, but was through the door a split second after Cindy. Mary and Jimmy followed; their weapons ready, fingers hovering over triggers, all their safeties off.

With the companions spread out on the loading dock platform, their eyes went wide as they took in what was sitting in one of the five bays before them. Polished steel and glass reflected the illumination of the multiple torches spread out across the dock like a hundred small stars, sending slivers of light to bathe the dock in an eerie glow.

"Oh my God, I don't believe it," Henry gasped.

Before any of the others could reply, gunfire filled the dock, echoing like cannon fire off the stone walls.

Diving for cover, the companions returned fire.

They were pinned down, just as Henry had feared, and as they fired back at their unseen foes, the conflagration roared through the hallways, like a mystical fire-breathing dragon, coming directing towards them and consuming everything in its path.

CHAPTER SIXTEEN

"COME ON, YOU bastards, hurry the fuck up and get that shit loaded!" Sterling screamed at the two men and one woman who were all that remained of his tribe of cannibals. The men and woman were busy loading supplies into the luggage compartment of a brand new Greyhound bus, shoving in all the meat and water they could manage. Boxes of ammunition were being loaded, as well, though most had no guns to be loaded with it. Sterling had found the ammunition on a raid to the city more than two months ago, but all the firearms had been long gone. So, hoping to find weapons later, he had taken the ammunition back to the hospital. Even if he never found another gun, the ammo would make excellent trade goods. Not to mention he could always take the rounds apart and make pipe bombs with the gunpowder, though that would be a waste of good bullets. Either way, the ammo was valuable. More valuable than gold in the new world market of death. The only thing more valuable than the ammo would be the weapons to fire them with.

Sterling shook his head as he fingered the .38 in his hand. The men and woman also had firearms, though all were of poor quality. The four of them were all that survived the assault of the armed attackers who had charged into the cafeteria spitting lead. He had seen his father go down with a head wound, the old man dead before he'd hit the floor. His throne had tumbled away from his body to bounce on the floor next to him, now just another piece of garbage.

Sterling had fired three shots at the attackers, but when they flipped a table over and were under cover, and began systematically killing his people, well; David Sterling's mother didn't raise no idiot. He accepted all was lost and high-tailed it out of the cafeteria, taking anyone still standing with him. They had made a beeline for the loading dock where they kept their vehicles. It had always been a difficult task to get in and out of the hospital with the cars and trucks. Usually, one of their number would run around and distract the zombies, running around the lot like a sick game of tag, and while the dead idiots chased their meal, the loading dock doors were opened and the vehicles would slip in or out. Once inside or outside, a rope would be sent down to the runner so he could get back inside the building. Of course this didn't always go as planned. Many times in the past year, one of the runners had been cornered or had slipped or tripped to be overwhelmed. The number of zombies would easily surround the hapless runner and had begin to tear the screaming shrieking person apart until there was nothing left but a large blood stain on the pavement. But still, the next time they needed to go outside, there would always be another volunteer.

After all, if they didn't leave the hospital to hunt, they would all starve anyway. At least being torn apart by the ghouls was preferable to starvation. Well, sort of.

Sterling studied the Greyhound bus, the rear bumper almost touching the loading dock door. The bus had been a find, that was for sure. They had been on a hunt a few miles from the city limits and were on their way back when the driver had spotted it on the side of the road. Other than a shitload of bloodstains on the inside of the passenger compartment, the bus was unharmed and started up on the first try. The big diesel had purred like a two dollar whore with a five dollar john and Sterling had personally driven the large bus back to the hospital. It had been a bitch getting the bus into the loading dock quickly and he'd panicked the doors wouldn't close, but in the end it had made it with only a few inches to spare. The bus had sat idle from then on, only being started to make sure the battery was always charged and to keep the fuel lines clean. The bus was his escape plan. If something ever went wrong in the hospital and he had to bail, he knew the rolling monster would be an excellent getaway vehicle. Though he had never realized he might actually need to use it, he was damn glad he did.

He was more than surprised when the metal door that led to the hallway and deeper into the hospital was thrown open and the same attackers from the cafeteria came charging through the doorway. And he was even more surprised to see Mary with them. The woman was still bootless, but she had a gun in her hand and a large machete in the other. Sterling recognized the machete as a weapon from one of his men. The dull blade was easily recognizable, though even dull, the blade could do some damage.

Barking a yell, he got the attention of the two men and woman. All three dropped their supplies and pulled their weapons from waistbands or unslung shoulder straps to level their rifles. Before the companions had fully entered the loading dock, Sterling's people were hiding behind whatever cover they could find, weapons already firing. He watched Mary and her three friends dive for cover themselves, each returning fire when they thought it was safe.

Each group fired at the other, neither scoring a hit, and when Sterling fired another of his precious rounds, he saw the smoke slowly coiling through the loading dock as it drifted into the overhead ceiling. The torches filling the loading dock fluttered at the touch of the smoke, but still burned brightly.

Sterling fired again, down to his last few rounds, then ducked when a bullet ricocheted near his head. He needed to escape the dock fast or else they would all die here.

Deciding he needed a distraction, he dropped to the floor and began crawling behind the Greyhound and to the loading dock door that would open to the outside. It was one of five similar doors and he picked the one second closest to the greyhound bus. Safe behind the vehicle, and still hearing the retort of gunfire, he reached up and grabbed the chain that would open the accordion-type door manually. With the sound of tortured metal, the door began to open. Slowly, one inch at a time, the door moved upward, and with each passing foot the waning daylight filtered inside the dock. But the light was dim due to the fact there were dozens of legs and bodies blocking the light. When the door finally rolled upward into the ceiling, more ghouls appeared. This was what the undead had been waiting for, a weakness in the hospital's security. When the door was six feet off the ground, the first ghouls poured inside, moaning and wailing like they were shoppers rushing into a store at an all night madness sale.

Sterling backed away from the door and crawled towards his men with a smile on his lips.

"That'll show 'em," he muttered to himself, proud of his idea. What he didn't realize was that the ghouls wouldn't be discriminating against who they attacked. They didn't care about Henry or Sterling. All they wanted was meat and all the humans inside the loading dock were fair game.

"All right, that should hold 'em. Hey, Smithers, get the rest of the shit into the bus, it's time to go," Sterling snapped at the balding man with a face full of pimples. Smithers sent another shot at the hiding companions and nodded, his jowls shaking like a bowl of jello.

"Okay, but cover me, those guys are pretty good shots," Smithers retorted and pointed to his left ear which was bleeding from a stray round that had come an inch away from entering his head.

"Fine, fine, just go, and hurry the hell up. I just let a bunch of dead fucks in here so we only got a few seconds."

"You what?" The woman snapped and spun around to glare at Sterling. "Why the hell did you do that?"

"Because we needed a distraction, now keep those bastards pinned down. In a second they're about to have company. The stairs are on their side. The dead pricks have to go up them to get to us. Why they're fighting we can get away."

The woman frowned, but nodded understanding the logic, then began firing a few shots with her old 22 rifle. The stopping power was low, but a head shot would still kill a live human and would usually scramble a zombie's brains enough to kill it.

The last man in Sterling's crew was a tall, thin man with a crewcut and a small mustache. He looked like a skeleton with meat still on the bones and his face was like a skull covered in parchment. Sterling always figured if the guy ever turned into a zombie he probably wouldn't end up looking that much different than he did now.

"Hey, Waters, how you doin' for ammo?" Sterling called to the skinny man. Waters was hiding behind the guard shack, taking pot shots when he could at the companions. Near head height, the shack was pockmarked with bullet holes from the near misses he'd been receiving.

"I'm okay, but what did you just say about zombies?" Waters answered in reply.

"Nothing, don't worry about it. Just stay down until the shit hits the fan, then go for the bus," Sterling ordered the thin man.

Waters nodded, and when he thought he had a shot, he swung around the shack and fired two more times, quickly jumping back as another round slapped off the corner of the guard shack, sending splinters into his hair.

"Damn, these guys are good," Waters called as he wiped his hair clean. "Who the hell are they, Sterling? What do they want with us?"

"It's that woman we took this morning. Those are her friends. The bastards found us somehow. But don't worry, once we're in the bus we're out of here, now shut up and keep firing. I want as many of them as we can gone before we run for it."

Sterling shot his last round and reached into his pocket to retrieve a handful of bullets. He had boxes of .38 ammunition and now had a weapon to use them with. Opening the cylinder, he emptied out the loose brass and began reloading the weapon one bullet at a time. When finished, he snapped the cylinder closed and prepared to begin firing again.

It was at that moment he noticed though the companions were still firing their weapons, they weren't firing at him and his men anymore. The ghouls had reached the stairs and the companions now had bigger troubles.

Sterling smiled, thinking about what was going to happen to the bitch, Mary, and her friends in seconds.

But before he could contemplate their fate, a loud explosion filled the loading dock and a white cloud cascaded across the cement floor, covering Sterling and his people as the billows of smoke joined with the ash gray fog of the approaching fires. It became hard to breathe and his vision was almost gone, the caustic fog irritating his eyes like tear gas.

"What the hell just happened?" Waters called from somewhere in the fog.

"Sterling, what's going on?" The woman yelled.

He felt someone brush by him and realized it was Smithers.

"Smithers," Sterling called as he coughed and cleared his throat. "Where the hell are you going? Get back here."

But Smithers wasn't listening, the man panicking in the chaos. Sterling had known the man for some time and knew he was a coward, but until this moment, he hadn't realized just how much of a coward he truly was.

Over the sounds of gunshots, the dead wailed and moaned. Sterling's smile had now become a long frown as he stared at the cloud around him, wondering what was hiding inside its roiling mass.

His plan to leave the loading dock and kill his attackers by using the undead had gone terribly awry. But how had it happened? What the hell had the companions done to turn the tables on him so badly?

These things and his own mortality ran through his mind like children playing tag at recess, while he waved his .38 around at anything he perceived as movement, and waited for whatever would come next.

CHAPTER SEVENTEEN

HENRY FIRED THREE rounds from his Steyr and dropped down behind a stack of boxes filled with hospital supplies. The boxes contained what appeared to be sheets, blankets, and paper, the puffed material of the sheets exposed where countless bullets had pierced the boxes. Releasing the expended clip, he slapped in one of his last remaining full ones and worked the bolt to chamber the first round.

"What the hell are we gonna do Henry?" Jimmy called from a few feet away. "They've got us pinned down."

"No shit," Henry replied as he stayed huddled behind the boxes. Rounds peppered the cardboard, but the copy paper and notebooks inside the containers absorbed the impacts.

"Well, we can't stay here forever," Cindy observed dourly as her eyes flicked to the open loading dock door. The smoke was pouring in from the hallway and it would only be a matter of minutes before the dock was so full of smoke that the lack of air would become life threatening. They needed to get out of the loading dock fast or else they would all die of smoke inhalation.

Henry's eyes darted around the dock, studying every piece of machinery and items littering the upper level. There was a forklift in the corner, but it was useless to him. Even if he made it to the machine safely, there was no guarantee it would start. His eyes drifted over the Greyhound bus again, the large vehicle reminding him of times long gone. It looked like it was in perfect condition, not even a scratch on its gleaming painted surfaces. The windows were all intact; the passenger ones tinted for maximum comfort for the paying customers now long dead.

The sound of metal rattling came to his ears around the staccato of gunfire and he realized one of the loading dock doors was being opened. Dusk was falling fast and the remaining sunlight streamed into the smoke-filled room.

"You hear that?" Jimmy called as he fired off a blast with his Remington. He waited for the accompanying cry of pain, but when it didn't come, he knew he'd missed again. Damn, but those cannibals were dug in.

"Yeah, one of the doors is opening to the outside," Henry commented as he studied the lower level of the loading dock. The door being opened was on the other side of the bus and he couldn't see what was happening, but when he began to hear the wails of the undead floating in the air and rebounding off the cement walls, he knew what was occurring and a chill went down his back.

"Shit, guys, I think we're about to have company," he told the others as they fired one at a time.

Mary was to his left and she swiveled in time to catch the first two ghouls as they rounded the rear bumper of the bus, two dozen following close behind. The stairs were just behind her and the ghouls were heading right for them, almost as if they knew the companions were there. Firing with the Ruger, she shot both lead ghouls, but neither shot was a headshot. The ghouls stumbled from the impacts of the rounds and then began moving forward again, an extra hole in each of them.

"Henry, we got deaders, a lot of them!" Mary called and fired again. She turned to Cindy. "Cindy, I need more ammo!"

Cindy nodded, rummaged in her backpack and tossed Mary a box of .32 caliber bullets. Mary held the box and shook it, only hearing a few rounds jingling inside. Frowning, she quickly reloaded the weapon, knowing every second could be her last. It was unbelievable. She was rescued from being killed and eaten by cannibals only to end up being trapped in a loading dock with ghouls and more cannibals still trying to kill her. She couldn't help but wonder if it could get any worse.

Henry swiveled behind the stack of boxes and shot the first zombie as it began climbing the steps. The heavy round struck the ghoul in the forehead, the back of the head exploding outwards to spray the ghouls behind it with black ichor and gray brain matter. Slumping to the stairs, the following zombies now had to crawl over their very dead comrade, the obstacle slowing them down.

Henry saw the dozen or so vacant faces following the first ghoul and knew he needed to do something quick or the companions would all be over run. It was then that his eyes spotted the fire extinguishers dotting the loading dock every fifteen feet or so. The bright red canisters were easily spotted even within the growing smoke from the burning hospital.

An idea struck him and he quickly got the attention of the others. Pointing to the fire extinguishers, he directed each of the companions to fire at a specific canister. Jimmy took the closest, the shotgun not good for long range targets, while Mary and Cindy took the others. Henry took the one across the dock, near where the cannibals were pinned down.

On a count of three, all four companions fired simultaneously, each warrior scoring their intended target.

The fire extinguishers exploded, the pressure inside released from the impacts of bullets on the pressurized canisters. A white fog erupted into the loading dock, and every surface became covered with a fine spray of white dust. Visibility was almost down to zero, only the first three feet in front of a person visible.

Coughing and trying to clear his throat, Henry ran to the others, slapping each on the back.

"Come on, now's our chance. Get to that bus. If we're lucky, we can get it started and leave in it!" Henry yelled over the noise. The crescendo of sound was overwhelming. Between the undead wailing and the cannibals shouting at the appearance of the white fog, the echoes bouncing off the stone walls to reverberate back, trying to talk and give directions was impossible as no one could hear you.

Taking Mary by the hand, who grabbed Cindy, who grabbed Jimmy's hand, the companions dashed across the loading dock, their destination the greyhound bus.

But their way was still blocked, some of the cannibals moving onto the platform as they coughed and hacked to get away from the exploding fire extinguisher that had gone off almost directly behind them. Smithers' bald head was now white and his pimples were hiding under a layer of dust as if he'd applied makeup. Henry was first in line, and as he led the others across the platform, he literally walked into Smithers, caught completely off guard.

Smithers was blinking his eyes clear of dust and smoke, and when he turned his head, he found Henry coming straight at him and his tear-filled eyes went wide in surprise. The man swung his gun up, prepared to shoot Henry at pointblank range when Mary jumped in front of Henry, the machete in her left hand already swinging in a flat arc.

The dull blade sliced into the man's neck, severing his jugular in a messy cut. Smithers' second mouth began spewing blood like he was throwing up and his eyes flared so wide it looked like his eyes were going to pop out of their sockets. Henry thought the dying man looked like a cartoon character in a Looney Toons cartoon.

Smithers' legs went limp and the man slid to the stone floor of the platform, a steady pool of red spreading out around him. He was still alive though, and he tried to speak his last word on this earth out of a blood-frothed lined mouth.

Henry said nothing to Mary; thanks could be done later if they made it out of the loading dock alive. Instead, he moved forward.

As Jimmy passed over Smithers, the man reached up, begging with his eyes for help. Jimmy never saw the man's plea, but stepped over his prone body and continued on. Ten seconds later, the first ghouls topped the stairs and quickly found Smithers. With the man breathing his last, he got to find out how it was to be on the other side of the dinner plate as hungry mouths and grabbing hands began to tear him apart and feed on him.

Just before the companions reached the bus, a filthy woman jumped out of hiding, screaming death threats at them. Cindy was the first to react. Spinning on her heels, she leveled the M-16 and sprayed the woman with a half-dozen rounds starting from her crotch and stitching the body to the forehead. When the last round entered the woman's face between the eyes, her body slumped to the floor, bleeding from a half-dozen wounds. Seconds after her body landed on the cold stone floor, ghouls reached her and began feeding on her still warm flesh. Animal sounds permeated the smoke clouds. Sounding like a pack of dogs or wolves had found a way into the loading dock to feed on the corpses.

"Come on, get in the damn bus!" Henry snapped as he shoved his friends into the opened door. The air was slightly better inside the bus, the caustic smoke not seeping in just yet.

Jimmy moved to the driver's seat, his eyes scanning the dashboard and pedals on the floor.

"Hey, this is an automatic. I can drive this."

"You sure, Jimmy? We don't have time for mistakes right now," Henry chastised him.

Shaking his head, Jimmy smiled. "No, old man, I'm telling the truth. It's just like driving a car only longer."

"So do it already," Cindy yelled while she tried to peer through the front windshield. The dock was so engulfed in smoke there was nothing to see. But if she stared hard enough, every few seconds she saw a limb or a head, but then it was swallowed back into the clouds of fog and smoke.

"All right, the keys are in the ignition!" Jimmy screamed, elated at the good fortune. He reached down and started the engine, the diesel motor turning over for a second before catching. Thick clouds of engine fumes poured out of the tailpipe, merging with the already smoke filled dock. The smell of the exhaust could be detected almost immediately, the only ventilation on the dock the open accordion door the ghouls were using. But there was almost no wind outside and the smoke laid heavy in the air, going where it wanted to, only being stirred by the moving bodies within it.

Suddenly, the left windshield had a hole on it and the safety glass began to splinter, spider web-like cracks appearing. No sooner had that hole appeared then another followed, a neat hole appearing a foot above Jimmy's head. He ducked down to avoid invisible bullets and gunned the engine as he prepared to leave the loading dock.

"Someone's still shooting at us out there!" He called while trying to shift the bus into reverse. Another shot entered the windshield and he ducked, the bus jerking as his foot left the brake.

Then like apparitions forming into cohesive forms, two men came out of the fog. One was taller than the other and he waved a revolver in his hand. Mary immediately recognized the taller man as Sterling and she cursed at the sight of her own weapon in his hand. Waters was next to him and the man waved his own handgun menacingly. Sterling's face was a mask of rage as he leveled the .38 to fire again. The round missed Jimmy by inches and the young man cursed a blue streak.

"Would someone please shoot those bastards before I get killed?" Jimmy barked as he tried to begin backing the bus out of the dock. He could see nothing and he was hesitant to just back up blindly.

"Jimmy, open the door," Henry ordered, moving to the door across from Jimmy's seat. Jimmy did as he was asked and Henry leaned out, firing a few rounds at the two approaching men. From his stance on the stairs and the angle, he knew he wouldn't be taking either of the men out, but that wasn't his plan. He just wanted the two men to run for cover, that way Jimmy would have time to get them out of the loading dock. After firing three rounds with the Steyr, he ducked back inside and Jimmy closed the door, sealing off the smoke.

And his plan worked, as both Sterling and Waters had no choice but to dive for cover as rounds flew by their heads like angry hornets. Waters ran for a stack of boxes and no sooner did he fall to the floor than he realized he wasn't alone. Turning around, he could see nothing in the thick clouds and had to wait for a coughing fit to pass before he could try to see better. Mucus ran down his nose in droves and his throat felt like it was on fire. With his gun in his hand, he tried to pierce the fog so he could shoot whatever was near him.

He blinked twice more to clear his eyes, and on the second blink, three faces appeared out of the smoke, like disembodied heads floating on their own accord. He fired at the middle head, the face receiving a new hole between the eyes, but then the heads moved closer and he saw all were attached to bodies. Rotten, desiccated, rag covered bodies with withered skin and teeth showing; lips dried and peeled back to expose gums and bad teeth. Waters fired again and again at the oncoming ghouls, but was soon out of ammo and clawing to free himself from grasping hands. In seconds he was overwhelmed and his shrieks of death echoed off the walls to join with the wails of the undead.

Sterling heard Waters scream, but he could see nothing. Picking himself off the floor, he spun around in a circle trying to see through the smoke. The Greyhound engine roared as the vehicle began backing up. But he could know longer see the bus, the smoke so thick visibility was down to a foot in front of his face. But his ears told him which way the bus was and he moved in that direction, his revolver ready to blow out a few tires and stop the thieves before they could leave with his cherished prize and escape vehicle.

Jimmy floored the gas pedal, throwing the three passengers across the seats. Cries of pain and aggravation filled the inside compartment and Jimmy winced.

"Sorry, guys, just getting the feel for it."

A few choice imprecations from the others told him how they felt about his driving.

"Jimmy, the door behind us is closed," Mary called out as she looked through a side window.

Jimmy turned to Henry who was standing just behind him. Jimmy used the large mirror over his head to gaze into Henry's eyes. The older man nodded. The door didn't matter. They would have to charge it.

"Go for it," Henry said flatly and Jimmy knew what he meant.

With a roar of the diesel engine, Jimmy slammed the bus in reverse and released the brake, then slammed his foot on the gas pedal. "Hold on! This is gonna get rough!" With a surge of motion, the bus shot backward, the sounds of screeching metal piercing the cab of the bus. The rear bumper shot out of the dock, the metal door flapping like a Venetian blind in an open window. But Jimmy had miscalculated and the bus swerved too much to the left. The entire left side of the bus rubbed against one of the many large stanchions supporting the ceiling of the loading dock. Metal and fiberglass were ripped from the left side of the bus and more than half the windows on that side caved in, safety glass pelting the companions like hail.

But no sooner did the bus drag across the stanchion then it was free, and a dim light fell upon the roof, the vehicle free of the loading dock door. Two foot pieces of fiberglass and rubber hung at odd angles off the side as Jimmy slowed to a stop fifty feet from the dock doors. Wreckage could be seen littering the pavement as pieces fell off to fall to the ground.

Henry frowned as he stared at the side of the bus, his head peeking out one of the missing windows.

"I thought you said you could drive this thing?"

Jimmy shrugged, flashing one of his patented shit-eating grins at Henry.

"I said I could drive it, just not too good. Sorry, I guess I didn't gauge our exit that well."

"Ya think?" With a shake of his head, Henry patted Jimmy's shoulder. "That's all right, pal, any crash you can walk away from and all that. As long as it can still drive, we're fine."

Another round penetrated the windshield, causing the companions to duck. Looking through the fractured windshield, Sterling came charging out of the smoke, firing at the front of the bus.

"Jesus, that guy doesn't give up," Henry said as he watched the man standing at the opening to the loading dock. To his right, the torn door hung and swayed back and forth, only the top of it still holding it up.

Sterling was about to fire at them again when he spun around at some unseen foe. The companions could only watch as more than a dozen ghouls came out of the smoke clouds billowing out of the open bays and surrounded Sterling. The cannie fired round after round at the approaching ghouls, punching and kicking once he fired his last shot. But there were far too many for him to fight on his own and he was quickly surrounded and pulled to the ground. But even lying on the ground, the man would not go into that good night easily. Still, he punched and kicked as teeth found their marks on his warm flesh.

Mary moved up to the window and watched as Sterling fought for his life, her face impassive.

"Jimmy, open the door again, will you?" Henry asked quietly. Jimmy did so and Henry stepped out onto the pavement. He made sure the area around him was clear of ghouls or any other threat and then brought the Steyr to his shoulder, his eye covering the scope.

When Sterling's head was in his sights, he shot one round. Sterling's head snapped back and the body slumped to the ground as the zombies began to feed unhindered. Lowering the rifle, Henry climbed back into the bus.

"Why did you do that? I wanted to see that bastard suffer," Mary said to him, anger on her face. "That asshole deserved to die hard and a hell of a lot more pain than he got!"

Henry's eyes were filled with sympathy as he touched her face with his left hand.

"I did it because it was the merciful thing to do, that's why. Maybe he deserved to be torn apart, I believe you when you say he did, but I don't want you to turn into me, Mary. I don't want you to have to do things that will corrupt your soul, your kindness and compassion to others. That's what makes you special. He's dead now, gone for good. Hopefully, you can put him behind you and look to the future."

Mary shook her head, crossing her arms over her blood stained chest. "I'm not a child, Henry. I can make my own decisions, you know. And I wanted to see that bastard suffer for what he did to me and some others who weren't as fortunate as I was to be rescued."

Henry nodded, understanding her. "Okay, then why don't we just say I needed some target practice and leave it at that, okay?"

Before Mary could reply, Jimmy gunned the engine, clouds of exhaust escaping out the back to float in the air.

"Come on, are we goin' or what? We're about to have company and I don't want any more passengers," Jimmy quipped as he watched the ghouls stumbling towards them. More than twenty were coming from the loading dock, their hands full of bloody human pieces while others from the surrounding area, hearing the noise of the bus and the gunshots, were approaching from the sides. In less than three minutes, the bus would be surrounded by bodies.

Mary broke her gaze with Henry and glanced out the windshield at the approaching zombies.

"Jimmy's right, Henry, we need to go now. But this isn't over; we still have a lot to talk about."

Henry smiled. "Sure, honey, just tell me when and I'll be there."

She nodded, and though she was far from happy, she accepted the topic as finished for the time being. Cindy moved next to her and studied the hospital out the window. All three floors were burning brightly, smoke rising into the air to join the clouds overhead. Around the hospital was a bright ring with a thousand embers floating out the shattered windows to float on the gentle air currents. It was very possible the burning hospital could end up setting the entire area surrounding it ablaze. Once the embers landed, if the surrounding area was dry enough, the whole city could become a raging inferno. It had happened before. With no one to squelch the flames, buildings would burn until the fires exhausted all flammable material. Across the deadlands, parts of entire cities were now nothing but husks of melted metal and blackened stone.

"Okay, Jimmy, get us out of here," Henry said while he slung the Steyr over his shoulder. Until they were truly clear of any danger, he would keep the weapon connected to him.

With a screeching of rubbing fiberglass on the left side of the bus, Jimmy spun the steering wheel and pointed the bus to the road leading away from the hospital.

Henry spared one last glance out the right side of the bus, night falling hard over the landscape, and his eyes hovered on the burning hospital. It was like a lonely candle in the night, burning brightly until it was extinguished.

When the bus reached the road that connected to the one leading to the hospital, Jimmy slowed and glanced to Henry.

"Which way do you want to go?"

Henry shrugged, and after looking at the others to make sure they had no opinion, he pointed to the right.

"Go that way, Jimmy and we'll see what's there to find."

With a shrug, Jimmy let off the brake, the airbrakes hissing softly, and swung the bus to the right. Stepping on the gas pedal, the bus surged forward, the billowing flames of the hospital slowly falling behind to become lost in the settling twilight.

CHAPTER EIGHTEEN

THE GREYHOUND BUS' headlights cut the darkness like a scythe as the large vehicle drove down the farm road paralleling Highway I-64. Frankfort was only a few miles from the companion's present position and all knew the perils of going near the dead city. Not to mention how crowded the main highways were even after over a year of no living souls actually using them.

The remnants of a fallen society still remained on the weed infested asphalt. Buses, cars and trucks still sat where their owners had left them on that fateful day when the rains came and turned innocent civilians into flesh-eating ghouls. Abandoned, the vehicles now choked the main arteries in and out of the city like cholesterol in a three-hundred pound man's veins. As for the highway themselves, after more than a year of no upkeep, the roads were cracked and splitting as vines and weeds forced their way to the surface, kudzu warming over everything. In a few more years' time, parts of the roads would be invisible from view as moss crawled across the pavement like spilled milk from a child's sippy cup, the greenery reclaiming the world from which was taken from it so many thousands of years before.

Despite the bus traveling on the back roads of Kentucky, barriers still slowed them down. More than once an odd truck or car was sitting in the middle of the road, and Henry, now at his turn behind the wheel, would have to force the wreck out of the way with the already dented front bumper.

On the last car shoved to the side, Henry had paused to gaze down into the rusting car. A skeleton still sat hunched behind the driver's wheel, minus a few limbs, tattered rags hung from the bleached bones in a few places and there was even a wedding ring glinting in the darkness on the right hand finger, reflecting the high-beams of the bus' headlights. A few cockroaches still scurried around the skeleton, hoping for one last morsel of food before giving up.

After studying the body for another second or so, he turned away, only giving the corpse a moment's thought before he revved the powerful diesel engine, touched his bumper with the rear of the rusted out hulk, and began pushing it to the side of the road. There was a steep incline on the left and the car slid into it, rolling a few times before slowing to a stop in a large cloud of dust that was invisible in the darkness. Then the bus was past the overturned vehicle and moving deeper into the night.

Inside the bus, spirits were high with the companions. They had saved Mary and had all managed to escape in one piece, of course with a few more bruises and bumps than they had begun with. Mary and Cindy were sitting in the middle of the empty seats talking to one another softly. Jimmy was near Henry, and the two talked quietly. There was no reason to speak in a hushed voice, but with the heavy darkness surrounding them like a living thing, it just felt right, like how one feels as they walk around a spooky abandoned house.

"We need to find someplace to rest for the night, but so far I haven't seen anything that looks safe enough," Henry said as he gazed out the front windshield. His speed was low and the wind whistled softly through the bullet holes in the fractured glass of the windshield and the missing windows on the left side of the bus. Every now and then another piece of the destroyed frame would fall away to be swallowed hole by the darkness behind them. Jimmy had managed to shove a few seat cushions into some of the empty window frames, thereby cutting down on most of the wind seeping into the cabin. Luckily, it was a warm night and the fresh air did no harm, in fact, with all of the companions needing showers, the extra ventilation was a boon to them all.

"Why can't we just stay in the bus?" Jimmy inquired while staring out the window at the road as it flowed by below.

"We will, but I still want to make sure we're hidden from the road. I don't want to wake up and find ourselves surrounded. We don't know this area at all. There's sure to be other gangs or scavengers or even more cannies around. Those bastards seem to be popping up everywhere lately." He was, of course, referring to the shopping mall in New England.

Jimmy didn't reply, instead focusing on the road in front of the bus. A soft fog had been growing, causing the headlights to work even harder to penetrate the darkness. Henry knew every second he traveled at night was a danger, anything could be waiting for them on the road and they wouldn't know the danger had befallen them until it was too late.

Jimmy's eyes lit up and he stood up next to Henry, peering through the front windshield, his nose almost touching the glass. "Hey, wait, what's that over there?"

Henry lessened the pressure on the gas pedal and applied the brake, the air brakes hissing in the night. Henry squinted slightly as he looked to the right where Jimmy was pointing. In the darkness, it was hard to perceive the full scope of what he was viewing, but the headlights chased away enough shadows for him to see what looked like the remnants of an old building a few hundred yards up the road.

"Don't know, but I think its worth checking out." Henry added as he yawned. "Besides, I'm dead tired." He glanced at the mirror above his head at the faces of Mary and Cindy behind him. Haggard and exhausted visages gazed back. "We all are. We need to get some rest. Unless this place is crawling with deaders, I think this'll be our camp for the night." As he finished speaking, he swung the bus into the gravel driveway and slowed to a stop, the sound of the air brakes reverberating off the deserted road and sounding like gunshots. Anything in the area would know there was a vehicle nearby, that was for sure.

The headlights of the bus played over the tattered remains of what looked to be a truck stop. But a fire had been in the building's past and there was nothing remaining of the actual structure but a few jagged teeth of burnt debris and steel rising from the ground like cavemen praying to the god of the moon. To the far left of the building was a sign that was still standing, though a few rusted bolts had snapped off, and the sign now hung drunkenly. It read: Sal's, Fuel and Eats, on one side and the other said the same only with a few of the letters missing. At one time the sign would have spun in a circle, the letters lit up for anyone driving by to spot easily. Now the sign was dark, just another faceless shape in the black of night. Polystyrene food containers, all crushed and stained the color of dirt blew about the area, one of the few survivors from the fire.

Henry secured the bus and turned off the engine, though left the keys in the ignition. That way whoever was first in the bus would be able to start it if danger reared its ugly head while they rested. It would be bad enough to have to make a speedy escape, but to have to wonder about who had the keys for the bus? That would be silly.

Jimmy moved to the door, wanting to step outside, when Henry held up his left hand for the younger man to wait.

"Now, hold on, Jimmy. Give it a second. If there are any deaders out there they'll be coming right for the bus. Let's give it a few minutes and see what pops up."

"Fine, Henry, fine. I guess another couple of minutes won't hurt," Jimmy answered.

"Hey, Jimmy, why don't you come over here and keep me company," Cindy said with a smile. Jimmy turned at the sound of her voice and nodded, set his shotgun against Henry's seat and walked back to Cindy and Mary. Mary stood up, and with a gentle smile of her own, let Jimmy take her seat. Jimmy plopped down next to Cindy and the sound of the blonde woman giggling filled the cabin. Mary knew when she was a third wheel and walked forward to where Henry was staring out the windshield. He had turned off the headlights, allowing his eyes to grow accustomed to the darkness. So far nothing had stirred around the battered vehicle and he was feeling positive that they were truly alone with the burnt-out wreckage of the truck stop.

When Mary reached Henry's side, she sat down in the right front seat. With Henry in the driver's seat all he had to do was turn his head slightly to the right and he could see her. When he did this, he didn't like the expression she wore.

"We still need to talk about what happened at the hospital," she said in a flat voice.

Henry yawned again, trying to act even more tired than he felt. "And we will, Mary, but it's been a long day for all of us, can't we talk about it in the morning?"

Mary shook her head, not being denied. "No, Henry now is as good a time as any." She paused for a heartbeat, and collected herself, wanting to use the proper words for how she felt. "I want to know why you shot Sterling and spared the man being torn about by those deaders. Henry, if you knew what that man was going to do to me and what he did to some other people he'd already captured you would never have done that. If anyone needed to suffer in this world it was him. He was as evil as they come."

Henry nodded, listening to her. "So his name was Sterling, huh?"

She merely nodded. Behind her, Jimmy and Cindy were giggling and Mary tried to tune them out.

Henry sighed, a long, tired sigh that had the weight of the world in it.

"Look, Mary, I'm sorry. I had no idea. All I saw was a human being who was about to experience pain in a way no human should ever have to experience it. I knew I could end his suffering and I did it." He turned to gaze out the front windshield, but it was as if his eyes were seeing the hospital again. "Would I have shot Sterling if I had known just how bad he was? Maybe, but I'll tell you this, Mary. Revenge and vengeance isn't an attractive cloak to wear and I don't want you to ever have to don one. Let me handle that, okay."

Mary shook her head, her eyes glittering with anger.

"No, Henry, it's not. And it won't be for a long time. You weren't there. You didn't see that bastard gut two human beings while I lay there and watched with the knowledge that I would be next. No, Henry, it is definitely not okay." She stopped talking when she realized Jimmy and Cindy were quiet, as well. Both had heard the tone in her voice and were now listening to the conversation. Mary sighed, one matching Henry's own sigh of a minute ago and then she continued. "Look, this isn't the same world as it used to be. I know you know that. Hell, you've told me it enough times. It's not like the police are gonna show up and arrest someone who tries to kill you or the rest of us. Now it's up to us to punish a crime or an obscenity. In the end, I guess it really doesn't matter whether Sterling suffered or not. In the end he's dead and we're still walking around breathing the air. And to tell you the truth, I don't think I'd feel any better if the prick had suffered more." Her eyes flared with intensity while she stared at Henry. "But it was still my decision to make and you took that away from me, Henry. So now I'll never know if I would have felt better watching the bastard suffer more or not."

Henry sat quietly, his eyes locked on hers while the bus creaked and settled around them. He saw one tear slide from the corner of her left eye and he nodded, finally understanding her point of view.

"You're right, Mary, and I'm sorry. I should have left it up to you. Can you forgive me?"

She flashed him a wan smile and cocked her head to the right. "Of course I can, Henry, but I'll just need a little time, that's all. Can you give me that at least?"

He stood up and she joined him. Opening his arms wide, she slid into them, Henry hugging her hard.

"You take all the time you want, Mar'. I can wait."

Jimmy's voice broke the moment as he stood up and moved over to the door. "Uhm, if you two are done with your bitch and stitch moment, I think we got company outside."

All eyes swung to the right side windows to see the undead faces glaring back at them. Skeletal hands clawed at the side of the bus, wanting the meat within as a few choice moans escaped withered lips.

"Dammit, I was hoping we were alone out here in the boonies," Henry spit as he watched the desiccated bodies moving about the ground outside the bus. Luckily, he only counted four ghouls so far and hopefully that would be all that arrived. If so, it would be easy to take care of the four that were now here and then they could bed down for the night.

Slapping hands against fiberglass reverberated inside the cabin as the ghouls tried to gain entry. Cindy stared at the rotting faces in revulsion. Only the interior lights of the bus were still on and they illuminated the undead faces and gave them a pallid-ethereal glow. It was like the ghouls were merely wraiths, which had come out of the ether to haunt the companions. But then another hand would slap the glass of the side of the bus to prove the ghouls were definitely real.

"What are we gonna do?" Jimmy asked while fingering the trigger of his Remington. Henry knew what Jimmy wanted to do already. He wanted to go outside and blow the walking dead away. But Henry knew that would be a mistake and he told them all in a few succinct words.

"No, we need to stay here and make sure there aren't anymore. If this is all that's around, then we need to kill them with hand weapons. No guns. The blasts would signal anything living or dead in a circular mile of us."

Jimmy looked at his shotgun with love in his eyes, but he nodded brusquely. "Yeah, you're right, I just thought it would be nice to just shoot 'em and forget about 'em. It's always the hard way with you, isn't it Henry."

Henry flashed him a broad smile as he picked up his Steyr and placed it on the driver's seat so it wouldn't fall in the aisle or into the stairwell. That would be unfortunate if they were all outside and the rifle was to end up lodged in between the door and the stairs. Jimmy could of course crawl into one of the missing windows, the frames more than large enough to accommodate him, but what might be happening while he was trying to gain re-entry?

More pounding sounded from outside and Mary noticed two more ghouls had arrived to join the others.

"We just got two more," she said flatly.

Henry followed her gaze and saw the two new arrivals. One was male, tall, with a yellow hard hat still on his head. The plaid shirt and denim jeans told of his past life as a construction worker. The other new arrival had been a housewife, that would be the best guess given her attire. She was barefoot and wore a floral housecoat with the front missing all the buttons. Her sagging breasts moved about on her torso like cow utters and Henry turned away or risk never wanting to have sex with a female again.

"So, okay then, if we're gonna wait then how long is that gonna be?" Jimmy asked, itching to do some killing. Ever since Henry had met Jimmy, he found the younger man took a certain glee from killing the undead. Though Jimmy could be compassionate, he usually erred on the side of shoot 'em in the head and let God sort 'em out.

Henry shrugged casually. "Don't know really. I'd say another ten minutes or so. By then whatever's in hearing distance should be here already."

"Great, ten minutes of standing here while those deaders pound and holler."

Cindy rubbed Jimmy's neck, massaging his shoulders. "Oh, relax, babe, there'll be plenty of killing to go around in a few minutes. You just have to have patience."

Mary barked a quick laugh as she turned to look at Cindy and Jimmy.

"Patient? Jimmy? Oh, please, I've never met a guy who could sit still for less time than Jimmy could."

Jimmy frowned as he pointed at Mary, but spoke to Cindy. "Are you gonna take that, Cindy? She's making fun of your man right in front of you."

Cindy moved away from him and stepped the few feet until she was next to Mary. She wrapped her left arm around Mary's shoulders conspiratorially "You want us to fight about it, Jimmy? Maybe in a pool of jello or mud?"

Jimmy's eyes took on a far away sheen as he imagined the picture Cindy painted for him.

"Well actually..."

"Forget it," both Cindy and Mary said simultaneously.

Hurt, Jimmy turned and walked away. "Well, I can still dream, despite what you say."

Mary turned to Cindy. "Oh great, now you've got him imagining me rolling around in a pool of mud. I don't even want to know what I'm wearing in his sick fantasy."

"Sorry, Mary, but you know him," Cindy apologized.

"It's a bikini, Mary; a very small one," Jimmy called from the rear of the bus. He decided he needed to go to the bathroom so he decided to check out if the one in the back of the bus was in working order. He'd learned the hard way about going into battle without using the facilities first. It wasn't like he could take a time-out if he had to go. So it was now or never.

Behind him, Henry, and the women talked amongst themselves, Jimmy hearing his name more than once. He smiled to himself, wondering what the topic of the conversation was. He knew Cindy would fill him in later.

Reaching the end of the aisle, he reached out to open the small doorway. More sounds of banging filled the interior of the bus, but he ignored it, assuming it was still coming from outside.

Because of this assumption, he never expected to open the bathroom door and end up staring at two pairs of eyes. Before he could so much as yell or reach for his sidearm, he felt the weight of soft bodies striking him in the chest. He was forced to the floor where his head struck a wooden hand rest from one of the chairs with a resounding crunch.

His mouth became filled with a dirty sleeve-covered arm and he tried to yell out, but with his mouth full of foul tasting clothing and his head spinning from the blow he'd just received, his vision blurry, he was all but helpless.

As one of the attackers climbed on top of him with outstretched hands, he couldn't believe this was how it was going to end for Jimmy Cooper.

How embarrassing.

CHAPTER NINETEEN

HENRY LOOKED UP from talking with Mary and Cindy when he heard Jimmy cry out in surprise. To his shock, Jimmy was on the floor and two people were on top of him. He couldn't see their faces, but he could tell immediately they were both women. One had a long mane of black, or midnight-blue, hair--depending on the light-- and was petite, wearing a torn polo shirt and jeans. The other woman was slightly larger, with a torn blouse and white slacks that were now all but black. She had blonde hair, but it was darker then Cindy's. Dirty-blonde was the description that came to mind. Where Cindy's golden tresses were like the sun, the hair of the woman attacking Jimmy had almost a brown tint to it in a certain light. He processed all of this in an instant, and was already climbing over the seats to get to Jimmy and help the man. His panga was sliding out of its sheath and he was bringing his arm back, ready to kill the two women with one heavy swipe of the blade, but when he was only a foot from them, both turned at the sound of his footsteps and Henry saw both women's arms were tied together at the wrists and both had bruises on their faces.

At the last second, Henry shifted his weight and the plunging panga sliced into the cushion near the blonde woman's face. Her eyes went wide as she stared at the long blade only inches from her head and she shifted her weight on top of Jimmy.

Jimmy took the chance and bucked his hips, the blonde woman falling backward to land heavily on the floor. But the black-haired woman, who Henry could see was only a girl, maybe fifteen or sixteen, continued trying to rip Jimmy's eyes out.

Pulling the panga from the cushion, he handed it to Mary who, with Cindy behind her, had rushed down the aisle after him. Then he turned and with both hands, grabbed the young girl by her torn shirt collar and hauled her off Jimmy.

She kicked like a banshee, but Henry shook her a few times, rattling the teeth in her head.

"Stop it, already, I won't hurt you. We're not cannibals, you're safe now." But the girl wouldn't listen and continued to squirm, her legs kicking out for whatever they could find. Her foot came up and glanced Henry's chin and as he swooned from the blow he wondered how the hell she had managed to do the acrobatic action. Deciding he was done playing around, he let her go with one hand, and when she dropped to the floor, his right hand slapped her hard across the face. The blow rocked her head to the side and her eyes glazed over from the slap. There was now a bright red spot on her left cheek and the blow seemed to take the wind out of her sails. Mary climbed over Jimmy and passed by Henry as she went over to the blonde woman lying on the floor with her back to the far wall of the bus. The woman crawled back in fear, her body bunching up and Mary tried to placate her, telling her she was safe, much as Henry tried to do to the younger girl.

The blonde woman seemed to take to the words more easily and slowed her crawling, sliding feet as she tried to press herself into the wall as if she could be absorbed into the metal by sheer will alone. Mary knelt down next to her and began untying her wrists.

As for Henry, it was like he had a hell-cat in his arms. The young girl had already shaken off the slap and was now trying to escape his arms with renewed vigor. Henry was about to really punch her to pacify her when Cindy moved up and grabbed the girl's swinging wrists. Henry was just glad her wrists were tied or he would have had even more of a handful.

"Calm down, we're friends. We won't hurt you," Cindy said to the girl, looking into her eyes and not breaking contact. The girl struggled for another few seconds and then seemed to calm down. Cindy had that effect on people. She was beautiful, with kind eyes and it would be hard for anyone to imagine that face wanting to do harm to another living soul. Of course, many had found her looks to be deceiving. Cindy flashed the girl a beautific smile as she touched her wrists, holding them tight, but yet gently at the same time.

The girl's eyes darted back and forth as she stared at each of the companions.

Henry felt her body tense and knew she was about to try and escape again when the blonde woman on the floor spoke up.

"Raven, stop it! I think they're telling the truth!"

The young girl spun her head around so she was looking at the woman on the floor.

"Why, because they say they are? Bullshit. They're with them, they have to be. Why else would they be driving this bus?"

"Because we killed all the cannibals and stole it, that's why," Mary replied while she moved away from the woman on the floor. Rubbing her wrists, the woman climbed to her feet. Mary nodded when she was standing, handing the woman a bottle of water.

"What's your name?" Mary asked of the woman.

The blonde woman drank deeply before replying. Once she'd finished half the bottle off, she seemed more confident, more sure of herself. Her posture was better, also. She was standing straighter, not flinching each time one of the companions moved.

"I'm Sue, Sue Anders, and this wildcat is Raven."

Henry still held onto Raven and now he pulled her a little closer to him. "Hi, Raven, I'm Henry. That's Mary over there and the blonde one is Cindy. That's Jimmy on the floor. Tell me, if I let you go do you think you could just wait a sec' before you try and kill me?"

Raven's eyes flared menace but she nodded, slowly.

"You sure now? Wouldn't want anyone to get hurt, especially me." As he said this, he eyed her nails which were almost an inch long and were honed to a sharpness resembling small razors. He knew she could do some damage with those nails if her hands were free.

"Promise him, Raven. What do we have to lose?" Sue said to her, trying to get the young girl to see reason.

Hesitantly, the girl nodded, and this time her eyes showed she might actually follow through with her promise. Prepared for her to act out, Henry released her wrists. Red marks were on her smooth skin from where Henry had gripped her and she eyed the bruises warily, flashing Henry an annoyed look.

Cindy moved next to Raven with a knife in her hand. Raven immediately jumped back, her mouth curled into a feral snarl and Cindy held up her free hand.

"Whoa, girl, I just want to cut you hands free, relax."

Raven's scowl faded, but she still remained in a crouch. Slowly, Cindy moved closer and held the knife out to the girl. Raven held out her wrists and Cindy quickly separated the rope strands in a few sawing motions. The rope fell to the floor of the bus and Raven jumped back again. She rubbed her wrists with her hands, alternating from left to the right.

"You okay?" Henry asked her.

Raven turned to glare at Henry, but she didn't attack him. Henry was glad for small favors and shifted position. Outside, the undead still pounded on the side of the bus and he knew they would have to be dealt with soon. Their constant moaning and pounding on the frame of the bus was a call to all ghouls in the area and that was a very bad thing if they wanted to spend the night here. And they should want to, as driving at night was almost as dangerous as walking at night. With no streetlights or other ambient light from anything but the moon and stars, traps could be anywhere, just waiting for unwary travelers.

With the girl right in front of him, Henry noticed Raven had deep brown eyes that seemed to turn green when she turned her head, the overhead lights in the bus catching her eyes just so. He studied her more closely, realizing she had the figure of a gymnast. There was almost no fat on her body and her muscles looked well toned. She was like a caged animal, only waiting for her chance to run the instant the cage door was unlocked and opened. She didn't look hurt, and that was always good as antibiotics weren't easy to find as a year ago. A small cut not treated and cleaned could become deadly real fast.

Raven caught him studying her and she snarled at him.

"What the hell are you looking at, old man?"

Jimmy laughed. "That's rich, she knows your name, Henry, how 'bout that!" He yelled with a grin.

"Shut up, Jimmy. If you don't want to be constructive, then please, just shut up," Henry snapped.

Jimmy looked hurt from the rebuke, but he remained silent.

"Well, if you must know, I was checking you for any signs you might be hurt. You sure act like you're okay."

"Well, I am. I killed three of those fuckers when they caught us and I would have killed more if they hadn't whacked me over the head from behind." She rubbed the back of her head where she felt a bump under her hair.

"That's true, she did. It was amazing," Sue said as she finished her bottle of water. She handed the empty bottle to Mary with a smile and a thank you. "It was unbelievable. Like in one of those karate movies."

"Oh yeah, you know how to fight?" Jimmy asked, interested.

Raven turned to him and frowned. "Yeah, I know how to fight, what of it? My Dad was a cop and he taught me how to defend myself. So what."

Jimmy held up his hands in surrender. "No, it's cool, good for you. So if you're so tough, then how come you were tied up in our bathroom and why didn't you let us know you were in there?"

"That was my idea," Sue said. "We heard people moving around the bus, but we just thought you were the cannibals. We figured we should just stay quiet so you'd leave us alone for as long as possible."

"No, Sue, you said that. I wanted to get out of the bathroom so we could try to escape."

"How'd you two get in there in the first place?" Henry asked while he sat down on an armrest bordering the aisle.

"We were traveling with two more people, a man and a woman. We were jumped on the road and they took us back to the hospital. Once there, they split us up and put us in separate rooms," Sue told them. Her voice trembled as she continued. "I heard them screaming sometimes; then everything would grow really quiet. I don't know what happened to them. When we began to hear gunfire, the big man..."

"Sterling, his name was Sterling," Mary added.

Sue nodded a thank you. "Right, Sterling. Well, Sterling came and took us through the hospital and to the bus with a couple of his people. There was a bald man with a skin condition, a skinny man and a woman with him. Said he needed to have us with him for when he got needs. Not to mention we could be food in a pinch."

"Piece of shit. If I had been free I would have ripped his throat out," Raven said as she flashed her teeth in a snarl of rage. As Henry watched the teenage girl, he had no doubt she would have if given the chance. Too bad she hadn't had the opportunity. If she had, then maybe things would have gone smoother for the companions. Still, they were all safe and now had a nice, big bus to move about with. At least until they ran out of fuel, that is. But the tank was more than half full and that would get them pretty far before they would have to abandon it.

"Well, Raven, those guys are all dead," Cindy told her. We killed most of them on our way out of the hospital. Hell, the few we missed are probably all dead by now, too. Either by the deaders or from the fire."

"The fire?" Sue asked meekly. Henry studied her face. She was in her very late thirties if he was correct and underneath the dirt and filth covering her face she was attractive. Twin lines of missing grime were under both eyes from when she'd been crying and her hair was a tangled mess in massive need of a comb.

Without realizing it, Henry felt a stirring in his loins he hadn't felt in quite some time. First he had lost his wife, Emily. Then, later in Boston, he had watched helplessly while Gwen was tossed off the roof of the shopping mall by the sadistic boss of the enclave, Barry. After that loss he had thought his heart was just going to explode with grief. He'd finally found someone to share his world with again and had lost her just as fast. After that he had resigned himself to bachelorhood, but as he stared at Sue, he couldn't help but wonder if it was possible to love again, and even if it was, should he even try?

Sue noticed him looking at her and she looked down shyly at the floor while the others talked around her. Mary was filling Sue in on the hospital and how it had been a massive inferno when they had left the loading dock. Sue had merely nodded. Henry now noticed she was sneaking peeks at him whenever possible and he found himself growing uncomfortable from the attention.

He was pulled from his thought by the shattering of one of the windows on the right side of the bus. A ghoul had picked up a stray rock and had managed to break the safety glass. More pieces of glass fell onto the seats to join the piles already laying there.

"Shit, that's it, we need to take care of those deaders now before they cause real harm to the bus," Henry said and moved to an empty window frame to look out on the heads of the ghouls. He would have liked to just reach out of one of the windows with his panga and simply chop the heads off of each one, but when he tried this, his shoulder barely fit through the opening. No, that would have been too easy, he thought as he pulled himself back inside.

Turning to the others, he frowned.

"It's no good, I can't fit out there enough so I can swing at them easily and I don't want to end up losing my blade or get bit. We'll have to go out there and take care of them one at a time."

Jimmy pulled his knife, waving it back and forth. "Sure, let's go, it's about time I kicked some undead ass," he joked and stood up, flexing his hands as he prepared himself for the battle to come.

Henry looked at the small knife in Jimmy's hand. "Not with that, you're not, Jimmy. You need something to fight with that won't let them get too close. Either that or you stay in the bus and shoot a few that get to close to the rest of us that are outside."

Jimmy looked at his knife and stopped waving it about, realizing Henry was right. Walking away from the group to the front of the bus, he looked around the cabin, trying to find something that would work in place of the knife. He began rummaging around behind the driver's seat, and with a cheer of happiness, stood up holding a tire iron. It had been wedged in a small compartment behind the seat, along with a few flares and a flashlight.

"Will this work?" He asked, swinging the tire iron back and forth like a baseball bat.

Henry nodded. "Yeah, I guess so, but just don't get careless. I don't want to have to kill you later if you get bit."

With a smile, Jimmy hopped onto the first seat of the bus, balancing his butt on the top edge. "Not on your life, Henry, I wouldn't give you the satisfaction."

Henry grinned back and nodded. All kidding aside, it would break his heart if Jimmy got bit. He loved the young man like a son, though he would never, ever tell him that. He and Jimmy had a more competitive relationship, though he knew Jimmy cared for him just as much. But being men, of course it could never be spoken.

"Uhm, look, I hate to seem ungrateful for you saving me and Raven, but do you have any food? Neither of us has eaten in almost two days and I'm absolutely famished," Sue said to the companions.

"Oh, my, I'm sorry," Mary said. "We should have figured that out for ourselves. Here, come with me and I'll get you something to eat. We don't have much, but you're welcome to what we have."

Sue smiled a thank you and moved off to the middle of the bus with Mary and Cindy, while Raven stood behind Henry. To be seen, she jumped onto a seat and climbed gracefully over others until she was eye to eye with Henry. She was like a cat, lithe and graceful.

"If you're going out there to kill those rotters then I want in," she told him.

Henry shook his head. "No way, nuh-uh. You stay here and get something to eat with the women. Me and Jimmy can take care of those deaders."

"Deaders?" She asked, then her eyes lit up with recognition. "Oh, that's what you call the rotters, oh okay, whatever. But I'm going out there, too."

Henry walked passed her and to the front of the bus. "No, you're not, you're staying in here."

She began climbing over seats like an acrobat, passing the women as she moved. When she passed Mary, her arm reached out and grabbed a piece of beef jerky. "Thanks, Mary," she said as she continued forward. She jumped off the last seat, her head brushing the ceiling and landed quietly on the floor next to the door controls.

"What did I just tell you?" Henry asked in a low growl.

She stood her ground, looking up at Henry. She was a full six inches shorter than him, but it did nothing to intimidate her.

"Look, Henry, is it? You're not my father. My father's dead and I do what I want. And what I want to do is go out there and dish out a little bit of what I've been getting for the past few days. If you don't like it, then tough shit. Stay in here with the women for all I care."

Mary looked up, not liking the word women being thrown around like it was a bad word. Both she and Cindy would he happy to go out there and take care of the ghouls, but she knew how Jimmy and Henry would want to do it, given their masochistic tendencies. Both she and Cindy had just learned to go with it and let the boys feel like men, like they were protecting them. Even though both Cindy and Mary had saved Jimmy and Henry's asses more times than either of them could count.

"Henry, let her go with you if she wants to. She's old enough to take care of herself. Besides, she just might be a help."

Henry frowned, glancing at Mary and then back to Raven.

"Hmmph, I guess we'll just see," he said flatly. "Before you go out there you'll need a weapon."

Raven smiled widely, and before either Henry or Jimmy could stop her, she opened the door and jumped out of the bus.

"I don't need a weapon! Come on, old man, let's go kill some rotters, and try not to break a hip on the way down the stairs!" Then she was through the door and was lost in the darkness surrounding the bus.

Jimmy prepared to follow her, and he turned to Henry, his mouth already open for a wisecrack.

"Don't you say it, Jimmy, or so help me..." Henry told him with the panga pointing at Jimmy's nose threateningly.

Jimmy slowly closed his mouth, relishing the moment, then turned to go down the stairs, but his smile never faltered. He jumped the last foot and was in the darkness, his grunts already filling the air as he whacked the first ghoul in the head with the tire iron, the meaty thwack drifting back into the bus.

Henry glanced at Mary and the other two women for a brief moment and Mary waved. "Good luck, don't get bit. One of us will be in the window in a second to cover your backs."

"Okay, Mary, thanks. We'll be back in a few minutes." He stepped down to the dust covered ground and closed the door behind him, pushing at an angle to get it to close properly. No sooner was the door closed then a shadow came out of the darkness, the odor of death and decay preceding it. Raising the panga, he charged at the shadow.

It was time to get to work, and with the darkness surrounded him like a cloak, he began the job of destroying every ghoul surrounding the bus.

CHAPTER TWENTY

HENRY PUNCHED THE first ghoul in the face that came for him. The short, dead man with a harelip staggered from the blow, but regained his balance and came forward again only seconds later. The dead man wore what looked like a fast-food restaurant uniform and the nametag on his breast had the name Steve imprinted on it. Henry immediately dubbed the man Harelip Steve and as he studied the face of the man, he saw that the harelip was his most attractive feature because half his face was missing and one eye had been punctured, a milky white liquid seeping out of the socket like rotten mayonnaise.

Harelip Steve charged at Henry, jaws snapping like a mousetrap.

Henry didn't hesitate. Without compassion for his walking dead adversary, he sliced the panga horizontally at the dead man's neck, severing it from the shoulders in a gushing flood of black ichor. The decapitated corpse dropped to the ground like an animal in a slaughter house, the head rolling across the ground to stop a few feet away. And so ended the tale of Harelip Steve.

Another rotting ghoul came at him from his left and Henry ducked an outstretched arm, spinning out of the way like a ballerina. When he was standing upright again, and in control of the situation once more, he stiff-armed the ghoul in the jaw. There was a crack, denoting either that the jaw had been dislocated or other bones had been broken, but the ghoul barely noticed.

Teeth flashing in the darkness, the zombie charged at Henry. But the punch to the jaw had given Henry the opportunity to get his panga into position. When the ghoul came at him again, he raised the long blade over his shoulder and brought it down heavily; slicing into the top of the zombie's skull and severing the head in half like a rotten watermelon.

Black blood sprayed from the mortal wound and the ghoul tumbled out of sight, the panga coming free as the weight of the falling body released it. Henry waved the blade in a circle, casting off stray droplets of blood while looking for his next target. He spotted Jimmy a few yards away and watched the man dance around multiple ghouls like he was playing tag. A middle-aged woman in a business suit was trying to catch him. Just when she thought she had her prey cornered, Jimmy spun around and cracked her on the side of the head. The meaty thwack carried over to Henry, who watched the dead lady drop to the ground with her brains spilling out like a bowl of red worms mixed with a healthy dose of slugs.

Jimmy spotted Henry watching him and flashed his friend a smile. Then he went back to the wet work with more pleasure than he should have felt.

Another ghoul, this time a pretty red-head in a bikini and one flip-flop, reached for Henry out of the darkness and he sliced her hands off at the wrists. Both severed appendages fell to the dirt and the woman kicked them across the ground with her feet. Henry couldn't help but notice her ample cleavage sitting under the small bikini top, but when she was so close he could smell her, whatever attraction he'd felt quickly dissolved. Still, despite the odor she was in fairly good condition for a zombie. She moaned at him and it almost sounded like a moan of sexual excitement, or was that just Henry's imagination? Shaking off the impure thoughts, not to mention just plain disgusting, he dropped to the ground and swung his left leg outward, knocking the bikini-ghoul off her feet. When she struck the ground, Henry was already up, and as she looked up into his eyes, he brought the panga down hard, the tip of the long blade sliding into the dead woman's left eye and into her brain. She twitched for a few seconds, then remained still. One of her breasts had become dislodged from the bikini top and Henry tastefully turned his gaze away.

The area around him was devoid of ghouls and he looked to his right to see Raven surrounded by the last three remaining zombies. If he had been worried about her taking care of herself, he needn't have.

Like a dervish with wings, she danced and jumped around the three ghouls, searching for her opportunity to strike. Grabbing one by the arm, she swung the ghoul around until it crashed into one of the others. While those two rolled around on the ground, she dealt with the last one standing. Henry could see from the dead man's uniform he'd been a policeman. And when Henry's gaze lowered down to the man's waist, his eyes lit up when he saw the dead cop still wore his weapon as well as a few clips still secured to his belt. Then the cop was hiding behind Raven as she charged the ghoul head on, knocking the policeman on his back in a spray of dust. Sitting on the cop's chest, with an accompanying scream of rage, she reached down, grabbed the man's head and twisted hard, like she was pulling an incredibly large apple from a tree.

There was a loud crack, the neck of the cop snapped, the spine split in half and the arms dropped limply to the dirt. Raven never stopped to admire her handiwork, but jumped off the supine body and charge at the last two ghouls who were climbing to their feet like two drunks after a brawl. Both were female, one about the same age as Raven, the other slightly older. Raven plowed into them, using her legs like lethal weapons. The young dead girl who was about her age received a sharp kick to the side of the neck that sent her falling away to roll across the dirt like a rag doll. The other dead woman never slowed, not really caring about her dead girlfriend. Raven didn't slow either, but punched the woman in the chest with her left and then right, fists clenched into small bludgeons. The blows were delivered like a boxer and the dead woman staggered backward. If the woman had been alive, it was very possible she would have cracked ribs from the battering she'd just received. But being dead, the woman could have cared less and was already coming back for more.

Raven was ready. As Henry and Jimmy watched, she jogged backward a few feet and then charged the woman like she was in an action movie. With her right leg extended, toes pointing out, Raven kicked the woman under the chin. The head was jerked to the side like she'd been hit with a battering ram and the rest of the body followed soon after. The woman landed in a heap of legs and arms, her head so askew it was a wonder it was still connected to the shoulders. The ghoul didn't get up and both Jimmy and Henry realized her spine had been snapped from the blow.

Brushing her hands as if to dry wash them, Raven strolled over to Henry and Jimmy like she was merely out for a walk under the starry sky.

Jimmy wore a wide smile as he watched her sway up to him.

"Damn, girl, you can really kick some ass," he said approvingly. "Where the hell did you learn to fight like that?"

She sneered as she looked up at him. She was a few inches shorter than Jimmy, though the size difference didn't seem to bother her in the least.

"I told you, my Dad was a cop. Since I was four, he would take me out into our backyard every night after work and teach me how to fight. The older I got, the better the training. He was into stuff like that and seems as I was his only child and not a boy, well, I got the training instead."

"Well, it sure looks like you paid attention, Raven, that was something to see, watching you fight," Henry added. When he thought back to only a few minutes ago when he'd first found her in the bus, it was hard to imagine this small girl could be such a killing machine

"So, is that how you managed to survive this long out here and not behind the wall of a barricaded town?"

She shrugged, checking her nails to make sure one wasn't cracked. "Yeah, I guess so."

"You fellas all right out there?" Mary called from one of the open windows of the bus. "Guess you didn't need me to shoot any, huh?"

Henry ran stiff fingers through his rumbled hair, dry washing his face to wake him up. It had been a long day, longer than usual, and he was praying it was truly almost over.

"Yeah, Mary, we're fine, no we took care of 'em, they went down pretty easy. Looks like that was the last of 'em, too. Just give us a few minutes to drag them away from the bus and we'll be right in," Henry told her.

She waved back, then disappeared from the window. Henry could see her moving about inside though, her head and shoulders silhouetted behind the tinted glass from the illumination inside the bus.

"Okay, Jimmy, we need to drag these bodies out of the area or we're gonna be smellin' them all night," Henry told him.

"Why can't we just move the bus a little more? It would be a lot easier," Jimmy shot back; not wanting to have to work if it could be avoided.

"Yeah, it would at that, but I don't want to start the engine if I can help it, that's why. The sound of that diesel will let anything else that hasn't heard us know we're here. No, better to try and stay quiet for the rest of the night. It looks like the area is clear of deaders so we can finally bed down for the night."

With a weary sigh Jimmy consented.

"Raven, you go back inside, all right? You've done enough. We can take it from here," Henry ordered her casually, almost making it sound like a suggestion. He had a feeling if he tried to give her a real order she would only argue with him.

Raven shrugged her small shoulders, brushed her long hair away from her eyes, and tossed out a: "Sure, whatever." Then she spun on her left foot and strolled back to the bus. Once she was at the door, she tapped on the glass and the door swung inward. She stepped inside and the door hissed closed again.

Henry turned to Jimmy, slapping his hands together at the same time.

"Well, pal, you ready to get to work?"

Jimmy answered Henry by flipping him the middle finger, but he turned and grabbed the first body by its torn shirt collar and began dragging it across the lot and into a ditch near the burnt out building, grumbling the entire time. With a chuckle at Jimmy for his actions, Henry began doing the same, starting with the body of poor Harelip Steve.

The small ghoul was easy to drag and when Harelip Steve was lying face down in the ditch, Henry went over to the prone cop. Bending over, he slid the officer's side arm from its holster and looked at the weapon in the wan moonlight of the night. It was a Glock, similar in design to the one he'd been carrying for over a year. Henry's Glock was a police issued weapon, as well. He'd found it on a dead policeman and the weapon had saved his life more times than he wanted to count. Hefting the weapon, he slid out the clip and checked to see if it was loaded. The clip was empty, but there were three more on the man's belt. With deft fingers, Henry slid each clip from its loop and pocketed them. With the exception of the last, which after checking to make sure it was full, slapped it into his own Glock. A feeling of safety suffused his body, the loaded weapon on his hip finally deadly once again. He had never realized how truly uncomfortable he'd been feeling until he had the pistol loaded with a full clip.

Something else caught his eye on the side of the policeman's belt and Henry slid it free of its sheath. It was a Leatherman. Henry had never owned one before, but knew the tool was of better quality than a Swiss Army knife. The tool could be converted into pliers, a knife, a file, screwdriver a few more that weren't worth listing. The two and a half inches of metal felt good in his palm and he plucked the leather sheath from the cop's belt, undid his own, then slid the loop of the sheath onto the belt. Sliding the Leatherman back into its sheath, he grinned. Not a bad haul, he thought. Someone must be looking out for him.

Jimmy's footsteps grew louder as he returned from dragging another body to the ditch.

"Hey, you gonna help or what?"

"Yeah, I'm gonna help, relax. I found ammo for my Glock and another one to boot. I can give it to Mary with a full clip."

Jimmy wiped his brow and he placed his hands on his hips. "That's great, Henry, I'm happy for the two of you, but if it's all right with you, I'd like to finish this shit and get back inside the bus."

Henry nodded, placing the extra Glock in the small of his back for safe keeping. Then he began dragging the dead policeman across the ground to the ditch.

Jimmy grunted, pleased when Henry got to work and then he did the same, dragging a ghoul by its torn pants.

The two worked in silence for the next ten minutes, while high in the night sky, a crescent moon and a thousand twinkling stars kept them company.

Inside the bus, the women were talking amongst themselves. Mary had watched Raven, Henry and Jimmy take out all the ghouls, then had opened the door for the girl. She had been amazed at the ferocity and skill the teenager displayed and was anxious to talk to her about it. But when Raven entered the bus, her visage said quite clearly she wasn't in the mood for conversation. Taking one of the few remaining water bottles piled on a seat; she strolled to the back of the bus and sat down, her feet propped up on the headrest of the seat before her.

"Your welcome," Mary said, annoyed at the girl's rudeness. Raven merely held up the water bottle and smiled a thank you.

"Don't let it bother you, Mary," Sue said askance of her. "She's always like that. You get used to it after a while."

Mary glanced at Raven one more time, but with the girl sitting down, all she could see was the top of her ebony hair.

"Maybe you can, but if she's gonna travel with us she better cut the shit," Cindy answered for Mary.

Mary nodded, agreeing with her friend.

"She's right, Sue. If you want to stay with us, then we all need to be civil. We don't need anyone running around like they know what's better for them than the others. We all walk together or we die together," Mary stated.

Sue's eyes opened a little wider. "You mean we can stay with you? I didn't even know that was an option."

Cindy looked at the woman as if she was an idiot. "Well, what else are we gonna do with you two? We're sure not gonna kick you off the bus and let you fend for yourself out there, though Raven seems to know how to handle herself pretty damn good." She glared at Sue closely. "How 'bout you? Can you fight?"

Sue shook her head. "No, afraid not. I never fired a gun before and I'm not much good with a knife. But I'm a damn good cook, so I did that and I would take care of the laundry and stuff. Someone has to do it, so it might as well be me."

Mary slid into a chair and looked at Sue. "So what did you do before everything fell apart?"

Sue looked down at her feet and answered, her voice low, as if she was embarrassed. "I was a housewife, that's all. My husband went to work everyday and I took care of the house."

"Any kids?" Cindy asked.

"No, no children. We tried a few times, but I never got pregnant. We were gonna go to one of those fertility clinics when everything began to get crazy. Then one day my husband never came home from work. That was near the end..." She trailed off, leaving the rest to the imagination. Not that she needed to. Everyone still left alive had their own story of loss and fear.

"What about Raven? What's her story?" Mary asked.

Sue shook her head again, her dark-blonde tresses covering her forehead. She casually brushed them aside while she talked. "Don't know really. She came into our town one day and of course we took her in. Wouldn't tell us much about herself. You know about as much as I do about her."

"So why were you on the road when the cannibals grabbed you?" Cindy asked, interested. "Seems like a stupid thing to do."

"In hindsight, yes, I have to agree with you. We were on a scouting mission to another town nearby. Prattville was about twelve miles away and we lost contact with them over a week ago. Me, Raven and two others, a husband and wife, agreed to go over there and see if they were all right, but we were run down and captured by the cannibals. We thought they'd left the area, but evidently we were wrong."

"Did you get to the town first or what?" Cindy asked, wanting to know more.

Sue shook her head again. "No, we weren't even halfway there before we were ambushed. Why, do you think you might want to go there? If you did, I can guarantee you safe haven. They'll know me and Raven by a few passwords we shared with each of the towns. They're good people there. All they're doing is trying to stay alive like the rest of us. They don't like strangers too much, but if you're with me, I'm sure they'll let you in."

Mary and Cindy exchanged a look at Sue's words. They both knew about what it was to be an outsider. Most towns frowned on strangers and travelers at their gates. Some wouldn't even let you enter the town's limits. Some were so hostile they would shoot you dead as you stood at their gate awaiting entry. Some were more civil and would at least shoot over your head first, giving you a chance to leave. But there were still a few scattered barricaded towns that welcomed strangers. With phone lines a thing of the past and the internet about as useful as a cigarette lighter under water, some towns welcomed strangers as a way to find out what was happening beyond their makeshift walls of old cars and steel fences.

A hard knock on the door of the bus pulled Mary and Cindy away from Sue. Mary stood up and moved to the front of the bus. Upon seeing Henry's scowling face through the tinted glass, she opened the door. With a hiss of pneumatic hinges the door swung inward and Henry and Jimmy climbed the steps. Both smelled of old sweat and something else...like rotten fruit.

Mary was the one to figure out it was the odor of the dead transferring from their filthy clothing onto Henry and Jimmy's clothes.

"Whew! You guys stink," she said while waving a hand in front of her face.

Henry pushed past her and picked up a water bottle, drinking half and splashing a few drops on his face.

"Well, excuse me. Next time I have to fight hand to hand with a bunch of deaders, I'll make sure to stay clean."

"Would you?" Cindy asked, but when Henry turned around, preparing to tell her to go to Hell, he saw she was grinning. His face lightened and he smiled back.

"Very funny, Cindy." He turned to Jimmy. "Hey, Jimmy, you got yourself a real comedian with this one," he said while the younger man drank deeply from a water bottle. He gargled a few times before swallowing, eliciting a stern look from Cindy.

"Yeah, Henry, I guess I'm rubbing off on her."

"That's never a good thing," Mary chimed in, a smile of her own appearing on her face.

Henry plopped down in one of the plush seats, finally pleased to be resting. "We need to post a watch just in case we're still not alone out here."

Jimmy brushed his statement off. "Why? Even if more deaders show up, all we have to do is drive away. I say we're fine with us all resting in here."

Henry sat straighter, hoping he wasn't going to have a rebellion on his hands. It had been settled many months ago that Henry would be in charge, the others deferring to him as the natural leader. Of course, all the companions had a say in what they did or didn't do, but at the end of the day, Henry's word would be final. Henry leaned forward in his seat so he could get a better look at Jimmy. Even in his new position, with Jimmy now sitting in another seat, he could only see the younger man's eyes.

"Okay, fine, we'll do it your way. But tell me this, Jimmy ... What if, in the middle of the night, a group of scavengers comes up on us and slashes our tires before we know they're there? Or how 'bout this one. What if, in the middle of the night, so many deaders arrive that the bus can't move? Or maybe some wolves or wild dogs? Remember the wild dogs, Jimmy? Hey that was fun. Hell, I almost kept one as a pet."

Jimmy shook his head, remembering a few months ago when the companions had battled for their lives against a pack of roving, wild dogs on the outskirts of Boston. What was once man's best friend had turned into nothing more than a pack of wolves in dog's clothing. They had barely escaped with their lives and Jimmy wasn't looking forward to meeting another pack of the wild beasts.

Holding his left hand up in surrender, Jimmy relented. "Okay, you made your point, we'll stand a watch." He looked at the other's faces. "So, who's first?"

They all discussed who would take the first watch and the rotation on how each of them felt. Cindy was feeling fairly good and so would take the first watch, followed by each of the others. Henry would take the last watch and would be the one to wake the others up in the morning. For thirty more minutes, the companions and their two new charges stayed in their seats, talking about this and that and getting to know one another a little more. Raven stayed in the rear of the bus, and when asked a question, would usually answer in one or two word answers. All the companions were learning she was a moody person with not a lot to say. In other words, she was like every other teenager to live since the beginning of time. The only thing missing from Raven's persona was an I-pod and a cell phone connected to her ear.

Susan, or Sue, as she liked to be called was a bit more forthcoming. She answered every question asked of her and even volunteered a few items on her own. Henry didn't talk to her that much, but instead merely watched the others chatting. But despite himself, he couldn't help but study the lines on Sue's face. Her cheekbones were high and she had thin lips, but not so thin they weren't attractive. Her skin was tanned slightly from being outside, one of the casualties of walking almost everywhere. Once again he found his gaze falling to her one leg that was casually stuck out in the center of the aisle. Her slacks on that leg had slid up, showing her ankle and her curving calve muscle. It was evident that under her clothing she had a firm body, with mostly muscle for body mass.

One time she caught him looking at her and Henry quickly turned away, feeling like a high school boy staring at the girl he had a crush on in Math class. But if Sue knew he was staring, she didn't seem to mind. When his eyes snuck a peek to see if she was still watching him, he was surprised to see she was. She only nodded and smiled at him pleasantly. He smiled back and then resumed his military ablutions. He had been loading the clips and also making sure the newly acquired Glock was in good shape for Mary to use. So far it just needed a good cleaning. He was lucky he hadn't lost his backpack, because all the cleaning supplies and gun oil for their weapons was inside it. His hands moved effortlessly over the weapons, sliding the parts together and slapping the clip into the butt of the weapon with a small click, satisfied when it seated properly. Sometimes he was still amazed at his own skill at the weapons that had become such a large part of his life. An old man, the armorer from the town of Pittsfield back in Virginia had taught Jimmy and Henry a lot about how to service their weapons. If not, then the weapons would end up misfiring. And that would be sure to happen at a crucial moment of life and death.

Not that an instance like that was such a major occurrence anymore. The world had changed to the point that a man could go from life to death in the blink of an eye or the snap of fingers.

Finished with his weapon and satisfied it was in as good a shape as it could possibly be, he gathered his gear and stood up to get the other's attention. "All right people, let's get something to eat from whatever we got left in the packs and then bed down for the night. I want to head out at the crack of dawn."

"Are we going to the town Sue was trying to get to?" Mary asked.

"I don't know. Does she know how to get there from where we are now?" Henry asked Mary while his eyes fell on Sue.

"Yes, probably. All we need to do is get to a major road. Once I see a road sign and know where we are, I can get us there. I grew up around here. In Florence, actually," Sue told him.

"All right then, I guess we have a destination tomorrow," Henry added. "Now, let's eat, I'm starving."

A few murmurs of consent and a little grumbling from Jimmy filled the interior of the bus as everyone got to work digging out the rest of their supplies. Once that was done, everyone stood up and began gathering food. Henry watched for a few seconds, just gazing at the people in front of him who had become his family. Then Mary called to him and he shook himself of his reverie and went to see what she wanted, plus, he already had the Glock in his hand to give to her. It was a surprise for her and he hoped she would like it.

CHAPTER TWENTY-ONE

HENRY PULLED HIS jacket closer to his body, shifted his butt to a more comfortable position, and stared at the darkness surrounding the Greyhound bus. With no ambient light coming from streetlights, passing cars and nearby buildings, the stars shone brightly in the sky, a naturalistic piece of art exposed for what seemed like an audience of one, namely Henry.

The sun having set hours ago, the temperature outside had dropped almost a full twenty degrees and more than half of that inside the bus. Henry was in the driver's seat again, only now he was on watch. Behind him, in the rear of the compartment, the others slept fitfully. The seats were uncomfortable for the sleeping companions, even with armrests pushed up so that a person could stretch out on the three seats. With all this there was still barely enough room for a stretched out body.

Henry gazed into the ebony night, watching a light mist hover over the earth like ethereal ghosts playing a game of tag or soft clouds cast off from the sky. The internal lights were off in the bus, and with the exception of Jimmy's snoring and the rhythmic breathing of the others, all was quiet. It was like the world had died and they were truly the only survivors. Merely lost souls on a journey to the road to Hell, with no idea where the next turn on their odyssey would bring them.

The austere landscape outside the front windshield seemed almost ominous with the roiling mist, and Henry could almost hear one of the musical scores from the late Bernard Herrmann playing softly in the background of his imagination; the man had scored many a Hitchcock movie, some of which were Henry's favorites. That was one of many things he truly missed, movies. He'd loved curling up on his couch and watching an old movie, sometimes with Emily by his side or sometimes alone after she had gone to bed for the night.

Henry shook his head, trying to stay awake. With nothing but the dark to keep him company, his eyes wanted to close again. He stretched in his seat, the imitation leather creaking softly. Apparitions danced across his vision, like a play where all the actors were dead. Countless ghouls floated by, past enemies he had thwarted. Leaders of towns who had tried to exploit him came to the forefront of his vision, only to flutter away out of reach.

Shaking his head harder, he dry washed his face with his hands. He needed to stay awake. Peering through the cracked windshield and checking the only remaining side-view mirror, nothing stirred around the bus. So far they were undetected by any threats of danger and he could only hope it stayed that way until the sun rose in another hour or so.

Movement in the bus from behind caused him to sit taller. Turning in his seat, he saw a shadow moving towards him. At first he couldn't tell who it was, but after a few more steps, Susan appeared from of the darkness.

"Hey, how's it going?" she asked in a whisper while moving to the seat directly across from him.

"Hey, yourself. So far all's quiet. What's wrong, why are you up?"

Susan shrugged slightly. "Not tired I guess. I got a few hours in though, but with everything that's happened to me today, well..." She trailed off, leaving the rest in the air.

Henry knew what she meant. Less than a day ago she was tied up in a bus bathroom waiting to be either raped or eaten. Now she was free, but the memories would take time to fade.

"Mind if I sit with you for a while?"

Henry nodded. "Sure, yeah, that would be nice. With nothing to do but stare outside it's hard to stay awake."

"Have you ever fallen asleep while you've been on watch?"

"No, never," Henry said, adamant. "This is war, you know. If I or one of the others fell asleep, we might end up waking up with our throats slit."

She only nodded slowly and an uncomfortable silence descended over the two of them.

Henry sat in his seat, wondering what he should say to break the silence between them. As he wondered, he was distinctly aware of her only a foot away from him.

Finally, he took a chance.

"So, you're married?"

She was looking down again, at the floor, something Henry noticed she did from time to time. "Yes, but though I don't know for sure, I'd have to say I'm probably a widow by now." She looked up into Henry's eyes, his face only a dim outline in the darkness. "You?"

"The same. But I definitely know for sure." He gazed past her into the night and she realized there was a story there.

But she didn't ask for him to elucidate and he was glad for it.

He decided to change the subject.

"So where are you from? You know, you haven't even told me your last name, and neither has Raven."

"Well my last name is Richardson and Raven has never said a thing about her last name. She's just always gone with the one name, you know, like those Hollywood stars and singers. As for your first question, it's a little double-sided. Do you mean now or before?"

Henry gave that a moment's thought. Wherever she was from and whoever she had been before everything fell apart was irrelevant. The only thing that mattered was the here and now. There had been many people who had taken the apocalypse as a chance to start anew, where the sins of the past were truly dead and buried. Unfortunately, there were others who had taken the same chance and twisted it, becoming something evil.

"I mean now. Where are you from now?"

"Well, I've been staying in a town called Ashland for the past seven months or so. Over five hundred people who live there managed to barricade a large section of the city and were living pretty well. I found them almost by accident and they took me in. That's why, when they needed volunteers to go out, I stepped up. I felt I owed them something, you know, wanted to pull my weight and all that. I can't shoot worth a damn and I'm really not a great fighter, so…"

Jimmy rolled over in his sleep, his snoring shattering the quiet. Mary woke up with a start and yelled at Jimmy, punching the back of the middle seat the young man was laying on to make him stop. Jimmy stopped snoring, but his breathing remained heavy. The uneasy silence returned.

Sue looked into Henry's eyes, only the gloom of the bus' interior separating them.

"How 'bout you? Are you from around here?"

Henry decided where he was from didn't really matter that much anymore. He was a child of the deadlands now, like his companions sleeping softly behind him. He mumbled something about being from the Midwest and then changed the subject, not wanting to talk about himself. He was more interested in hearing about her.

"So, what do you think we'll find at this town tomorrow, what was its name?" He asked softly.

"Prattville, the town's called Prattville."

"Oh, right. So, as I said, what do you think we'll find there?"

Sue shook her head, her tresses falling across her face. She had washed up slightly, but there were still smudges of dirt on her cheeks. Henry had hopes of finding an untainted well or fresh water spring where they could all get cleaned up and wash their clothes. Hopefully, it would prove smoother than the last watering hole they had found.

Brushing her hair from her face, she looked into Henry's eyes again, locking her gaze with his, and he felt he could become lost in those twin pools of twinkling azure orbs.

"Honestly, I just don't know. We had ham radios to talk to one another, but about a week ago they just stopped answering our calls. Fearing the worst, we decided to go check on them, but I'm not hopeful. They had more than one radio at their disposal, so it couldn't have been an equipment malfunction. Before I left, the leaders of my town were talking about the infection maybe having gotten into Prattville. Maybe the town was invaded by them and now they're all dead, or worse, they've turned into them."

"Yeah, it's possible. And it wouldn't be the first time it'd happened," Henry commented.

There was movement outside the bus, caught by his peripheral vision, and Henry immediately stopped talking, his hand gripping the Steyr tightly. Ignoring Sue, he gazed out the front windshield, trying to peer through the darkness.

"What's wrong?"

"Shhh, I thought I saw something," he said in a whisper, despite the fact even if he had spoken at a normal tone it was highly doubtful anything stirring outside the bus would have heard him.

She did as she was told and Henry continued to study the area in front of the bus. Deciding it was clear, he stood up, the bus creaking slightly from his weight, and moved to one of the side windows. He was on the side that was still intact and he pressed his nose against the glass. Then he saw movement again and he squinted harder, trying to see into the darkness. A furry blur moved by the bus, heading towards the pile of corpses. Henry had a brief glimpse of a hairy body and a long tail, then the shadow was gone. Deciding it was most likely a wolf or a wild dog, he moved back to the driver's seat with one eye now on the landscape at all times.

"What is it, what did you see?" Sue asked hesitantly.

Henry shook his head. "It was nothing, a wolf possibly, or some other scavenger. We're fine."

She nodded, concern written all over her face. Henry held his gaze on her for another moment and realized she was shaking. He reached out and touched her arm, then slid his fingers down to her hand. He squeezed her hand softly, reassuringly as he smiled. "Hey, we're fine, really. Look, my friends and I have been on the road for a long time and so far we've done a pretty good job of taking care of ourselves. And now that you're with us, well, that goes the same for you, too. And Raven."

She looked up into his eyes and her face softened. "Thank you Henry, that's good to know."

"Will you two shut the hell up? I'm trying to sleep over here!" Jimmy snapped from the rear of the bus. After his outburst, both Cindy, Mary and even Raven joined in, though they were yelling at Jimmy for waking them up.

"What are you yelling at me for? Henry is the one gabbing away like a junior high kid on a date?"

"Well, maybe he is, but it was your big mouth that woke us up," Cindy snarled back.

Jimmy sent a few choice imprecations into the air at God and whoever else wanted in on the argument and then slid his head under a seat cushion salvaged from an unused seat.

"Sorry, Jimmy, we'll be quiet up here," Henry called back, a smile creasing his face while everyone yelled at one another in angry banter. He glanced at Sue and she grinned back meekly, feeling bad about waking Jimmy.

"Oh, don't worry about it, Sue. Jimmy's a big baby when it comes to getting his beauty sleep."

"Shut up, shut up, shut up! God it's almost light out!" He growled in exasperation. "Christ, I was quiet when you were sleeping!"

Henry and Sue stopped talking, and everyone quieted down again, and in minutes Jimmy was snoring fitfully like he'd never been woken. Cindy, or perhaps it was Mary, even kicked him once to stop him from snoring too loud again. Henry couldn't see who it was that had made the kick, as he only saw the boot reach out, the shadows still complete inside the bus.

Sue reached out and took Henry's hand again, her eyes creasing into a beautific smile. She mouthed the word sorry and Henry nodded in reply.

The two sat next to each other for the rest of the night, until the first faint rays of the morning sun appeared, holding hands like two teenagers on their first date.

CHAPTER TWENTY-TWO

THE NEXT MORNING saw the bus cruising down one of the many circuitous back roads of Kentucky once again, while inside the passenger compartment the companions and their two new additions talked and relaxed.

After a quick meal of rations, each person made a quick bathroom break while at least one other stood guard. By the time they were ready to leave; more than a dozen ghouls had arrived and were trying to gain entry into the bus.

Keeping to the small country roads, the bus made good time and the scenery was beautiful. Overgrown farmland, surrounded by high, lush trees and swaying wheat moved back and forth in the wind, as if the high stalks were waving to the bus' occupants. Each was lost in his or her private thoughts and at the moment Henry was driving.

Neither Cindy nor Mary was too keen on driving, so Jimmy and Henry had taken turns.

Jimmy walked down the swaying aisle and plopped down just behind Henry, leaning forward so Henry could hear him over the noise of the diesel engine. Though the engine was in the rear of the bus, it was making noise, small damage sustained in the escape from the hospital.

"So what's up with you and Sue? You were getting pretty chummy last night," Jimmy said slyly while he gazed out at the lonely road in front of him. He had that sly grin on his face that told Henry he knew exactly what was up, though he still wanted Henry to spell it out for him.

Henry glanced up into the rear view mirror to see the top half of Jimmy's face, from the nose up.

"I have no idea what you're talking about," Henry replied. He pressed the brake and slowed while he drove around a pile of telephone poles lying in the middle of the road like a child's discarded Lincoln Logs. There was plenty of room on the shoulder and he passed the obstruction easily. Two minutes later, they came upon an eighteen wheeler with a large empty flatbed, the straps hanging off the side like impotent snakes, the buckles at the ends swaying softly in the wind resembling the heads of those same snakes. This was where the poles had come from. Henry slowed the bus when he passed the cab of the semi, but all he was rewarded with was an empty cab with dried, brown blood splattered on the front windshield. Deciding there was nothing more to see, he pressed the gas pedal and continued on. They were only a few miles from Prattville and Sue was keeping tabs on his driving from the rear of the bus while she chatted with Cindy and Mary.

Raven was an island unto herself, the teenager still sitting alone in the last row of seats like she was on a school bus and wanted to hang in the back so the driver wouldn't see her.

"You don't, huh? Listen, Henry, it's all right if you like her. She's pretty cool and she's about your age, too. You should go for it. After all, it's been a while since you, well, you know, how do I put this delicately? Since you bumped uglies, did the horizontal mambo, made the beast with two backs…" Henry cut him off.

"Jimmy, will you please stop it? She might hear you. Christ, you're such a jerk sometimes." Henry stared at Jimmy, his visage grew serious and his voice went down a pitch, almost becoming a growl. "Look, Jimmy, whether I like her or not, it's none of your concern; now leave it alone, will you please?"

Jimmy nodded and stood up, knowing he was pushing Henry a little too far and slapped him on the back. "Fine Henry, I'll stop, but I'm telling you right now. Don't let this opportunity pass you by, not again. You're a good guy, you deserve someone." Then his face grew serious as well and he creased his eyes. "I don't even want to think about what I would've done if I hadn't met Cindy. She makes it all okay, you know? Even when it gets bad."

"Yeah, Jimmy, I know more than you might think," Henry answered as he thought back to Gwen and how good he'd felt in the brief time he'd known her. But it wasn't meant to be and he'd lost her so fast. Maybe that was a blessing in disguise. He had found her and lost her so quickly that maybe his loss wasn't as bad as it could have been. Only God still knew he felt a hollow spot in his heart when he thought of his late wife, Emily.

Sue's voice caused him to focus on the here and now once again and he looked up to the rearview mirror over his head to see Sue standing there, holding on to the pole running from the back of his seat to the ceiling.

"There, Henry, take a right at the next four-way intersection. Prattville is about a mile and a half away," she told him as she swayed to the motion of the bus.

"You got it," he said and she flashed him a warm smile in return. She stayed behind him as he drove, and he was acutely aware of her standing there. Sometimes when the bus would hit an imperfection in the road, she would lean into him and he would immediately come alive by her touch. He forced the feelings down. Now was not the time to feel like a school boy on his first crush. For now, he needed to stay focused.

The bus reached the intersection and made the turn easily. Cars were everywhere and it was apparent the town's limits were close. Once they had passed through the four-way intersection, buildings began to sprout up, like wild weeds. The signs on the buildings listed everything from dry cleaners to video stores At the end of this long road Henry slowed to a stop, the air brakes hissing like an out of shape old man after a long hike.

In front of the bus was a large wall of debris, reaching over six feet high, and in a few other places, nearly topping eight or nine easily. The wall seemed to be made out of whatever had been gathered in a small amount of time. Old tires were one of the main components, but there were plenty of washing machines, refrigerators, and scrap metal. Even the kitchen sink was there, the faucets still attached and the copper piping hanging from the bottom like dead vines. There were countless bodies scattered around the wall and it was apparent by their condition and clothing they had once been ghouls. Spent shell casings reflected the sunlight, attesting to how the bodies had been put down. Smack dab in the middle of the wall, right in the middle of the road, was an opening large enough to drive an average automobile through. A large panel truck was pulled to the side and it was apparent this was the actual gate. Sheet metal had been welded to the lower chassis to prevent attackers from going under the truck. The left side, facing out, was a solid wall of metal and would do well to hold off the undead.

Mary and Cindy joined the others at the front of the bus and they all studied the area.

"They left the gate open, that can't be good," Jimmy commented from the right of Henry. Henry nodded, his eyes scanning the prone bodies, waiting to see if any were going to move, but so far they were immobile. Midnight-black crows and a few vultures had found the dead meat and were feasting happily, tearing away at the soft tissues. One particular crow popped its head up at the sound of the bus and Henry saw it had a juicy eye ball in its beak. The crow squeezed its beak closed, severing the orb in half, then scooped up each piece with relish.

"That gate should be closed and there should be guards behind it. This is wrong, very wrong," Sue said while she leaned over Henry's shoulder to eye the opening. Henry felt his heartbeat flutter when her hair cascaded over him. Then she realized where her hair was and pulled it back with one hand, mumbling an apology to Henry.

"What do you think, Henry? Do we go check it out?" Mary asked mildly.

Henry glanced to Sue. "What do you want to do, Sue? You know these people better than us. Can you even think why they might have abandoned the town? That's got to be one of the only reasons there's no one around." He pointed to the bodies. "See those? If they had been overrun then we would see at least a few deaders moving about. So far there's nothing."

"I want to go in and see what's happened. So, if you're asking me what I want to do, then my answer is yes, go inside."

Henry looked at the other companions in the rearview mirror.

"All right, people, I've got one vote for checking it out, how 'bout the rest of you? Jimmy?"

Jimmy bit his lip as he gave the question a moment of thought, then he nodded. "Yeah, Henry, let's see what's up. Maybe they left some food or ammo behind. We need both, ya know."

"Jimmy's right," Cindy added, "we need both badly. I say we see what's what. If it looks like trouble, we can always turn around and leave."

"Okay, that's three for going in, Mary?" Henry asked.

Mary shrugged. "It's okay with me. Go or stay, I'll go with whatever you guys want to do."

"Okay, then, I guess we're good to go. Raven, you got an opinion?" Henry called to the girl who had never left her seat in the rear of the bus.

"Whatever," was all she said and Henry snickered at that.

"Ah, the indifference of youth," Henry chuckled. "Then, it's settled, we go in. Okay, there's room for the bus and it looks like there's a wide open area past the wall so I'm gonna take the bus inside. Jimmy and Mary, you take the left side and stay sharp. If it moves, kill it. We'll worry about asking questions later. Cindy, you keep watch on the right and give a yell if there's trouble." He glanced back to Raven who still hadn't moved a muscle. "Okay, Raven, why don't you stay back there and watch the bathroom," he said sarcastically

Raven waved a hand casually, then was hidden again behind the headrest she sat behind. If she picked up on the sarcasm, she didn't show it.

Jimmy and Mary nodded and moved to the middle of the bus, then took positions at a window each, while Henry let out the air brake. The bus began rolling and he slowly took it through the gate, moving at an easy four miles an hour, which would be about the speed of an average walker. Sue leaned forward, studying the street, her breathing becoming shallow with expectation.

About a hundred feet past the opening; Henry slowed the bus and reapplied the air brake. The bus idled softly and he turned off the engine, sliding the small rectangular window to his left open. The first thing he noticed was the odor of burnt wood. There had been fires here recently, and now that he scanned the buildings lining the road, he could see the scorched marks covering the stone structures and the wooden ones were nothing but charred husks. The entire road for as far as he could see was nothing but blackened storefronts and residential homes.

His eyes took it all in at a glance and he instinctively lowered his hand to his Glock. There was a bad feeling in the air, the dread a palpable presence.

When there was no sign of an enemy, whether alive or dead, he nodded to the others, who each told him the same thing. All was dead quiet.

Deciding they had seen all they could from inside the bus, he stood up, pocketed the keys and opened the accordion door.

"Let's go see what the hell happened here. Whatever it was, it was some bad shit," he said as he led the procession off the bus.

The companions followed, and soon all were standing on the asphalt a few feet away from the front grille. The sun was high overhead, shining across a sky of unsullied blue. Heat waves hovered over the road as the sun cooked the world with its rays, the air above the pavement seeming to scintillate with the heat of the day. On top of the smell of smoke, there was a heavy odor of scorched tar. "There was one hell of a fire here," Jimmy said, moving away from the group. He shouldered his Remington while he walked across the road and stopped when he was standing in front of a shattered storefront. The façade was charred, the sign hanging over the hollow door now nothing but cinders.

"Okay, everyone spread out and see what you can find," Henry said, "but stay in the middle of the street. There's no way of knowing if there's anything still inside any of those buildings."

"Yeah, I know. How come there aren't any deaders around?" Cindy asked while she studied the empty buildings, fingering the trigger of her M-16 uneasily. From where she stood, the road went straight for almost a thousand feet before curving away deep into the town, though every building she saw was burned and hollow. Whatever had caused the fire had been massive, enveloping the entire town in its warm embrace.

"I know, I was just thinking the same thing," Mary added, moving to join the blonde-haired warrior. With the two together, they set off to investigate a nearby storefront, Mary carrying her new Glock at her side. Rubble lined the street in front of the shattered plate-glass windows; a clear clue an explosion had taken place here. The question was: was the explosion before, during, or after the fires had begun?

Henry glanced to Sue. "Hey, you want to come with me? Keep me company? Maybe you might see something unusual that explains what the hell happened here."

She nodded and moved next to him. Together, the two moved perpendicular to the bus. There was a wide open area opposite the wall and there appeared to be more than a dozen cars and trucks mingled together. None looked serviceable. Every one of them was missing parts, and tires on many were either gone or flat. They had obviously been out here to use for spare parts. Henry took the lead, with Sue only a foot behind him. With potential danger around every corner, he knew he was going to have to get the woman a weapon, even a stick would be better than nothing.

With the Steyr leading the way, he moved between the stripped cars, feeling like he'd come upon relics of history. He expected an attack around each turn and was still surprised when he reached the end of the vehicles and nothing had jumped out at him. A loud buzzing sound had been filtering slowly into his ears, and when he moved out of the line of cars, the noise grew louder.

The wind shifted and began blowing toward him and he stopped and turned away, holding his breath as the vile redolence of decomposing meat struck him hard in the face. His stomach rolled inside him, the spasms threatening to send up his meager breakfast, and it took all his will to get his fragile insides under control. Sue wasn't as strong and he heard the sounds of her retching. She vomited her breakfast onto the hot cement beneath her feet, the soup-like substance steaming in the warm air.

When nothing more would come up, she began to dry heave, but slowly she began to regain control of herself. Henry had already regained his composure. Normally the odor, no matter how disgusting, would have barely fazed him. He'd smelled and seen too many things over the past year to be fazed anymore about what he found while roaming the deadlands, but every now and then his guard would be down and something would get by him.

This had been one of those times.

"You okay," he called to her as she leaned over the hood of a Datsun. Standing to her full height, she wiped her mouth with her sleeve. She kept her arm over her nose and mouth, trying to filter the odor.

"Yeah, thank you, I'll be okay, it's just..." She opened her mouth like she was going to vomit again, but then stopped herself, turning away and covering her face yet again. "It's just...that smell...good God, Henry, what is that?"

"Rotting meat. Human or animal, it all smells the same in the end. You can stay here if you want. You don't have to come with me any further. Go back to the bus and wait for me there if you want," he told her.

She shook her head, her hair flowing across her face. "No, I'll be okay. It's just... It took me off guard, the smell, I mean. It doesn't bother you?"

Henry gave her a wry smile. "Yeah, a little. But you'd be surprised what I've seen and smelled these past few months. You get used to it after a while. Try breathing through your mouth. Leave your nose out of the equation. It helps a little."

She did as he suggested, and with her arm still over her nose, she nodded. "Yeah, that does help, thanks."

He nodded. "Okay then, let's keep going. One way or another we need to find out what's making that stench." His jaw grew taut. "It can't be good, I'll tell you that much right now." He waited while Sue moved through the remaining cars, and while Henry waited, a bad feeling he already knew what was making the awful stench slowly crept up on him.

Sue stopped when she was next to him, her eyes cast downward. "What's wrong?" He asked her.

She shrugged slightly, her eyes still staring at her feet. "Nothing, I was just thinking that a few seconds ago wasn't one of my best moments, that's all."

Henry smiled, nodding, understanding completely.

"Forget it, Sue, it's not a big deal, really."

"Yeah? You mean that? You're not just saying it to be nice, are you?"

Henry shook his head. "No way, doesn't bother me at all. Tell you what; you can toss your lunch whenever you feel like it, all right?"

She smiled bashfully. "Oh Henry, now you're just being silly."

"Yup, I am, now come on, let's keep moving."

With Sue next to him once again, they began walking and it was near the wall, at an angle to the parked cars that Henry found what he expected.

Corpses, more than sixty or more were spread out on the ground in different poses of death. Sue raised her hands to her face in absolute shock and turned again and vomited. Her stomach was empty and she mostly dry heaved, only a small amount of spittle escaping her open mouth.

Henry was handling it better. The aroma of death, sickly sweet and sour, was like a solid wall in front of him, but he ignored it, moving across the forty feet that separated him from the first line of bodies. Yelling at the top of his voice, he chased the murder of crows away, their cawing at their displeasure of being interrupted filling the air surrounding the bodies. They took flight, but didn't go far, all resting on the edge of the wall, waiting for when it would be safe to return to their meal.

He stopped upon reaching the first corpse and went down to one knee, careful not to get his boots or knee in the dried pools of blood that had been cascading from the bodies at the moment of death. In between the other bodies, gallons of dried--and in some small places where the bodies shielded the sun, still sticky--blood painted the ground like someone had spilled a hundred cans of brown and maroon paint. Maggots squirmed in the plasma, sharing the sweet liquid with ants and other forms of insect life. Flies were absolutely everywhere and he waved them away from his face, wincing when they landed on his flesh. He knew he would have to be quick, before they attacked him en mass. His eyes investigated the scene like a detective from an old movie. He studied the frozen visages of death intently, filing many items away for later inspection. Leaning forward, he picked up a spent shell casing. There were dozens of similar casings sprinkled around the bodies like confetti, the metal reflecting the bright sunlight like small mirrors, and the debris filled wall was riddled with bullet holes.

Henry rolled the spent shell casing in his hand for almost thirty seconds, then let it fall from his hand. It bounced on the road twice and finally lay still. His eyes roamed over the faces of the dead again, his gaze lingering on each face. There were small children, the elderly, and even a few babies. It was all so overwhelming he just wanted to close his eyes and pretend he'd never seen any of it. But he couldn't. With one last look, he stood, turned, and walked away.

Sue was waiting for him and her eyes were red and filled with tears.

"Oh my Lord, Henry, are those people from the town?"

"Yeah, I suppose so, though there's only about sixty or so, give or take. There were a lot more than this living here, right?"

She nodded. "Of course, hundreds more, why?"

He shook his head. "Not now, later. I want to talk to the others about this. Come on, let's get back to them and fill everyone in. Maybe they found something a little more positive than we did." He began working his way back to the line of wrecked cars.

"But what about all those bodies?" She asked as she stared at his shoulders. "Surely, we can't leave them like that."

Henry stopped walking and turned half-around to gaze at her. His face was hard, but his eyes were soft. "Sue, there's nothing we can do for them now. They're dead. But I'll tell you this. They weren't just killed, deaders didn't do this; they were executed. There's signs of bullets on the wall behind them and spent brass everywhere. Someone lined them up and slaughtered them like diseased cows."

Sue's face was one of consternation. "But who would do something so heinous; so barbaric?"

Henry turned away from her again and began walking back to the bus, his gait steady. "That's what I'm gonna find out," he growled over his shoulder and picked up his pace.

Sue realized she was going to lose him in a moment when he entered the first row of the parked cars, so with one last look over her shoulder at the pyre of bodies, she began running after Henry, her back itching in the belief that if she dallied long enough, something would climb out of the pile of corpses and chase after her.

CHAPTER TWENTY-THREE

U PON REACHING THE bus again, Henry saw the others were already waiting for him. As he moved closer, he could see Jimmy waving his arms in agitation while he was speaking. Moving closer still, Henry caught the tail end of his words.

"...there's nothing but burned out buildings in every direction. By the way everything is charred; I'd guess someone set the place on fire. There's no other excuse for everything to be so burned up."

"But that's crazy, Jimmy," Mary said askance of him. "That would mean someone came in here and did it. Who would have any reason to do that? What would be the purpose to burn down a whole town?"

Jimmy raised his hands in the air in a: I give up gesture. "How the hell should I know? I'm just telling you what I saw."

Cindy shook her head back and forth, her mane of golden tresses flowing about her face until she brushed them back. "Something weird happened here, I'll tell you this." She looked around at the blackened buildings and a chill went down her back. "This place has a weird vibe to it. I think we should leave, and as soon as possible."

"Cindy's right," Henry said, walking up behind them. He wasn't surprising any of them, all the companions having watched their backs. They had seen Henry emerge from the cars and had gone back to talking amongst themselves as he made his way to them.

"There's a pile of bodies on the other side of those cars and they looked like they'd been lined up and shot, like what the Germans used to do to the Jews in World War 2. Another thing I discovered, and let me tell you it was pretty hard to look at, was that all I saw were old men and women and really small children. No one under the age of seventy or older than six or seven years of age. Did any of you find anyone in that age bracket?"

Everyone shook their heads. "No, we did find a few bodies in the rubble, but they were too badly burned to know how old they were," Jimmy told him as he eyed the parked cars warily. Just knowing what lay beyond its borders sent a chill through him.

Henry frowned, long and deep. "Some bad shit happened here and I've got to say I agree with Cindy. There's nothing here for us. We should go before whoever did this comes back. With the amount of spent ammo I found on the ground, they're more than we can handle." He turned to Sue. "I'm real sorry about all this, Sue, but there's nothing we can do."

She nodded, her eyes gazing at the wreckage of homes and businesses. "No, Henry, I understand." She shook her head. "It's so horrible. All those people, dead."

"Maybe not everyone," Henry replied. "As I said, I didn't see anyone over seven and under seventy or so. That means anyone who was in the middle of that and was young and healthy isn't here."

"If they're not here, then where did they go?" Mary asked.

Henry shrugged. "Who knows? Maybe they evacuated the town and couldn't take the old and young with them. Maybe they had an outbreak and had to destroy the whole damn place."

"That sounds pretty far-fetched, Henry," Cindy snorted. "You want us to believe they burned their own town and then...what? They killed all the old and young because they couldn't leave with them? That's crazy."

A cloud of anger fell over Henry as he stared at the young blonde woman.

"Sorry, Cindy, if my ideas don't make sense, but what the hell do you want me to say? I wasn't here; I don't know what the hell happened!"

"Whoa, Henry, all right, Cindy didn't mean anything by it. Let's all agree this is a really screwed up situation and leave it at that, all right?" Mary said, trying to calm Henry down. She was as mystified as the rest of them and she was feeling mighty uneasy. That felling of uneasiness for Henry had become a short temper.

Henry's face softened and he nodded, then mumbled a small apology to Cindy. She nodded, letting the entire discussion go.

Suddenly, the sound of falling wood from behind the bus caused the companions to spin on their heels, weapons tracking in the direction of whatever had been heard.

"You hear that?" Jimmy asked, his Remington pump in his hands, leveled, the muzzle tracking for danger.

"Yeah, what the hell was it? A deader maybe?" Henry suggested.

"Could be, but we were over there already and I didn't see anything. If there had been, it wouldn't have stayed hidden," Mary whispered.

That was one of the advantages the companions had over the walking dead. The ghouls had no reasoning capacity. If they were near prey, they would attack, not lie in wait for a better time to attack. If a ghoul had been waiting somewhere in the rubble, it would have lunged out immediately upon sensing the companions.

"Well, let's go see. Standing around in the middle of the road won't get us shit," Jimmy said and began moving towards the disturbance.

"Jimmy, dammit, get back here, we don't know what's in there!" Henry yelled at the younger man. Jimmy was being impetuous yet again, acting first and worrying about the consequences of his actions later.

Cindy took one look at Henry and Mary and then took off after her man. She wasn't going to let Jimmy walk into danger without her by his side.

"Cindy, where are you going?" Henry called to her.

"To be with Jimmy, stay there if you want to."

"Dammit," Henry grumbled, "doesn't anyone listen anymore?" He spoke to Mary, who only smiled sideways.

"Sorry, Henry, you know how he get's. Come on; at least let's give him backup if he needs it, both of them."

With a weary sigh, he nodded and the three of them moved off after Jimmy and Cindy. Then he stopped Sue, holding her upper arm gently.

"Sue, why don't you get inside the bus and stay there. Raven will watch with you. Yell if there's trouble."

Sue nodded in understanding and moved to the stairs of the bus. "Be careful," she called.

He nodded curtly. "Always," and then was moving with Mary by his side, the Steyr level in his hands.

Jimmy had reached the crumbling, charred wreckage of one of the dozen buildings lining the road. He was about to step into the area when Henry reached him and placed a hand on the back of his shoulder.

"Will you wait a second, please? Jesus, Jimmy. That whole thing could come down on your head," Henry pleaded as he scanned the damaged structure. "Let's take this slow."

Jimmy made a face, like a small child who was impatient to go on a ride at the carnival, but he did stop.

"Fine, Henry, fine, we'll do it your way," he replied.

"Good, that's real good, Jimmy," Henry told him and cast a glance at Mary and Cindy. "You two stay sharp, and Jimmy and I will check out inside, okay?"

Mary and Cindy both nodded their approval and rechecked their weapons. Henry nodded; pleased at least they were listening to him. He turned back to Jimmy and gestured with the tip of the Steyr at the shadows inside the wreckage.

"You ready?"

"Hell yeah, old man, I've been ready," Jimmy quipped, anxious to investigate. On the tail of his words there was another small noise, like a can had fallen off a shelf or perhaps a loose piece of wood had slipped from its mooring.

"Well then, lead on," Henry told Jimmy with a slight grin.

Jimmy took a second look at Henry, wondering what the grin was for. It was like Henry knew something he didn't and was now wary of entering the burnt-out structure.

Jimmy stood to his full height, throwing his shoulders back and ran his left hand through his hair. Now prepared, he strolled into the shadows of debris, Henry at his back.

The odor of burnt wood and other items, such as plastic and insulation, came to his nose and he scrunched it up, trying to breathe through his mouth. The entire inside of the building was blackened and there was no inclination of what the building had been used for.

The pungent odor of chemicals seemed to hang over everything, the thick miasma hovering near the floor like fog. Henry kicked a piece of wood aside and noticed a small amount of smoke puffed out, the small cloud now free of escape its prison.

"Shit, Jimmy, I think there might still be some hot spots in here," Henry told his younger companion.

"Yeah? That means it wasn't that long ago that the town was burned down, right?"

"Sure. A good rainstorm would put out the fires exposed to the weather, but inside here, where it would be protected, the heat from a fire like this could last for days. Hell, maybe even a week."

"Really? No shit," Jimmy added.

Henry grinned. "Yeah, no shit. I could be wrong, though. I mean, I'm not a fireman or anything, but by the looks of those bodies I told you about, this town was still here a week ago."

Jimmy stopped moving through the rubble and stared at Henry. "That means whoever did this might still be around, right? You know, like, still in the area."

Henry's smile was lost at the thought that whoever had been ruthless enough to set fire to an entire town and slaughter all those innocents could still be close enough the companions could run into them unannounced.

A shifting of debris deeper in the building caused Jimmy to swing around, shotgun barrel tracking the noise. Henry was by his side and gestured with the Steyr.

"Over there," he mouthed, not wanting to call anymore attention to himself. He realized both he and Jimmy had been sloppy. They'd been talking and chatting like they were having a beer at a local bar instead of focusing on what could be mortal danger. He resolved right then that playtime was over. He'd learned a long time ago, that in the new world he was living in, one careless moment could be his last for himself or someone close to him.

Taking the lead from Jimmy, he moved ahead, cringing every time his boots crunched or crackled, wary where he set them down, concerned about tripping on the hidden debris under the ash and soot that covered the floor like carpeting.

There was what appeared to be a hallway with a four way junction ahead. A large blackened beam had fallen in the middle, but there was still room to move around it. Sliding under it, bits of charred wood trickled into his hair. Henry ignored it, keeping his attention on what was ahead. Dark shapes, surrounded by darker ones, filled the corridor and Henry slowly moved forward. The noise came again and he spun around, realizing he was going the wrong way.

Jimmy, having been behind him, took the lead again and the two men began working their way passed the beam and down the opposite hallway from where they'd been going.

Another junction was in front of them and Henry noticed the partial paintings hanging askew on the walls. They were almost entirely gone, only a few spots untouched, and he saw a peaceful lake and trees with birds flying in a clear blue sky. The rest was ash, the flames having consumed it.

Jimmy was the first to discover the noise and he let out a small gasp that had Henry's finger squeezing the trigger of the Steyr, prepared to compress that one-eighth of an inch more and send a steel jacketed round into whatever lay ahead.

"No, wait, Henry, it's okay, there's nothing to fear here," Jimmy said, raising his hand.

Henry couldn't see what Jimmy had spotted, as he was still behind the man and the junction. Moving up next to Jimmy, Henry looked down on what had been making the noise that had attracted their attention.

He wished he hadn't.

On the floor, buried under some wreckage, all charred a deep charcoal, was what had once been a man. Now the body was a deep black color with spots of red seeping through cracks in the roasted skin. Every single inch of the man's flesh had been cooked away and Henry couldn't even imagine the agony the man must have endured while being cooked alive. At least, he assumed it was a man. With no hair or clothing on the body, the true gender was unknown.

Henry couldn't help but think of beef jerky as he stared down at the prone form.

But it was when the eyes opened, a stark whiteness in contrast to the blackened face, that Henry almost fired the Steyr directly into the poor bastard's head. He would have, too; assuming he was looking at one of the undead, but then something happened that immediately told him the crispy critter was still human.

It talked.

The mouth opened slowly and two words slid from the mouth like syrup.

"Help me," the mouth spoke; the words harsh-sounding, like a saw blade striking a nail when it's cutting through a piece of wood. No doubt this was because of inhalation of smoke and the high heat of the fire, burning the vocal cords so it was a miracle they worked at all. Inside the mouth, the red tongue moved about over still white teeth.

"Water," the mouth gasped. The breathing was hard and shallow, each breath a struggle

Jimmy turned to glare at Henry, his eyes asking the older man what to do.

Henry shook his head no. Neither of them carried water on them, and it was possible if either of them tried to get back to the bus to retrieve a bottle of water, the immolated soul would be dead long before they returned.

Henry leaned down close to the body. From the size, he was fairly certain it was a man, though age and color were still a mystery. From the accent, he appeared to be a local.

"I'm sorry; we don't have any water for you. Is there anything else we can do for you? Maybe try to make you more comfortable?"

The burnt man raised his left hand, particles of blackened flesh falling off his arm to fall to the floor. The man winced in pain, but not as much as Henry would have expected. Later, Mary would tell him it was probably because every nerve in the man's body had been burned to the point there was no feeling left.

The raised hand pointed directly at Henry's Glock.

"You can shoot me with that...stranger... and right quickly...too," his harsh, raspy voice said in a dull whisper. "I can't tell you...how much pain...I'm in." Every word was a chore.

Henry glanced to Jimmy, but the young man said nothing.

Standing up, Henry slung the Steyr over his shoulder and pulled the Glock from its holster, flicking off the safety with his thumb.

"All right, mister, I'll do it. I'll put one right in your head and put you out of your misery, but first I need you to answer something for me."

"What do you...want to know?"

"What the hell happened to this place? Why are all those old men and women and small children dead near that wall? Where is everyone else and why are you in here? Why didn't you get out when the fires began?"

The man wheezed a hard sigh, then bellowed a few wracking coughs that sent blood shooting from his mouth, staining his white teeth red.

"I ain't got much time left...but I'll tell you what...you want to know. Just keep your promise...with that gun."

Henry nodded. The man seemed to dig down deep from inside himself, wanting to share his story so Henry could end his pain. Though still hoarse and harsh, the man spoke smoothly, only his eyes showing any emotion he may have felt.

"Almost a week ago a convoy arrived. It was the army. We thought we were saved, that the government was finally coming to help us after over a year of hearing nothing. But they were worse than the dead ghouls that haunted us outside our homemade walls. I heard his name once, but I can't remember it. Sorry. I think he was a captain or a colonel. Well, he took all the men, women and children that were of strong age to join his army and then killed the rest so they wouldn't become ghouls." He began coughing again and Henry reached out to help him, but when he did, Henry's left hand brushed the man's shoulder. The man cried out in anguish from the touch. When Henry's hand had slid across the man's shoulder; the burnt skin had slid off his back like it was attached with butter. Where Henry's hand had been there was now a bright red spot on the man's shoulder; glistening drops of scarlet beaded the wound, clear to see even in the shadows of the corridor.

"Oh, Jesus Christ, I'm so damn sorry," Henry told the man, wiping his hand on his pant leg. The charred skin stuck to his hand like burnt skin from barbecued chicken.

Jimmy looked like he was about to vomit, and Henry realized if the younger man did, he would probably join him.

"So, where were you when all this shit happened and what about the fire? The entire town is nothing but ash," Jimmy asked, wanting some answers. Sweat beaded on his forehead and he wiped it away.

"The captain or whatever he was set the town on fire. He used explosives. He told the town he was doing it so the ghouls couldn't take over. With the buildings destroyed there would be no place for the ghouls to hide. Said he was covering his tracks." He began coughing again and Henry and Jimmy had to wait for the bout to pass.

"So where were you when all this shit happened?" Jimmy asked again when the coughing fit had finally passed.

"I'm sorry to say I was scared, so when they began taking people, I hid in here. Even with the fires, I stayed hidden, because I knew if I left my hiding place they'd get me, too."

"Yeah, that worked out good for ya, didn't it," Jimmy sneered as he gazed down at the rack of grilled ribs that resembled a man just barely. "You hid like a coward while your entire town was killed and taken away as slave labor." He shook his head in disgust. "Looks to me like you got what you deserved."

"Jimmy, please, not now," Henry chastised.

"No, your friend is right," the man told Henry. "I did hide and I'm a coward, but what else could I do? I was only one man and there were so many of them." He began coughing again and this time he couldn't stop. He began to spasm and his eyes stared at Henry, the eyelids open as wide as they could go. Whatever well of strength he'd been using had gone dry.

"The...pain...kill...me...please!" The man gasped each word, barely able to make them comprehensible.

"Go ahead, Henry, shoot the poor fuck. Better than he deserves, though," Jimmy growled as he watched the man twitching on the floor. With each scrape of his skin against the floor and surrounding debris, pieces of blackened flesh peeled away to expose the red muscles and tendons beneath. The man began making a mewling sound that bounced off the walls of the hallway.

With a look of pity and disgust, Henry aimed the Glock at the man's head and put a bullet right between his eyes. The gunshot was loud in the confines of the hallway and the charred head snapped back to the floor, blood pooling under the neck to spread into the ash covering the floor.

"Jesus Christ, that was somethin' else," Jimmy said as he watched the blood spreading out in strange shapes that would make a psychiatrist orgasm in his pants.

"Yeah, it was, the poor bastard. Coward or not, though, no one deserves to go out like that." He turned to gaze at Jimmy, the two making eye contact, his face hard. "No one, Jimmy."

"Yeah, maybe you're right, Henry, maybe you're right." He spun on his heels. "Come on, let's get back to the girls, they're probably wondering what that gunshot was about," Jimmy said and began walking away.

Reholstering his Glock, Henry nodded in return. Without another word, he followed Jimmy away from the prone, blackened corpse; the hallway now as good a tomb as any for the hapless man.

CHAPTER TWENTY-FOUR

MARY AND CINDY were waiting nervously on the sidewalk and relief flooded their face when Henry and Jimmy exited the wrecked building.

"Oh, thank God, we were about to go in after you. We heard a shot," Mary said in a quick tone. The worry and concern was apparent on her face.

Jimmy went to Cindy, wrapping his arms around her, the two talking quietly, while Henry went to Mary.

"Everything's fine, Mar', really. We found someone inside there, though," Henry said and then quickly filled her in on what the burned man had said and the final shot that had ended his suffering.

Mary's eyes creased in thought as she weighed Henry's words. Halfway through his tale, Jimmy moved closer with Cindy, and they had both listened to the rest of Henry's story, Cindy nodding at what she'd just learned from Jimmy only seconds ago.

"Do you think this colonel or captain is really in the army? If he is, it sure as hell doesn't sound like any military I've ever heard of," Cindy said.

"No shit," Jimmy added. "This guy's doing like the military did in Vietnam; conscripting people to be in the army whether they want to or not."

Henry nodded, rubbing his chin. It was rough from more than a day's worth of growth and he was confident he wouldn't be shaving anytime soon.

"Yeah, you're right, Jimmy, not bad," Henry told him, impressed with the younger man's knowledge. "It looks like this guy has instituted a draft. Makes sense in a morbid way, though. If anyone's gonna try and get things back together, they're gonna need manpower. With everyone only out for themselves nowadays, it makes sense he'd have to institute the draft by force."

Mary's eyes flashed with anger, she couldn't believe Henry was taking this mysterious commander's side.

"And what about all those bodies you found? Huh, Henry? What about all those little children he slaughtered because they weren't old enough to work yet or he didn't want to feed them. Are you okay with that!"

"No, Mary, of course not, I'm just saying, hard times call for hard measures. He's justifying anything for the greater good, or so he must think. And if it does hold real rank in the military, then he might just be the last one still running around in the states. We've come how far in our travels and found almost no military presence? When things hit the fan last year, the soldiers took off for their own families, not that I could blame them."

Jimmy shrugged, giving Henry a depreciating smile. "I don't know, Henry, this guy sounds like just another megalomaniac with delusions of grandeur. Whether he was once a real general or captain or whatever doesn't matter anymore. He's a murderer and he needs to go down."

Mary and Cindy nodded their heads, agreeing with Jimmy's words. Cindy patted Jimmy's shoulder, whispering in his ear how proud she was of the big words he'd just used. Jimmy smiled widely like a student who'd been praised by his favorite teacher.

Henry held out his hands, palms out, trying to keep the peace. This discussion was getting out of hand. "Look, it doesn't really matter what we think. This guy has a lot of firepower behind him, so the last thing we want to do is get caught up in whatever crusade he's trying to do." He looked at Jimmy, Cindy, and Mary, his eyes lingering on each one for an extra second. "We can't save the world guys; all we can do is watch our backs and keep surviving until whatever's happened to the world finally ends."

He turned and began walking back to the bus. Sue was waiting and he was sure she was worried. "I'm going back to the bus. Let's get out of here. The sooner the better, just like Cindy said."

As he moved away from the others, he could still hear them talking. He decided to let them discuss whatever they needed to and later, when tempers had cooled, perhaps they could continue where they'd left off.

Henry was more than halfway back to the bus when the horn blared loudly; breaking the silence of the empty town like an explosion had gone off. Until hearing the horn blast, Henry hadn't given it much thought, but now realized the town had been deathly silent. Almost like a tomb; a fitting reference, he thought.

The horn blared again and Henry began running. Footsteps sounded behind, attesting to the fact the others were now racing behind him; as they too, wanted to investigate why the horn was blaring like the bus was stopped in a traffic jam with an annoyed driver behind the wheel.

Henry found out a moment later, when he rounded the corner of the bus. He was facing the opening that led out of town and he muttered a few choice curses as he spied the score of walking dead now shuffling through the gaping portal the bus had traversed less than an hour ago.

Watching the ponderous, yet determined, movements of the animated corpses, he realized the town had been devoid of any mobile ghouls; all of them in the area having been put down. But like maggots to rotting meat, any surviving ghouls in the area would eventually come to the town and that was what was most definitely happening at the moment.

Just their luck, Henry thought, they had to arrive at the town just when more deaders were popping up. If they had driven into the town yesterday, they would have been able to investigate and leave with never a shot fired.

But now they were in for trouble.

Jimmy and the girls slowed to a stop next to him, the soles of their footwear slapping the warm concrete.

"Oh, shit, that's just great, that's all we need," Jimmy snapped while staring at the horde of undead moving towards them like senior citizens out for a morning constitutional.

"Actually, we've been lucky to make it this long without seeing any," Mary commented idly.

Jimmy flashed her an annoyed look. "Thanks for bringing that up, Mar'. I feel a lot better now."

The shambling mockery of humanity sent up a wail that filled the air with uneasiness. Henry studied their decayed forms, seeing all walks of life mixed together. There was a policeman, a doctor and a nurse, next to a corpse in what was once a two-thousand dollar suit.

There were Mexicans, whites, and blacks, walking side by side with Asian and Korean. It was a regular United Nations of ghouls.

Sue was at the door to the bus now and her face was filled with fear and terror. Upon seeing Henry, she jumped down to the road and ran into his arms. Cindy and Jimmy shared a conspiratorial smile at the sight of the two of them. Henry hugged her for a second, then pushed her out of his arms.

"Whoa, calm down, Sue, relax, everthing'll be fine."

"But what about them?" She asked, pointing over her shoulder at the approaching crowd of death.

Henry calmly shook his head, as if he was talking to a child.

"What about them?" He asked her almost idly.

She looked confused. "What about them? Why, they're coming in here, we're trapped!"

Henry chuckled and then waved to Jimmy and the girls. "Come on, guys, let's get out of here," he said casually, like he was preparing for a road trip instead of trying to escape a town of the dead. "Everyone get back on the bus."

Jimmy nodded and moved closer to the front bumper. He raised his Remington and pointed the barrel at the first ghouls in line. They were no more than a hundred feet away and closing rapidly, despite their almost trepidatious gait.

Henry stopped him from firing, gesturing for him to get onboard.

"Forget about it, Jimmy, don't waste the ammo. We'll just drive through them and be gone, piece of cake."

Jimmy was saddened by the loss of shooting a few deaders, but he nodded, realizing Henry was right. They were low on ammunition and it would be foolhardy to waste it.

"Fine, Henry, but I get to drive," Jimmy told him as he stepped onto the first stair.

With a sigh, Henry nodded. "Fine, Jimmy, fine, just as long as we're leaving." Mary and Cindy joined him at the stairs and one at a time they climbed inside in a casual gait like they were school chaperones on a field trip. Henry was last, and with one more look at the burnt shells of the buildings of the once thriving town, he climbed inside the bus and closed the doors with a slight hissing of hydraulics.

Meanwhile, the crowd of undead had grown closer, only fifty feet now separating the first ones from the front of the bus. Realizing their prey was so close, the first few seemed to put on a burst of speed, almost jogging as their legs transported them forward. Behind them, the others followed suit, and soon the crowd was waddling forward like a fun run for the March of Dimes.

Looking out the front windshield of the bus, Henry thought all the group needed were paper numbers taped to their chests, signifying each runner.

The bus' engine turned over on the first try and smoke belched from the exhaust. Vibrations flooded the frame of the vehicle and Jimmy grinned as he let off the air brake.

"This is gonna be good," he said like a kid playing with his first firecracker.

Henry grimaced while gazing at the approaching crowd of walking corpses. Then he spun around to the others.

"All right, this ride might get rough; everyone sit down and hold on tight." He turned back to Jimmy, slapping the younger man on the back. "Go for it, Jimmy."

Jimmy nodded, sent up a loud whoop, his cry of excitement becoming contagious. Raven was still in the rear, but now she was on her knees instead of sitting on her seat, wanting to get a good view of the upcoming minutes.

Jimmy put the bus in drive and floored the pedal, the engine surging to life, the massive vehicle rolling forward. The first ghouls in line were only bumped out of the way, though one unfortunate soul was caught under the left front tire. He exploded like a water balloon, black ichor and bits of bone coating the tire like mud as the tires churned the body to mush. Others were tossed aside like paper toys, the bus slowly gaining speed with each yard it covered. Jimmy veered to the left, catching three stumbling ghouls head on, their bodies catapulting into the air to land in a tumbling heap of fractured limbs. Eyes spun in sockets and tongues hung out of slack-jawed mouths. One ghoul, the policeman, Henry saw, landed so hard his tongue was torn off from his snapping teeth. The slug like appendage twitched in the warm sunlight, seeming to almost steam on the hot pavement. Then the bus was passed, still moving forward. By the time the bus reached the last group of undead, Jimmy was going over forty miles an hour. He hit the horn in fun and rolled into the half dozen ghouls, shattering bones and breaking necks on impact. The front and rear tires were a red and black mess of bone and gore, the expelled fluids shooting out the rear tire wells like rainwater covering a road after a heavy storm.

Then they were through the crowd and Jimmy drove through the open portal, clipping one last ghoul as he sped out and into the open road once again.

"All right, that was awesome!" Jimmy yelled from the driver's seat, pumping his right arm in the air like a cheerleader. Now that he was done plowing over bodies, the ride had smoothed. Before, as body after body had been pummeled under the wide tires, it was like he had taken the bus off-roading.

Henry moved up behind him, his face still grim. "All right, hotshot, slow it down some. We don't need an accident out here. The closest tow-truck is a long ways from here."

Jimmy used the rearview mirror over his head to look at Henry, and though he was still pumped from the ride, he acknowledged the reasoning and slowed the vehicle, the engine vibrations also slowing to a more respectable droning.

Henry patted Jimmy on the top of the head like a dog. "There's a good boy."

He leaned forward to gaze out the windshield at the road ahead of them. With the exception of a years worth of weeds sprouting from every crevice in the asphalt, it looked like it always had, empty and quiet.

"You all set?" Henry asked Jimmy, making sure the younger man was through fooling around.

"Yeah, old man, I'm fine. But I do have one question. Where the hell are we going to now?"

Henry let his lips crease into a large smile while he looked down at Jimmy. "We're going down there and don't stop till we get there." He turned away then and walked back to the middle of the bus where Sue was waiting for him. Mary and Cindy had been together, talking, and now Cindy stood up, grinned at Henry and passed him on her way to Jimmy. When she reached him, she leaned over and gave him a big, wet kiss on the cheek, then sat down in the first seat on his right. The two engaged in idle conversation while Jimmy drove the bus.

Mary leaned back in her seat and closed her eyes, exhausted from everything that had happened to them. With nothing to do but rest, she was more than happy to take advantage of the lull in their normally action packed days. In the past year it seemed she had been either running from, or running to, some form of life threatening danger. Sometimes, in the middle of the night when she only had her thoughts to occupy her, she wondered how she'd managed to deal with everything that had happened to her. She heard Henry talking and she smiled to herself. He was one of the main reasons she had managed to deal. He'd become a second father to her and the two were closer than most fathers and daughters ever were. Jimmy had become the brother she had never had, and after knowing him for more than a year, never would have wanted. Cindy had become her sister, forged in their battles for survival. She'd managed because she had friends to lean on when times became rough and knew they would do anything for here, and she for them. Leaning back in her chair, she tried to get more comfortable, and with the bus slowly rocking from side to side as it drove down the lonely road, the engine droning on like a large air conditioner, she fell into a deep sleep.

Mary came awake with a start.

Something wasn't right. For one thing the engine of the bus was off and as she looked forward to the front, she saw the vehicle wasn't moving.

She was alone.

With mild concern, her hand on her new Glock, she climbed out of her seat, stretched quickly to loosen tight limbs, and moved down the aisle, her eyes scanning the side windows. The accordion door was open and when she stopped at the top step she nearly jumped out of her skin when Jimmy's grinning face popped up from the side of the open door.

"Hey there, sleepy head, we were wondering when you were gonna wake up."

"Good God, Jimmy, you scared me half to death," she scolded him. Her eyes looked over his head to an empty road. "Where are we? Why have we stopped?"

Jimmy gestured with his head by swiveling his neck to the rear of the bus. "We pulled over for a bathroom break and to stretch a little. Come on, everyone's out here." His head disappeared and she was alone again, though now she could hear the sound of voices mingling and every now and then a laugh.

Holstering her Glock, she climbed down the stairs and stepped out on the road.

Her eyes roamed over the landscape and she breathed in the fresh-smelling air. They were parked in the middle of a country road, only the thin yellow line proof that the road had once been part of the highway system. To the left of the bus were waist high weeds and a few yellow shrubs were scattered about like anemic alien creatures. Trees lined the road, as well, but they were growing more a few hundred feet away. Telephone poles lined the opposite side of the road, the defunct wires still connected, resembling a mammoth clothesline for Titans.

Her eyes shifting to the bus, she saw everyone gathered near the end of the long vehicle, seeming to be engrossed in the open compartments. The luggage hatches were all opened wide and Jimmy stood under one of them, shielding himself from the sun while he chatted with Cindy. Upon seeing her, he waved for her to come over and join them. Raven was sitting on the side of the road with a plastic bucket under her butt, idly inspecting her long fingernails. Sue was digging through bags of stuff while Henry tossed out more from inside the luggage compartments. Jimmy ripped open a box and held up an unopened bag of potato chips for her to see.

"Look, Mar', we found all this shit in the luggage holds. There's water and ammo, too."

She walked the few yards until she'd joined them and stuck her head inside the luggage compartment Henry was working in. Inside, a sweaty face gazed back at her. Henry smiled and decided it was time for a break anyway, so he climbed out, pointing to Jimmy to take over for him. Jimmy frowned, but he did as he was asked, climbing inside the hot compartment.

"Hey, Mary, how you feeling? You were sleeping so soundly, I figured we'd just let you sleep."

She scratched her head and brushed hair from her face. "Yeah, I guess I was pretty tired. What's all this?" She gestured to the piles of bags and boxes.

"Pretty great, huh? It's about time we had some luck. The cannies must have packed all this in here so they would have supplies." His face sank slightly from disgust when he gestured to a pile of burnt and dried meat on the side of the road. "Some of the stuff we didn't need.":

Her eyes followed where he was pointing and she recoiled slightly at what the pile was. It was body parts, cured and smoked like beef jerky. Bad memories of her time with the cannies flooded back and she felt weak in the knees.

Henry saw this and reached out to her. "You okay?"

She nodded. "Yeah, just a little light-headed. I'll be fine in a sec'."

Sue walked up to her and handed her a bottle of water. "Here, honey, drink this. It's hot out here and you gotta be careful you don't dehydrate."

Mary accepted the water with a slight grin for a thank you and drank a few inches of the warm liquid. If both Sue and Henry thought she was dehydrated then that was fine with her. Some thing's she needed to keep to herself and the ordeal with the cannies was one of those times, though she knew she would have to fill Henry in on the basics of what had occurred later. But some of what had happened would stay with her till the day she died, no one the wiser.

Jimmy poked his head out of the luggage compartment, wiping his forehead with the bottom of his shirt. "So what do ya think? Will you look at all this stuff we found?" He asked Mary cheerfully.

She nodded. "Yeah, Henry was just showing me. How'd you know to look in there?"

Jimmy climbed out of the compartment and moved next to her with a proud look plastered on his face. "That was me, too. When we pulled over to stretch our legs and stuff I thought I'd check inside and ta da, this is what I found."

"Oh, Jimmy, stop bragging about it. Even if you hadn't found everything, I'm sure one of us would have looked in there eventually," Cindy told him. She'd been hearing about his glorious find for almost half and hour and it was getting real old, real fast.

Jimmy flashed her an annoyed look, but other than that ignored her. "You're just jealous that I found the stuff first, that's all," he said, turning to the pile of boxes lined up in the shadow of the bus. "There's ammo for all our weapons in here along with some calibers we don't need. Talk about a stroke of good fortune."

Henry had gone back inside the compartment to resume working when Jimmy had exited and now he poked his head out again.

"Yeah, we can use the calibers we don't need for trade at the next settlement we come across. We'll live like kings for quite a while with all the rounds we've got." A few voices agreed with him and he ducked back inside, rummaging around some more. He continued working for another five minutes, lost in the simple act of physical labor. He piled items to the side and moved ones that weren't as important in the back, humming to himself while he worked.

Outside on the road, he could hear the companions talking amongst themselves and at first he didn't notice when all conversation stopped. Buried inside the luggage compartment, he barely gave it any thought, but continued working, tossing out boxes when he saw they were valueless. The cannies had packed a wide assortment of goods, some worthless to the companions. Boxes of Playboys and Penthouses were worthless to them with the exception of now being good kindling for starting a fire, though he did set one or two aside for personal use. He was a man after all and the draw of pictures of beautiful women could not be denied, but the rest was just wasted space.

While Henry worked, moving the rest of the boxes aside to check what was in the last ones stacked on the bottom of the piles, he felt himself growing thirsty.

"Hey, would someone toss me a bottle of water, please. I'm dying of thirst in here."

He waited for a reply, expecting one of Jimmy's wise-ass remarks, but when no answer came, he stopped working, curious as to why no one had answered him.

"Hello? Hey, what's going on out there?" He called again, and when he received no reply, he placed his hand on his Glock and moved to the front of the luggage compartment. Poking his head out into the sun, he stopped short when he felt the cold metal of a gun barrel pressing against his neck.

"Move one fuckin' muscle and your head's gonna paint the side of this bus red, grey hair," a man's voice said, a definite Kentucky accent hidden in the words. "Get 'em up and keep your finger off the trigger of that gun if you want to live passed the next three seconds," the voice added and nudged him out of the luggage compartment and into the light of the day.

Henry did as ordered, moving slowly, not wanting to spook whoever had him dead to rights. The Glock was ripped from his hands, and a second later he felt his panga taken from its sheath. It was then he saw that the man who had him cold was at least sixty, with what might have been laugh lines or crows feet around his eyes and mouth. He had a long beard that made him look like ZZ Top and Henry thought all the man needed was a pair of dark sunglasses to make the look complete.

Henry creased his eyes from the glare of the sun and gazed at his friends and the men who now held them hostage. There were five men, all hard looking and disheveled, with scraggly beards and about a year's worth of filth on their skin. Two of them looked to be well over sixty; the other two in their thirties, except for the fifth who was barely out of puberty.

Looking to his left, Henry saw his fellow companions were all lined up against the bus. He quickly realized, in the positions they were in, backs against the bus' side, they were lined up like they were in a firing squad. That did not bode well and he knew something would have to be done before it was too late.

One of them, a short, round man with a large wart on his nose and another smaller one on his chin, moved up next to Cindy and ran his hands over her chest. "I like this one, Jasper, I call dibbs on her," he said with a chuckle.

The man who still had the barrel of his weapon pressed against Henry's neck nodded. "Fine, she's yours then. Doesn't matter, it's not like you can get it up anymore."

The other men all chuckled, but the small man ignored it, only having eyes for Cindy. He clapped gleefully and pulled out a set of blood-stained handcuffs. Before Cindy or Jimmy could do more than protest, he slapped one end of the cuffs on her left wrist and the other to his right.

"There ya go, darlin', now you can't run away," he grinned, his parting mouth showing a toothless smile.

Jimmy squeezed his hands into fists and was about to punch the old man in the face when Henry called out to him, stopping him cold.

"No, Jimmy, wait! Don't do it!"

Jimmy stopped, the barking order penetrating his anger and he turned to look at Henry.

Henry said nothing this time; only shook his head back and forth. But his eyes bore into Jimmy and he mentally sent him a message. *Wait, the time's not right.*

Whether it was something about the way he stared at Jimmy or perhaps he somehow picked up mentally what Henry was telling him was unknown, but Jimmy did stop, his shoulders slumping as he stepped back against the bus.

It was then that Jimmy saw the third man in the posse, a wiry fellow in his late teens. The teenager stood with an old Smith & Wesson rifle in his hands, the muzzle aimed directly at Jimmy's chest. If Jimmy had gone through with striking the man with the large wart on his nose, he would have been shot down like a dog before he'd taken his second step. The teenager wore a bright red shirt with the picture of a stick of spearmint gum on the front and Henry mentally thought of him as Red.

The shotgun barrel pressed hard against Henry's neck as Jasper pushed him closer to Mary. Henry did as he was told, letting the man push him around. He noticed out of the corner of his eye that Jasper carried an old shotgun good for two shots at a time. After that he would have to crack the weapon and take out the spent cartridges to reload. That would use valuable time in a firefight if it came down to it.

The fourth man, a skinny man in his late thirties that resembled the scarecrow in the Wizard of Oz, picked up Henry's Glock and panga and added them to the small pile on the shoulder of the road. Henry could see the companion's other weapons there, also, all tossed like dried sticks waiting for the fire. The man Henry thought of as Scarecrow grinned like a pig in shit as he admired the pile of weapons. He decided to take Henry's Glock as his own.

"What are we gonna do with 'em, Jasper?" This from the round man with the wart. Henry dubbed him Wart Nose for easy identification.

"What we do with all outsiders stupid enough to come down our road."

The four men began to laugh at Jasper's words and Henry knew it wasn't good.

"What about the women? Can we have some fun with them first?" This came from Scarecrow.

"That'd be great. It's been a while since we had some fun," this came from the last man. He looked young, maybe in his early thirties, and wore army BDU's similar to what the companions were wearing. Henry decided to call this last man G.I. Joe. The man wore a beard, but it was clipped short, as was the dark black hair on his small head. A set of dog tags hung from his neck and Henry guessed he'd once been in the military. Whether he'd deserted or had just left when things began to fall apart beyond repair was irrelevant. As long as he pointed the M-16 he had taken from Cindy at Henry and the others, he was an enemy.

"I got dibs on the one with black hair," Red said with a leer as he eyed Raven. So far the girl had done nothing, merely stood silently against the bus. Sue was frightened to the point she was shaking. She had known coldhearts like these men before and had heard of convoys being attacked. She knew this encounter wouldn't end well for her or her new friends.

"Fine, fine," Jasper snorted, "but I get the brunette. I likes 'em with brown hair." He licked his lips as he eyed Mary, and Henry saw Mary flex her wrists and squeeze her hands into tight balls, the anger inside the woman growing with each passing second.

"All right, boys, let's get rid of this excess baggage and then we can have some fun with the sluts," Jasper yelled loudly. He swung the shotgun barrel away from Henry and stepped away three feet so he wouldn't get hit with most of the blowback from when he shot Henry in the face. "Kill them, now!"

Henry knew it was now or never.

Jasper had made the fatal mistake of not moving far enough out of arms reach of Henry and the deadlands warrior used the man's mistake to his advantage. Before Jasper could react, Henry dropped and wheeled, going under the barrel of the shotgun. Jasper reacted quicker then he expected, but Henry was already under the barrel. He used his forearm to drive the barrel upwards just as Jasper fired off a burst. The steel pellets peppered a window on the bus over Henry's head and small shards of safety glass rained down on his head.

Henry never stopped moving, and when he forced the weapon upward, he saw Jasper had a small hunting knife strapped to his belt. Henry reached out with his free hand and ripped the blade from its sheath. In one fluid motion, he flipped the blade over in his hand and jammed the tip of the knife into Jasper's crotch, the blade sliding in three inches until it stopped at the pelvic bone. The old man screamed in pain, and when Henry twisted the blade to the right, his screams became higher. His face went slack and he fell over to the pavement, his mouth hanging open as he tried to gasp through the utter agony he felt in his groin.

When Jasper fell to the ground, Henry reached out and grabbed the barrel of the shotgun, the warm metal burning his palm. He ignored it, knowing to hesitate was to die. Jimmy was about to get a brand new hole in his chest, the teenager, Red, about to fire the revolver in his hand.

Red was only three feet from Henry and the shotgun was pointing the wrong way. Jumping at the teenager, Henry slammed the butt of the shotgun into the teen's face, shattering teeth and breaking his jaw. Red dropped the revolver and yelped in pain, his hands reaching up to his shattered face. Henry didn't let the teen suffer long. Spinning the shotgun in his hand like a baton in a parade, Henry jammed the muzzle of the shotgun into Red's bloody mouth and squeezed the trigger on the confiscated weapon.

The back of Red's head blew apart to send gray matter and skull across the pavement, his brains riding on a chunk of skull to skitter across the ground like a blue plate special would slide across the counter by a waitress at a local diner.

The brains steamed on the hot asphalt, cooking in the sun and Red swayed for a moment, like a willow tree in a gentle breeze, then tumbled to the earth to remain still.

Raven wasn't one to sit still while her life was in danger, and she lunged at Scarecrow, her right hand flat like a karate chop. Her razor-honed fingernails sliced across Scarecrow's throat, severing the man's jugular in one swipe. Blood squirted from the mortal wound, and the man moved back and forth in panic, resembling a lawn sprinkler, his blood spewing about him to rain onto the ground. He dropped Henry's Glock and began making weird, gargling noises as he tried to breathe. He sounded like a dog trying to swallow a chicken bone, his face becoming white as blood seeped from the wound, unable to reach his brain, and a red froth seeped from the corner of his mouth to drip down his chin. His eyes rolled up into the back of his head and he fell over, his head striking the ground with a meaty thwack. He didn't notice, though, he was already dead.

Jimmy had hesitated for barely ten seconds, the shock of seeing the tables turned on his captors so completely slowing his reflexes, but he knew he needed to move quickly and finish off the rest of the men before one of them got off a lucky shot and ended up killing one of the companions.

To his right stood Cindy, fighting with Wart Nose and the man tried to control the she-devil he now found himself handcuffed to. Cindy was trying to punch the small man in the face and head with her free hand, but she couldn't get enough momentum to hurt him. Wart Nose laughed and slapped her across the face, Cindy reeling from the blow.

Jimmy charged the man, his head held low as he knocked him over, both of them tumbling to the road. Cindy was pulled down with them, and the three of them rolled around, each trying to get in as many punches as they could. But Wart Nose was over matched, and in less than a minute, was lying on the road with a bloody nose and a dazed expression on his face. Jimmy would have shot the man then, but there was no weapon nearby, the man's gun having fallen out of reach. Deciding to stay put, he continued to sit on the small man, his knees pinning his arms while Cindy held Wart Nose's legs down with her handcuffed arm stretched at an odd angle.

While Henry and Jimmy were attacking their adversaries, Mary went into action. Her nerves had been taut and she knew Henry wouldn't merely let them die. So when Henry attacked Jasper, she moved, dropping low and charging G.I. Joe.

The man wasn't ready for her. He was still staring at the sight of Red's head disappearing in a pink mist, and before he could do anything to protect himself, Mary barreled into him, the two tumbling to the ground. Mary was unlucky enough to land wrong and her left shoulder sent waves of pain through her body, causing her to gasp out in agony. Taking the advantage, G.I. Joe rolled on top of her.

G.I. Joe was the first to react and he reached out and wrapped his hands around her throat, beginning to squeeze the life from her. Mary choked as the oxygen was cut off from her brain and her face began to take on a bluish tint, and though Henry had taught her many ways to fight in hand to hand combat, at the moment she panicked. G.I. Joe's eyes went wide and he grinned down at her as he increased the pressure. While struggling to breathe, she felt the distinct pressure of the man's penis which had grown hard while he squeezed the life from her. She had no way of knowing the man had been into torture porn his entire life and killing her was one of the best turn-ons he'd ever experienced.

Mary's vision began to become cloudy and she realized she was about to pass out. Just before she lost consciousness, the pressure on her neck suddenly was gone and G.I. Joe fell onto her, his weight crushing her chest. She sucked in a ragged breath, sounding like a terminal lung cancer patient after a lifetime of smoking cigarettes.

Blinking the tears from her eyes, she looked past G.I. Joe's head to see Sue standing over her. In her shaking hands she was holding the head-sized rock she had used as a bludgeon. There was a small spot of blood on the bottom of the rock. Sue tossed the stone aside and grabbed the dead weight of G.I. Joe, Mary also pushing the body away from her. The man rolled onto the ground, landing on his side, and Mary sat up, breathing easier now that her chest was free of burdens. There was a red ring around her neck where the man had tried to strangle her and she massaged it gently, wincing at the rawness of the skin. Looking down on the dead man, she could see there was a large crack in G.I. Joe's head. Pink brain matter was seeping out like pudding squeezed from a plastic bag and the front of his pants was still pushed out; the man taking his hard-on into the afterlife.

"Thanks, Sue, thanks a lot," she said in a hoarse whisper.

Sue smiled slightly. "Glad to help." She reached a hand out. "Here, let me help you up."

Mary took the proffered hand, and on unsteady legs gazed around her to see if the danger was over, their adversaries slain.

Henry was standing over Jasper, going through the raider's pockets. After less than a minute, Henry stood up with two new shotgun shells in his hand. Cracking the shotgun, he took out the expended shells and popped the new ones into the chamber, then closed the breach.

Jasper was curled up in a fetal position, his hand holding the handle of the knife still stuck in his groin. He whimpered softly, tears running down his cheeks.

After snapping the shotgun closed, Henry kicked the prone man in the side, eliciting another whimper from Jasper. Using his foot, he made Jasper roll onto his back. Henry raised one foot and brought it down so he was now straddling him. Jasper's filthy face was awash with pain, but Henry ignored it.

"So, you were gonna kill most of us and then take and rape our women, is that right?"

Jasper shook his head back and forth, denying everything, and pleading for his life. Henry ignored the man's words. He turned his head to look at each of the companions. Mary was standing with Sue. Jimmy and Cindy still had Wart Nose pinned down and Raven was in the process of cleaning blood from her fingernails, casually leaning against the bus like she was with a tour group that was just taking a quick break at a rest stop.

Henry turned away from them and gazed back to Jasper.

"You know, I've seen a lot of cruel shit since everything fell apart, but you, my friend, are one of the sleaziest. If you had asked us for some food, we would have given it to you. Hell, we could've even given you a ride if you'd wanted it, but instead you attack us and then try to slaughter us just because you could." Henry leaned forward slightly, his eyes staring at Jasper. "Well, you got anything to say? An apology, maybe?"

Jasper whimpered some more, but said nothing, his eyes now showing defiance despite the pain he was in.

Henry sighed. "If I was somehow stupid enough to let you go, you'd only gather some more men like yourself and then just start doing what you do all over again. Am I right?"

Jasper shook his head no, mumbling about how he wouldn't. How he'd go straight.

"Bullshit. That's bullshit and you know it. Hell, you'd kill me right now if I gave you the chance. Lucky for me and my friends, you and your idiots aren't as good as we are in combat. If you were, it would be me on the ground right now instead of you." Henry yelled his next words. "Am I right?"

Jasper turned his head slightly, wincing at the anger in Henry's voice. He gazed into Henry's eyes but saw no compassion there, no mercy. Any chance of mercy had been forfeited when he'd given the order to slaughter the companions.

Henry looked up, across the road to the trees beyond and seemed to be thinking, pondering something that weighed heavy on his soul. For almost a full minute his brow was furrowed and he seemed to struggle with a decision.

Then he nodded to himself, and looked back down at Jasper.

"Eat it," he spit, jamming the muzzle of the shotgun into Jasper's mouth. Jasper screamed in terror, two of his front teeth cracking off from the steel shoved into his mouth and he began to squirm under Henry, his legs kicking up and down with impotence.

"Henry, no! Don't do...! Mary yelled, but her words were drowned out when Henry switched the shotgun to fire both barrels simultaneously. He squeezed the trigger and both barrels of the shotgun discharged directly into Jasper's mouth.

The back of Jasper's head disintegrated like an egg being dropped from a ten-story building. It was like some kind of sick magic trick. One moment it was there, and then...poof, it was gone; nothing but a red mist remaining to spread out on the road.

The shotgun muzzle was still in the man's mouth, though there was nothing behind it, and Henry slipped it free. That had been the last ammo for the weapon and now it was useless. He tossed it to the side of the road and stepped over Jasper's twitching corpse.

No one spoke, all stunned by the brutality Henry had shown them, but despite this, each knew he had done what had to be done. In the new world, justice was dispensed at the end of a firearm, and there would be no appeal.

Henry picked up his Glock and holstered it, then walked to their pile of weapons, retrieved and shouldered his Steyr and picked up his panga, sliding back home in its sheath.

He waved Sue over to him, and when she was by his side, he told her to gather the rest of their weapons and pass them back out to the others. Then he walked over to Jimmy and Cindy.

"Get off him, Jimmy," he said coldly.

Jimmy nodded. "What are you gonna do? You gonna do the same to this fucker?"

Henry didn't answer. Wart Nose looked up at Henry's face and grinned widely.

Cindy was to his side, their arms still attached by the handcuffs, both of their wrists lying on the road.

"What are you gonna do, huh? If you kill me, too, then you gotta drag my body with you as there ain't no key for the cuffs here with me. I got the key back at the camp." He chuckled slightly, secure in his cleverness. "I got you, buddy, I got you good."

Henry said nothing, but as Wart Nose watched, the right side of Henry's lips curled into a snarl. While the small man had been taunting Henry, the warrior had pulled the panga from its sheath and now held it in his hand, and before Wart Nose realized what was going to happen, Henry raised the sixteen inches of razor-honed steel into the air, and slammed the blade down hard onto the prone man's wrist, severing the limb from the body like he'd sliced through a bar of soap.

For one split second there was utter silence. No one spoke and Cindy's jaw went slack as she gazed down at the separated hand.

Then Wart Nose screamed, his wails of pain rendering the air like a siren. Blood shot from the stump and he climbed to his feet, his free hand wrapped around the pumping wound, trying to hold back the blood. His eyes were as wide as they could go and dark blue veins covered his forehead as he shrieked in utter shock.

Pulling his Glock, Henry pointed it at the man.

"I suggest you get a tourniquet on that quickly or you're gonna bleed out. Now get the hell out of here or I'll shoot you dead right here."

Wart Nose stared at Henry, his face filled with both shock from his amputation and relief he wasn't going to die right there on the road. Blood squirted from the jagged stump with each beat of his heart. Henry took a step towards the man and Wart Nose jumped back, realizing he was about a second away from death. With his seeping stump cradled against his chest, only his other hand keeping the blood from spilling out and killing him, the small, round man backed away into the shrubs and disappeared from sight. His stumbling footsteps could be heard as he crashed through the brush until that, too, eventually faded away.

Jimmy walked over to Henry with Cindy in his arms. She'd kicked the severed hand away from her and now stood with the free cuff dangling impotently by her side.

"Why didn't you kill him, too?" Jimmy asked.

Henry shrugged. "I don't know. Truth is, unless he gets real lucky he's either gonna die from blood loss or get an infection from that wound even if he manages to cauterize it. Either way, with one hand I think he'll be harmless. It was Jasper there that was the ringleader. Without him the lowlifes usually slink back into the woodwork.

"Yeah, until another ringleader pops up to take control again," Mary added while she moved closer. She was carrying Cindy's M-16 and she handed it to the blonde woman who took it with a silent thanks.

"That's how the world works, Mary, whether now or before. There's always another asshole waiting to take over when one goes down," Henry said and gazed around the road, seeing all the bodies of the raiders.

"Let's get moving and pack this stuff up. With all that shooting there's bound to be a few deaders around here. I'm surprised we've been let alone for as long as we have been." Henry also knew a lot of that had to do with the isolated country road they'd chosen to park on, but the undead were never too far out of reach.

Everyone got to work, packing the food and water back into the bus. But instead of placing it back into the luggage compartment, they carried it into the passenger compartment, placing it on the empty seats in the back. Henry wanted everything of value close to them, just in case something happened.

Any extra weapons worth keeping were salvaged, though a few were beyond hope, even from a master weaponsmith's point of view. The Smith & Wesson revolver was so dirty and the barrel clogged with debris, Henry wondered if the gun would have fired at all, but instead merely blown up in the shooter's hand.

The two barrel shotgun was taken, Jasper not needing it anymore and it was tossed into the luggage compartment with the rest of the items that could be used for trade. Perhaps at the next settlement they came across. With only two shots at a time, it wouldn't be a weapon any of the companions would want to use. Many times it had only been the amount of lead they could send at their enemies that had allowed them to survive for as long as they had.

When the last box was placed on the bus and everyone had gathered inside, Henry dropped down into the driver's seat. With a brief glance at his friends, he started the bus and drove off; leaving the dead bodies of the raider's to rot in the sun.

When the bus had disappeared over the crest of the road and the scenery returned to normal, three ghouls stepped out of the brush. They had been a half mile away and had been attracted by the sound of gunfire. Stepping onto the road, they gazed down at the five dead bodies of the raiders. The bodies were still warm, the hot sun only helping to keep them that way.

Without hesitation, the ghouls moved across the road and knelt down, each ripping a piece of flesh from the body of its choice.

With a few birds chattering in the trees, and flies festering on the bodies, the zombies dug in, a smorgasbord of flesh, just waiting for them to sample.

CHAPTER TWENTY-FIVE

THE BUS ROLLED across the deserted road, bumping and bouncing over the cracked asphalt while the wind whipped through the shattered windows, blowing everyone's hair about their heads.

The day was over and the darkness surrounding the lone vehicle was almost complete. Inside the passenger compartment, all the companions were sleeping. After eating from their newfound stores of food and water, they each found themselves unable to stay awake, and one at a time had drifted off into a restless slumber.

Jimmy was in the driver's seat again, having switched with Henry more than two hours ago. He was restless as he drove and he knew with the darkness almost complete, he should pull over and park the bus for the night. But truth be told, he didn't want to stop. They were making good time and he wanted to cover at least another twenty miles or so before he finally stopped for the night. It didn't seem to matter to Jimmy that he didn't really have a destination; he just wanted to get there fast, wherever that might be.

Outside, in the falling shadows, shells of old homes and structures of unknown identities loomed empty and unwelcoming.

Jimmy frowned as he passed the next batch of buildings. There had to be somewhere nearby where he could park the bus in relative safety, but so far nothing had shown itself.

Still in the back roads, Jimmy had seen very few of the undead. Most would turn at the sound of the bus and Jimmy would easily drive around them. Henry had scolded him for trying to run over every deader he spotted, telling him to just go around them. Only if there was no choice was Jimmy to plow them over.

Slowing at a fork in the road, the bus' headlights illuminated a four car pile up in front of him. He swung the bus to the right, toward the only open route available.

Perhaps he should have woken Henry or one of the others and asked their suggestion on what to do next, but Jimmy had always prided himself on making his own decisions. So, swinging the bus around the tight corner, the bus' bumper only inches away from the first wrecked car, he turned down the new road, revving the engine as he shot forward, free and clear.

When the bus had leveled out and was headed down the road, Jimmy was unable to see the flattened street sign lying on the dusty, weed covered, shoulder. It had once stood tall on steel posts, but had been knocked over during the riots that had taken place after the first zombie outbreak.

Perhaps if Jimmy had seen the sign, he might have stopped the bus and woken Henry up to ask him what he should do, but he didn't, and so he continued on into the night, only the headlights of the bus cutting through the inky blackness.

For the sign had read: Lexington, 22 mi. Interstate 75.

And if Jimmy had known this he could have told Sue, who would have told him that Lexington was the second largest city in Kentucky. That would have made Henry immediately make Jimmy turn the bus around for it had been established almost a year ago the need to stay away from the big cities of America.

But Jimmy didn't know any of this and he leaned back in the driver's seat, humming a song to himself, smiling. All the while not realizing he was driving straight to a city with over 270,000 walking corpses just waiting for him to get there.

Henry was dreaming about his wife, Emily. But not just about her. Gwen was there, too. Though the two women had never met each other being two entirely different parts of his life, the two women were now standing side by side, arguing over who would get Henry.

Henry tried to talk to them, but every time he tried to get a word in, they would both turn and tell him to be quiet. Cowed like a five-year-old being disciplined, he stood silently, while the two women continued arguing his fate.

Suddenly, his world began to shake and he found himself struggling to stand up. Out of nowhere a large hole opened up in the ground, and before he could do anything but shout a warning, both Gwen and Emily were swallowed whole, their cries for help falling away to be lost.

Then he heard them again, and with hope in his heart, crawled to the edge of the deep pit. There were Emily and Gwen, each on opposite sides of the hole, hanging on to a jagged edge. Both were calling for help, and Henry realized in an instant he couldn't save them both.

He could only choose one life.

But who would live and who would fall to their death?

Henry became frozen, not able to decide who to save. The women pleaded for him, each reaching out with one free hand to coax him forward. "Save me, I'm the one you love," they screamed.

But the world was still shaking and Henry found himself falling to the ground. Before he could do anything about the lost women another hole opened up near him and as the earth began to crumble away; he starting sliding into the widening hole which now appeared to resemble a giant mouth.

He cried out once, his hands reaching for purchase, but there was none. A large rock was sliding toward him and before he could move, it crashed into his chest, sending him spiraling into the massive orifice. He managed one yelp of terror and then felt himself go weightless as he began to tumble into an abyss that seemed to have no bottom. While he fell he looked up above him and with the wind whistling around his head he watched as the mouth closed, large blackened teeth slamming shut like a monster trap.

Then another jolt tossed him in his seat and he bumped his head against the window frame he'd been leaning against, causing him to snap his eyes open and growl in pain.

"What the hell?" He asked as he looked around the darkness. Behind him and to his side he could hear the others complaining. Sitting up and trying to clear his vision from sleep, he realized the bus was at an odd angle, the front end leaning forward like it had tried to drive over a five foot hill and the middle of the undercarriage had become caught on the ridge.

The engine was revving and the vibration filled the entire vehicle, but he didn't get the feeling they were actually moving. Wiping the corner of his mouth clear of drool, he shook the last vestiges of his dream away and stood up, then dropped back down when the uneven floor caused him to lose his balance.

"Jimmy? Where in the hell are you?" He called out.

"I'm up here, Henry. And I think we've got a problem."

"No shit," Henry mumbled and crawled out of his seat again to try to stand on the uneven floor, this time making sure to get a good grip on the seat in front of him.

"Henry, what's going on? Where are we, what's wrong?" Mary asked from nearby.

"I don't know yet. Just stay with everyone else and I'll see what's happened," he told her and then proceeded to make his way down the center aisle. His bladder was full and the pressure was uncomfortable, but there were more important things to worry about at the moment.

Upon reaching the front of the bus, he gazed down at Jimmy and then at the road in front of them. Or what was left of the road.

There appeared to have been an earth shift or flooding in the recent past. With no work crews on the roads to fix the highways and thoroughfares anymore, whatever damage a road sustained was there for good.

Which is what had happened to the two-lane road the bus was presently on. There were large cracks in the asphalt, bisecting the road like jagged scars and thick growths of kudzu and weeds seeped up to swallow the pavement whole. A thin layer of moss was growing in some places and in another year the asphalt would be completely hidden. There were abandoned vehicles here and there, mostly on the shoulders, as if the drivers had known to pull over to let others pass when the world had crumbled.

But that wasn't the real problem.

The real problem was the bus had driven over a sinkhole and the asphalt had collapsed under the weight of the bus, sinking the front end into the deep ravine. The rear wheels of the bus were three feet in the air and spun impotently while Jimmy continued to step on the gas, trying desperately to escape.

Less than two miles in the distance, the dark outline of the buildings of Lexington could be seen against the lighter night sky, like abstract art for a post modern America.

"Jesus, Jimmy, what have you gotten us into?" Henry asked as he stared at the fractured road.

"It's not my fault. I was just driving and then the damn road fell apart. How the hell am I supposed to stop that?"

With a deep frown, Henry realized his friend was right. "Where the hell are we? Do you even know?"

Jimmy shook his head no. "No, man, there haven't been any signs. I had to take a detour two hours ago when the way was blocked by cars, but other than that, it's been smooth sailing."

"Well, turn off the damn engine at least; you'll alert anything in the area for miles around that we're here with all the racket the motor's making."

Jimmy did as instructed, turning the engine off. The instant the engine stopped, it seemed the silence descended like a torrential rain shower, seeming to envelop the companions like a blanket. With nothing but moonlight filtering through the shattered windows, everyone's faces took on a pallid, anemic look.

With the interior lights of the bus now off it took a few seconds for Henry to gain his night vision, but once he did, he gazed out into the surrounding darkness. Shadows were everywhere, the road lined with tall trees on both sides. Birches and maples acted like a massive fence, helping to reduce sound to the outlying farms that could just be seen through the thick tree trunks. Henry couldn't help but let his eyes wander back to the outlines of the tall buildings in the distance. He grimaced heavily as he stared at the sharp lines and square frames.

"Good God, Jimmy, you drove us right to a city. Do you know what that means?"

Jimmy did and his mouth opened and closed frantically as he tried to think of a reply that wouldn't have Henry yelling at him. But he knew there was none. He had inadvertently carried them within walking distance of a city and that could only mean one thing.

Zombies; and a hell of a lot of them.

Henry stood tall and spun around to face the darker shapes of the others, all still in their seats.

"Wonder Boy here managed to drive us right to the edge of a city. We're in deep trouble, guys," he said calmly, but under the calm the tension was clearly heard by all.

"Which city is it," Henry? It could be a half dozen," Sue asked out of the dark.

Henry shook his head. "It doesn't matter what the name of the place is, Sue, they're all the damn same. Filled with more deaders than we could ever fight. We need to get this bus pulled free and get the hell out of here before we're surrounded. I'd guess we have a half hour, maybe less before it'll be too late to do anything more than run."

"But what about all the supplies we found? Christ, Henry, we finally have a good load of stuff and now we'll have to leave almost all of it behind, that sucks," Cindy said from the shadows next to Sue.

"Hey, don't blame me; blame your boyfriend up here who isn't smart enough to stop for the night. Thanks to him, we might all be dead by morning." He turned to glare at Jimmy and the younger man frowned.

"God, Henry, thanks for the support. I didn't do it on purpose, I swear!"

Mary climbed from her seat and moved up next to Henry. She leaned forward and gazed out the windshield, holding herself up by holding onto the headrests of the seats lining the aisle.

"Look, it doesn't matter whose fault it is. What matters is that we're in trouble. Now, we can stand around poking blame or we can get to work." Mary finished her sentence by staring at Henry and Jimmy.

"You're right, Mary, I know that. Okay, enough about how we got here. Let's see about getting us free and away," Henry said and turned around to look at Jimmy again. "You," he ordered, "go outside and see how bad it is. Keep the parking lights on, but not the headlights. They'll only illuminate us like a spotlight to anything in the area."

Jimmy nodded, eager to please, hit the door release and jumped down, his Remington in his hand just in case there was something waiting for him in the moonlit shadows.

"Okay," Henry said, "let's figure out how in the hell we're gonna get free if Jimmy does come back with good news."

The companions all gathered together in a rough circle in the middle aisle and began to discuss how to free themselves, while outside in the deep night, Jimmy began to inspect their predicament and the damage to the bus.

Jimmy stopped at the bottom step on the stairs and waited, that primordial fear of the night all humans have inside them overcoming him. When it passed, he looked around himself, straining to peer into the shadows. The moonlight overhead was slight, but it was enough to make out dim shapes, and as he looked down at the dark pit the front of the bus had sunk into, his heart sank.

They were really screwed.

Jumping across the five foot divide that separated the stairs from the lip of the sinkhole, he landed hard and off-balance, rolling onto his side and coming up in a crouch.

He turned around and looked behind. All was dark, but the voices of Henry and the others could be heard floating through the broken windows. The moonlight reflected off the jagged dents on the side of the bus and he frowned, knowing he had done those, too, when he'd backed out of the loading dock of the hospital. Well, he would never get any medals for driving, that was for sure.

Sweeping the Remington back and forth in front of him, he studied the road and surrounding landscape. With the exception of a few night birds calling in the nearby trees, all was silent. Walking to the rear of the upended bus, he shook his head at what he saw. The entire rear portion of the vehicle was stuck in the air. Moving close to one of the large tires, he slapped it with his fist, the flexible rubber like a trampoline, his hand rebounding.

Backing up a few yards, he tried to get the big picture, to see if there was any way he and the others could somehow get the bus free of the sinkhole he'd driven into. Maybe they could use rope or push it free. But as his eyes scanned the entirety of the situation he knew it would be impossible without a crane, or a very large tow truck, like the ones he saw towing transit buses in his hometown.

"Well, Jimmy, how's it looking?" Henry called from one of the shattered windows. His face was just another dark shape among count-less others.

Though Jimmy hated to admit it, he knew he might as well just fess up, as there was no way to get around it.

"We're fucked, that's how it's looking. The entire front end is in the sinkhole and the back is sticking up in the air like a friggin' Piñata. You know that already, too, you can feel how it is inside there, right?"

"Yeah, I figured as much. That's why I didn't come out with you. What was the point? Well, Jimmy, it looks like we're walking from here on in, so come back inside and help us load up the supplies. We're gonna try and take as much with us as we can."

Jimmy nodded, understanding. They would be loaded up with the supplies, but a lot will have to be left behind. It would do no good to be weighed down with so much that if trouble appeared, they wouldn't be able to move fast enough to react. Carrying too much could be just as dangerous as carrying too little. You had to be able to move fast if needed, not be bogged down by gear that would probably be useless in a firefight. If they were trying to outrun a crowd of ghouls, the lighter the better, as the zombies would never stop until they were either destroyed or left so far behind they couldn't pick up the trail of their prey.

Henry's shadowed face disappeared back into the bus, followed by more raised voices as Mary, Sue, Cindy, and even Raven, gave their opinions on their new situation. With the sounds of their conversation, Jimmy began walking back to the open door. He had to be careful, though. His footing was uneven. The weeds were like ropes, crawling around the road, reaching out to entangle him in their spindly growths. Plus, the pavement was uneven; multiple places more than suitable for him to stub his toe or trip, like when tree roots grow too big on the sidewalk, pushing the cement upward like an underground monster is trying to break free from its subterranean prison.

When he was halfway there, he heard a scraping sound coming from his right, just along the tree line. At first he didn't give it that much credence, assuming it was just a bird or an animal. Besides, everyone inside the bus was making quite a racket while they discussed what had happened to them and what would be happening next. Jimmy heard his own name mentioned more than once and cringed inwardly.

Boy, he'd really screwed up this time. They'd been all set, with a working vehicle and a good supply of food and weapons and what did he do? He had to crash the bus into a sinkhole. And if that wasn't bad enough, he had inadvertently driven far too close to the city limits of a large metropolitan area for comfort.

More scraping sounded from his right and this time he gave it the credence it deserved. Stopping, he whipped around; the shotgun leveled, and stood perfectly still, his eyes now studying the area he thought the sound had come from. He held his breath, and when Henry raised his voice inside the bus, he wanted to yell out for him to shut up, but knew he needed to remain silent and motionless.

Suddenly, the trees parted and a low shape emerged, seeming to materialize out of thin air. Jimmy didn't move, his eyes trying to piece together what he was seeing. As the shape moved closer to him, the parking lights helped illuminate the shadowy form and Jimmy let out a small sigh when he realized it was only a dog. The dog stopped below the rear bumper, its head looking up at the elevated wheels. It was a poor specimen, with its ribs showing through its fur and one ear ripped from a past fight.

The animal's eyes seemed to stare into Jimmy, mocking him, and Jimmy could imagine if the animal could talk what it would say. The dog canted his head to the side and seemed to be saying: Well you really screwed this up, didn't you, Jimmy.

Annoyed, Jimmy felt his anger growing inside him. Some for the dog who told him what he already knew and the rest for himself, frustrated with his screw-up for himself and his friends.

Jimmy slapped his foot on the ground and made a shooing noise with his lips. "Go on, get outta here, ya mangy mutt," he whispered in a stern voice. "I don't need your opinion."

The dog stared at Jimmy, who repeated the shooing noise again. Then it lowered its head, not perturbed in the slightest. Jimmy was about to slap his hands together, hoping to scare the dog away once and for all, when the animal seemed to gaze passed Jimmy. Suddenly, it raised its hackles, then took off, spinning around quickly and running down the road. Its nails clicked on the asphalt for a half-second and then the sound was gone, swallowed by the night.

Jimmy chuckled to himself, a little embarrassed. Being spooked by a dog, he should know better. At least Henry or the others hadn't seen him. They would have only used the incident to heap more abuse on him, especially Mary who was always looking for a reason to tease him like an older sibling was wont to do.

Deciding he should get back inside the bus and see what the others had planned, he turned back around to cross the few remaining feet that would bring him to the edge of the sinkhole and the stairs leading inside the bus.

There was a cool breeze blowing passed his face and he relished the sensation.

Spinning on his heels, he was taken aback to find the road in front of him was not deserted anymore. In fact, it was quite crowded.

Not believing his eyes, Jimmy paused for one brief instant, too surprised at what had transpired while he'd been occupied with the dog.

While he'd been looking to the rear of the bus, more than a dozen ghouls had come out of the surrounding brush, with none of them making the slightest sound. With the breeze blowing away from him, Jimmy never detected the stench of decay and death that preceded zombies wherever they congregated.

One of the first ghouls in line, a shaggy blonde-haired woman with a missing right cheek, pale flesh and sunken eyes, had managed to get within a foot of him, and just as Jimmy spun around to try and raise the Remington in his defense, he already knew it was going to be to late to avoid the blackened, diseased ridden, rotting teeth already leaning over to sink themselves into his left arm.

CHAPTER TWENTY-SIX

WITH A YELL on his lips, Jimmy gazed at the descending jaws, his nerves already preparing to feel the bitter bite of death.

So it took him completely by surprised when the forehead of the woman sprouted a black hole and her head snapped backward like she'd been kicked under the chin.

Jimmy's face swiveled to the side, back towards the bus and his eyes went wide when he saw Mary standing on the stairs, her newly acquired Glock in her hands. Even in the darkness surrounding them, Jimmy could see the slim wisp of smoke swirling around the muzzle of the gun.

"So, are you going to stand there all day or are you gonna get in here?" Mary asked almost casually. Before Jimmy could answer, she swiveled to her left and shot two more approaching ghouls, both head shots. She felt pride as each body dropped to the ground. When she'd first found herself in a world of the undead, she had barely known how to hold a gun, let alone fire it. Now she could drop a body from twenty yards, sometimes better depending on wind and sun conditions.

Jimmy took her words to heart and charged across the remaining space separating him from the edge of the sinkhole, lunging for the stairs when his foot was about to go into the hole. Mary fired round after round, dropping zombies whenever one moved too close to Jimmy.

Jimmy caught movement on the edge of the approaching crowd and saw other shapes appearing. There were a lot more out there and they were now converging on the bus.

Reaching the stairs, Jimmy pulled himself inside, and Mary fired one last time, another head falling away with pieces of scalp missing and brain spilling to the ground. Stepping up the stairs, she pushed the door shut just as the first ghouls slammed against the glass. They fell into the sinkhole first and then their arms reached up to slap the door; rotting teeth grated against the tinted glass, incisors separating from rotten gums to stick to the door, then slide downward like pale-yellow snails. Split, brown and black lips still sucked against the glass and Mary found her stomach spasming inside her. Every now and then one particular disgusting sight could be too much for her to take.

Inside the bus, the companions were moving about, lining up at the open windows to begin shooting the ghouls as they made their way to the sides. Fingers slapped against the sides of the vehicle, fingernails peeling off fingers as the appendages scraped across the fiberglass and metal. The sound of a hundred chalkboards being scraped filled the interior of the bus, only to stop suddenly.

With fingernails bent and broken, the noise was impossible to make anymore. Now the moaning began; the song of the dead filling the passenger compartment, the horrible song enough to drive even the hardiest souls mad. Henry fired again and again from the small, driver's front window, the Glock barking in his hand. When the clip went dry, he reached for the Steyr, firing repeatedly until he had to reload. He thanked himself internally for having the foresight to keep the supplies inside the bus. At least they had all the ammunition they could need. But as he fired again and again at the oncoming bodies, he realized there were far too many to shoot, even if the companions had an inexhaustible supply of bullets.

Like a heard of cattle being moved to market, the undead flowed out of the shrubs and trees lining the road, surrounding the bus on all sides. Cindy had taken the left side, opening one of the passenger windows not already broken. She fired round after round with her M-16 at the shapes surrounding them, careful to use single fire to conserve ammo.

"Jimmy, put on those damn headlights! We need all the light we can get!"

"But what about them knowing we're here with the lights on?"

"It's a little late for that, don't you think?" Henry snapped back and then returned firing. With each fallen body, the next zombie would climb on top of its vanquished brethren, and they were slowly making steps of dead meat that was bringing them closer to the windows. Henry jumped back for an instant when a rotting head filled with maggots and missing one eye popped into the window, mouth open and closing as it dreamed of sinking its chompers into Henry's flesh.

Henry jammed the muzzle of the Steyr into the ghoul's mouth and fired, sending the back of its head riding on a spume of blood and gore. It fell away from the window to be swallowed by the crowd below, but now there was another step leading to the bus' vulnerable windows.

Multiple hands were banging on the door, and Jimmy was the first to see the hairline cracks appearing on the glass. As for the ghouls, they never ceased their pounding, even when fragile wrists and fingers snapped apart and fell to the ground. They just continued pounding with the ends of their arms, the fractured bones now protruding. The sounds of sticks on glass filled the bus and the door was covered in black and brown gore from blood that had long stopped pumping through withered hearts and veins.

"Shit," Jimmy mumbled. "Hey, Henry, they're getting through the door!" He yelled over the noise. Between the cacophony of guns firing and the moans of the undead, it was impossible to be heard inside the passenger compartment.

"Well, just hold them off for now," Henry shot back, too occupied with his own window to worry about the door. If he stopped firing for more than a few seconds, they would be inside the bus in moments. Next to him, Sue was whacking any heads that appeared with a steel frying pan she'd found in one of the boxes of supplies. The metal twang of each blow was similar to music and Henry found himself trying to piece the gongs to a song he'd heard once.

Raven had found herself a long knife, a machete, the blade the same one Mary had used inside the hospital, and she was near the rear of the bus, slashing at anything that showed itself. Body parts went flying and the window she was defending was bathed in blood, the effusive liquid flowing over the sill to pool on the floor, resembling a dark syrup.

"We can't keep this up, Henry!" Mary called as she fired round after round at attackers. She cycled dry, popped out the spent clip and slapped in a new one like a pro. Chambering the first round, she continued firing, almost every shot a kill shot.

But still they came, pouring from the nearby city to surround the bus in a sea of the dead. The bodies were more than twenty thick on both sides of the bus and Henry realized they were truly screwed.

There was just no way to destroy that many bodies, unless he had high explosives at his disposal. And even then, the resulting blast would probably take out the occupants inside right along with it.

The bus' door bent inward under the onslaught of bodies and Jimmy began firing at the first ghouls in line. One at a time they dropped to the stairs, only to be pulled out of the hole so others could fit.

One ghoul, faster than the others, scampered over the fallen bodies and charged up the stairs. Jimmy stared at the creature that had once been human, shock in his eyes.

The ghoul's visage resembled the face of leprosy, far advanced, and pustules of yellow ichor seemed to pulsate in the dim light of the bus' running lights. The mouth was champing and slavering for some meat and its eyes moved back and forth, like two restless black buttons on a child's doll. Its shirt and pants were caked with dried gore and flies hovered around it, waiting for the ghoul to stop moving so they could settle down and feed again.

Lowering the Remington, Jimmy fired point-blank, delivering a thundering dose of double-ought buckshot to the creature's face. The head dissolved into a red mist, the headless body tumbling backward to land on the others behind it. The arms still twitching in death, the body was consumed by the undead as more made their way up the stairs.

The next monstrous form to appear had an exposed ribcage, the ribs sticking up like Pungi sticks in a trench, and it punched and kicked as it fought its way up the stairs. What amazed Jimmy was the inside of the chest cavity was empty. There were no internal organs to keep the ghoul moving. Everything was missing. He believed if he could have yelled into the cavity, it would have sent his voice back in an echo. The pale-blue face, with skin stretched like rotted elastic rubber bands over its cheeks, looked on while it stumbled up the stairs, and Jimmy kicked it away to fall back to the ground below.

More took its place, each fighting to get up the stairs. It was like a Three Stooges' movie, none giving another a chance to go first and all clogged in the doorframe. Jimmy shook his head, thankful for the idiocy of the undead, and then fired three more rounds, exploding expressionless faces and heads like watermelons. In the brief cessation of attack, he quickly pulled shells from his pockets and began reloading the Remington, knowing there was more killing to do before the night was over.

No sooner did he have the weapon reloaded, then the next wave of undead began to crawl up the steps. With a weary sigh, Jimmy began firing again, knowing to stop was death.

Henry knew how Jimmy felt. He had cycled dry twice and had to reload on the cuff as Mary and Cindy covered for him. Sue was yelling something and he tried to see what she wanted. Turning his head the first chance he got, he saw a ghoul crawling through a shattered window in the middle of the bus. Sue was whacking the rotting corpse that had once been a very large man across the head, but her blows were ineffectual at stopping the large zombie. Deciding her threat was more imminent than the ghouls at his window; Henry spun and yelled for her to get out of the way.

At first she didn't hear him, concentrating on fending off the large, ham-size hands, but eventually Henry's voice penetrated her mind and she jumped out of the way, a piece of her shirt staying in the ghoul's hand.

Henry waited for the second it took for Sue to remove herself from the equation and then fired two quick rounds from the Glock, double-tapping the trigger.

The first round grazed off the ghoul's forehead to zip into the shadows of the rear of the bus. The second round found the large zombie's right ear and the bullet sunk in like a knife through butter.

But the man was so large there was no explosion of brain matter or missing chunk of skull. The bullet rattled around inside the massive skull, chewing the brain to mush and the zombie simply stopped moving, like he'd been an electrical appliance that had been plugged in before and then someone had pulled the plug out of its socket by accident. He slumped over the seat he'd been climbing on and was silent. The entire time it took him to die; he never made a sound, no moans or wails, just silence. Henry felt it unsettling as ghouls were usually quite vocal.

Sue was panting with panic, her breathes coming in quick gasps as she stared at the large zombie only a foot away from her. Henry wished he could go to her, hug her, and tell her it would be all right, but there was no time.

"Get back to that window and keep them out!" He yelled at her like a boot camp drill instructor. She was pulled from her terror and nodded, hefting the pan over her head as she began smashing rotten hands and arms when more tried to enter the windows. Henry watched her for another second, proud of her resilience. She may have been scared, but she was still able to push herself to do what she feared most. Some people couldn't do that, even if it was their own survival at stake.

A middle-aged woman with half her face missing tried to get past him and he shot her in the face. As the bullet hole expanded her sinus cavity, he thought the new look was an improvement for her. He raised his right foot and kicked her back out into the crowd. Next came a woman in her twenties, with dark red hair and so much make-up on her face she looked like a clown. With the exception of the jagged wound on the base of her neck, she was in almost perfect condition. He was sure her skin was pale from death, but with the thick layer of foundation on her skin it was impossible to tell. She opened her mouth to snarl at Henry and he saw something glitter in the shadows inside her mouth. When she opened her mouth again, he saw it was a tongue ring. Perhaps at one time the jewelry might have been sexy, but with her tongue now thick, bloated and black, it was one of the most grotesque things Henry had seen in a long time.

He shot her in the forehead and watched her slump back through the window.

Three more ghouls came at him from the windows next to the one he'd taken position at and he shot two in the face, the third making it inside with him. In the confines of the bus he was hesitant to fire, not wanting to risk shooting one of his companions, so he pulled his panga from its sheath and with one slice, decapitated the ghoul. The head rolled away to become lost on the floor and the body toppled like a felled tree onto one of the seats. A small amount of black gore and ichor seeped from the wound, but the geyser of plasma he'd expected didn't come. This ghoul had been undead for so long the blood had congealed in its body.

Ignoring the fallen corpse, Henry returned to the window. More were coming through and he began firing with his Glock and slicing with his panga, in multiple successions, his breathing becoming labored from the continuous activity.

"There's too many of them, Henry! We can't keep this up forever!" Mary called as she fired into the face of a young boy of no more than ten. The small face disappeared to be replaced by three more snarling, grunting countenances.

At first, Henry didn't answer her, though he was beginning to come to the same realization. Chancing a look out the window he was protecting, he saw nothing but a shifting mass of heads and arms in the darkness. His heart sank in his chest at the utter hopelessness of the situation, but he forced those feelings away. Somehow they would get out of this mess, he knew they would. Since the dead first began to walk, Henry and his fellow survivors had been in more scrapes than he could count. Some had been so dire they all should have died, but each time, with their will alone, they had overcome the obstacles in their path to live another day.

But as Henry gazed out at the ocean of dead faces, he was starting to believe maybe this time they might not be so lucky.

CHAPTER TWENTY-SEVEN

A SNARLING FACE, covered with detritus from its past battles appeared in front of Henry. Swiping overhand with the panga, the head was severed at the neck, a small amount of bile and ichor spraying onto the seat in front of him.

Instinctively, he jumped back, not wanting to get any of the effusive liquid on him, then swiped at another mock visage of humanity.

So far all the companions were holding their own, but only just. With more and more bodies swarming onto the sides of the bus, it wouldn't be long before there were so many there would be no way to ever hold them off.

The bus shook on its shocks as wave upon wave of dead humanity pushed against it. The air was rendered with the shouts of his fellow warriors as each fought a private battle in the larger war for survival.

When three ghouls clambered through the window frame and only luck enabled Henry to stop all three before the next wave entered, he made a decision, and prayed it was the best one.

"Okay, people, that's it. This shit is getting deep in here and we need to fall back!"

"But where do we go?" Cindy called as she shot four ghouls in the face one at a time like she was duck shooting at a carnival.

Henry had been giving that serious thought as he fought for his life and there was only one place to go.

"Up! We go up!"

"What? What the hell are you talking about, old man!" Jimmy yelled and fired at a half dozen bodies as they tried to force their way up the stairs.

"The roof of the bus, dammit, that's where. There's no place else to go, if you hadn't noticed!"

Jimmy flashed him a deprecating look, but he didn't add to it by voicing his thoughts. Instead he concentrated on firing his weapon. An ambitious zombie sneaked by the others and Jimmy drew his .38, stuck the muzzle in the ghoul's left eye and squeezed the trigger. The head snapped back and the body fell to the stairs, slowing the ones behind it for half a second.

To his left, the front windshield was cracking further, as a few more ambitious ghouls got the idea to try and go through the window. Their bloody fists pounded on the glass until the darkness outside was all but invisible, but their ministrations were working and soon the glass would concede to their continuous onslaught. Jimmy realized he didn't want to be anywhere in the vicinity when that happened.

Henry turned away from Jimmy and called out to Sue.

"Sue, get that roof hatch open and start passing boxes of ammo and food up there. Raven, you help her!" He ordered the teenager. He was relieved when she sliced the last ghoul in her window and then jumped to the task at hand, not arguing with him. Evidently, even she realized this was not the time for disobedience as all their lives were on the line.

Sue climbed onto some of the boxes near the hatch, and after a few seconds of playing with the lever, forced it open. Raven pushed her through the hatch and then began passing boxes through the hole while Sue grabbed them and began piling them on the roof. She felt like she was on a boat in the middle of storm-tossed waters as the bus shifted to the left and right as the zombies below pushed on the sides of the vehicle. The roof had a steep slant thanks to the rear axle stuck in the air and the footing was treacherous. She looked out on the sea of bodies and swallowed a knot in her throat. She didn't want to even hypothesize what would happen if she lost her balance and tumbled into the undead horde below, but she had a good idea.

Down inside the bus itself, Henry gave the two women only the briefest of looks, to make sure they were not having trouble and then returned to the grizzly work at hand. The panga was coated with a thick layer of gore as he hacked and slashed at heads, arms, and hands. Below his feet, littering the floor, were numerous body parts and he had to be careful or risk slipping on the viscera spread out everywhere.

After almost a full minute, he decided it was enough time for the girls to load what they could on the roof and he called out to each of the companions.

Mary was first to go, and when she got the order, she jumped away from grasping hands and charged for the open hatch. Climbing the boxes, she was welcomed by Sue and Raven, who were waiting for her, and was pulled through the hole, her boots disappearing like she'd been sucked through a reverse hole.

"Okay, Cindy, you next!" Henry told her as he shot three more faces to puddles of red jelly. He'd lost count how many bullets he had fired and was waiting for the inevitable click on a dry chamber.

Cindy sprayed the M-16 across the four windows she'd been protecting, and no sooner did she back away, the bodies began trying to force their way inside the windows. Cindy darted past Henry and was up the box stairs and sliding up into the hatch.

"Okay, Jimmy, now you go, and watch your step, there's shit everywhere!"

Jimmy shook his head. "No way, old man, you go next and then I'll cover you while you get up there."

Henry was about to argue with him when a decaying face appeared in front of him, teeth snapping like a baby bird. He jammed the muzzle of the pistol under the ghoul's chin and fired the gun, the flesh muffling the report. The 9mm slug erupted out of the top of the deader's head and the rotting brains jetted upward to dance in the air, pink clouds of glistening puff floating in the air for the briefest of moments.

The body toppled backwards, a small burp of arterial blood spurting from the jagged hole in the ghoul's crown.

Henry cursed under his breath when the Glock cycled dry.

Reholstering the weapon, he began swinging the panga with renewed force, wary of where to place his boots. The floor of the bus was riddled with spent brass, just waiting to trip him up, and the air was murky from gun smoke.

"Dammit, Jimmy, there's no time to argue, now go!" He yelled, finally having a second to speak. The battle was unbelievable, with more and more bodies trying to enter the bus. It was a seething mass of decadent humanity, all wanting one goal, namely, to feed on the companions.

Muttering a few choice imprecations of his own; Jimmy shot the first ghouls climbing on the stairs and then turned and darted down the aisle. He swung his body around Henry and charged up the boxes. A ghoul had climbed in from Cindy's unprotected windows and grabbed him by the ankle. Jimmy kicked out and used the butt of the Remington as a club, then continued up the box-stairs and when hands reached down for him, he grabbed one of each to be pulled through the hatch, his legs kicking like a schoolchild at play.

Henry was the only one left and he saw he had seconds before he was surrounded. Every window once protected by the others was now exposed and bodies were climbing through, falling onto the seats in a tangle of arms and legs.

With one final slash to a pair of hands, he turned to the pile of boxes leading to the roof hatch. Unfortunately, just as he prepared to make his break, a pair of ghouls, unstable on the soft seat cushions, fell into the boxes, knocking them over to fall into the aisle.

Jimmy was in the hatch and was looking down into the shadows when he let out a scream as the boxes tumbled away.

"Henry, oh Jesus, the boxes!"

"Yeah, no shit," Henry called back and elbowed a face that was about to try and bite his arm off. His eyes scanned the aisle in front of him and the roof hatch overhead. A small square piece of night sky could be seen and he wanted to get to it badly.

More bodies were swarming into the passenger compartment and he found himself trapped. With Jimmy not covering the stairs, the ghouls had climbed over their fallen brethren and were even now crawling onto the first landing. The front windshield finally shattered, bodies tumbling inside to land on the ones trying to climb the stairs.

Henry could hear his heart pounding in his chest and he wanted to vomit. He'd aced death many times, but to be trapped inside a bus and then overwhelmed by deaders was one of the least ways he would have picked to die.

Ghouls filled the aisle in front of him, some climbing over seats like children at play, while behind him they were moving down the center aisle, like tired commuters preparing for the ride home from work.

His throat moved up and down as he swallowed a large lump of fear and his mind raced for a way to escape the certain death that was only moments away.

Then an idea struck him like a bolt of lighting as his brain began to place bodies in front of him in a certain order like building blocks or the game Tetris he used to play on his computer at work after the boss had gone home for the day.

"Jimmy, shoot the first three deaders near the hatch, and do it now!" Henry yelled to Jimmy.

A half-second later the booms of the Remington filled the air and the ghouls dropped and swayed from the barrage.

Henry sliced at the first two in front him and they fell to the floor. The second ghoul fell halfway against the seat to his right and Henry grinned widely.

Perfect.

Taking a step backward to get a running start, he avoided grasping hands and charged for the hatch. When he reached the first fallen ghoul, he jumped onto its body, his left boot landing hard on the back of the ghoul's neck. Before he lost his balance, he was stepping onto the next ghoul, the one that had fallen onto the seat. His right boot slammed against the rotten cheek and pressed downward as he used the head as a springboard to keep moving.

With boxes littering the floor, the ghouls Jimmy had shot had fallen onto them and the still forms were higher off the floor than normal. Henry used each fallen body as a stepping stone, only his momentum keeping him from tumbling to the floor where he would be torn apart by undead hands. When he was at the last zombie facing him, the one that stood under the hatch, he kicked the ghoul in the stomach. The ghoul bent over, as if on instinct, and when it did, Henry jumped onto an arm chair rest and placed both feet onto the ghoul's back, springboarding straight up to the opening of the night sky above him framed by the square sill of the hatch.

As he reached up and jumped, he prayed Jimmy would be ready for him.

He was in luck, Jimmy already reaching down to grasp his outstretched hands and locking instead on his wrists. Henry swayed back and forth, his feet only a few feet off the floor and he heard the sounds of moaning below him. He waited with baited breath to feel the sharp pain in one of his legs when a set of decayed teeth sank themselves into his calf or ankle, but then Jimmy was hauling him upward, with Mary and Cindy holding Jimmy's belt for added support. Henry could feel rotting hands raking his boots and he cringed at the thought. The barrel of the Steyr almost stopped him from going through the hatch, but he shifted his weight and the weapon slipped to a better position on his shoulder.

Without realizing it, he found himself breathing in the night air, and though filled with the reek of death, it was still a hundred times better than the atmosphere inside the bus.

Jimmy pulled him the rest of the way through the hole and promptly dropped to the roof exhausted.

"Christ, Henry, lay off whatever the hell you're eating, you're one heavy bastard."

Henry lay there gazing up at the starlit sky and laughed, long and loud. He was deliriously happy. He was still alive when this time should have been the one to finally send him on the last train to Hell.

But he knew there was no time to rest and quickly rolled to his knees, stopping when vertigo overcame him. Closing his eyes and waiting, his heartbeat filling his head with its steady rhythm, he opened his eyes to see the world was stable once again.

"Okay, how we doin' up here?" He asked Jimmy while he slowly scanned the area around the bus. If he thought it was a dismal view from the inside, then on the roof, with more to see, he was even more depressed. With the darkness fully descended, the shadows of heads and bodies, with nothing but the moonlight and the small parking lights of the bus to see by, the surrounding road looked for all purposes like a storm tossed sea, with the bus the only floatable object for miles. The front headlights had been shattered by undead hands and Henry knew in time, the batteries in the bus would run low and die, too.

There was no road, no shoulder or land in view, only bodies upon bodies, all fighting to be the first to reach the companions. It was one of the most horrific scenes Henry had ever witnessed, and he truly believed if he somehow lived through this ordeal, it would be the one memory he would take with him to his grave whenever that might be.

He pulled himself from his thoughts as Jimmy pointed around them, waving his hands in the air.

"We're fucked, Henry, okay? I think that one word about sums up our situation. The only thing going for us is that we seem to be safe up here. So far they haven't figured out how to climb up." The roof of the bus swayed for a moment and then stopped, but then moved again. It only added to feeling of being lost in an ocean of the dead. The rear of the roof shifted, the sinkhole becoming unstable. But the tremor subsided and they seemed to be safe for the time being.

"Oh yeah, and be careful; or you'll end up over the edge. They keep pushing the bus back and forth. But I don't think they can tip it over."

Henry nodded. "I don't think that was them, Jimmy. I think that's the damn hole we're stuck in."

"Yeah, well, like I said before, at least they can't get up here," Jimmy added, wanting to get the last word in.

Henry nodded, agreeing with him.

No sooner did he think this then Cindy let out an angry yell, her M-16 firing in single burst. Henry and Jimmy turned to the left, rear, side of the bus in time to see a head blow apart, then tumble away to fall back into the milling crowd below.

"What's up?" Henry called to the blonde haired woman.

Cindy shook her head. Next to her, Mary, Sue and Raven all sat on the roof, Mary watching the opposite side of Cindy.

"One of them climbed up, that's what. Either they're using the broken windows on this side as a ladder or just stepping on top of each other. Doesn't really matter, anyway. All that does matter is now they're gonna be climbing up."

Mary held her hand up, pointing down at the shifting heads.

"I got this side, Henry, and Raven is gonna take the back. Why don't you two stay over there and hopefully we can keep them at bay." She turned to Sue. "Why don't you go with Henry and Jimmy. Another set of eyes would be good up front."

Sue nodded, then on hands and knees, as she was petrified of falling, she crawled up to the front of the roof. Henry took her hand and pulled her to him, trying to show her a reassuring smile in the gloom. Then he turned to Jimmy, wondering why it was so dark. Surely the running lights on the bus should have been adequate to push some of the night away. He asked Jimmy and the younger man shook his head, spitting over the side for emphasis.

"No go, Henry. Most of them got busted, along with the headlights. I don't know whether it was on purpose or not but they're shattered. I think it happened when we were climbing up here."

Banging could be heard from below, even louder than the moaning and the pounding coming from outside. Henry moved to the open roof hatch and peered into the gloomy interior. He saw a packed aisle, ghouls crawling over the seats as they tried to figure out how to reach the companions. With a snarl and a curse, Henry slammed the roof hatch closed.

"Shit, we won't be going back down there, that's for sure."

"So what's the plan?" Jimmy inquired. His eyes roamed over the edge of the roof where it curved slightly to the sides. So far no other heads appeared. In the middle of the roof was the small pile of boxes Sue and Raven had managed to carry up with them. So far the shifting roof wasn't moving so much that the boxes were threatened of going over the side, but that could change in a flash.

"Plan? What plan? How 'bout we stay alive for the rest of the night?"

Jimmy frowned. "Well, that's a given, Henry. But we need to figure out a way out of here."

Henry gazed out at the land of the dead and shook his head.

"Jimmy, I don't know what to tell you. We're surrounded on all sides by hundreds of deaders." He leaned closer to him so his words wouldn't carry to the others. Even then he had to raise his voice over the moaning and the pounding "I think this might be it for us. Once our ammo runs out, all we can do is use our knives and feet to keep them off the roof. And we've only got so much food and water and we're damn lucky to have that."

Jimmy's mouth slid open an inch as he stared at Henry and then at Sue who was listening quietly.

"No way, old man. This is not it. There's got to be a way out of here." He said this with resolve, but as he joined Henry's gaze across the shifting undead below, he felt self-doubt creeping in.

A small thought penetrated his mind, though he was wont to listen to it.

Maybe this was the end, only none of them knew it just yet.

He turned to look back at Henry who only nodded. Looking over Henry's shoulder, he could see Cindy guarding her section of the roof. When she saw him looking at her, she flashed him a slight smile and waved, blowing him a kiss. Mary noticed this and made a face, rolling her eyes upward. Raven had her back to them, so had missed it all. Jimmy figured the moody teenager wouldn't have cared anyway.

He glanced down at his Remington, the powerful weapon only as good as the last shot in its chamber, and realized Henry might be right.

Trapped on the roof like cats up a tree, it was like they were on a small island in the middle of the ocean with no possible hope of rescue.

But instead of sharks, patiently waiting in the water for the opportunity to rip their prey apart, the companions had hundreds upon hundreds of ghouls to deal with.

Jimmy didn't answer Henry as all this poured into his mind, but instead turned away to stare out at the shifting, undulating shapes of dead, pale faces, each one a lost soul that would never be retrieved again.

His legs felt weak and he slid to the roof, careful to stay away from the edge.

As he sat on the roof of the bus, staring at the vacant faces below, he couldn't help but wonder if he would be joining them anytime soon.

CHAPTER TWENTY-EIGHT

THE MINUTES SLOWLY turned into hours, the companions sitting on the roof of the stranded bus with nothing but hordes of the undead for company.

The night had passed relatively without incident, only a few adventurous ghouls clever enough to find a way to scale the wrecked and dented sides of the bus.

Whenever a slack-jawed, pale visage would appear, it would be met with a kick to the face or a simple bullet to the forehead. Ammunition was a concern for all of them, but with each ghoul shot, there would be one less to deal with later.

The dawn had just broken the night, the crimson and orange sunrise kissing the horizon.

Weary eyes looked on, and the companions struggled to stay focused. It had been a long day and night and now, with a new day dawning, the possibility of rest was a doubtful thing.

Henry began to organize rest periods, where two people at a time could sit in the middle of the roof and try to get some much needed sleep.

None of them believed they could actually fall asleep with the constant moaning, the pounding of dead flesh on the sides of the vehicle, the carrion breeze flowing passed them, and the reverberating sounds of intermittent gunshots, but each fell asleep almost instantly, exhaustion taking its toll. When the sun grew high in the sky, a small shelter was fabricated from some of the boxes. It was rickety and threatened to blow away at each gust of wind, but as long as someone kept a hand on it, the structure stayed put.

The undead never ceased their advances, seeming to ebb and flow like the tide. Sometimes an hour would pass without one head appearing and then the next hour would see more heads and hands than any of them could count.

Henry had got to the point he didn't bother wiping his panga clean after each wave attacked, as no sooner did he finish, then another limb would appear to be lopped off like a tree branch in the jungle.

Morale was low, each warrior wrapped in private thoughts as they contemplated the future. Jimmy was the only one who seemed to deny what was happening. He went out of his way to shoot and kick as many ghouls as he could reach. The others tired to stop him at first, but as the hours lagged on everyone gave up. Eventually, even Jimmy stopped, too exhausted to continue.

When night began to descend, finishing their first full day stranded on the roof, Mary walked over and sat down next to Henry at the front of the vehicle. Henry's boots hung over the edge, his heels touching the small bits of windshield still connected to the frame. Below his feet, by only a few inches, wrinkled fingers stretched in vain to reach him. He ignored them, knowing he could pull his boots away at anytime. With darkness descending, Henry realized the surviving parking lights were off. The battery had finally died and only the partially exposed moon would give them any light to see by.

Mary settled next to him, but made sure to keep her feet under her. She wasn't about to dangle her legs off the side like a worm on a hook.

"Hey," she said while she gently nudged his left shoulder with her right.

"Hey, yourself," he answered back, wincing slightly from the shoulder wound he'd picked up from the battle with the cannies. The Steyr was resting across his lap and the Glock was half out of its holster, ready for a quick draw if needed. The bloody panga rested on the roof next to him, a small pool of blood spreading out from the sixteen-inch blade.

She saw him wince and leaned forward so her eyes were boring into him.

"You all right? And the truth, Henry, none of that macho crap you men are so fond of."

He chuckled slightly. "Yeah, I'm fine. My shoulders still a little tender, but you fixed it up good. Just needs to heal, is all."

Below on the ground, trios of ghouls were circling like sharks, pushing and shoving the others out of the way. Their eyes were glued to Henry's boots and they reached up ineffectually again and again.

"So, are you gonna tell me what happened back at the hospital?" He asked, and when he saw her face change, the smile washing away from her lips, he immediately regretted it.

She nodded though, and her eyes stared down at the sea of undead. But she wasn't looking at them. Her eyes took on a faraway look and she shrugged her shoulders slightly.

"Yes, Henry, I will, but first I need to sort out everything that's happened." Her voice dropped so low he could barely hear her over the moaning and wailing. "Things happened to me in there. Things that I thought I would never have to experience in my life. I… I just need to work some more of it out, okay?"

He nodded, reaching for her right hand with his left.

"Sure, Mary, whatever you want to do is fine with me." He squeezed her hand, gently. "I'm just glad you're all right and we all got out of there in one piece."

She smiled back and the two shared a quiet moment together. Well, as quiet as they could get with an army of the dead below them wailing and moaning for their flesh. Still, their bond grew tighter with each passing day and he wondered what he would do if he ever lost her. If he'd ended up with children, a daughter, actually, Mary would be the exact vision in his mind of what she should be. Perhaps that was why they had grown so close. About a month ago, Mary had shared her thoughts about her parents. Her father especially, and Henry found out that he and Mary's father were very similar. If they had ever been fortunate enough to meet, Mary believed they would have become good friends.

Footsteps on the roof behind them caused both Mary and Henry to turn slightly.

Sue was moving towards them and she carried two bottles of water and a couple bags of assorted snacks salvaged from the supplies. She smiled widely when Henry looked up at her and Mary knew when she was a third wheel. Before Sue could say anything, Mary stood up, preparing to leave.

"Where're you going?" Henry asked, not understanding why one woman was arriving and the other leaving.

Mary shook her head, amused at Henry's naiveté, and only pointed to the rear of the roof.

"I'm gonna go check on Cindy. Make sure she's okay." With another smile directed to Sue, she walked away, her arms out to balance herself. The rocking had settled as the night had turned to morning, but a steady jolt could come at any time.

Sue watched the younger woman walk away, then sat down next to Henry, her feet now swinging next to his. If she thought she was in any danger, she didn't let on and Henry didn't give it much thought, still thinking about Mary's words to him. Gazing down at the undead faces, she made a disgusted face.

"Ugh, they are so disgusting," she said with a scowl. "And the smell. I don't think I'll ever get used to it."

Henry only shrugged. "You'd be surprised what you can get used to when you have no choice," he said idly as he watched the churning bodies, trying to palliate the mood. "Take garbage men for instance. They get used to the smell of the dump and the trucks eventually. It's like they don't even notice it after a while."

He made eye contact with one of the trio of zombies that were more persistent than the others, but quickly looked away. There was something unsettling about staring into those undead eyes. They were so soulless, a bottomless well of despair and decay that seemed to hypnotize you if you stared for too long. It took him a few seconds to realize Sue was talking to him again.

"I brought you these," she said and Henry snapped out of his trance to take the bottled water and bag of pretzels from her hands.

"Huh? Oh, sorry, guess I went away for a sec' there. Thanks, I was getting thirsty." He glared up at the sun overhead, now a bright yellow circle that hurt the eyes. It was warm out and threatened to become warmer as the day progressed. The heat only added to the miasma that hung over the area like a clouds of smoke; the animated dead literally rotting on their feet.

"Do you know what's going to happen to us, Henry? Are we going to get out of this safely?" Her voice cracked slightly, as if she knew the answer to her question, but still hoped to hear something different.

Henry shook his head. "I don't know, Sue. I mean, I really just don't know. My friends and I have been through some tough times together and we've always managed to get out of them in one piece. But this time, with all of this," he gestured to the undead below. "Well, I just don't see how to save us. We're trapped with nothing around us. There's no trees or buildings close enough to try and reach. There's no sewer system to get underground and escape. There's nothing around here for miles except them." He pointed again at the zombies. "I'm sorry to say it, and I wish there was another way, but I don't have a goddamn idea how to get us out of this."

"That's what I thought," she said. "We were all talking a little while ago and Jimmy was saying how you always come up with a plan to get them out of danger. But this time even you wouldn't be able to figure something out. He said under different circumstances he'd be happy. The great Henry Watson finally got stumped. He just wished he didn't have to die for it to happen."

Henry smiled and looked over his shoulder at Jimmy.

"Yeah, that sounds like something Jimmy would say."

"So what happens next?"

Henry shrugged, not knowing the answer.

"I guess we just wait until we run out of ammunition, food and water." He held up his Glock then, showing her the weapon was cocked. "Don't worry, though. If it comes to that, I'll make sure I save a bullet for each of us. It'll be quicker."

She shook her head and then nodded, trying to come to terms with what he'd just said. But then the strong façade cracked and Henry saw the emotion welling in her eyes and he reached out and wrapped his arms around her. She literally fell into his waiting arms and the heavens opened, the tears coming hard and fast. Her shoulders shook as she crushed her face into his chest and he slowly rubbed her shoulders, saying soothing things that were meaningless, but still he felt the need to say them. Superfluous liquid seeped out of each nostril and the tears became rivers while she sobbed into his body. Eventually, the shudders slowed and she pulled herself away from him, wiping her eyes with the back of her sleeve.

"Oh, God, I'm such a woman. I didn't want you to see me like this. I wanted to be brave, like Mary and Cindy."

He smiled at her, his eyes sparkling in the sunshine.

"Oh, don't put it past them to cry, too. I've seen them let out a tear when the need arose. Hell, so have I. Sue, its okay to be human."

"Well, still, I want to be more like you guys. Like Raven. That girl is as tough as nails."

"Yeah, I've noticed. She's one hard girl."

"I guess you have to be nowadays, what with the state of the world and all." She looked into his eyes, hers still puffy from crying. "Do you think things will ever go back to the way they were before? Do you think we'll ever be able to just lay our dead to rest?"

That was something Henry thought about often.

He only gave her his patented shrug, feeling it served as an answer.

She processed the shrug, then nodded, as if that was an acceptable answer. Henry decided it wasn't enough.

"Look, Sue, whatever happens, happens. In the mean time, you've got to be brave. We're not dead yet, you know. Where there's life, there's hope."

She smiled wanly, his words soothing her and Henry was about to add a few more tidbits of wisdom when a yell rang out from the rear of the roof.

"Henry, we got problems over here!" Jimmy called out as he fired down at what Henry could only assume was more attackers. Raven was by his side and Henry could see her hacking and slashing with the machete she still had in her possession. Mary and Cindy moved to the rear of the bus, as well, helping Jimmy and Raven with the climbing ghouls that were even now scaling the back of the bus in force.

Unfortunately, when the two women abandoned the sides of the roof, it was the perfect opportunity for a few mountainous ghouls to try and scale the unguarded sides of the wrecked vehicle, as there was no foot to kick them off or muzzle to place a bullet in their heads.

Before Henry was barely on his feet, the sides of the bus disgorged body after body, all climbing onto the roof with outstretched hands. Sue let out a scream and Henry pushed her behind him as he began moving forward, the Glock in his right hand and his panga in the left, ready to begin taking out the first struggling ghouls on the roof. That was the time to hack them up, when they were still horizontal, just having cleared the edge.

With his attention focused on the middle of the roof, he didn't see the five ghouls begin climbing the grille and frame of the front of the bus and slowly begin clambering onto the roof behind him. It was only when Sue screamed loudly, a rotting hand wrapping around her ankle like a snake, that he realized she was in trouble and was now surrounded.

Spinning around to save Sue, he then hesitated upon hearing Jimmy call out, yet again, in need of his assistance. He was needed in two places at the same time and he couldn't make a decision. If he chose wrong, either Sue or one of the companions would be killed, lost under the decaying, ravenous bodies even now swarming onto the roof like a swarm of locusts.

Inside his head, he could almost see a metronome ticking back and forth, or the sands of time slipping through an imaginary hourglass.

But still he needed to make a decision.

CHAPTER TWENTY-NINE

HENRY HESITATED FOR less than three seconds, then went into action, knowing to falter would be death for someone close to him.

Deciding Sue was the most in need, he jumped the few feet separating her from him and almost flew through the air, the panga in his left hand already coming down like a scythe.

The blade flashed in the sunlight and came down so fast it was nothing but a blur. It sliced into the appendage holding her ankle and the strength of the blow was so powerful, the edge of the blade sank deep into the sheet metal roof. The severed hand remained on her ankle, still squeezing, but the rest of the ghoul fell back to the milling crowd below.

With his Glock in his right hand, he squeezed the trigger, sending three rounds into two heads. The first ghoul got the double-tap. The first round penetrated its cheek and then ricocheted off bone harmlessly, but the second bullet plowed into its forehead, the bullet hole blossoming on the pale brow like a magician had waved a magic wand. The back of the skull exploded outward, bits of brain matter raining down on the ghouls below. Some bent over and began chomping on the detritus, just glad to have something to eat at last.

The third round went straight into an old woman's left eye, the seventy-year-old ghoul's head absorbing the bullet until a greater force prevailed and her head seemed to explode from the inside out like a watermelon with a cherry bomb stuffed inside it. The white-haired scalp danced in the air, spinning like a plastic bag caught in an updraft, for a brief moment in frozen time, then the scalp plummeted back to earth. Her jagged neck stump shot crimson and twisted back and forth and her skeletal hands reached out for the empty air, then she fell back amidst the crowd below her.

Grabbing Sue in a vise-like grip and picking her up from the roof from where she'd stumbled in terror when the hand latched onto her, he yanked her to her feet. With Sue safe for the moment, he spun around to see Jimmy and the women in dire trouble.

All four companions were trapped between two hordes of crawling bodies closing on them from both sides of the roof. Every time a ghoul was shot, it would roll away, only to have two more take its place. Stuck in the middle, Jimmy and Cindy had their backs to Raven and Mary, who were facing Henry. Raven was using the machete, slashing at faces and arms. She knew not to use the large blade as a stabbing instrument. The risk of getting the knife caught in bone was to risky, so instead, she was hacking and slashing, splitting faces open and taking off limbs like she was carving a path through the Amazon jungle. The roof was awash with spilled blood, some fresher than others. So far it looked like all the blood was from the ghouls. With the slant to the roof, their footing was becoming treacherous as each struggled to stay standing, much like they were fighting on a slab of ice.

As Henry watched the visceral tableau, he knew the struggling companions only had enough survival time as their ammunition would allow. Once their weapons ran dry, there would be no time to reload and all would have to resort to hand-to-hand tactics. There was no time to reach them, either, he needed something instantaneous to turn the tide of battle in the companions' favor.

For the moment, his part of the roof was empty, having knocked all the climbing bodies back to the ground below.

Holstering his Glock and resheathing the panga, cringing as he slid the blood soaked blade into its leg sheath, (if he lived, what a mess that would be to clean), he swung the Steyr off his shoulder. Bringing the scope to his eye, he racked the bolt and searched for the first pale face to put in his crosshairs. Even in the wan moonlight, the scope was more than ample to see by and he gritted his teeth as he searched for his first target.

A young boy of perhaps thirteen or fourteen with half his face missing was trying to reach Mary. The five foot ghoul's back was to Henry, and he could see the boy had a haircut that made him look like a jock. He wore a red shirt that had his high school's name emblazoned on it and the blood-stained sneakers on his feet were once one of the most expensive brands in the corporate world.

Henry lined up his sights with the hairline on the back of the boy's neck and fired off a round. The bullet struck where he'd aimed and the round destroyed the boy's spine, severing any connections to brain to body. The ghoul seemed to twitch and dance in the subtle moonlight, then lost its footing and toppled over to disappear from view. The dead boy was already forgotten as Henry lined up the next shot. He fired seven more times, having to stop near the end to manually load each round. He had run out of rotary clips and now had to do things the hard way. But with him picking off specific bodies while the rest of the companions continued firing at others, it wasn't long before they regained the upper hand.

When the last zombie tumbled over the edge, leaving the entire roof painted a dull maroon color which became sticky almost immediately; Henry carefully made his way to the others, Sue next to him the entire time.

Jimmy wiped blood splatter from his face with the tail of his shirt as he gazed at Henry. He was lucky; none of the fluids had gone near his eyes or mouth. Though it was very unlikely for him to get infected by blood splatter, he was wont to take the chance. Months ago, both he and Henry had been covered in bodily fluids from dozens of ghouls and had actually burrowed under the bodies to escape the rounds from a machine gun. After the shooter had departed, both Henry and Jimmy had crawled out of their meat shields absolutely dripping in gore. None had spoken of what might happen next and days later both were relived to still be breathing. Henry had postulated about it one night and his only answer was that the virus was in the mouth, or the saliva or teeth.

"Shit, that was close," Jimmy said and continued wiping blood from his skin.

"What the hell happened?" Henry asked.

Mary spoke up, reloading a new clip as she talked. "

"They just started climbing up. I think one got the idea and the others followed. Before we knew it, they were swarming up the sides like monkeys."

"So far it's okay," Cindy called from the rear of the bus. She was standing watch, hesitant to move. When she was completely sure it was clear, she carefully moved to the others, popping out the spent mag of her rifle to slide in a new one. She saved the empty magazine, as she could reload it later if time allowed. And so far all they had was time.

"That's good," Henry said and shouldered the Steyr. He turned to gaze out into the sea of dead faces, all moaning and squirming to reach the companions. How do you fight an enemy that never stops, never tires, never sleeps, and never knows fear?

"Wow, will you look at them all? I swear there's more now than from last night. You know, if they try that in any real force we'll never be able to keep them at bay," Mary said askance of Henry.

"Tell me something I don't know," Jimmy sneered while he reloaded his Remington, and once finished, began reloading his .38. He was down to his last few bullets and when the tide had turned in his favor, he was really beginning to believe it was game over. But he kept his fears to himself, not wanting to show his weaknesses. If he had known that the others were feeling as vulnerable as him, perhaps he might have opened up, but as it was, he was keeping silent.

"Okay, let's see what we can do to make sure that doesn't happen again, and then we'll start a rotation of watches." Henry said to everyone then turned to Sue and lowered his voice so only she could hear him. "You okay?"

"Yes," she replied, "just a bit shaken up, is all. Thank you, Henry. If you hadn't decided to help me first, well I…"

"Shhh, its okay, you don't have to say anything. I'm just glad I was able to save everyone…this time," he added. "Come on, let's get you washed up. We still have a little water we can use for bathing. But after that I think we'll have to only use what we have left for drinking." He took her arm and the two moved to the boxes of supplies while Jimmy passed them as he made his way to the front of the roof.

Henry knew wasting one drop of water on anything but consumption was foolish, but he also knew the amount of water they had left would be irrelevant compared to the amount of ammunition remaining. With the army of ghouls below becoming bolder with each passing hour and learning from their mistakes, running out of water was the least of their problems. But knowing to mention this would only cause more concern, he kept his own counsel.

For now at least they could concentrate on the simple things like washing up and eating.

* * *

The hours passed once again, the monotony grating on all their nerves. A few times over the hours some of the ghouls tried to climb onto the roof once again, but they were easily knocked back down. A few more aggressive ones had to be shot, thereby lowering their reserve of ammunition.

Henry had decided everyone should use blades and feet whenever possible, thereby saving the ammo for when it was truly needed.

But even with this in practice, the times when bullets were the only deterrent was growing with each passing hour.

The heat was oppressive, as well. It was in the high eighties to low nineties and the stink of death was so oppressive a few of the companions took to covering their noses with spare rags torn from clothing. Even with the rags in place the odor was only muffled slightly. Sue had even vomited once or twice, the redolence of death too much for her weak stomach to take.

Henry knew how she felt and was doing everything in his power to keep his stomach settled.

The only thing of any interest to happen to break the monotony was when Jimmy took a pee off the edge of the roof, spraying his urine into the waiting undead crowd below like he was a rock star at a benefit concert. Cindy yelled at him like an overworked mother and everyone else had a good laugh. Jimmy, his lips spread wide with his patented shit-eating grin, took a bow when he was finished, all the others clapping. But the event was soon forgotten and boredom set in once again.

So the day wore on with the companions sitting, fighting and sitting some more, like castaways on a deserted island or a raft lost in the middle of the Atlantic Ocean.

On the second night trapped on the roof, after a meager dinner of saltines, warm water, the last bag of jerky and miscellaneous bags of salty snacks, Henry and Jimmy moved off alone to discuss their situation. The two men hadn't talked for hours and now was as good a time as any to try and figure out a way to escape their present predicament.

"Come on, Henry, you gotta have something, you always do," Jimmy pleaded with his older friend.

Henry could only shrug in response.

"I wish I did, Jimmy, but the truth is, we're really screwed here. I think this might be the end for us. There's no way for any of us to escape. Even if some of us tried to sacrifice ourselves so the others could escape, there's nowhere to go. We're surrounded on all sides." His head dropped as he stared at his boots, stained and crusted with dried blood. "I just don't see any other way."

"Shit," Jimmy spit, then lowered his voice when the women looked over to him. He didn't want to spook them anymore then they already were. Cindy had shared her thoughts on their situation with him earlier and she was as scared as the rest of them. Jimmy could only hug her and tell her they would get out alive, that she just had to have faith. Something he didn't know if he still had given their dire circumstances.

Jimmy turned to glare at Henry, his eyes full of fire, his right index finger stabbing at Henry's chest accusingly.

"Look, old man, I'm not ready to die yet. This can't be the way we finally go down. Not after everything we've seen, after all we've done. There has to be a way out."

"Well, if you find one, then I'm all ears," Henry told him, his jaw set tight. As the hours passed by, he'd slowly begun to accept his fate.

Jimmy was in one of the earlier stages: denial. But as time passed, he too, would learn to give in to their reality, as would the others. Either way, whether they accepted what was coming or not, the end would be the same, the only question was how to go down. And in that sense, Henry had already squirreled six bullets into his pocket so he would have enough for them all.

Jimmy nodded, soaking in Henry's words.

"Fine, I will. You just wait. If you aren't gonna get us out of here then I will." He turned and stormed to the opposite end of the roof, where Cindy was waiting for him. The two began to talk quietly, though by the way Jimmy was moving his arms and hands in the air, it was a one-sided discussion. Turning away, he scanned the edge of the roof, deciding to let Jimmy work out his mortality on his own. The roof was empty, only the dull stains remaining from the earlier attack. It had been quiet for hours, no ghoul attempting to climb the sides of the bus, but as each minute passed, he could tell something was going to happen. The zombies closest to the bus were becoming anxious, even attempting to climb the vehicle only to slide back down. But soon they would learn what their predecessors had learned. The zombies were stupid, yes, but even like the slowest animal, they adapted, and in time would begin attempting the climb again.

Henry vowed to be ready, for if the ghouls managed to climb onto the roof faster than before, it was highly probable the companions wouldn't be able to stop them this time and would simply be washed off the roof to land in the moaning crowd below. If that happened, there wouldn't even be time to swallow his gun for a quick shot to the head to spare the torture of being eaten alive.

Sue waited for Jimmy to move away, hovering near their perimeter while the two men talked, and walked over to him once Jimmy was gone. Her arms were wrapped around her tightly, the woman hugging herself in fear. Her face was a mask of terror as she looked out on the sea of undead faces below.

Without saying a word, Henry opened his arms wide and she slid into them. Both stood there on the edge of the roof, close together, relishing the nearness and comfort of another human being, while beneath them, hundreds of undead mouths moaned their song of despair and hunger under a clear blue sky.

CHAPTER THIRTY

THE NEXT TWO days passed with times of violence, followed by lulls where the undead did nothing but mill about like the homeless after getting rousted by the police.

Bodies were stacked like cordwood against the wheels of the bus and it was only a matter of time before the last wave of ghoul's would finally swallow the companion's whole.

The stench of death was overwhelming.

The water and food was gone, only a few crumbs left in a pile of wrinkled plastic bags. If the companions had been under more shelter, out of the sun's direct rays, Henry was sure they would have been able to last much longer, but as there was almost no protection from the heat, all they could do was roast on the roof like Christmas turkeys in a giant oven.

The sheet metal of the roof soaked up the sun like a sponge and became so hot an egg could be fried upon its painted surface with ease. Because of this, none of the companions could stay seated for long, even with spare clothing used as a damper between their bodies and the metal. The cardboard shelter had been gone for almost a full day, blown away at the first strong gust of wind. Some of the full water bottles had gone with the shelter, furthering their already dire circumstances. Everyone's face and arms had become beet red, a few blisters appearing here and there from the constant exposure to the sun. Dark circles were under their eyes from exhaustion and a drawn, haggard look covered their visages as each one of them dealt with their private piece of hell.

Henry's mouth felt as dry as the desert, his tongue nothing but a piece of sandpaper. A faded nickel lay in the corner of his mouth, a substitute for the pebble he would normally have used. But with the ground unattainable, the coin would have to suffice. All the companions sucked on coins, trying to keep their mouths lubricated. Talking had stopped more than a day ago, words only used when absolutely necessary, and even then in clipped, short sentences.

When each word was torture to utter, it was easy to be short and to the point.

Sue was lying on the roof near Henry with her arm draped over her eyes and he looked down at her again, checking on her. He stood so his body shielded her from the harsh sun, but he could only block a small portion of it. She lay with her eyes closed, her chest rising and falling slowly as she slept in utter exhaustion.

Behind him, spread out on the roof, the others sat, guarding the edges from reaching hands. Jimmy and Cindy were together at the rear of the roof, guarding any unauthorized attacks from that direction and Mary and Raven were in the middle, looking down on the dead faces as they ebbed and flowed like a tide. Some of the closest were crushed, their arms and legs broken in multiple places from the weight of their brethren pressing against them.

Henry watched as a pale and blistered face appeared below Raven and the dark-haired girl kicked it firmly in the chin. Teeth went flying from the rotten mouth and the head snapped back. The force of the kick was so strong the body flew off the side to land on three other zombies below. They all fell to the ground in a loose pile, already struggling to regain their footing once again.

Raven turned to Henry and flashed him a slim smile, pleased with her work. Henry nodded in her direction and the girl went back to her vigil. Another head appeared in front of Mary and she used the butt of her Glock to crack it on the top of its skull. When that did no good, she stepped on the fingers when blackened hands tried to crawl onto the hot roof. She pressed hard with her heel, twisting her foot and grinding the flesh and bone onto the hot metal. When the fingers were shattered to the point they wouldn't function, the ghoul slipped away, the bits of meat and flesh still sizzling on the roof.

Henry turned to the front of the bus in time to see his own climber struggling to reach him. He waited for the ghoul to make it all the way to the top, so that all it had to do was swing its legs over. Henry raised the panga and swiped at the exposed neck, severing the tendons and skin right down to the spine. The body jerked like it was being electrocuted and fell away from the edge. Henry had already forgotten about it, prepared for the next one. Jimmy used the butt of his Remington to crack another head like a melon, the brains oozing out of the wound as it slumped against the roof and slid back down to the blood-soaked road. But there were more behind it and Henry realized the next onslaught was about to begin.

For some reason, it took only one or two zombies to figure out how to climb up the side of the bus and then once they did, the others would mimic the action, following in their dead footsteps. This had happened multiple times over the past days with the companions fighting them off each time. But with each day that passed, the companions were growing weary, to the point where merely raising a hand in self-defense was a Herculean effort. And with exhaustion setting in, that would mean mistakes would happen. One mistake could be fatal; there would be no chance to make two.

"Get ready!" Henry yelled; his voice raspy and hoarse. "I think they're gonna try again!"

No one answered him, but he made quick eye contact with each of the others, making sure they'd heard him. Sue was thrown awake and she looked about herself, forgetting where she was for a moment before consciousness took over completely. Henry leaned down and grabbed her shoulder so she would see him and not roll off the edge of the roof. That would bring falling out of bed to an entirely new level.

"What's the matter, did you yell?" She asked this with unfocused eyes, her head darting back and forth like a frightened meerkat guarding her den.

"Yeah, they're about to come at us again, I can feel it. Get in the middle of the roof and stay ready for whatever comes next. Go to whoever needs the most help. Use your feet, not your hands. Remember that. Don't let them bite you."

She nodded, knowing that already, but did what she was told, swaying back and forth like a drunkard as she slowly woke up and came to her senses. The bus was moving again, rocking on its shocks, like it was on a slightly churning ocean with only a few waves to move it back and forth. But it could get worse at any moment and Henry spread his legs wide, planting his boots firmly, just in case.

So far the sinkhole had remained stable but that, too, could change at anytime.

And then they came, swarming over the edges like a sea of rats deserting a sinking ship except heading in the wrong direction. Henry was ready for the first ones and he raised his panga in the air and brought it down on the first head that came into view. His aim was off and he shaved off an ear like he was carving a rump roast; the ghoul barely noticed.

Following through with the swing, he used the momentum and let it whip over his head to come back down in a backward arc. The panga bit deep into the zombie's neck, severing head from shoulders in a spray of blood. The body fell away and the head was kicked to the ground to be lost under shuffling feet. Another ghoul appeared on his right at the edge of the front corner of the roof and he fired the Glock, puncturing an eye with the round. The ghoul's head snapped back and fell away. After that, they came at him in two and threes and he lost count as he swiped and shot at pale and bloated bodies again and again.

Mary fought valiantly, kicking and punching each zombie that came at her. Cindy was behind her and she could here the blonde woman fighting, her grunts and shots filling the air with sound. Mary knew if she stopped for one second, or missed one face that popped up, it would all be over before she could so much as pray to God for it to be quick. Kicking a head away, and then firing the Glock into an upturned mouth, she continued fighting for her very life.

Cindy never stopped firing, the M-16 growing hot in her hands. The zombies were climbing the dead corpses like a macabre meat staircase and she was taking the brunt of the attack. She sprayed the rifle back and forth, the 5.56 tumblers shattering skulls and destroying faces. Bodies barely made it onto the roof before they danced a jig of death as they were ripped to shreds of dead meat. Falling back to the ground, many took their climbing brethren with them, but with each wave she destroyed, dozens more were waiting for their chance to chomp at the bit.

Her gun cycling dry, she dumped the spent mag and slapped a new one in. Flipping the charging handle quickly, she resumed firing, the entire action taking less than three seconds. But it was two seconds too long and when she squeezed the trigger again, the next ghoul had managed to come within two feet of her. Blowback bathed her face in red as the torso of the zombie erupted into spent intestines and viscera. Turning her face away and wiping her eyelids clear with her free hand, she gritted her teeth and began firing again, knowing her ammunition was drastically disappearing with each round fired.

Jimmy was between Cindy and Henry and he was trying to cover both sides of the bus at the same time. The Remington was a crowd pleaser and he fired shell after shell, pumping the weapon one handed as he used his knife to slash at anything that came too close to him. But as the minutes wore on, he began to grow tired, already feeling the weight of lack of sleep, food and water. Tensing his arm, he pumped the next shell into the chamber and fired at the next climbing ghoul; the blast taking half its head off in a brilliant display of blood and gore.

The loud moaning of the dead was maddening and he tried to focus his hearing elsewhere. But the more he tried to tune it out, the more the wailing penetrated his mind until it felt like he was going crazy. Shaking his head to clear it, he fired at the next target, blowing off an arm and then finishing with a shot to the head that disintegrated a face. His resolve returning, he continued the fight.

Whatever would happen, he knew he wouldn't be the first to go down. He would not fail, not for him, but for Cindy and the others who were relying on him to hold his position.

Raven slashed and hacked with her machete, slicing arms and limbs off bodies like she was trimming a tree. One ghoul managed to make it to its feet and as it came for her, fingers outstretched for her face, she pivoted on her heel and let it pass her by. When the ghoul was past, she slid the machete into its side, then yanked up with all her might. The sharp blade sliced upward, opening the side of the ghouls' torso. Severed organs spilled out of the open wound to land on the hot roof, the meat steaming in the sun like liver in a frying pan. The ghoul stumbled to the roof, but it was far from dead. The internal organs it had once needed to live were nonessential and the body was already struggling to rise. That was when Sue appeared, swinging the frying pan she'd salvaged from inside the bus days ago. The pan cracked the dead-head hard, shattering the skull like a dinner plate. The corpse dropped to the roof, immobile. Raven and Sue shared a quick smile, but then Raven had to defend herself again as three more walkers came for her. She slashed at each one, going for their eyes and ankles. The sounds of her wet work filled the rooftop, sounding like she was chopping cabbages in two. But there were no vegetables on the roof with her with the exception of the zombies and she hacked at each one until the pieces stopped coming for her. Kicking the body parts off the roof, she braced herself for the next onslaught, her dark hair billowing behind her like a cloak of darkness.

But for all the courage the companions showed, there were simply too many foes to battle. Slowly, Henry was driven back to the rear of the bus, and when he joined Mary and Cindy, along with Sue and Jimmy, they all continued moving backward, fighting with each step lost. The ghouls had completely swarmed over the rooftop, now only the rear of the roof still relatively empty thanks to the rear of the bus angled higher in the air, the wheels off the ground.

Raven was a dervish, wheeling and kicking with exotic acrobatics that made her limbs blur at what seemed the speed of light. But even she was no match for hundreds of attackers that felt no pain and only stopped when they were either beheaded or received a puncture to the brain by either bullet or sharp instrument.

Gathering in a small circle, they each prepared for the end.

Sue moved next to Henry and huddled against him, shivering. He wanted to comfort her, but there was no time as he fired repeatedly with his Glock. When the gun clicked empty, he shoved it into his waistband, swung the Steyr around to fire the only bullet loaded in it and then began using the weapon as a club, the heavy butt more than adequate to cave in heads. He continued until the weapon became entangled in the arms of a zombie that tried to grab him. He let go of the rifle and swung the panga once again, careful to only hack, not wanting to stab and risk the blade becoming stuck in a ribcage or bone.

Huddled on the edge of the roof, the companions made their last stand, eyes hard, jaws set tight. They were warriors of the new world, and if they were going to die, then they would make sure they sent a thousand ghouls to hell before them.

While Henry fought, his hand slowly reached down for the last six bullets remaining in his pants' pocket. While he contemplated the only result of the battle they were slowly losing, the companions continued to valiantly fight off their attackers under a clear sky of untainted blue.

CHAPTER THIRTY-ONE

THE COMPANIONS STOOD back-to-back on the dark-stained, steaming roof, forced there by the mass of rotting bodies slowly encroaching on their last refuge of safety. With gritted teeth and adrenalin pumping, they fought for their lives. Below them, the sea of bobbing heads and waving arms never ceased, always more to replace the ones taken down.

Each of them was covered in gore from countless killings and they resembled their attackers more than anything that was once human.

Breathing hard and heavy, feeling like they would fall over at any moment, each charged up their spirit and continued to battle on, fighting back the fatigue that filled each one of them with dread.

A tall ghoul charged at Raven, its eyes bulging and putrid; a goo like vanilla pudding running from the sockets. As it raised hands to wrap around her neck, she jumped off her left foot to gain some height on the tall foe and snap-kicked her right. The toe of her right sneaker connected with the chin of the ghoul with a loud crack and its head snapped back to become off-center on its shoulders. Blood-filled froth spilled forth from its open mouth and it stumbled around for a moment, lost, until it fell away to tumble into the bodies below in a tangle of twitching limbs.

With a wild snarl on her lips, Raven spun around, prepared to take out the next threat.

Henry caught only a small amount of her acrobatics and was impressed nonetheless. The girl was a natural fighter, with whip-like instincts that none of the others could compare too.

Then he had problems of his own when two pale faces popped up in front of him, separating themselves from the pack, with more right behind them. He kicked the faces away with the bottom of his boots with bruising force, feeling the impacts in his thighs as his heavy soles crushed bone and skull. When faces dropped away, the distinct imprint of the bottom of his soles was pressed into their faces. His panga slashed down, severing a head from its shoulders in one clean swipe. The shapeless zombie had been one of the first, and after a year of wandering the land, it was nothing but dried tissue and bleached bone. As the head rolled away, puffs of dust followed it, until a foot kicked it off the roof like a soccer ball.

Henry never saw any of this; he was already swiping and punching at the next face in line. A dead face came so close to his nose he could smell its fetid breath. But the exhausted air didn't come from its mouth. The ghoul had a torn out trachea, and harsh gasping sounds could be heard as air worked its way through the throat wound. Disgusted, Henry used the shaft of the panga to punch the ghoul in the nose. Dried cartilage collapsed, and with a kick to the knee, the ghoul slipped away to be lost in the onrushing horde. The next face appeared and he stabbed at its left eye, the long blade sliding through vacant orb to exit the rear of the skull. The ghoul twitched and spasmed for a moment and then sloughed off the blade, severed arteries that had once fed the brain pan spurting blood everywhere. Henry pulled his blood-varnished knife clean from the ruined face and turned to the next foe in front of him. His arms were tired and he knew even if they held off the ghouls forever, sooner or later he would get to the point that his arm would not be raised, that the panga would feel like a lead weight in his hand. Then the time for contemplation was over and he charged at the next ghoul in line.

No one spoke, there was no time as each fought on, never slowing, never giving up. Mary and Cindy were bunched close together, with Jimmy doing his best to keep them safe, but with each passing second, the amount of room on the roof shrunk by half.

Henry looked past the undead foe he was struggling with to glance out and over to the walking dead below. They were like locusts, swarming over the road and land beyond.

His only regret would be he wouldn't be around to see them destroyed like the scourge they were. Whatever had happened to turn good people into monsters was irrelevant now, a thing of the past. It had happened, that was all that mattered. The fact was every ghoul was nothing more than a virus on the earth, destroying what was good and right.

The living dead did not have towns or communities; they did not grow food and till the land. They did not try to better themselves in any way. All they did was take and take, unending eating machines that fed on human flesh. They were unspeakable evil in all its glory. They were humanity if it was nothing but a stagnant pool of water.

And he wouldn't be around to see their destruction, despite the fact he had tried so hard over the past year. Henry's mouth and throat were bone dry from the knowledge of death hovering so close to them all.

The circle grew tighter and Henry knew it was seconds before one of their number was either bit or thrown from the roof. As he was making his inner piece, his left hand reaching down to the six bullets in his pocket to save them all the pain that was coming, he heard a rumbling overhead that was low at first and then began to grow in pitch.

And then he heard something he thought he would never hear in the middle of a battle.

Music.

Loud and long, blasting across the hillside.

Slowly but surely the music was growing louder, the decrescendo seeming to float on the wind, and then the sounds of helicopter rotors could be heard, as well, just behind the music.

The lilting, blaring music boomed from unseen speakers, until suddenly, like the phoenix rising from the ashes, two large military helicopters appeared, cresting over the treetops and zeroing in directly on the companions position. The raging sound of the music filled the area, drowning out the moans and wailings of the undead. The sound of the drums, strings and brass shook the bus on its foundation and Henry recognized it as Wagner's "Flight of the Valkyries."

The helicopters were of two different designs. The first, the smaller and more agile, was an AH-64A Apache attack helicopter complete with 30mm cannons and Hydra rockets. It was capable of carrying sixteen laser guided AGM-114 missiles and was fitted with anti-tank armor. The second was a CH47D Chinook. Its twin engine, tandem rotors, blew debris everywhere, causing a small cyclone to appear, agitating the ghouls even more than before. The large aircraft was able to carry up to forty-four troops at one time and carry 26,000 pounds of storage. Inside were three cargo hooks, waiting patiently if needed. One door was open wide and a machine gun muzzle was hanging out, the .308 caliber belt fed M-60 bolted to the inside of the deck. The machine gunner was strapped into a black harness and his face was hidden behind mask and goggles, but the green and brown uniform was a dead giveaway. The man was either in the army or had stolen the uniform, which seemed highly unlikely as he was flying in the cargo hold of a military chopper.

All the companions, every ghoul on the bus' roof and on the ground turned to look up as one at the two helicopters. For one brief moment, the battle was halted as the living humans and the dead ones stared at the swirling blades spinning like scythes above each copter. A subtle silence descended, but only for the slightest instant.

No sooner did the battle stop, only the wash of the rotors and the booming bass of the music filling the road, then the thundering music abruptly ceased.

But it was immediately replaced with a crescendo of death as the M-60 opened fire and the Apache began firing rockets less than a hundred feet from the bus.

In a roaring explosion of gravel, rocks, and body parts, the crowd of ghouls dispersed as they were evaporated in the ensuing inferno. The machine gun sent tracers over the heads of the undead, and once the gunner had his bearings, he sent the steel-jacketed rounds straight at heads and torsos, shattering bodies like they were made of nothing more than paper-mache.

On the roof of the bus, the companions went to their knees, trying to remain on the roof as the first gust of the shockwave from the rockets swarmed over them, pelting them with bits of debris. The ghouls standing on the bus weren't so fortunate. With no reasoning skills, they didn't realize they were exposed and were blown off the roof to fall into the milling crowd below. A few were on their knees and were spared the fate of their brethren. Crawling towards the companions, their mouths opened wide for the feast to come.

Henry raised his panga, prepared to hack at an oncoming ghoul when the head of said body suddenly exploded like a dropped egg, spraying him with bits of bone and blood. Turning towards the Apache, Henry saw a sniper in an open side door. The man looked up from his sniper rifle and waved to Henry, who waved back half-heartedly.

Then another rocket went off and surrounded the bus in smoke. Jimmy couldn't believe what was happening and was almost the victim of a bite from a crawling zombie. Just before the ghoul sunk its teeth into his arm, Raven sent a snap-kick at the head, knocking the body away. Jimmy jumped back and fired his .38 at the pale face, blowing out the right eye and destroying the brain. As the cadaver fell away, Jimmy turned to Raven.

"Thanks, kid, I didn't see that one coming at me."

Raven frowned. "Don't call me kid; and you're welcome."

Jimmy chuckled at her, the comment reminding him of how he and Henry used to go at it. Then he had to whack another crawling ghoul on the shoulder and kick it off the roof. Mary finished the last one off by punching the zombie in the face, crushing the nose and sending the corpse rolling off the blood splattered sheet metal.

For a moment, none of the companions could believe they were alone on the roof, and they each held their vigil in case it wasn't true.

Around them, the two helicopters continued pounding the massive sea of undead, blowing body parts into the air and setting hundreds on fire. The smell of charred meat overwhelmed the sweet, cloying smell of death and the smoke chased away the swarms of flies that had been an ongoing nuisance since the first of the walking corpses arrived.

For fifteen minutes the barrage continued, the steady staccato of machine gun fire filling the land with death, dropping bodies like ten pins, the ghouls twisting and thrashing in their final death throes. But eventually the gun slowed and only the twitching bodies covering the road remained, the sheer carnage hard to imagine by anyone living in the twentieth century.

Scenes of Jewish concentration camps, piles of bodies stacked like trash, came to mind as Henry gazed down at the chaos of dead humanity now thoroughly destroyed.

The sniper continued firing, putting down the few remaining ghouls that appeared to still be mobile along with the 30mm cannons. Once all the walkers had been thoroughly stamped down, the Chinook rotated 180 degrees and set down between two small craters, the edges of the crater riddled with body parts and gore like the shore of an ocean. The Apache continued to hover above them, the M-60 firing in single shot at each threat the gunner perceived.

Henry was the first to stand up, careful to wait for his balance to return. There was still movement on the sides of the bus and he had no doubt if he was foolish enough to fall off the roof, he would suffer a painful and gory death.

The Chinook hovered three feet off the ground and the cargo doors flew open, disgorging men in military gear, all armed to the teeth.

They jumped onto the wet ground, their combat boots splashing in the puddles of gore, and began to fan out, shooting the ghouls up close and personal. Some used the bayonets on the ends of their rifles, and when a few soldiers were close enough, Henry was surprised to see some of them were carrying shiny new AK-47's instead of the traditional M-16As he expected to see.

The Kalashnikovs looked brand new, their blue-steel barrels flashing in the sun, and the polished wooden stocks shone bright with polish. The rapid-fires used the same ammunition as Henry's Steyr and his hope went up he might be able to trade for some new ammunition.

The soldiers were sure and methodical, working through the undead crowd and taking down any twitching bodies. The bayonets sliced into skulls, piercing eyes and ears as they sliced brains in half.

The entire time the soldiers were working, the companions merely stood on the roof, not moving, only watching what was happening below them. A couple of surviving ghouls climbed onto the roof, still hungry and Henry and Jimmy kicked them off again, the crack of the zombie's necks loud enough to filter down to the closest soldiers.

The soldiers moved though the pile of dead until they were standing below the bus. Each man was wearing a mask; eyes, nose and lower jaw covered. Henry could see it was a filter of some kind and he was immediately envious. The stench of death and burning ghouls was unbearable and he would have given almost anything for a filter to cover his face with.

The first man in line glanced up to Henry and removed his mask. His face was grim; a hard face that was used to doing wet work.

"It's safe. You can come down now," the soldier said in a gruff voice. It was apparent to Henry and the others he was not asking, merely being somewhat polite. The companions looked at one another and then decided they had nothing to lose. Each one knew they had just been saved from certain death, but in the new shattered and lawless world, even a rescuer could become your enemy at the drop of a hat, as each man and woman alive usually had ulterior motives for whatever actions they took.

"Go 'head, I'll cover you guys," Henry told the others. He quickly loaded the six bullets he had left into his Glock, thankful they weren't needed for what he'd intended. One by one the companions began crawling off the sides of the bus. Halfway down, they had to use the piles of bodies for steps. Their feet sunk into open cavities and blood seeped into their boots and socks, but none of them complained. Blood and death were a part of them now, as much as the sun and the sky.

As Raven was making her way down, a zombie that wasn't quite out of the picture yet rose up from under the pile of bodies it was buried under and tried to bite her leg. Henry saw this and was about to shoot the ghoul in the head when she spun around, kicked the ghoul in the face and brought her sneaker down on its head, the coup de grace crushing the rotting, soft skull under her heel. She ground the head into the body of the ghoul below it, and when finished, continued down the pile of corpses like she was picking daises on a hillside, her face placid and emotionless.

Reaching the bottom, she jumped off and moved past the soldiers who acted like what she'd just done was of no interest. Raven stopped only when she was next to Sue who was waiting for her with the others. When everyone was down, Henry began his descent. He jumped off the bus and landed almost calf deep in blood and gore. The smell of bloated gases and viscera, bile and puke, flooded his olfactory senses and it took every ounce of willpower he could muster not to vomit. He definitely did not want to throw up right now. He believed that would be perceived as weakness in the eyes of the soldiers, and at this critical time in their meeting, it was important the companions appeared strong.

Turning his nose away from the worst of the odor, he pulled one leg up and out of the meat. A sucking sound filled the pile of corpses and Henry gently set his gore-soaked boot on more stable footing. Once done, he yanked the other leg out. A string of intestine had caught on his toe like a garden hose and he had to use his panga to cut it away. Once finished, he carefully made his way down the stinking, maggot infested, pile until his boots touched ground once again. Once down he climbed out of the sinkhole, a soldier with a waiting hand helping him over the lip.

The lower half of his pants was all but hidden behind the coating of blood and gore. Stomping wetly to the others, he waited for what would come next.

The soldier, his mask on his face again, walked over to the companions and gestured for them to move away from the bus. With a soldier in the lead, they crossed the carnage until they were next to the Chinook. The wash of the rotors blew smoke and returning flies in every direction and the odor was slightly better under the spinning blades. Soldiers stood at five foot intervals around the helicopter, guarding it from any unwanted attacks. A single gunshot sounded ever few seconds as soldiers disposed of ghouls shambling their way to the aircraft. Only the perimeter around the bus had been decimated. Further away, the ghouls were even now navigating the blast craters. They were on the move and the helicopters would either have to leave soon or send another barrage of missiles onto the road. Inside the bus, the packed passenger compartment showed dozens of the undead as they hung out the windows and slapped the remaining unbroken windows.

The lead soldier spoke into a microphone on his collar and the Apache helicopter moved into position near the bus. A second later a whoosh resounded below its undercarriage and another rocket was exploded. Its fire trail was quick, the distance short and a second later the bus exploded into a blazing fireball that broke the vehicle in half as it rose off the ground. Falling back to the earth, it lay on its side, a blazing mass of junk. The piles of corpses around it were incinerated, some tossed away from the force of the blast to roll on the ground.

It was the closest thing to Hell Henry had ever been and he hoped it would be his last.

As if that wasn't enough, the sinkhole opened wider, the unstable ground weakened further from the blast, and finally giving way. The burning wreckage of the Greyhound bus was swallowed hole, the deep pit under it seeming to act like a giant mouth, consuming metal, rubber and dead bodies with glee. A pillar of black smoke poured out of the hole and Henry swallowed hard, imagining what would have happened if the companions had been on the roof when the sinkhole had finally fallen in.

Satisfied with the results of the explosion, the lead soldier turned back to Henry and gestured for the companions to move to the Chinook.

Henry balked for a moment, not wanting to go inside the helicopter without knowing who his benefactor was, but when each soldier surrounding them raised their rifles in the companions' direction, his mind was pretty much made up.

"Looks like we're going for a ride," Henry said to the others. Jimmy only nodded, understanding completely.

"Hey, it's got to be better than where we were a little while ago, Henry. Way I see it, we can only go up from now on," Jimmy said as he eyed the closest soldier. The soldier was a foot to his left and he gingerly reached out and touched the point of the soldier's bayonet with his finger, testing the sharpness.

"Ooh, that's pointy," he said with a grin. The soldier never moved, and behind his face mask, his eyes hidden, he could only imagine what the soldier was thinking.

Cindy and Mary returned Henry's gaze and both nodded. There was no choice, and truthfully, anywhere had to be better than where they were now.

Sue was standing near Henry and he wrapped his arm around her. Raven was on her other side and her face showed nothing. She would do whatever the others wanted to do. It made no difference to her.

"Enough talk, get in there," the soldier ordered.

"What about our weapons?" Henry asked, concerned. A man without a weapon was a dead man; he just didn't know it yet.

"You can keep them, but keep them holstered and slung...or else."

"Fair enough," Henry relented as he moved toward the aircraft. He knew keeping their weapons was irrelevant. With so many armed men surrounding them, to try and blast their way out would have been tantamount to suicide. But he still felt better staying armed.

One at a time, the companions moved to the open cargo doors and climbed inside with the help of another soldier. Once inside, each of them fell to the floor, exhausted, still believing it was some form of dream and not true reality.

When the last of them was inside, the lead soldier raised his hand in the air and spun it over his head in a circle. Immediately the men on the ground closed ranks and began filing back one at a time into the Chinook. One soldier who wasn't watching his back found himself tripped up when a stray bloody hand reached up and pulled him to the ground. The hand grew until a shoulder appeared and soon the entire ghoul had crawled out from under the pile of viscera that had buried it. The ghoul climbed up the man's prone body and sunk its teeth into the side of his neck. The soldier screamed for help, but the instant the lead soldier saw what was happening, he spoke into his collar radio.

The M-60 roared and the soldier and ghoul were chopped to pieces. A bullet set off one of the hapless man's grenades strapped to his web belt and the entire area exploded with sound and light. Gobbets of flesh peppered the side of the Chinook and then other soldiers turned away from their fallen man.

Now more wary, each soldier climbed into the Chinook, and when the lead soldier climbed aboard, the cargo doors were slammed closed.

The sound of the engine began to whine and the rotors began to spin faster, the Chinook lifting into the air. The Apache hovered nearby and flanked the Chinook, guarding its rear. Henry looked out one of the windows and down on the smoking sinkhole and surrounding road. From his height, small bodies could be seen swarming over the battlefield as they began seeking out anything worth devouring.

It was utter devastation, with fires burning sporadically and the entire area around the sinkhole seemed to be painted a dull red and brown from the gallons upon gallons of blood that had been spilt.

Then the Chinook banked away from the carnage and moved off over the land, leaving the distant dead city behind, its empty buildings to rot and the destroyed bus to smolder alone with the undead in its makeshift grave.

Now Henry could see the rolling grassland of Kentucky bluegrass. He saw untilled farms where tobacco, corn, soybeans and wheat grew unattended. On the horizon, he saw what appeared to be a field of Golden Rod, the state flower of Kentucky, blowing gently in the wind, like they were waving to the helicopters.

Turning away from the windows, he glanced down at his exhausted companions. Jimmy and Cindy were huddled close together and Mary was leaning against the far bulkhead, her eyes closed and her head moving slightly from the motion of the aircraft. Raven was staring at the soldiers sitting on benches behind them, her eyes reminding Henry of a watchful guard dog. Sue was looking straight at him and he nodded to her, smiling slightly. She grinned back, and after brushing her disheveled hair from her eyes, stood up on unsteady legs and walked over to him. Henry's eyes went to the soldiers, but the men didn't seem to mind Sue moving. When she was close enough, Henry reached out to her and she fell into his arms.

"Where do you think they're taking us?" She asked loudly so she could be heard over the twin engines.

Henry shook his head. "Don't know, but I figure it can't be worse than where we were; nowhere could."

She nodded that she understood him and leaned against his chest, ignoring the blood and gore covering them both. She gazed out the window and Henry joined her.

While Henry and Sue stared down at the rolling landscape below, he would soon learn to regret those casually spoken words.

CHAPTER THIRTY-TWO

FIVE MINUTES BEFORE the Chinook set down on the ground; one of the soldiers stood up and walked over to Jimmy and Cindy, squatting down so he was face to face with them. He didn't look a day over eighteen

"So, are you guys in the army or what?"

Jimmy looked perplexed, not understanding the question. "What do you mean by that? We're not in the military."

"You sure? If you're not, then how come you're wearing those uniforms?"

Jimmy looked down at his torn and blood stained BDU's and realized he did look like a soldier. So did the rest of the companions.

"You think we're in the army?" Jimmy asked, confirming the soldier's question. The soldier nodded.

"Well, I'm sorry to say we're not. We're just wearing these as clothes. As far as we knew, there was no more army. Hell, it's been more than a year and none of us have seen anything remotely resembling the United States military."

"Except for you guys, that is," Cindy added as she smiled at the soldier. "What's your name?"

"Private Marshall, ma'am. Originally from Indiana. When all hell broke loose last year I was stationed at Fort Knox. Still am, I guess."

Jimmy realized this soldier was a friendly sort and knew this was as good a time as any to try and get some information on where they were going and what would happen next.

"Is that where we're going, to Fort Knox?" Jimmy asked.

Marshall nodded that it was.

"Cool, maybe we can get some gold while we're there. Oh, and thanks for saving us, by the way. You probably saved our lives," Jimmy told Marshall over the whine of the twin engines. "And what was up with the music when you guys flew in?"

Marshall grinned from ear to ear, looking like the typical good ole boy. He had dark brown hair and ears that looked too big for his head. On top of that he had freckles covering almost every inch of his exposed flesh, especially his face. Jimmy knew he probably had sensitive skin and direct sunlight probably made the freckles worse.

"You liked the music? Cool, huh? That's the Major's idea. Says it distracts the stenches so we can zip in and blow 'em to hell." Marshall said. "That's Major Maddox, actually. He saw you guys on the roof of that bus while we were passing by on patrol and with you wearing those BDU's and all, he thought you was one of our other patrols that had somehow gotten lost and trapped. He radioed to base and the CO told him to save you at all costs. That's our commander. He can be tough as nails at times, but overall he cares about the men under him."

"Who's this CO? What's his name?" Jimmy asked, trying to squeeze more information from the freckle-faced soldier, but just as Marshall was about to answer, another soldier walked over and clapped Marshall on the back hard enough to make the man gasp. He was the lead man and he towered over the small frame of Marshall.

"That's enough, Private. Get your ass back to your seat, now! We're about to touch down," the soldier said. The man still wore the lower half of his mask and all Jimmy could see were his black, piercing eyes. He saw no kindness there, only a hardness that said he would put up with no foolishness.

Marshall gained control of himself, smiled wanly at Jimmy and Cindy and quickly stood and moved back to his seat with a quick: "Yes, Major."

The lead man glanced at Jimmy and Cindy. Then let his eyes roam over a sleeping Mary and a scowling Raven. He turned his head to glare at Henry and Sue, making sure they were all looking at him.

"We're about to set down at the base. Do what you're told and you'll be fine," he said brusquely. "And wake her up. Everyone needs to be alert. You can sleep later after you're processed," he said, gesturing to Mary. Then he went back to his seat, sitting down and crossing his arms over his chest.

Henry, with Sue by his side, moved over to Jimmy, crouching down low so he wouldn't have to shout.

"What was that all about," Henry asked Jimmy.

"Don't know. The kid was just being friendly. Then the other guy came over and told him to leave. Henry, I think these guys are the real deal. They're definitely the real army."

"Yeah, I was thinking that, too." He frowned deeply. "This may or may not be a good thing. Up till now we've been going it on our own and you know what happened the last time we had to deal with the military."

Jimmy nodded, knowing full well what Henry meant. More than a year ago, when the outbreak first began, Henry, Jimmy and Mary had been trapped in their hometown with a trigger-happy military shooting anything in sight. After realizing there would be no help from them, Henry and the others had traveled deep into the woods to avoid the blockade and were very possibly the only survivors of the infected town. Since then, they all had a tense paranoia and wariness of the military and their shoot first ask questions later philosophy.

The twin engines changed pitch and the helicopter shifted slightly to the right. Standing up, Henry walked back to the window, gazing out at the rolling landscape sliding by below.

His jaw dropped open as he stared at what was most definitely a military base. He saw the north edge of the base, a tall perimeter fence surrounding it, the tops draped with concertina wire. Hundreds, if not thousands, of zombies railed against the fence, some climbing over one another to gain access. The fence held, the steel pylons holding the chain link in place, the twisting mesh of reinforced metal more than enough to stop the frail and rotting bodies, even in their high numbers.

When the helicopter passed over the fence, Henry was able to see streets and buildings. Most structures no more than one story, though a few were two and three, though all the taller ones were on the perimeter of the base.

To the west of the base he saw large parts set aside for farming. Human forms could be seen tilling the land, and when the helicopter flew over them, drawn and tired faces gazed up for a moment, then quickly returned to their labors.

The Chinook banked to the left and slowly began to descend.

Henry was told to get to his seat and he did so, joining his companions. Mary was awake and she looked around with bleary eyes. When her eyes met Henry's, he nodded to her. She returned the greeting, but otherwise remained immobile. To her left were the soldiers, sitting on the seats in threes and fours. So far, with the exception of the freckle-face private, none had spoken a word to them.

The Chinook touched down and an instant later the cargo doors were thrown open, letting in the warm Kentucky air.

The lead soldier was the first off the chopper and he directed the companions to disembark. Once all were out and standing in a loose circle, he directed them to follow him. The man still wore his mask; his true features were unidentifiable. The companions did as they were told, not having a choice in the matter. Behind them, eight soldiers with weapons aimed at them followed, and all knew one false move and a firefight would be the end result. Behind them the other soldiers began the chores of refitting and refueling the Chinook and the rapidly descending Apache.

Following the back of the lead soldiers head, Henry and the others were led through a maze of one-story buildings. At one point they passed an open courtyard and Jimmy was the one to stop dead in his tracks. Cindy, who was walking behind him, crashed right into his back, and was about to chastise him for stopping when she, too, followed his gaze and gasped in shock. Soon, all were staring in the same direction and it was Sue who turned away to vomit. Behind her, the soldiers chuckled, the grotesque scene nothing new to them.

In the middle of what was once a small grassy courtyard there was now a small stage and gallows, occupied by one lone form swinging back and forth from a noose. To the right of the swinging corpse were three poles, ten feet high and about as thick as an average man's arm.

On each of these poles were the remnants of three more human beings, long dead by the looks of them. Though hard to believe, it appeared they had been placed on the sharp tips of the poles with their anus' on the tips. When they had been set loose, their own body weight had forced the sharp, thick spears to slowly move through their bodies, slicing and puncturing organs while they slowly slid down the poles. Eventually, the tips of the poles had slid out of the corpse's mouths, making the bodies look like they'd been skewered like a pig for a barbeque. The impaled bodies were full of buzzing flies and maggots and a couple of crows still sat on their shoulders, trying to find any last remnants of soft tissue worth taking.

The arms and legs moved softly in the wind, making them look as if they were still alive. The barbaric ritual was something seen in the Middle Ages and was the last thing Henry or the others would ever have thought to see, especially on what appeared to be a truly functioning military base with real soldiers in charge.

"Oh my God, how can that be?" Mary asked as she stared dumbfounded at the wanton act of cruelty. "Who could do something so evil?"

The lead soldier spun around, stopping short, and Henry finally saw his full countenance for the first time. His dark complexion was ruggedly handsome, but his eyes were hard and black. A scar ran from the right corner of his mouth and curved up to the halfway point on his cheek, and his short-cropped, coal-black hair framed the cold visage. Standing so close to Henry, it was easy to gauge his height. He had to be at least six feet and was well built, his muscles straining under his clothing; his bull neck was lined with taut tendons that made him look like a weightlifter. Henry read the name tag stitched to his breast, the name Maddox stitched in black thread. On a holster on his left hip he carried a .45 long-barreled Colt Army Special and on his right hip was a Buckmaster survival knife.

The knife was used mostly by Special Forces. The handle was hollow, the blade razor sharp and curved on one side. On the upper half of the opposite side, the edge is wickedly serrated so that when the blade is removed; the wound is torn, not sliced. Inside the handle were detachable anchor pins used for grappling hooks and the skeletal handle can be used as a knuckle duster. The fact that this man owned this knife meant he either stole it or had earned it before the world collapsed. It told Henry either way to be wary of him.

"Those men," Maddox pointed at the dead and tortured bodies, snickering slightly, "were deserters. They were made examples of by my commander. Follow the rules and you won't end up feeding the crows, but if you decide not to..." He grinned as he gazed back at the swaying bodies. A few crows cawed with annoyance, their dinner disturbed, and then went back to feeding.

None of the companions said anything. There was nothing to say.

Maddox turned and began walking, and after at a few gentle jabs by some of the soldiers, the companions moved on, following Maddox's wide shoulders.

They walked for another ten minutes and Henry and the others studied their surroundings. They soon came upon what were obviously the buildings used for the barracks. But instead of soldiers, they saw children, men and women, all with tired faces and some wearing nothing but rags.

"What's the deal here, Maddox? Why are all these civilians here? Are they the families of the soldiers?" Henry asked.

Maddox chuckled slightly, but it came out like the sound storm clouds make before they release their payload.

"Not exactly. Those are conscripts. They've been drafted for the good of the nation. There are buildings all over the base that house them."

"What do they do here?" Mary asked from behind Henry.

Maddox shrugged. "A lot actually. They clean and service our vehicles. Some work in the south and west fields we've set up to grow food, and others do whatever we need them to do, whether its body disposal or something else." He turned to glare at Mary, his left lip rising slightly. "Some of the things to be done are only for the women folk. Maybe you might want to be a part of that?"

Some of the other soldiers chuckled and Mary and Cindy gave them a dirty look. Mary knew exactly what he was talking about and would be damned if she'd wind up in a brothel.

"Thanks, but no thanks; I think I'll stay with my friends."

"Suit yourself," Maddox said, as if her decision was irrelevant. He turned and moved on, the companions following close behind.

Two blocks over from where the impaling posts and gallows were located, the companions slowed yet again. In front of them there was a large crowd of people of all shapes and sizes and they appeared to be waiting for access to a large, hangar-like, building. At the entrance to the building were five metal desks with men sitting behind them. Large stacks of paper and computer laptops were spread out on the desks, the cords for power trailing away into the hangar. The crowd was being filed and stamped here, each person in line was giving their names and where they had lived before arriving on the base.

Henry's eyes went wide at the sight of the electronics.

Wait a second, computers? This base had working computers, too? He thought while moving closer.

It appeared the base was functioning the same as before the holocaust, with power and a command structure still in place.

Soldiers with AK-47s and a few M-16s surrounded the edges of the crowd, keeping people in line. The noise was deafening, hollering and yelling competing with hundreds of conversations, all trying to speak at the same time.

Maddox pointed to the end of the crowd, a cruel smile on his lips.

"Go over there. This is the line for processing. From here you'll be given a number and sent to a barracks. After that you can grab some chow. And later the commander wants to meet you, Watson isn't it?"

Henry nodded. "Yeah it is."

"And then what happens?" Cindy asked as she gazed over the milling sea of humanity.

"Then you get to work with whatever we need you to do," Maddox snarled. "All right, you men, move out!" He yelled at the top of his lungs so the escort soldiers could hear him.

The companions were ushered to the end of the line where other soldiers now took watch over them. Henry still found it odd that the companions were allowed to keep their weapons, but as he snuck a peek at each soldier guarding them, he realized their keeping the weapons was really nothing special. If they even tried to shoot their way out, they would be caught in a crossfire, suffering countless casualties.

No, whatever was going on, they would have to play their part, at least for the time being. Once they knew the lay of the land and how the base operated, perhaps then they could try and escape.

Henry studied some of the people in line in front of him and he saw a few carried firearms, as well. He didn't recognize all different make and models, but all the guns looked serviceable. Almost every person in line had a weapon of some sort, whether it was a sharpened broomstick or a blade.

While they had walked through the base, jeeps had trundled past and he had seen convoy trucks and half-tracks parked in front of buildings. This base had fuel and fuel meant a possible way to escape, though they would then end up in a running battle across Kentucky if they were pursued. Anyone who would go to so much trouble to draft people would not let them get away so easily.

The sounds of rotors could be heard and Henry and the others looked up in time to see another Apache come into view overhead. It hovered for a moment, as if the pilot was scanning the crowd, and then flew off, the wash from the rotor blades stirring up dust and causing more than half the crowd to cough and choke as they tried to filter the dusty air from tortured lungs.

Henry frowned and Jimmy moved closer to him.

"You thinking what I'm thinking?" Jimmy asked as he watched the Apache disappear over the nearby buildings.

"Maybe. I'm thinking that even if we steal a truck we'll still have to deal with the helicopters. They'd chew us to bits before we got a mile away."

Jimmy nodded. "Yeah, that's what I was thinking. But what about if we stole one of the helicopters?"

"You idiot," Cindy quipped. "None of us knows how to fly a helicopter, that's stupid."

He nodded. "Yeah, but maybe one of us can see if we can get into some kind of training. Surely they need more pilots. It's worth a shot. I mean, how hard can it be?"

Henry nodded. "Okay, then Jimmy, that's your job."

Jimmy grinned. "Done, you'll see. I'll be flying in no time."

"Sure you will," Cindy sneered.

"I still can't believe this, Henry, it all seems so unreal," Mary said from behind him.

"Yeah, it doesn't make sense," Cindy said askance of Mary. "Hey, do you think this is where that captain came from? You know, the guy who torched that town?"

Henry shook his head. "Don't know, Cindy, but I promise you this, I'll do my best to find out. Everyone just keep your head down for a while, we don't know how things work around here." He looked over to Sue. "You all right?"

"Yes, Henry, I'm okay, Raven said she'd look out for me, you just worry about getting us out of here." Behind Sue, Raven nodded to Henry, signifying what Sue said was true. Henry returned the gesture then glanced back to Sue

He smiled to her, but it was a cold smile, filled with concern for them all. "You can count on it, Sue."

The crowd moved forward a foot and the companions followed, everyone shuffling forward twelve inches. Behind them, more recruits were arriving and the companions had to keep their voices down. Who knows who was listening and would take back what they might hear for favors or a better position in the army.

More subdued, the companions continued working out their plan of action, while the crowd slowly shortened, and they moved closer to the hangar bay and the desks with their working computers.

CHAPTER THIRTY-THREE

THE COMPANIONS SLOWLY made their way down the line of people, while behind them the crowd continued to grow. Overhead, choppers flew by semi-frequently, some hovering like large flies searching for food.

The rotor wash was welcomed as it blew the stink of more than a hundred unwashed bodies away from them.

When the companions were no more than eight people away from the desks with the soldiers divvying out names, a small occurrence began that sent ripples through the crowd of waiting people.

A man in a torn sweatshirt, faded denim jeans and an unshaven face began yelling about his wife. Henry was the first in line of the companions and he moved slightly closer, wanting to hear what was happening. Any little bit of information could be crucial in their escaping and what this man did could have drastic effects on the group.

The man was waving his arms in the air, demanding to know where his wife was. The soldier behind the desk, his face emotionless like a good bureaucrat, told the man to calm down and in due time his wife would be located. But the man wouldn't listen. He reached down and with one sweep of his hands, pushed the laptop and papers covering the desk to the pavement, the laptops screen shattering with a small discharge of glass shards. Soldiers guarding the crowd moved closer, weapons aimed directly at the disturbance, but the distraught man was so upset he never noticed the mortal danger he was in.

Mary was about to move closer, wanting to help the hapless man, but Henry quickly reached out and grasped her arm firmly in an iron grip. She opened her mouth to protest, but Henry shook his head, his eyes boring into hers. All Mary would succeed in doing if she tried to help would be to draw unwanted attention to them and possibly get herself killed or imprisoned.

With a huff of acceptance, she stopped struggling, and though her hands were balled into fists at her side, she watched the tableau play out before her.

After the irate man had swept the laptop and papers to the floor, he attempted to climb over the desk, wanting to charge the shocked soldier sitting behind it. Before the man could so much as get his first leg over the top, a staccato of gunfire ripped through the man's back, sending scarlet ribbons and bits of flesh exploding out his chest. The soldier behind the desk was splattered with gore and he lunged out of the way of the falling man. The once irate man's mouth flapped open and closed like a fish's and he fell heavily onto the desktop. Blood pooled under him to drip onto the pavement and the crowd erupted in chaos. But the soldiers quickly regained order, shoving anyone foolish enough to try and break free of the line. The companions stood firm, their backs to one another, hands on weapons as the crowd seethed and flowed like the incoming tide against them.

A few hands were raised to the deadlands warriors, but once the attackers saw the hard-set faces and cocked weapons on hips, all moved on for easier game.

Five minutes after the slaughtered man was taken down, order was restored. Four women came out of the hangar with buckets of water and quickly washed the gore from the table, while two more men in civilian clothes picked up the corpse, tossed it onto a wheeled dolly, and rolled it away. Another laptop was brought to the soldier, and in no time it was like the incident had never happened, only the pooling blood and flies on the pavement proof that the altercation had ever existed.

The line began to move again and in no time it was Henry's turn.

"Name," the bored looking soldier asked. Henry read the name on his shirt, the name Burns written in indelible black marker.

"Henry Watson."

"Place of birth," the soldier asked.

"Indiana," Henry said. This wasn't his actual birthplace, but he was curious to see if the soldier would notice. That answer would depend on what information was stored in the computer. But if the soldier detected fraud he didn't let on, and typed the information into the laptop.

"Age," the soldier asked.

"Forty-four," Henry said, giving an age very close to his actual one.

"Skills," the soldier asked, looking up from the keyboard and into Henry's eyes.

Henry shrugged, not knowing what to say.

"Well, I used to write software, you know, before things fell apart."

"Uh-huh," the soldier said uninterested.

"But what have you been doing since then?"

"Surviving, what have any of us been doing?"

The soldier actually smiled then.

"Good one, Watson." Then a red flag appeared on his face. "Wait a second. Says here the commander wants to speak with you after you get situated. Major Maddox initialed it, so I guess it's true." He gazed back at Henry. "You must be someone important if the CO wants to talk with you. Usually he doesn't see anyone except Maddox."

"Sorry, I don't know what to tell you. I don't know your CO."

The soldier typed in a few words that Henry couldn't see and then handed Henry a small metal tag similar to dog tags, only this had a number stamped on it.

"Here, put this on and keep it on. It's your pass to be on the base. If someone stops you and you don't have this on, you'll be shot on sight."

Henry took the tag, nodding. "Got it," he told the soldier.

The soldier pointed to his left.

"Your berth is that way, third street over on the left, building 35. Once you've cleaned up, get some chow and then go to the CO's office."

"But I don't know where that is," Henry said.

"Don't care, oh and welcome to Fort Knox," he said with a sneer.

Henry was going to tell the man thanks for nothing, but the soldier had already dismissed Henry and was looking behind him for the next person in line, which was Mary.

"Just ask anyone in uniform, they'll tell you where to go," the soldier said and then began interrogating Mary the same way. Henry moved, stepping away from the tables. But he didn't leave. He wanted to wait for the others.

As he waited, a soldier with a shiny new AK-47 moved up next to him.

"What are you doing, recruit," he asked in an authoritative voice.

"Waiting for my friends. They're next in line."

"I don't give a flying fuck if you're waiting for the President of the United States. Get moving or I'll kick your ass up and down this parking lot."

Henry squeezed his hands together, his right hand hovering over the handle of his panga. The soldier was only an inch taller than him and he knew he could have his blade out and have the man's right arm lying in the dirt, his bloody stump pumping his life's blood all over the place. But he held himself back, knowing the instant he committed the brutal act, he would have five muzzles aimed at his head. With a brief glance to the rest of the group, still working their way through the line, he decided to move on and do what he was told. Hopefully, they could all meet up later, out of the watchful eyes of the soldiers.

Repositioning the strap for the Steyr on his shoulder, he moved off, following the directions the desk soldier had given him.

After Mary, Sue and Raven had worked their way through the line and had each received an identification tag, it was Jimmy's turn.

Strolling up to the desk, he casually leaned against the edge and almost tipped it over, spilling the contents onto the ground. The soldier sitting behind the desk frowned, long and hard. Jimmy could tell the soldier was bored with his job, the menial task of taking names and addresses grating on his temper.

So, of course Jimmy thought he'd have a little fun with the stressed out soldier.

"Name," the soldier asked, not looking up from his keyboard as he waited for Jimmy to speak.

"Abraham," Jimmy replied and the soldier began typing. Jimmy paused for dramatic effect and then said, "Lincoln, the third."

The soldier was still typing and then stopped and gazed up into Jimmy's smiling face.

"Abraham Lincoln, that's your name?"

Jimmy nodded. "You betcha, and boy oh boy, did I ever get ribbed in school for it, too."

The soldier wasn't buying what Jimmy was selling, but he wasn't totally a nonbeliever yet.

"Okay, then, Abraham, where were you born?" The soldier was looking back down at his keyboard, prepared to begin typing again.

"In a log cabin, sir, why do you ask?"

The soldier's fingers hovered over the keys momentarily and then he took them away. This time when he looked up at Jimmy there was a glittering of anger in his eyes.

"What are you, some kind of an asshole?"

Jimmy grinned back. "Yeah, some kind of, why? Is there a problem?"

The soldier waved over one of the nearby guards who were watching the crowd.

"Hey, Lou, this guy won't give me his name and shit. Do me a favor, will ya? If he doesn't answer me the next time I ask, will you blow his fucking head off his shoulders?"

The guard answered by hefting the weapon to a better position on his shoulder, the muzzle now aimed point-blank at Jimmy's forehead.

Jimmy swallowed a large lump in his throat and stared at the round opening on the end of the barrel. A few ounces of pressure on the guards trigger finger and Jimmy's head would be mush. The wide grin he had been sporting suddenly dissolved like the morning fog when the sun came out.

The soldier now grinned, slightly, confident in his authority. "Now, buddy, what is your real name and where are you from?"

Jimmy quickly rattled off his name and where he was born and the soldier typed the information in quickly. He then handed Jimmy his tag, told him where he was berthed, and waved him away with another grin.

With a new frown on his face and looking like a whipped puppy who'd been disciplined for peeing on the carpet, Jimmy moved away from the desk. He eyed the guard for one brief moment, waiting for the soldier to lower the rapid-fire. The man seemed to hesitate, as if he wanted an excuse to take Jimmy's head off, but eventually the guard lowered the weapon.

Jimmy flashed the guard an insincere grin, then moved off, following the path the women had taken only minutes ago.

While he walked, he decided maybe he would keep his big mouth shut for a little while, telling them he was a pilot was lost, as he realized the desk soldier wasn't going to be fooled. It seemed these soldiers didn't appreciate his witty sense of humor.

The women walked side by side with Cindy in the lead. Raven was trailing slightly behind the others, taciturn as always. As they passed other buildings, they were able to peer inside. They saw what looked like a gypsy camp, men and women, each in their own barracks, living and sleeping and cooking. It was more like a giant camp than a military base, the first impressions as they had flown in the choppers deceiving. If the soldiers weren't wearing military style uniforms, the base would be no different than a hundred other fortified towns the companions had come across on their travels through the deadlands.

The four female companions weaved their way through the winding streets until finally reaching the building they'd been issued as their sleeping quarters. Stepping inside the doorway, partially opened already, their senses were immediately assaulted by the odor of unwashed bodies and heavy perfume, mixed with the smells of cooking meat and boiling vegetables.

With Mary in the lead, they strolled down the center aisle of the large room. On each side of the aisle were beds, two rows each. On these beds were a wide assortment of women and children, though the latter appeared to always be over seven years of age and most were covered in filth. It seemed cleanliness wasn't much of a necessity to most of the people in the barracks. Near the back of the room, small cookfires had been set up, positioning them under ceiling vents to suck out the smoke. Old women, though not ancient, stirred a brown and green sludge around the steel pots hanging from poles of metal. The fragrance reminded Mary of how she used to feel when she walked through Chinatown or other ethnic parts of California before she had moved to the Midwest. She saw some were armed with firearms though none seemed to be of the same caliber of either the soldiers or the companions. Once again it was odd that everyone who wanted to was able to carry firearms inside the base.

Looking up, Mary noticed all the lights were on across the ceiling. This building had power. No one else in the large room seemed to notice or care, just taking it in stride. If the base had power, then where was it coming from? She would have to remember to bring it up when she joined Henry and Jimmy again.

Faces of all ethnicities stared back at them while they moved slowly through the room. When they were halfway down the aisle, a rotund, burly woman in her late forties stepped in their path. A hunting rifle was slung over her shoulder and a large butcher knife hung from a makeshift sheath from her right hip. She stank of dried sweat and pork products and her brown, stringy hair was held back behind her large ears by a small, faded blue scrunchy.

"Who the fuck are you?" The large woman spit, showing the two front teeth she was missing. Her eyes glittered hatred and the companions knew there would be trouble. Both Cindy and Mary had seen enough to know when they were being challenged, the trick was, whether they should just shoot the large woman down in cold blood or let her make a move first. A quick glance over Mary's shoulder at the three soldiers standing near the front door told her they would have to do the latter, at least then they would have the excuse of self-defense.

"Look, we don't want any trouble," Cindy said. "We just got assigned here. Let us get a couple of beds and we won't bother you."

"Damn right you won't be no bother," the large woman spit back.

"You tell 'em, Bertha. Put 'em in their place!" This came from someone to their right, the owner of the voice unknown.

"Look, Bertha," Mary said, now knowing the woman's name and hoping to score some points by sounding like she knew the large, angry woman. "My friend said we won't bother you or anyone else, now we can do this the easy way or the hard way, your choice. But let me tell you this. Either way you'll be lying on the floor sucking your last breath." She spoke in a low voice so no one else could hear her except Bertha, and while she talked, she lowered her hand to her Glock, the weapon now partially drawn. Bertha's eyes gazed downward and her eyes creased into two slits at the partially drawn gun. Next to Mary, Cindy had already dropped her hand to her Ruger, as well, and would have it out and firing in less than a second.

Bertha began chewing her lip, while she mulled the situation over. She stared hard at Mary and Cindy, and then at Raven and Sue standing behind them. None of the companions flinched, though Sue did look away when Bertha stared too long. Finally, Bertha nodded, then moved out of the center of the aisle so the four women could pass. None of the companions said a thing, only moved on towards the rear of the room. In the far left corner were a few made beds with no personal items near them. Deciding they had to be unoccupied, the women moved to them, setting their items down on the floor and bed.

Once the companions were near the back of the room, conversation began again, the situation diffused. Crying children, yelling and talking commenced, Bertha already forgotten.

There was only one problem with the way Mary had handled the situation. While wanting to save Bertha's pride by not calling the woman out in front of the other occupants in the room, and not causing the large woman to fight merely to save face, Mary had not shown the other bullies in the room that the companions were people not to mess with.

So no sooner did they begin shrugging out of their gear and plopping down on their beds to rest, then another woman moved up behind Raven. This woman had the look of the classic lesbian, with short-cropped hair and a strong face, almost masculine. She wore a pair of men's blue jeans and her shirt was a man's button down with the sleeves cut off, the thread hanging and aged like a shag rug around her biceps. She was wide in the hips and waist, some of it muscle, some only fat, but she was more than twice the size of Raven.

As Raven set her things down on one of the beds, the woman leaned over and slapped the items away, knocking them to the floor. The machete went spinning across the linoleum to strike the wall.

"Hey, little sweetie, that's my bed. Get another one."

Raven's eyes flared with anger and she spun to face the woman, but she said and did nothing, only stared at the larger woman. Mary immediately went to her aid, Cindy right behind her. Sue was just sitting down on her bunk and hadn't realized there was another problem.

"Look, lady, we don't want any trouble. We're sorry if this was your bed, she'll get another one," Mary told the lesbian. The soldiers were still at the front of the room, but they couldn't see what was happening from where they were. Mary didn't know if that was a good thing or a bad one.

The large woman acted like she hadn't heard Mary.

"It's too late for that, bitch, she already got it dirty when she dumped her shit on it. Now she's got to pay."

"That's bullshit and you know it!" Cindy spat, moving so close to the woman she could smell her breath. It smelled like road kill with a touch of garlic and Cindy's stomach lurched inside her, the taste of bile rising in her throat. She forced it back down.

Cindy's hand was reaching around her back to the small hunting knife hidden there. The instant the woman tried something; Cindy planned to stab her in the side, trying for her kidney or spleen. But she never got the chance. With Cindy's last words leaving her mouth, the large woman reached back with her left hand and clubbed Cindy on the side of the head, sending the blonde woman rolling across the next bunk and tumbling to the floor in a tangle of limbs.

"What the hell are you...?" Mary began and then felt a roundhouse punch to the side of the head from the woman's right hand, the blow sending her mind spinning like she had just taken a ride on the biggest rollercoaster in the world. She stumbled backward and plopped down on her butt like a toddler trying to walk for the first time, her head filled with fog.

Pleased that the opposition was out of the way, the lesbian reached out to wrap her hand around Raven's wrist.

"Come with me, sweetie, you need to pay me back for messing up my bunk. You and me are gonna have some fun."

But Raven didn't let herself be grabbed, but instead jumped onto the closest bunk and bounced on it with her left leg like it was a trampoline. When she was as high in the air as she could reach, she snap-kicked with her right foot; the sole of her sneaker connecting with the larger woman's chin. The lesbian was knocked backward and the sound of cracking jaw filled the back of the room, causing the closest residents to stop and watch, realizing something was happening. The lesbian rubbed her jaw and shook her head to clear it.

"Why you little bitch. I was gonna go easy on ya, but now it's gonna be rough. That's okay, though, I like it rough."

Quicker than her size belayed, she lowered her head and charged straight for Raven, resembling a mad bull. But as the woman ran at Raven, the teenage girl wasn't occupying the same space as a second ago.

When the lesbian lowered her head and charged, Raven jumped onto the closest bunk and used it like a trampoline yet again. But this time as she reached her peak in the air, she spread both her legs like a gymnast. As the lesbian ran under her, Raven placed her hands on the woman's back and sprung over her like she was on a balance beam. But as she flew past, she spun in the air and used her sneakers to kick the woman in the butt, forcing the lesbian to lose her balance and go crashing into the far wall. The other residents watching began to chuckle and the lesbian picked herself off the floor, the anger in her face apparent. She was so red she looked like a giant beet with hair and she let out a yell that should have woken the dead.

"You are dead, you little bitch!"

Raven landed on another bunk and rolled off it with ease. Standing up, she crouched low, her nails extended outward, ready to slash the lesbian's throat on her next attack.

But before the large woman could take more than her first step, a loud clang filled the back of the room and the large woman stopped in mid-stride. She swayed like a mighty oak in a storm for a brief second, then toppled over to the side like the same felled tree. There was another bunk there, but it was occupied. When the woman fell on top of the bed, the sleeping occupant rolled away with a high-pitched squeak. The lesbian's head landed directly on the pillow, and with the exception of the small blood spot on the back of her skull and the large lump accompanying it, the woman appeared to be sound asleep.

Both Mary and Cindy were on their feet and both stared at Sue standing where the lesbian had been. Sue was holding the large skillet she had previously used to fend off attacking ghouls when they had been trapped on the bus. She gazed down at the unconscious woman, still shocked at what she'd done.

"What the hell? You still have that thing?" Cindy asked while moving closer.

Sue nodded. "Yup. I brought it with me. I figured it did a good job before, so why not now?"

"Well, it sure did. Good job, Sue, That woman was a big one. I thought we were gonna have to kill her."

"I had her," Raven said as she lowered her hands.

No one doubted Raven would have been able to take the larger woman, but it was still better there was no bloodshed.

Mary leaned over and checked the unconscious woman's pulse, nodding when she found it. "Yeah, she's still with us, but she's out cold."

The sounds of heavy bootsteps filled the room and the four companions looked up as three soldiers ran over to them. Either someone had told them what had happened or they had figured it out for themselves.

"What's going on here?" One asked as he looked to each of the women. His rifle was aimed down to the floor, as were the two other soldier's muzzles.

Raven said nothing, her face devoid of emotion and both Mary and Cindy shrugged. Sue hid the skillet behind her back, smiling politely at the soldiers. She looked like someone's mother, her visage angelic.

"Nothing's going on here. Why do you ask?" Mary said and began fixing her bed.

"We heard there was a scuffle going on back here," another soldier said.

"Nope," Cindy shook her head. "We're good. Figure we'll grab a shower and change before we get something to eat." Cindy walked over to one of the soldiers, turning on the charm. "Would any of you like to join us?"

The soldier blushed. He was no more than sixteen and he looked like he was about to faint.

"No, ma'am, it's against orders. Major Maddox said we'd be on the poles if we even think about touching one of you ladies."

Cindy sighed. "Oh, well, that's too bad, you're kind of cute." The solider blushed even harder and tried to clear his throat.

"Okay then, if everything's all right, then we'll be gettin' back to our posts."

"You do that, but don't forget if you change your mind, you know where we are," Cindy said in a sexy voice.

The soldier nodded slightly, swallowing hard, and after grabbing the other two men who were seriously considering Cindy's offer, they stomped away, chatting amongst themselves in a quick tone.

Mary stepped up next to Cindy, a wide grin on her lips. "You are so evil," she said.

Cindy only shrugged. "Nah, I knew they wouldn't take me up on it. If they could, they would have done it with someone else long before us and I could tell by the way the other woman looked at them they weren't that afraid of 'em."

The lesbian moaned in her sleep and rolled over, the previous occupant of the bed staring down at her.

"What do I do now?" the middle-aged woman asked, now bed less.

"Sorry, honey, not my problem," Mary said and turned away to look at Cindy, Raven and Sue. "Come on, let's grab a shower and a change of clothes before we eat, I'm starving."

Working out a cycle so that one of them was always watching their weapons and gear, the women began undressing; looking forward to the warm shower and hot water they were told was available. The entire time they showered, dressed and saw to any wounds they had incurred from either the cannies or the battle with the ghouls, the unconscious lesbian snored away merrily, sawing logs in her sleep.

CHAPTER THIRTY-FOUR

STEPPING INTO THE men's barracks, Henry scanned the faces looking back at him. He didn't like what he saw. Every face looked hard, and underneath was a layer of exhaustion. He saw no children, only adult men, and as he began walking down the center aisle, all eyes were on him.

A small man with a receding hairline, wire-rimmed glasses and a friendly smile stepped up and joined Henry while he moved down the aisle.

"Ignore them, friend, they're just looking to see who you are. In a second or two they'll forget about you. We get so many new people here; strangers are no big deal anymore." The small man held out his hand. "I'm Ralph, Ralph Whitman."

"Henry," came the reply. There was no need for a last name. Nowadays, last names were a frivolous thing, much like an appendix or an odd growth on a person's back. It was a thing of the past.

"Nice to meet you, Henry. Welcome to Fort Knox, the largest slave labor camp in what was once the United States." He slowed near an unmade bunk. "Ah, here we go, you can have Clancy's bunk. He died the other day and no one's claimed his bed."

"Oh, yeah? How'd he die?"

Ralph shook his head. "That's a story for another time, when you've settled some." The small man changed the subject. "Have you eaten yet?"

Henry shook his head no. "No, and I was hoping to grab a shower. I heard there were new clothes here, too."

"Oh yeah, we got clothes coming out our asses. This base once held over 23,000 soldiers, their families and civilians. If you don't mind wearing army uniforms then you're good to go." Then Ralph took another look at Henry's blood-stained clothing and at the warrior's weapons. They were so covered in gore the actual pattern on the clothes were indistinguishable. "Oh, I see you're already wearing some. Looks like you were in quite a battle. Are you a soldier already?"

Henry replied no and left it at that, despite Ralph's prodding.

Henry roamed his gaze over the faces who were watching him one last time. His eyes took in the assorted weapons each man carried. He saw M-16's and the out of place AK-47s as well as a jumble of handguns and serrated blades. Turning back to look at the door he'd entered from, he saw two soldiers standing guard. Both were acting very casual, smoking cigarettes and leaning against the doorjamb. By the time he pulled his eyes away, the other men in the room had gone back to what they were doing, Henry already forgotten.

Ralph pointed to the back of the room.

"The showers back there. We got hot water, too. One of the few perks to being here." Henry began undressing, already wondering how he would be able to guard his weapons while showering when a new man entered from the same door Henry had used. With the sun at his back, the man's face couldn't be seen, but as he began walking into the room, Jimmy's wide, smiling face appeared.

"Jimmy, over here!" Henry called out, relieved to see his friend. Ralph said nothing, watching the new man enter.

Jimmy strolled down the center aisle like he was a Hollywood celebrity walking down the Red Carpet. He said quick hellos to the men closest to the aisle and nodded to others, like he was an old friend returning from some errant trip.

No one returned his greetings and Jimmy was frowning by the time he reached Henry.

"Tough crowd," he said unhappily. "Hey, Henry, what's up?"

"Not a damn thing, Jimmy, I'm glad you're here. Now I can shower while you watch my stuff. Then I'll do the same for you."

"Fair enough. Gonna do that now?"

"Hell, yes, look at me, and you, too, for that matter. We stink like a slaughterhouse."

"Okay then, let's go, I'm starving. A guy outside told me where the cafeteria is located. But we need to get there soon before they stop serving."

Henry nodded and the two men moved off to the showers. Jimmy noticed Ralph following them and gestured to Henry, asking who the little guy was.

"Leave him be, he's harmless. And he might just be of use to us for info," Henry whispered as the two men entered the showers. There were a few men already there, but they were just finishing up. With a wary eye at the newcomers, they all wrapped towels around themselves and left.

Jimmy studied the showers and the pile of towels sitting on a cart in the corner. Small clouds of steam billowed across the white tile, tantalizing and inviting.

"Wow, just like home. Never thought I'd see something like this again."

"Oh, yeah, the CO makes sure we have the few amenities he can give us. The hot water and power comes from a nuclear reactor a few miles away. He secured it and found a few scientists to run it so we have all the power we want."

Henry nodded and began stripping.

"Me first, Jimmy, then you," he told him as he shrugged out of his shirt. Ralph's eyes went wide when he saw the gash on Henry's upper arm near his shoulder. It wasn't bleeding, but it was puckered, like the lips of a fairytale monster. The bandage had slid off and was now hanging by a small piece of white tape.

Henry winced as he touched it with his fingers, remembering the sharp pain when a cannie had shot at him. A few inches higher or lower and he could have been killed by the severing of a major artery.

"Wow, what the hell happened to you?" Ralph asked. "On second thought, never mind." He held up his hand for Henry to wait a second and then ran off back into the barracks.

Jimmy pointed with an overhand finger at the little man's back.
"What's his deal?"

Henry lifted his shoulder slightly, then turned to the showers. Jimmy nodded, understanding. Henry didn't know or care about the little man. If he was interested in them that was fine with Henry, just as long as he didn't cross the line. Besides, it was always good to have someone with you who knew the layout and workings of a town or fort. Less chances of stepping on the wrong toes.

Henry stopped under the warm spray and felt his weariness wash away. The water sluiced off his broad shoulders, washing the dirt and grime away. Jimmy sat in a small chair near the edge of the shower, the pile of weapons and gear at his feet. He was feeling clammy with the steam penetrating his clothes and was looking forward to his own turn in the shower.

Henry soaped up and washed every crack and crevice, enjoying the cascading water. He took a little extra time on his shoulder wound, peeling off the bandage Mary had placed on it and rubbing the soap into the opening and causing it to bleed slightly. But the wound seemed clean with no sign of infection so far. Mary had doused the gash liberally with antiseptic and the medicine appeared to be working.

Henry had always been a quick healer and had almost never had to deal with infections. His body had an uncanny knack for fighting off unwanted bacteria, and in a world where the local hospital was a morgue, that was a valuable talent to have.

After being under the water for a full ten minutes, he felt his stomach rumbling so hard he thought it would just break out of him and go off seeking food on its own. Turning off the spray, he picked up a towel and began drying off, feeling wonderful for the first time in a long while. Even bathing in the lake wasn't up to the simple experience of taking a real shower.

Wrapping another towel around his waist, he gestured for Jimmy to go ahead and get undressed. Jimmy stripped like he was in a contest, and then charged into the showers, almost slipping on the slick tiles. Henry continued toweling himself dry as Jimmy turned on the spray and began singing. Henry shook his head and chuckled at this friend.

Ralph was standing behind him and Henry looked down at the small man.

"I went to get you something," Ralph said and moved closer to Henry.

At first Henry was wary, but then realized Ralph was trying to help him and he lowered his guard. Ralph moved so he was leaning over Henry's wound and he held something in his hand.

"If I may? I can close that up for you."

"How? You got a needle and thread?"

"Better," the small man said and showed Henry the small bottle of Crazy Glue in his hand. "You remember what happens when you got some of this stuff on your fingertips? Well, this is the same thing only better."

Henry frowned deeply while he considered the man's idea of first aid.

"Trust me, it works."

Deciding he had nothing to lose, Henry nodded and Ralph leaned over and touched the tip of the glue to the edges of the wound, Henry wincing slightly. Then he pressed them closed. The wound sealed like the man had used professional skin glue hospitals used and Henry nodded as he touched the wound gingerly.

"Hey, that's not bad. Thanks, Ralph, appreciate it."

Ralph smiled, pleased to be of help. "No problem. It works great on weapons, too. Only it doesn't last as long. But it's great in a pinch. Here," he said handing Henry the tube. "You take it, I got more."

Henry took the tube of glue and set it on the floor with his other items.

Ralph stood quietly, like a puppy waiting to be told what to do. Henry ignored him, standing and walking over to the small shelf full of uniforms. There were socks, underwear, new BDU's and a small pile off boots. Some looked worn, but others were brand new. Henry grabbed a set of what he needed and quickly dressed. He decided to keep his own boots as they were broken in and had a lot of miles left in them. But he did use one of the towels to try and clean them, rubbing the dried blood and bits of gore out of the laces. By the time he was done, the white towel was covered in brown from the all the blood and gore caked on the boots. But the inside of the boots were still damp with blood, and with a weary sigh for wasted effort, he tossed them into the corner, then found another pair his size. After trying them on, he found they were almost a perfect fit.

Standing tall, Henry looked into one of the tall mirrors lining one wall of the showers and gave it considerable thought if he should bother shaving. There was four days worth of stubble on his face and it felt like thick sandpaper when he rubbed his chin with the palm of his hand. Deciding it was worth waiting until there was more to worry about; he crossed the floor and began checking his weapons. He unpacked the gun oil and the few rags he had so he would be ready to strip and clean them upon returning to his bunk.

"Come on, Jimmy, you're gonna look like a prune!" Henry called out.

"Yeah, yeah, I'm comin'," Jimmy answered back. The shower went on for another two minutes and Jimmy finally pulled himself away. The steam was everywhere and Henry had to wave it away from his face. It was like a fog bank had rolled into the barracks from some unknown source.

Toweling off, Jimmy walked over to Henry and Ralph, who was standing quietly, watching them.

Jimmy had a towel on his head, but otherwise was naked.

Henry averted his gaze as Jimmy walked to within a few feet of him.

"Do you mind? I don't need to see your wang today if it's all right with you. Cover up, will ya?"

Jimmy had done this in the past, not shy about being naked.

Snickering, Jimmy wrapped the towel from his head around his waist. "You're such a prude, Henry. The human body is a beautiful thing, revel in it."

"Yeah, okay, tell you what. You revel in it. I'll stick to wearing clothes, now come on and get dressed. We need to clean our weapons and then I want to eat, I'm starving."

Nodding that he understood and agreed on the eating part, Jimmy went over and grabbed his own share of clothing. When he was dressed, he wore a clean white T-shirt and green army pants, compared to Henry who wore the green uniform with matching shirt and pants. Jimmy grabbed a cap, placing it on his head and Henry thought he looked just like a recruit, though his hair was a little longer than authorized by the military manual.

The two warriors gathered their gear and walked back to their bunks, Ralph right behind them. Henry stopped and Ralph almost walked into him.

"Look, Ralph, we need some time alone, okay? Thanks for all your help, but we're good for now."

Ralph looked dejected, but did as he was asked, tossing furtive glances over his shoulder while he moved away. He went to a small group of men like himself, all looking studious with glasses and thinning hair. He began talking to them, waving his arms in the air as he gave the others the scoop on the newcomers.

As for Jimmy and Henry, they went to their bunks, dropped down their weapons and gear and began stripping each weapon one at a time. Between the continuous use and the blood and gore covering them, they had their work cut out for them.

While the other men in the barracks went about their business, the two warriors talked quietly about where they were and what had happened. Henry's stomach rumbled again and he had to slow himself down, not wanting to rush the cleaning of the weapons. But he knew as soon as they were finished, they would head to the cafeteria for some much needed food. And hopefully, when they got there, they could find Mary and the others and decide what to do next.

CHAPTER THIRTY-FIVE

WITH WEAPONS CLEANED and oiled, Henry and Jimmy made their way to the cafeteria for some much desired food, and were promptly stopped just as they were exiting the barracks. A pair of soldiers stood with their rifles aimed at Henry and Jimmy's chests and the two warriors raised their hands immediately. The two guards on watch at the door stood motionless, watching the tableau play out.

"Whoa, what's up guys? We do something wrong?" Jimmy asked as he stared at the small black hole at the end of each gun barrel.

The first soldier took another step closer to Henry and pointed to his right down a small cement path leading deeper into the base.

Major Maddox told me to come and get this guy," he gestured to Henry with his rifle. "We're to escort him to the CO immediately."

"But we were just going to get something to eat. Come on, guys, can't it wait a while? We're starving," Jimmy protested. He slowly reached out with his right index finger and gently pushed the muzzle of the rifle closest to him away from his chest. "And how 'bout pointing that thing somewhere else, please. You're making me a little anxious."

The soldier yanked his rifle away from Jimmy's finger and jabbed it at him even harder.

"I have my orders. All I was told was to get you there. He didn't say what condition you had to be in when you made it, though." He was talking to Jimmy, but his eyes looked straight into Henry's eyes, the threat obvious.

Henry patted Jimmy on the shoulder, calming him down.

"That's okay, Jimmy, relax and go get something to eat. I'll be there when I'm done with the head honcho. Just do me a favor and save some food for me, okay?"

Jimmy frowned as he looked at Henry and the two soldiers. He really didn't have a choice in the matter and that was what was so aggravating. Finally, his shoulders slumped and he nodded.

"Fine, I'll go, but if you're not back in a half hour or so I'm gonna come looking for you."

Henry nodded, smiling slightly. Good old Jimmy, loyal like a hound dog. He had no doubt that if Henry didn't return in a timely manner; Jimmy would go through as many soldiers as he could to find him.

"I'll be fine, just go. We don't want trouble. 'Sides, they did save us from certain death, you know."

"Yeah, don't remind me," Jimmy said and pushed past the two soldiers, knocking their weapons away from him like he was swatting troublesome flies away.

Henry watched Jimmy round the path and disappear from sight, then he turned back to his two armed escorts.

"Well, gentleman, shall we go?"

The first soldier nodded, then gestured to the Steyr and the Glock Henry carried.

"We need to take those from you. You'll get them back after your meeting with the commander."

Knowing better to argue, Henry nodded, not mentioning to the two men when they overlooked the panga riding his hip. It wasn't a firearm, but it was better than nothing in a pinch. The two soldiers moved out, Henry sandwiched in the middle.

The two men on guard duty watched Henry go, then began chatting about women and the latest fight at the ring; Henry already forgotten.

With nothing better to do, as there were only nondescript buildings on both sides of the path, Henry stared at the back of the lead soldier's head while they made their way to a waiting jeep. Climbing into the back, the two soldiers climbed into the front, the lead soldier sliding behind the driver's seat. Turning over the engine, the jeep roared away, leaving a spray of grit and smoke behind it.

All Henry could do was hold on and wait and see what came next.

The fifteen minute jeep ride exposed new districts of the base. Henry watched the military part of the base disappear behind him and then nothing but wide open pastures of unkempt lawn. Near the end of the lawn, he saw one man on a large riding mower. Henry guessed that by the time the man finished cutting all the grass, he would need to start again at the beginning. The man's job was like something a landscaper would find if he went to Hell, a never-ending lawn that he would be mowing forever.

The jeep turned onto a single lane road and Henry caught the street sign when the jeep zoomed by.

Bullion Blvd. he read in neat print.

The jeep flew up this road until it slowed at a large wrought-iron gate. A soldier came out of a guard shack, and when he saw the driver of the jeep, he nodded, then disappeared back inside the shack. A moment later, the gate began to open, the guard pressing a switch or button inside the shack. The jeep drove through the gate and followed the road for three more minutes until it pulled up in front of a nondescript building with a large horseshoe driveway.

The soldiers jumped off the jeep and gestured for Henry to do the same. The lead soldier escorted Henry to the only door set in the building, while the other one remained behind to watch over the jeep, and hopefully, Henry's weapons. Just as Henry entered through the door, he turned and saw the other soldier pull out a car magazine from his back pocket as he prepared to wait for Henry to return and deliver him back to the barracks.

Upon entering the building, Henry was blasted by cool air.

The air conditioning still worked!

Soft lights recessed into the ceiling illuminated a long hallway, covered with a rich red, but short weave, carpet. Planters with plastic ferns lined the hall on each side, trying to give the space the semblance of life. The soldier gestured for Henry to go first, so he did. While Henry walked the length of the hall, he admired the paintings adorning the walls. The hall continued for fifty feet and then doglegged to the right to a small foyer. A lone desk sat unobtrusive in the middle of the small room, and an elevator stood behind the desk.

A man in a crisp army uniform sat behind the desk, complete with cap and ribbons.

Henry stopped in front of this new soldier and turned to see his escort hadn't followed him, but had stopped at the end of the hall where it touched the beginning of the room.

"So what's up? Are you coming?" Henry asked, mystified.

"No, I'll be waiting here, just do as directed and you'll be taken right to the commander."

Henry stared at the soldier for another three seconds, then turned away. The desk soldier was now watching him, his eyes never wavering. The man reached across his desk and pressed a button on the left corner and the elevator doors behind him slid open silently.

"Please board the lift, sir, and you'll be met upon arrival," the soldier said in a bored tone.

With nothing else to do but follow orders, Henry walked around the desk and boarded the elevator. Turning around, he saw the desk soldier and his escort already talking together, then the doors slid closed like a vault and Henry began descending.

There was no numbers pad for picking floors, only a door open button. The elevator was so smooth Henry could barely tell he was moving. Muzak played on the hidden speakers, some unidentifiable ballad he'd never heard before, and he felt like he had just walked back in time a year ago and was now riding in the elevator of any office building in any city in America.

What seemed like forever, but was in fact only two minutes later, the elevator came to a gentle stop. The doors hissed open and Henry let out a gasp.

An incredibly long and high chamber stood before him, and when he stepped out of the elevator, not noticing when the doors slid shut behind him, he gazed in awe at the rows upon rows of gold bars stacked like wood in individual shelving units. The gold glistened in the soft light that filled the massive room and seemed to reflect the light waves back, so it was like there were a thousand small suns stacked neatly, just waiting for some cosmic being to come along and use them in creating some distant galaxy.

So in awe of his surroundings, Henry at first didn't notice there was new music playing, a lilting ballad that was filled with sorrow and love and happiness all at the same time. Turning in a circle, he let his eyes roam over the vast store of riches, a nation's treasures, its very foundation, all around him.

The heavy steps of boots didn't pierce his senses for a moment and he only realized someone was standing in front of him when the man was so close he could have kissed him.

Henry blinked in surprise and looked the man directly in the face. The man had brown eyes set deep and his eyebrows were large and bushy. He was the same height as Henry, perhaps an inch taller, but he stood like a man who was taller in his mind, if not in body. He wore a crisp military uniform, complete with ribbons; much like the desk soldier upstairs, but this man had enough ribbons to make a salad. Despite the dress uniform he wore, a SOG desert dagger was strapped to his belt, the six inch blade suitable for hunting or close combat. A set of .357 Colt Magnum Pythons rode each hip and his brown hair was cut close to his head, almost like a high and tight, which was what most military personnel preferred. The hair was close shaved on both sides and only a small amount of fuzz was on top, with the area around the ears devoid of hair. The man smiled his perfect teeth as Henry stared at him, but his brown eyes stayed hard. Was it Henry's imagination or did he detect just the hint of madness swimming around in those dark orbs?

"Do you like the music, Mr. Watson? I picked it out personally for our meeting. Do you know classical music?"

Henry shook his head that he didn't. He had never gotten into the classical stuff, as it would usually put him to sleep. He compared it to opera, which also bored him to tears.

"This is Mozart, Don Giovanni to be exact. Down here the acoustics are incredible, don't you think? If only I had something better than my small cd player."

Henry followed the man's gaze to see a small table about twelve feet away. On it sat a boom box, though now there was no tape player attached, only a cd player.

The speakers spouted the music which filled the massive room, the sound bouncing off the walls and ceiling like they were inside a giant cavern.

Henry looked back to the man in front of him, waiting for what he would say next. Henry had to admit he was feeling slightly out of touch with what was going on. This place was incredible, and the cool air ruffled his hair, feeling good. He couldn't remember the last time he'd felt real air conditioning on his skin. He had figured it was just one more thing he would have to live without for the rest of his life.

I am Colonel George Miller and I called you here because I believe with your help and other men and women like yourself, I can bring back the old days, before the apocalypse." He held out his hand for Henry to take and Henry did so, shaking three times before Miller let go. Henry was still trying to wrap his mind around the massive vault.

He was actually standing inside Fort Knox, the largest gold repository in the world.

"So, what do you think of *my vault?*"

"Impressive," Henry said, missing the words *my vault*.

"Yes, it is. With what I have here I will rebuild America, but this time I will build it the way I see fit. The entire nation's gold reserve is down here. This is why I chose Fort Knox as my base. It was almost empty when I arrived, you know. All the personnel and civilians had evacuated when one of the perimeter fences had collapsed. But I cleaned the base up, fixed the fence and restored power. Did you know there's an underground nuclear reactor below us? No, of course you wouldn't, how could you, its top secret. No one knows about it except my most trusted advisories. The civilians above us think the power comes from a nearby reactor near the city, but that is a rumor I propagated. This base will have enough power for all my needs for years to come. With this base as my home, I will scour the land of those dead bastards and take back what is rightfully ours; what's mine. I will restore America to its former glory, only this time I will rule the land instead of some hopeless bureaucrat. I am someone who knows how to get things done."

A light went on in Henry's head and he realized something.

"Wait a sec'. Was that you who destroyed the town of Prattville?"

"Yes, that was one of many rescue missions, why?"

"Why? You killed all those people, slaughtered them like animals, why would you do that? You're supposed to be the army for Christ's sakes! You're supposed to help people!"

"And I am, Mr. Watson, in my own way. Those people had to die, they were nothing but extras. My resources only go so far right now, but in time they will grow and I will be able to save everyone. They died because they were either too young, too old, or too weak for my purposes. Mr. Watson, to retake America, we as a country, as a family, need to be strong, to be hard, to make sacrifices we would never had made a year ago. We need to do the distasteful as well as the heroic. I don't need people that can't work, can't contribute. I need strong backs and minds if I am going to make my dream a reality. Once things are running smoothly again, we can have more babies, more children to fill the large voids the dead have created. But first I need to destroy them all, send them back to Hell where they belong!" He gestured for Henry to follow him. "Come with me, please, I want to show you a few things I think will help to make my point."

Henry followed the man as they exited the large vault and walked down a small hallway. At the end of the short hallway was a steel door with a small keypad on its right side, mounted to the wall. Miller typed in the access code and the door slid open like something out of a sci-fi movie. Miller strolled through the doorway, without checking to see if Henry was following.

Once inside, Miller turned and gestured for Henry to look around. The room was the size of a small school gymnasium, which compared to the massive vault, seemed small in comparison. On one side were file cabinets, wall units and security monitors, images of the base there for Miller to keep an eye on, and on the other wall hung paintings. More than twenty paintings, all looking old and valuable, hung in three neat rows and Miller walked to the first one near the bottom right. He held up his hand to the painting like he was giving a tour at a museum, and Henry could see the madness sparkling in the man's eyes.

This is an original Van Gogh, Mr. Watson. Do me a favor and tell me what you see, will you please?"

Henry gazed at the painting for almost a minute, studying the brushstrokes and dark colors of grays and dark greens. It was a painting of a family sitting around the dinner table. All were eating potatoes and the figures seemed to be almost entirely shrouded in darkness. One lone light hung in the middle of the ceiling over their heads and their faces looked long and haggard, as if the life they led was slowly killing them, wearing them down until they finally succumbed to death.

He saw the small wall plaque and read it. The Potato Eaters 1885 by Vincent Van Gogh.

"Well, Mr. Watson? What do you see?"

"A painting. I don't know what you think I'm supposed to see, but it just looks like a painting to me."

With an aggravated sigh, Miller pointed to another painting. "Fine, then, how about this one? Tell me what this painting does for you."

Henry looked where Miller was pointing and studied the new painting. Where the Potato Eaters was dark and dreary, this new one was full of life, yellow seeming to be the predominant color. It was a painting of a corn field, the houses and piles of corn spread out under a clear blue sky, with not so much as one cloud to mar its beauty. He read the plaque below it: Harvest at Le Crau 1888 Vincent Van Gogh.

It was a picturesque painting and it filled Henry with hope. He told Miller as much.

"Hope?" Miller asked. That's all you see." Shaking his head, Miller pointed to a painting on the top row. Henry had to crane his neck to see it and Miller told him to tell him what he saw once more. Tired of playing Miller's game, Henry did so one more time, studying the painting intently.

It was a portrait of a man. The man wore a deep blue suit and the lighter sky behind him helped to emphasize his pale face. He was leaning on an elbow at an odd angle and had a melancholy visage as he stares back at the viewer. On the table before him, the purple flower of a foxglove, a medicinal herb used to treat nerve disorders indicated the man's profession. Henry read the plaque under it.

Portrait of Dr. Paul Gachet.1890 by Vincent Van Gogh.

"Well, what do you think?" Miller asked, impatient that Henry hadn't finished studying the portrait yet.

"I think it's a painting of a guy, so what?" He turned to face Miller. "Look, what the hell am I doing here? What do you want from me?"

Miller's face creased in anger, but he forced it away. He walked a few feet away from Henry and then spun around abruptly.

"I brought you here because I thought you were of the same mind as me. I heard about how you survived on that bus roof for days and it inspired me. I need men like you, and women, perhaps even some of your companions. The fair haired woman looked interesting to me."

"You mean Cindy?"

"Ah, is that her name? She's strikingly beautiful."

"Yeah she is, but she's taken. She's with Jimmy."

"Jimmy? You mean that young man you came in with? Surely he doesn't appreciate her the same way someone with my power, my intelligence could. I could make her a queen, my first lady." He walked back to the paintings and raised his hands over his head.

"These paintings, Mr. Watson are from one of the greatest painters of our time. But when he was alive, actually painting these works of art, he was nobody. He was a pauper, and if his own brother had not supported him, he would have wound up homeless. No one realized his brilliance until ten years after his passing. A hundred years after his death the portrait of Paul Gachet sold for 82 million dollars at auction and his painting of Still Life With Sunflowers sold for 29.9 million dollars.

"Yeah, so what? What the hell does this all have to do with me and my friends?"

"My point, Mr. Watson, is that during Van Gogh's life, he wasn't appreciated for his talent. And so goes the same for me. I don't expect accolades now, but I believe, nay, I know, that after I am gone future generations will come to see me as a genius, a savior that ended the undead scourge and brought The United Unions of America back from the brink of destruction." As he finished his speech, spittle accumulated on the corners of his mouth, making him seem rabid. Miller's eyes were wide as he told his tale and Henry took a step backward. This man was stone crazy. He believed he was the messiah for America, right down to renaming the United States.

Miller saw Henry's face and he calmed down slightly. Wiping the spittle from his lips, he crossed the few feet separating them.

"By your look of consternation I see you don't agree with my vision, am I right?"

"That's a fucking understatement. You can't be serious. You think you're the next Van Gogh? Please, your nothing but another small-minded man who was fortunate enough to grab a small piece of power before everything fell apart. Do me a favor and leave me and my friends out of it."

"Oh, I can't do that, Mr. Watson. You see, you are now part of my army whether you like it or not. But I'm a magnanimous man. If you do not share in my vision, I will forgive you for being misguided. Perhaps, in time, you will come around. When you do, come see me. My office is on the south side of the base, any of my men should be able to show you where to go, I try to be accessible to them."

"Don't count on it," Henry breathed. He was already wondering if he could take out his panga and slice this crazy bastard's head off and then get out of the vault, collect his friends, and hightail it the hell off this base, but the more he considered it, the more he realized it was a foolish idea.

For the first time, Henry noticed there was a small call box in Miller's hand, and when the colonel pressed it, four soldiers stepped from hidden alcoves around the large room, each holding a sniper rifle. Henry nodded, understanding. Leaving him with his panga had been a test. If he had tried to attack the colonel, or threatened him in any way, he would have been shot before he could have brought down the first blow.

"I believe our meeting is finished, Mr. Watson. It's too bad you're not a visionary like me. When I heard about your valiant survival on the rooftop of that bus, I thought you were something more than an average grunt. I see I was mistaken." He gestured to the closest soldier. "Escort him back to the barracks or where ever he wants to go, but have him report to Maddox in the morning for his assignment with the others taken in."

"Yes, sir," the soldier said, saluting smartly. He moved up next to Henry and gestured with the barrel of his rifle for Henry to get moving.

Without a glance behind him, Henry did as he was told.

"One more thing, Mr. Watson," Miller called just before Henry had exited the room.

"Yeah?"

"I'd watch my back if I were you. Though I try to maintain order, my base has a few undesirables I still need to weed out."

"That sounds like a threat, Colonel, is it?"

"No, of course not, merely a warning. What you choose to do with the information given you is entirely up to you."

Henry stared at Miller for a full minute, sizing him up yet again. Why the warning? If he wanted Henry dead, he had no doubt all the man had to do was snap his fingers and one of his soldiers would do it for him. All the men seemed like drones, merely doing what they were told. Henry couldn't blame them, really. They were on the top of the food chain, a safe place to live and food in their bellies, why rock the boat for a stranger if you didn't have to?

"Come on, move it," the soldier said, poking Henry gently in the back. Henry complied and headed back to the elevator. Walking back into the grand vault, he once again gazed at the gold. It was still there, of course, shining like a thousand suns.

For some reason, though, Henry thought it didn't seem to shine as brightly as before.

CHAPTER THIRTY-SIX

THE JEEP PULLED up in front of the cafeteria and Henry climbed out without a thank you. He reached back and grabbed his Steyr and the soldier sitting behind him handed him his Glock.

Taking the weapon, he walked down the small cement path leading to the cafeteria, and behind him, the jeep drove away with a cloud of smoke and the fading voices of the soldiers. Henry stopped for a second, looking around himself and listening to the vibrant sounds of life. All around him the sound of the military base filled the air. He could hear singing coming from a few buildings over and somewhere nearby women were laughing merrily. Further off there was the distinct wail of a child crying and a half-starved dog ran down the street with a piece of an old chew-toy in its mouth, three boys ages ten to thirteen chasing after the animal, laughing and clapping. The aromas coming from the cafeteria caused Henry to turn around, his stomach rumbling once more. Enough sightseeing, he was starving.

No one was going into the cafeteria, but many were leaving and Henry hoped he wasn't too late to get something to eat. He was absolutely starving and would settle for whatever he could get.

Stepping into the bustling room, his eyes scanned the people sitting down at the large picnic-like tables and others standing in small groups, talking loudly. The room was only half full, the complement of men and women nothing compared to what was once served at daily meals when the base was fully operational and manned. Trash barrels were spread out across the room, more than one of them overflowing with trash. Large flies filled to capacity crawled everywhere, eating whatever crumbs were left behind and sometimes entire plates of slop left by their owners. Small children, all no younger than seven, moved about the room, cleaning off dirty plates from tables and washing them clean.

Walking over to the food line, Henry frowned to see there was nothing sitting on the steam tables.

"Great, I missed the meal," he said to himself. There was an older man wearing a hairnet working behind the counter, wiping things down with a dirty rag.

"Sorry, pal, your ten minutes late and we got strict rules on not feeding late arrivals. If we didn't, no one would come on time. The next meal is tonight at six, though. You gotta wait a few hours. Next time get here on time."

Henry opened his mouth to explain to the man why he was late and decided what would be the point. Turning around, he wondered what the hell he was going to do for food when Jimmy waved from a far table near the back of the room.

Smiling at seeing Jimmy's cheerful face, Henry crossed the cafeteria, zigzagging around the men and women who were finishing up and leaving. He watched one of the children cleaning the tables, wiping them down with rags from filthy buckets of water. No one seemed to care or would be complaining anytime soon. The Board of Health was long dead.

Upon reaching Jimmy, he saw the rest of his traveling companions, as well. He smiled at Cindy and Mary, but Raven barely noticed him, too occupied with playing with her food, and he sat down next to Sue, who wrapped her arms around him and leaned her head against his shoulder.

"We were so worried about you. We're so glad you're all right," Sue said into his ear.

"Is that we or just you talking?" Henry asked with a grin.

"Both," she said.

"Here, old man, I saved you some grub. I figured you might not make it in time before they closed down the line."

Henry looked down at the plate of food in front of him and his eyes went wide. It was nothing but some kind of brown stew with fatty pieces of some unnamed meat floating around in it. The vegetables were mainly potatoes and carrots, all cooked so they fell apart when touched. A stale piece of bread came with it and Jimmy had managed to score a bottle of soda from somewhere. Despite the lackluster meal, Henry dove in with a vengeance, quickly devouring the stew and cleaning his plate with the stale bread, which was easier to swallow once it had soaked up some of the brown gravy. At least there was salt and pepper on the table, and Henry loaded up liberally with both, trying to improve the taste.

Six minutes after he had dug in his first spoonful, he was sitting in front of an empty plate, leaning back and relishing the rest of the soda.

"God that was good, even if it wasn't the best meal I've ever had. Still, it fills the empty spot that was gnawing its way out of my stomach. Thanks a lot, Jimmy, I owe you one."

They all agreed with him of the condition of the food and now that Henry had finished eating, the questions came at him with full force. He fielded each one, trying his best to get to the point and not mince words. He told them about what Colonel Miller had said and how he had saw Cindy and had taken a liking to her. He shared the colonel's visions of a new America and how he planned to get to that point. Sue's face was wreathed in anger while she listened; realizing the same man responsible for saving her life had committed mass murder on a grand scale.

Jimmy suggested they find a way to kill Miller, take him out before the man could do anymore damage, but Henry told him no. The commander of the base was too well guarded and for the five of them, at least one in no way a warrior, to try and kill him and escape would be suicide. No, better to just bide their time and try to sneak out of the base at the first opportunity.

A vote was taken and everyone agreed that would be the best course of action, though Jimmy couldn't help but protest a little more. Henry knew he was angry for two reasons. The normal reasons of wanting to take out another wannabe dictator, but also because Miller had stated he had eyes for Cindy.

"Well, whatever we're going to do, how 'bout we do it tomorrow?" Mary asked while standing up. "We've got the rest of the day off and I know I want to sleep for a week." She leaned forward and gathered some of the plastic food plates from the others. "Here, let me take those," she said and piled them on top of one another like a seasoned waitress. When she had as many as was physically possible, she turned and walked to a nearby trash bin.

Zigzagging through the people moving about, she almost tripped over a bucket of water left by one of the children, but she managed to regain her balance and continue on with only a slight misstep.

There were four soldiers and one civilian, all men, standing near the trash barrel, oblivious of the flies buzzing about, and as Mary dumped her load into the overflowing barrel, she smiled slightly at the men. Three soldiers and the one civilian looked at her with ambivalence, but the fourth soldier's eyebrows went up in admiration when Mary turned away, her hands now free of trash. The soldier's eyes dropped to Mary's firm buttocks, slim waist and long brown hair and he immediately reached out and grabbed her left arm, almost yanking her off her feet and spinning her around.

"Whoa, there, darlin'," he said in a slow, southern drawl, "Just where do you think you're goin'?"

Mary was surprised and shocked and was taken completely off guard by the soldier's actions. She thought at least here, on the military base, where the soldier's actions had consequences, she could let her guard down slightly. Too late she realized she was wrong.

"Get your filthy hands off me, you big ape," she snapped at the man, trying to yank her arm free, but the soldier's grip was tight and he only squeezed harder, causing Mary to yelp in pain.

"Looks like we got us a fighter here, boys," the soldier said to the other men who only chuckled at Mary's discomfort. Mary realized none of them were going to help her. Knowing she had to act fast, she brought her free hand up and slapped the soldier hard in the face. The resounding clap of palm against cheek was like a cannon shot in the room. The soldier's eyes went wide and his jaw set into an ugly scowl.

"Why you little…" he said as he raised his right hand over his head and prepared to slap Mary so hard her teeth would hurt for days.

Just as the soldier's arm came down, another arm came up, blocking the man's blow. The soldier was stunned to see Henry standing next to him, his forearm now connected to his, saving Mary from the battering only inches from her face.

"Take your hands off my friend right now, pal or you and me are gonna dance."

The soldier answered the threat by letting go of Mary, and spinning to strike Henry with his now free arm. The hand curled into a fist and was coming directly at the side of Henry's head. But the warrior wasn't there, already ducking low and kneeing the man in the balls. The soldier fell over, wheezing as he tried to suck in the expelled air that escaped him upon having his testicles pushed inside his abdomen. His face turned red and he went to one knee. Henry raised his arms over his head, hands locked into one large fist, prepared to bring them down on the back of the soldiers' neck and thereby knock the man unconscious, when one lone gunshot sounded throughout the cafeteria.

Everyone stopped moving, and Henry held his blow. Turning around, he saw Major Maddox standing in the doorway to the cafeteria, framed by five soldiers, all with AK-47's aimed at Henry and the wounded man at his feet.

"What the fuck is going on here? There is absolutely no unauthorized fighting allowed on this base," Maddox barked at the top of his voice. He strolled across the cafeteria, kicking buckets of water out of the way instead of merely stepping over them. The children cowered in fear under the tables, scared after hearing the gunshot, and anyone not needing to be in the cafeteria quickly left, almost dissolving into thin air. Henry stood his ground, unclasping his hands as he waited for Maddox to reach him. The soldier was still bent over, sucking in air.

Maddox stopped three feet in front of Henry and glanced down at the fallen man. Pointing at the man, he signaled for his men to pick the wheezing soldier up.

"What the hell is going on here, Corporal Wagner? And you better not jerk me around."

Corporal Wagner sucked in a heaving breath and stood taller, six feet two to be exact, not wanting to appear weak in front of his superior. The redness in his face slowly faded away until Wagner was looking slightly better. Sucking in another breath, he turned and gestured to Henry.

"This asshole came at me and sucker punched me for no reason, Major. I was just trying to defend myself."

"What!" Mary yelled. "That's a lie!"

"Silence!" Maddox screamed. "I'll get all your statements when I'm ready." He turned back to Wagner.

"Corporal, do you want to go to the brig or settle this in the ring? And be quick about it, I'm not in the mood for any bullshit. But someone is gonna pay for this insubordination."

"I'll take the ring, Major. This jerk needs to be taught a lesson how we do things around here."

Maddox nodded, then turned to one of the soldiers near him. "Go get the bone," he told the soldier, who promptly spun on his heels and ran out of the cafeteria.

Maddox turned to Henry, his dark eyes locking onto him and he frowned.

"What's the matter with you, Watson? You haven't been here for a day yet and you're already picking fights with my men. Well, don't you worry; I think you'll find that was a big mistake on your part."

"This is all crap and you know it, Maddox," Henry said tersely. "That guy tried to hurt one of my friends and I stopped him, end of story. He's telling you a lie. Ask anyone who was here; they'll vouch for the truth."

Maddox looked around to see the cafeteria was empty with the exception of the companions and the soldiers Wagner had been with. Maddox interviewed each of the soldiers and all took Wagner's side. When he was through, he turned to Henry again.

"Well, it seems your idea of what happened isn't very truthful after all," Maddox sneered

"This is all horseshit. Henry, we can't let this go on," Jimmy said from behind him. He was fingering his Remington, but so were the soldiers fingering their own rifles. Jimmy was angry, but he wasn't stupid enough to get into a firefight where the chances of survival were below ten percent.

The soldier Maddox sent away returned suddenly, stomping his boots as he ran into the cafeteria with something in his right hand. When he reached Maddox, he handed the small item to him. Taking the object, Maddox handed it to Wagner.

"Here ya go, Corporal, you know the rules."

Wagner nodded, took the object and then held it in front of Henry's face.

"You have disrespected me, asshole, and I challenge you to battle in the ring."

"The what? What the hell are you talking about?" Henry asked as he stared at Wagner and then Maddox. "What are you playing at here, Major?"

Wagner shoved the object in his hand closer to Henry's face and Henry saw it was a small bone, a deer bone to be precise. Wagner took an end in each hand and snapped it like a pencil. With the two separated pieces in his hands, he dropped them in front of Henry, the pieces falling to the floor and landing between his boots."

"We have a challenge!" Maddox yelled out, loud enough so everyone in the cafeteria could hear. Faces suddenly appeared at the doorways, and people now came back inside, confident there would be no shooting and it was safe.

"A challenge? For what?" Henry asked as three soldiers moved in, grabbed him around the arms and collar and stripped him of his weapons. Henry saw Jimmy moving into position to try something and he shook his head no.

"No, Jimmy, wait. It's too dangerous."

"A wise choice, Watson. We let you keep your weapons because you'll be needing them soon. Don't mistake my act of generosity for weakness. If one of your people so much as twitches a finger near their weapons, I'll have them all shot." He leaned in so close Henry could smell what the man had eaten for lunch. "Do I make myself clear?"

Henry nodded, understanding perfectly.

Maddox grinned, an evil grin that said volumes for the man's character. Looking at the soldiers holding Henry, he gestured for them to take him out of the cafeteria.

"Take him to the ring and get him ready. I'll be there shortly. There's plenty of time, though. I want there to be enough time for the men to gather. It's been a while since the last one and they need to blow off some steam." He turned to another of his men still standing behind him. "Oh, and go tell the commander what's happening, sometimes he likes to come, too."

"Yes, Major," the soldier said, then took off to find a two-way radio.

"And you, Wagner, go get ready. And you better put on a good show."

Wagner squeezed his hands together, cracking his knuckles, then glared at Henry. "Don't you worry, Major, I'll do us proud."

"Good, now get going, and get ready."

Wagner was off, his three soldier buddies right behind him. They were all whooping it up like they were going to a pep rally.

With Henry being dragged out of the cafeteria, the companions moved to block his egress. Instantly every soldier in the room raised their weapons, rifles cocking and safeties flicked off. The companions held their ground, ready to sacrifice themselves for one of their own.

"Leave it, guys. It's okay. I'll be fine. Just watch your backs until I return."

Mary moved close to Henry and touched his face. "Just be careful, and know we'll be right behind you."

He nodded and then Maddox ordered the soldiers to leave, Henry in the middle of them.

"That's very touching, but he's mine now. But never let it be said I'm not generous. Be at Patriot Stadium in one hour and you'll see him again."

"But where's that?" Cindy asked.

Maddox was stepping though the doorway and he slowed, turning to look at Cindy. "Just follow the crowd, when there's a battle, everyone not working shows up. It's what we do for entertainment around here. Plus, on top of the impaling and hangings, it helps to keep everyone in line."

"In line, how? Where did you take Henry, tell me!" Sue asked.

Maddox grinned lecherously. "You'll have to wait and see." Then he was gone, his soldiers following. A moment later, a jeep started outside and drove off, leaving the cafeteria quiet again. All eyes of the other occupants were on the companions as everyone whispered back and forth excitedly.

Jimmy grew tired of being the center of attention and moved towards the door, calling the others to follow. "Come on, let's get out of here, these vultures are pissing me off, and if we stay, I might do something I'll regret. Besides, we need to go find where they've taken Henry; I'm not waiting around for someone to tell me what's happening. Maybe we can get lucky and get him out of whatever's going on."

Cindy joined him, and Mary, Raven and Sue followed. As they left the cafeteria, the whispers followed them, causing each of the companions to get a shiver down their backs, though they didn't understand why.

CHAPTER THIRTY-SEVEN

HENRY SAT IN the rear of the jeep as it jumbled over the dirt road. On both sides of him people were running, yelling and generally acting like they were going to a celebration. In the front passenger seat of the jeep, Maddox sat stock still, like a statue, and Henry turned to look at the soldier on his right. He had a man on either side of him, both with pistols jammed into his side. It seemed they were concerned he was going to try something. Perhaps maybe make a break for it.

Both soldier's faces were hard and cold, their eyes like two rocks sitting in pools of water. Henry smiled at the right-hand man, trying to get him to smile, but it wouldn't happen. Eventually, he gave up and turned forward again. Deciding he needed more information, he poked Maddox in the middle of the back, the major turning slightly to see what he wanted.

"What do you want?" Maddox asked like he was dealing with a petulant child. "Just sit quietly and we'll be there in a few minutes. The stadium is at the far side of the base."

"Stadium? Look, when are you going to tell me what the hell is going on here? If you think I'm gonna do some tricks for you or kill someone, then you got another thing coming."

Maddox chuckled softly. "Oh, I think you'll do exactly what I want you to do. If you don't, you'll be dead." He shrugged slightly. "You'll probably end up dead anyway. You picked the wrong man to piss off. Wagner has been in the ring twice before this and obviously he's come out the winner. Either way, it'll make good entertainment. Now be quiet or I'll have you knocked unconscious until I need you."

The two soldiers on Henry's sides each pushed the muzzle of their guns into his side, adding to Maddox's words. Henry leaned back and crossed his arms, gritting his teeth in frustration.

The jeep wound through the one and two-story buildings, and the crowds followed. New people joined the procession, spilling out of open doorways like a leaky faucet. Henry only stared, not fully understanding what was going on.

Turning around in his seat, he saw the top of Jimmy's head. Then Cindy's mane of blonde hair came into view and soon he could see the other companions as they jostled after the crowd, trying to keep the jeep in sight.

The jeep pulled up behind a set of bleachers and Maddox climbed out. Then it was Henry's turn and he slowly stepped over the ridge of the jeep's side and planted his feet on the cement.

"Come with me, Watson, and don't try anything funny." His eyes creased as he looked Henry up and down. "I have a feeling you're not a man to reckon with lightly and I'm not taking any chances. The colonel told me about his meeting with you. That was a big mistake telling him no. No one tells Colonel Miller no."

"Well, I did and I'm telling you to go fuck yourself and this circus you call a military base."

"Hmm, we'll see just who is fucking who in a few minutes." Looking at the soldiers, he pointed to the opening between the bleachers. "Take him in there and put him on the right side. That way everyone can get a good view of him."

The soldiers obeyed and shoved Henry forward. He noticed the driver of the jeep was carrying his weapons, Even his panga had been taken from him and he felt naked with nothing but his hands for defense. But he could do a lot of damage with just his fists as he searched for a chance to make a break for it. Scenarios floated through his mind. Grabbing a soldier's rifle and spraying the rest with round after round, shredding their bodies like paper. But each scenario ended with him dying in another spray of bullets as other soldiers arrived to gun him down.

No, brute force wouldn't be the way to escape whatever Maddox had in store for him. He realized he would just have to go through with it and come out the other end intact, then he could try for an escape. Jimmy and the others would be nearby, as well, and perhaps one of them could cause a distraction. But at the moment it was all hypothetical and he knew he needed to deal with his reality.

He was led through the bleachers and the path came out where there had once been a rich, green field of grass. Football games had once been played here and parade functions for the base. Now the ground was denuded, hard packed earth and as Henry crossed it, he noticed darker stains mixed in with the brown. If he was unsure what they might mean, the flies buzzing around the stains gave it away.

Blood, spilled sometime in the near past.

The entire area near the bleachers was fenced in. A ten foot high chain-link fence made a circle that ended with one of only two entrances. Henry was ushered through the far entrance and handcuffed to the fence. As the two soldiers finished securing him, they sneered at Henry.

"Good luck, buddy, you're gonna need it," one of them said before they both exited the ring, chuckling at an inside joke. Behind the fence, Henry could see the bleachers were filling up. On both sides of the metal circle, the bleachers gave a perfect view of the ring and Henry could see why the ring had been built here. Henry yanked on the handcuffs, and though the fence wasn't a permanent structure, it didn't move in the least from his efforts. He looked down at one of the posts and saw it was anchored with cement. The metal fence that made up the ring was now as much a permanent structure as the bleachers and Henry knew whatever was going on, whatever he had stumbled into, it wasn't good.

He studied the faces in the crowd as they piled onto the bleachers. It was a party atmosphere and Henry's jaw fell open when he saw children holding balloons and near the entrance to the bleachers a cart had been set up, the vendor selling something resembling hotdogs or sausages. Nowadays, meat on a stick was a relative term and you could be eating rabbit or whatever road kill had been found out on the highway; killed by a predator or by illness.

He spotted Major Maddox and Colonel Miller as the two men made their way through the crowd. Half a dozen armed soldiers were near them, their eyes roaming the crowd for possible signs of trouble.

Both men walked up the stairs of bleachers, so they were directly behind Henry, and then sat down. The soldiers stood around them, creating a barrier from the revelers. The crowd was almost finished finding their seats and soldiers stood at intervals around the ring, directing men, women and some children to their seats.

Henry could only wait for whatever was going to happen next.

He spotted his friends sitting about halfway up the bleachers across from him. Jimmy stood up and waved, wanting him to know they were there. With his free hand, Henry waved back, letting him know he could see them. A look of concern was plastered on Mary and Sue's face and the two women talked amongst themselves. Raven glared at the people on the bleachers, uncomfortable with so many people surrounding her.

Henry looked up when a horn sounded and a bugler walked into the center of the ring from the only other door in the fence. He played long and loud, and slowly, with each passing note, the crowd grew quiet.

When talking had ceased, Maddox stood up and gestured with his hand to Colonel Miller.

"Ladies and gentleman and enlisted men, I give you, your commander in chief, Colonel Miller!"

As Miller stood up, there was sparse clapping here and there. A few catcalls and boos could be heard and when the soldiers at the bottom of the bleachers raised their rifles and aimed them at the crowd, suddenly the applause grew louder and cheers for the great Colonel Miller could be heard.

Henry watched this all with a keen interest. The people on the base were not that happy and why should they be? Miller had taken them from their homes, killed the old and weak of their families and had brought them here to work for him. They were prisoners without walls holding them in, but prisoners nonetheless. Henry wondered if it would be possible to start an uprising. The amount of civilians far outnumbered the soldiers and only the soldier's superior firepower and the civilians' lack of organization stopped them from overthrowing Miller and his men.

Colonel Miller stood up, opening his hands wide and waving his arms over his head like he was Mussolini giving a speech.

"My friends, we are here today to see two men work out their differences. In today's lawless world, with no true morality to follow, only we can keep civilization alive. Only we can be true to what are forefathers created all those years ago. It is our heritage that we must be faithful to. And that is why we are here. On this base, fighting is not allowed. If we battled each other whenever we want to, we would be no better than the lifeless husks that even now prowl our perimeter, wanting nothing more than to gain access to this base and kill us why we sleep. So that is why we are here today, to bear witness to this battle. Remember, all of you. If you do not follow the rules, you too, will end up in the ring. All right, then, I've said enough. Take what you see here and learn from it. Let the fight to the death begin!"

Henry's eyes went wide at that. To the death! Oh shit, that wasn't good.

There was more clapping and the bugler played a different tune. The gate the bugler had entered now had a new figure standing there. Henry watched as Wagner strolled into the ring, waving his hands in the air like a pro-wrestler. The crowd cheered for him and whether they agreed with Miller or not, this was someone they could relate to. Another soldier like them, who was forced to do what he was told. But if Wagner acted like he was under duress, it could have fooled Henry. The man had stripped down to his white T-shirt and camo pants. He was unarmed and he pointed at Henry with eyes filled with contempt and teeth flaring. "You are dead, Watson, you hear me? Dead!"

Henry felt the handcuffs being pulled and he turned to see a soldier unlocking them from the other side of the fence. "Good luck, buddy, you'll be dead in about two minutes."

Henry ignored the man and with his wrist free, he rubbed the chaffed skin the handcuff had irritated and moved away from the side of the fence, giving him as much distance from Wagner as he could. Up in the far bleachers, he could see his friends cheering for him. Sue was worried sick and he waved to her, trying to act nonchalant. If only he really felt like that.

While in no way a coward, Henry wasn't a fool, either. Wagner had almost a foot on him and was twice the chest size and muscle mass of Henry. Henry had been lucky the first time they had tangled, getting in his blows before the larger man knew they were coming.

But Henry knew size didn't always matter. A smart fighter could use that mass against his enemy, but the trick was to stay out of the enemy's grasp at the same time. Since traveling the deadlands, Henry had learned to fight hard and quick. He had been taught by men better than him and was never too embarrassed to ask pointers when he met a more superior fighter. With more than a year's worth of training, Henry was confident he could take Wagner, just as long as Wagner didn't get his mitts on him; which seemed very unlikely given the fact he was trapped inside a metal ring with no way of escaping until one of them was dead by the other's hands.

Wagner roared to the sky and charged at Henry, head low like a charging bull. Henry ran to the right, dodging the sweeping arms and tripped on a small hole in the ground. He rolled like a ball and came up quick, facing Wagner again. Wagner grinned at Henry's close escape, but was far from finished. This time keeping his head up, and his eyes on Henry, Wagner came at him again, but slower. Henry backpedaled until his back came up against the fence and he realized he was trapped. Wagner lunged at him, and when he was no more than a foot away, swung back his left fist for a blow to Henry's head. But Wagner was a street brawler and he telegraphed his punch long before he was swinging and Henry ducked under the fist. Wagner's fist punched the fence and he yelled in pain. Looking back to the spot his fist had connected to on the fence; Henry saw blood and a few bits of skin left behind from torn knuckles.

"Ooh, that's gotta hurt," Henry jibed, dancing away again.

Wagner growled like an animal and spun on Henry, charging at him once more. He plowed into Henry, wrapping his large arms around his waist and picking him up in a bear hug that had Henry wheezing to suck in another breath of air. Wagner laughed while he squeezed the life out of him and Henry could feel his ribs starting to crack. Ignoring the pain, Henry raised both his arms wide, palms open, and slapped Wagner's ears like Henry was holding cymbals. Wagner screamed from his pummeled eardrums and dropped Henry to the dirt. Henry sucked in a breath of dusty air and it never tasted so good. Crawling away from Wagner, the larger man shook his head clear of the pain and ringing in his ears and charged at Henry again. Rolling to his feet, Henry danced to the side, sticking his left foot out and grabbing Wagner by his right arm. Yanking hard, he sent Wagner over his leg and watched the man tumble to the dirt. Step one, use your opponent's superior mass against him.

Wagner rolled in the dirt and lay sprawled on his back, staring up at the sky. Henry was about to go over to him and try to end this for good when Wagner rolled over, and with one knee bent, pushed himself up. Henry quickly backpedaled away until he had as much room as he could get.

Wagner moved closer, though now more wary of Henry. He'd seen what his opponent could do and Henry thought he saw a small amount of respect in Wagner's eyes. Wagner fainted once or twice and Henry jumped away. Laughing at Henry's nervousness, Wagner turned and waved to the crowd, once again showboating. Henry knew it was a trap. The instant he tried to attack, Wagner would spin around and grapple him, so Henry waited, knowing his chance would come.

Realizing Henry wasn't taking the bait, Wagner turned around and bent down to fix his bootlaces. He did something with his right hand, but Henry didn't see what it was, distracted by the man tying his laces. Wagner stood up again and moved toward Henry, careful not to go too fast. Henry had no choice but to engage him and moved off the fence, not wanting to become trapped.

When both men were facing one another, Wagner swung his left hand again, his fingers curled into a fist. Henry was ready, but then Wagner shifted and with his right, he threw dirt into Henry's eyes, the payload scooped up while he was tying his laces.

Henry yelped in pain and turned away, blinded, but Wagner's plan had worked and he dove in, hitting Henry in the kidneys. Henry doubled over, and before he could do anything, he felt another punch to the side of his face, his inner cheek splitting in half.

Rolling away, Henry was in a world of pain. His vision was gone and he could hear nothing with the crowd cheering. Spitting blood, he moved away from where he thought Wagner was and came up against the fence. Blinking his eyes again and again, he slowly saw dim, foggy shapes. But no sooner did he see his first shape and a small amount of light then his head rocked to the side from a ham-fisted punch from Wagner. Falling to the dirt, Henry reeled from the blow and the stars floated in front of his vision like a thousand galaxies were dancing for his amusement.

He fought to remain conscious and shook his head to clear it from the fog descending over him. Looking up, he saw a shadow amidst other shadows. Taking a chance, he kicked out with his left boot and was rewarded with the feeling of bone giving way. Wagner yelped in pain and went to one knee, the other shattered thanks to Henry's lucky shot. Both men crawled around on the ground while each tried to recover first.

Blinking his eyes clean, rivulets of tears running down his cheeks, Henry finally regained his sight. Climbing to his feet was agony, but he did it, and as he swayed back and forth, he saw Wagner doing the same. He was limping now, but that was the extent of his wound.

"I'm gonna rip your fucking head off!" Wagner hissed through gritted teeth.

Henry saved his breath, not feeling the need to reply. Bravado was useless, all that mattered now was who would win. Hobbling away on weak legs, Henry tried to get some distance from Wagner. He needed to catch his breath, try to regain more of his vision. The sliding footsteps of Wagner caused him to look up and he moved away again. With Wagner's bum knee, he couldn't move fast enough to cut Henry off and this game of cat and mouse went on for more than five minutes before Wagner screamed at him.

"Stay fucking still, you little prick!"

Henry managed a chuckle at that, but still remained out of arms reach.

Up in the bleachers, Miller shifted with nervousness.

"Major, this isn't going at all the way I'd hoped. These two could continue this dance for hours. Make it more interesting, will you please?"

"Yes, sir, I know exactly what to do." He stood up and climbed off the bleachers until he was standing near the fence. He called a soldier to him and handed the man something, then quickly climbed back to his seat next to Miller.

The soldier moved around the fence until he was directly behind Wagner. He called to get the man's attention, then pushed something through one of the holes in the fence.

A dagger dropped to the dirt and Wagner smiled from ear to ear. Walking the few feet, he picked it up and held it high, the blade reflecting the sunlight and bouncing it in all directions like it was fine crystal. The crowd oohhed and aahhed at the sight of the lethal weapon.

"Now we'll end this shit," Wagner snarled and began walking directly for Henry, blade in front of him.

"Shit," Henry muttered to himself and quickly undid his shirt, wrapping it around his arm as a makeshift defense. He tried to get away from Wagner, but the man had a new confidence and barely limped anymore.

He moved in close and Henry weaved out of the way, kicking out with his boot to try and knock the knife from Wagner's hand. But the blow went wide and Wagner danced away, then darted back in to try and slice Henry's stomach open.

Henry jumped backward, and his back came up against the fence. With victory in his eyes, Wagner raised the blade overhead and charged. Henry crossed his arms and blocked the blow, the dagger hovering over his left eye. Wagner brought up his other hand and was now using both to press the advantage. Henry set his jaw and forced the blade away, but with each second the point moved closer to his eye.

The blade was no more than an inch from his eye and he knew he wasn't going to win, so he changed tactics, remembering he couldn't go head to head with Wagner. He watched Wagner flex his arms, prepared to push as hard as he could and when he did, Henry went limp. The blade came down fast, but so too, did Henry, falling to the dusty ground. The dagger missed his eye and slid a centimeter from his cheek, but still connected with his shoulder. The dagger pierced flesh and Henry yelled in pain, then managed to roll out from under Wagner who was off guard by the odd move.

Running to the opposite end of the fence, Henry placed his hand over his wound. It was bleeding, but not that badly, and besides the sting of pain in his shoulder, he felt fine. He was lucky. An inch or so deeper or an inch to the right on his shoulder and the ballgame could have been over with a severed artery.

Wagner climbed to his feet and tossed the dagger to his other hand, entertaining the crowd who clapped and cheered. Henry heard Jimmy's voice through the cascade of voices but he couldn't look his way. Leaning against the fence and sucking in air, he felt something in his back pocket. Reaching behind him, he pulled out the Leatherman he'd taken from one of the cannies in what seemed like months ago. The tool was equipped with a small blade and with the Leatherman behind his back; he flipped it open, struggling with the blade. The damn things were always hard to open and it was like you needed a tool to get the tool open. Literally cracking his thumbnail with effort, he managed to open the blade, but kept it behind him. Wagner was moving towards him again, slicing the air with the dagger. The bloodstained blade arced back and forth like a scythe and Henry waited for Wagner to move closer.

Henry slumped more than he needed to and used his right hand to cover his wound, acting like it was worse than it was. Wagner smiled, thinking Henry was wounded to the point he couldn't put up much of a fight and he charged ahead, knife to the side, confident in his victory.

When he was only two feet away, Henry dropped to the ground, and sliced with the small blade on the Leatherman. Wagner was off balance, not understanding why his opponent had fallen to the ground and only realized he'd been fooled when he felt sharp pain in his lower, right thigh. The Leatherman plunged to the hilt and Wagner screamed, jumping away. The Leatherman was ripped from Henry's grasp and Wagner hobbled away, screaming and yelling curses.

Standing up, Henry moved close to Wagner, following him like a hunter who had wounded his prey and was waiting for it to die of blood loss. But that wasn't to be the case and Wagner spun around, the dagger in front of him.

"Stay back, you fuck. Son of a bitch, you stabbed me!"

Henry decided it was a moot point that Wagner was trying to do the same thing to him and already had once.

With the dagger in front of him, Wagner was safe from Henry's attack and Henry was easily able to avoid Wagner when he tried to go after him. With the limp in his knee and now a blade in his thigh, the man was hobbling like an old man with arthritis. Once again the battle was at a stalemate.

Up in the bleachers, Miller slapped the metal bench, muttering obscenities.

"Dammit, Major, this isn't working. Do something or so help me you'll be in there next!"

"Do I have permission to do whatever I want, sir?"

"Yes, yes, just get this fight back on track. Look around you, we're losing the crowd."

And they were as men and women began booing, and worse, some were now cheering for Henry where before only Wagner was applauded. Henry was becoming the underdog, the man who was smaller and yet was still holding his own. All the civilians could relate and their fire was returning as this unknown man continued to turn the tables on his adversary.

Major Maddox spoke into his two-way radio and in quick, terse words gave the soldier on the other end instructions. When he was finished, and had his answer he placed the two-way radio down and turned to his commander.

"Sir, five minutes more and you'll get what you're looking for. I've given the orders."

"Good, Major, you better have," Miller said, the warning obvious.

The next five minutes went by slow as Henry and Wagner danced back and forth in the ring. Henry stayed away from Wagner and the larger man couldn't reach Henry. So the dance continued until a large wooden box was rolled up to the far gate, similar to a coffin, but made of pine or similar wood.

The crowd grew silent and, so too, did Henry and Wagner as each stared at the box at the far gate.

"What the fuck is this? This isn't supposed to happen," Wagner said to Henry.

Henry could only shrug, not knowing what should or shouldn't happen.

The gate was opened and a soldier climbed onto the top of the seven foot box. When he was on top, he reached over the front and raised the sliding door. As the door began to rise, Henry saw boots, then ankles, then legs, and then a waist. Next came a large chest and two ham-sized fists that dwarfed Wagner's. As the door was raised as high as it would go, Henry saw the face for the first time. The skin was a mottled black and was pulled tight against the skull. The eyes had sunken into a caveman brow and the hair was cut close to the head on the sides and was in cornrows on top, with the exception of where the scalp showed through in a few places and the cornrows had come undone over time.

At first glance at the man, Henry had missed the large circular chest wound placed directly in the middle of the man's sternum. Cracked ribs were sticking out at odd angles and internal organs could be seen hanging at odd angles inside the wound. Maggots squirmed around the hole, feeding on the dead flesh and when the giant figure moved for the first time, both Henry and Wagner jumped a step backwards.

With one large, size thirteen boot at a time, the tall, muscular ghoul exited its small prison and into the light of day. Opening its mouth, it hissed at Henry and Wagner, trying to decide who to go after first. Henry had to look up at the tall zombie who had to be at least six-six, six-seven easy. He couldn't help but wonder if this black man had been a basketball player in his former life.

Then, before either Henry or Wagner could do anything, the zombie charged, his long legs eating up the distance separating them from him in less than a second.

Gritting his teeth, Henry raised his fists, realizing this battle to the death had taken on a whole new deadly turn.

Chapter Thirty-eight

THE GROUND SHOOK as the giant ghoul turned and headed straight for Henry, muscular arms open wide and brown teeth flashing in the sunlight. There was a brighter flash in the zombie's mouth and Henry saw it was a gold tooth. Then he was rolling to the side as the ghoul lunged for him, missing him by inches. He came up near Wagner and his eyes popped out of his head when Wagner took a swipe at his exposed arm with his dagger.

"What the hell are you doing, you fool, we need to fight this deader together!" Henry yelled as he rolled the opposite away, feeling the wind of the dagger's passing.

Wagner ignored his protests and charged at Henry, hoping to take him out now that his attention was divided. Henry rolled to his feet and managed a snap-kick to Wagner's chest, causing the man to drop the dagger and stagger backward and off balance. The wound from the Leatherman was slowing him down some, and his busted knee only added to his fading agility.

Meanwhile, the giant ghoul had recovered his charge and was turning around. The large humanoid was stiff from decay and his speed wasn't there. If he'd been fresher, and faster, neither Henry nor Wagner would have stood a chance. Still, trapped inside the ring, the giant zombie was still a formidable opponent. And worse, the dead black man would never tire, never want food or water. He would keep coming until he'd finally sunk his teeth into either Henry or Wagner.

Running to the opposite end of the ring, Henry leaned forward, hands on knees and sucked in a few quick breaths of air. His ribs ached from Wagner's bear hug, but there was no wheezing so he was fairly sure there were no broken bones. Still, it hurt to breathe, so he closed his eyes and worked through the pain, trying to fill his lungs with as much oxygen as possible. His adrenalin was pumping and he wondered for how long he could continue fighting and running. Sooner or later he would tire and that wasn't worth thinking about, at least, not yet.

The zombie moaned so loud it came out as a roar and the crowd around the chain-link fence applauded, yelling and screaming for their favorite. A few even cheered for the zombie. This was something new to the spectators. Normally two men, and sometimes two women, went into the ring and only one exited. No time in the past had a zombie been introduced to the mix. It amped up the excitement a hundred fold. Who would live, who would die, and who would be bitten to come back as one of the walking dead?

Henry shook his head and ran to the side just as the ghoul lunged, missing him and plowing into the fence. He was just so big, and if he had worn a basketball jersey, Henry thought he would have looked a lot like Magic Johnson. That is if Magic had died and come back as one of the walking dead.

Still, Magic, as Henry dubbed him, was angry and was becoming frustrated he couldn't grab a meal. For all his bluster, Wagner was a good fighter, but Henry knew he couldn't trust him.

Magic pulled himself free of the fence and turned vacant eyes on Henry and Wagner. Deciding Wagner was closer, he charged the wounded man, feet falling in front of him like a Frankenstein extra. Wagner had recovered his dagger and he sliced at Magic, tearing a long gash in the ghoul's right arm. Nothing but dust seemed to seep out of the wound and Wagner rolled away. He spotted Henry a few feet away and ran at him, dagger leading. Henry knew if he tried to fight Wagner, then Magic could sneak up on them both, so he ran around the zombie, putting Magic between him and Wagner.

"You fucking coward, letting a damn stench fight your battles!" Wagner yelled at Henry.

Henry smiled and shrugged. His shoulder wound made him wince and he realized his other wound, the one Ralph had crazy glued, had opened again. His shoulder was coated in red, but the blood seemed to be slowing. It wouldn't be fatal if he could get both wounds looked at soon.

His shirt was still wrapped around his arm and he undid it, waving it in front of him like a bullfighter. Magic snarled and flared his teeth, then turned to face him. Henry slowly backed up, not really having a plan, but knowing something had to be done, and soon.

Magic decided Henry was the choicer meat and stumbled toward him. Henry realized he was painting himself into a corner and he looked to the left and right for somewhere to go. Magic was growing closer and Henry looked up, realizing the fence could be climbed. Turning, he jumped up and scurried up the fence, but the toes of his boots were too wide to fit inside the mesh of the fence. But he managed to crawl slightly higher than the ghoul and he held on for dear life. Magic tried to reach him for a few seconds and then gave up. There was still prey inside the ring, no reason to go after some that's out of reach.

Magic turned and moved towards Wagner as the man waved the dagger in front of him.

"Come on, ya dead fuck, bring it on!"

One of the soldiers climbed on another one's shoulders and used the butt of his rifle to knock Henry off the fence. With nowhere to go, Henry dropped down to the ground, his hands hurting from holding his body weight. He rubbed them together to get the circulation back while he struggled to figure out how to end this. Wagner ran around Magic and charged Henry.

Henry dodged the charge and spun around, kicking Wagner in the back with the sole of his boot, the man stumbling forward to crash to the dirt head first.

"You stupid bastard, will you stop trying to kill me for five damn minutes! We need to take out that deader or we're both dead!"

Wagner spit dirt and rolled to his feet, wiping his forehead clean of dust and sweat. Magic had turned and was coming for him again. Henry studied the fence and realized there were a few small holes spaced here and there where the mesh had been cut or broken over time. No more than four inches round, the holes were right where some soldiers and civilians were standing. One hole was about waist high and Henry saw a soldier standing in front of it. And the soldier had grenades on his web belt.

An idea came to him, and he darted across the ring, avoiding Magic and then hitting the fence hard. He was a few feet away from the soldier with the grenade, so he scooted along the fence. The soldier cat-called to him and clapped, enjoying the fun of the battle, and before he realized what was happening, a hand reached through the hole and snagged one of the grenades on his belt, plucking it from the soldier's chest like picking an apple.

He jumped away as the soldier yelled, his voice lost in the cacophony of the crowd. Magic was right behind him and Henry spun around, pulled the pin on the grenade and jammed it into the open cavity on Magic's chest.

Two things happened at the exact same moment. The first was Magic stopped cold and looked down at the open wound in his chest. He then looked up at the faces around him and a look of consternation crossed his undead face, as if he understood the implications of what was about to happen. The second thing to happen was Henry ran at Wagner, plowing into the man and pulling him on top of him as they both fell to the denuded ground. Wagner's face was elated, thinking Henry was throwing himself on the sword so that Wagner would win the match, and he raised his dagger high to bring it down into Henry's chest. But his arms never descended when the grenade went off and the ghoul nicknamed Magic Johnson disintegrated into an explosion of blood, bone matter, and gore. Shrapnel tore through the chest cavity and blew the ghoul into bloody smithereens while the crowd closest to the fence was splattered in blood and bodily debris. Bits of shrapnel and slivers of bone sliced into bodies, adding to the chaos.

On top of Henry, Wagner's face took on a world of shock when his back was ripped to shreds from the multiple shrapnel impacts. Henry felt his body go limp and watched the spark of life leave the man's eyes.

After the explosion had subsided, the crowd was utterly silent, with the exception of the screams of pain from the wounded. Anyone who was unhurt stared at the carnage, still trying to take in what had just happened. Even Miller and Maddox were dumbstruck. The companions were in shock, thinking Henry had just died, ripped to shreds from the shrapnel of the grenade. Already, Mary and Sue had tears in their eyes and Cindy was falling into Jimmy's arms, the grief overwhelming her.

Then Wagner's body began to stir and the crowd began to murmur.

Wagner was alive! The crowd went wild!

He had survived yet again to be victorious.

The man was unstoppable! He was the king of the ring!

Wagner looked like he was coming to his knees, but then he rolled to the side and fell back to the earth again. Blood from his shredded back soaked into the dirt, one more dark stain to join the dozens already there.

Lying on his back, his face covered in Wagner's blood, Henry sat up. Wiping his hands clean as much as he could, he climbed to his feet, swaying slightly.

The crowd went deathly silent, then Jimmy sent up a cheer. In seconds, the crowd joined in and with the sun high overhead, and his ears ringing after being so close to the grenade blast, he at first didn't realize he was hearing his name.

As the ringing in his ears dissipated, he could make out the chant the crowd was using. They were chanting his name and stomping their feet on the bleachers in a steady rhythm of We Will Rock You. Still groggy from the blast, Henry raised his right hand in the air and the crowd went crazy, clapping and cheering at his victory.

The gate was thrown open and people charged in, picking him up and carrying him out of the ring to the open field next to the bleachers. He could only go along with the crowd, as there were far too many hands to be stopped by himself.

Eventually, they grew tired of carrying him and he was set down. When he turned around, peering through the dozens of faces, he saw Jimmy and the companions, all with smiling countenances. Mary came at him and wrapped her arms around him hard, hugging him tightly and then she let go, so Cindy, Sue and even Raven could give him a quick hug. Jimmy slapped him on the back, careful of his wounds and Henry tried to answer the questions they asked when they came at him.

Suddenly, the crowd parted and a score of soldiers pushed through, using the butts of their rifles if necessary for those who were too slow or too stupid to move in time. In the middle of the men, all with rifles held at waist level, Miller and Maddox walked.

Upon reaching Henry, Colonel Miller nodded, approving of the victory.

"Well done, Watson. I'd never have expected that outcome. Highly unorthodox. You know, you wounded eight of my men and ten civilians with your little escapade, not to mention Wagner.

"Sorry, Colonel, it couldn't be helped," Henry said to him.

"Hmmph, I guess not. Well, you won fair and square and you're free...for now. The rest of the night is yours, but I want you to report to the helipad at 0700 tomorrow morning. You're flying out on a mission to the city. I need men like you, men who can handle themselves."

"Yes, sir, Colonel, I'll be there," Henry told him.

Miller turned and walked away, the soldiers parting the crowd for him and Maddox.

Maddox wore a look of disproval and Miller stopped to question him on it. "Something wrong, Major?"

"Yes, sir. Why in God's green earth did you tell Watson to report to the helipad? I thought only the best fly out on patrols."

Colonel Miller nodded, agreeing completely. "Of course you're right, Major, but did you hear how that crowd was chanting his name? That is very bad for my grand scheme. I already told you Watson and his friends are malcontents. They won't bow down to my way of life here. It was a mistake saving them, but of course how could you know that at the time. No, if he stays here, he could stir up the civilians I've brought here. There could be a revolt. No, he needs to disappear, quietly and cleanly. No martyrs will be made by my hand. So what better way then for him to disappear on a training mission? Or better yet. Why not take out that chopper that is having all that trouble. You said it won't fly, is that right?"

Maddox nodded. "Yes, sir, number 32. It flies, but it's unstable. As you know, our mechanics are only apprentices and we were lucky to find them. No matter how hard they try, they just can't figure out what's wrong with it."

"And we don't need it for spare parts, is that right?" Miller asked.

"That's right. We have a warehouse full of parts, more than enough."

"Good, then send Watson and any other malcontents with him. Once you're over the city, shoot them all down. No survivors, Major, do I make myself clear?"

"Yes, sir, absolutely, sir. We even have a pilot. He's a new recruit and he just can't get the hang of it. I was about to scrub him from the program."

"Good, at least this way he does some good. It'll make it look more convincing if the pilot goes down with his chopper."

Miller turned and began walking again, then slowed. Maddox moved next to him. "Oh, and have that blonde-haired woman traveling with Watson sent to my quarters. She...interests me. Be discrete about it. I don't want any added attention."

"Yes, sir, I'll have it done immediately."

Miller smiled and began walking, leaving the bleachers behind him. A jeep was waiting for him and he climbed into the passenger seat, while two soldiers climbed behind him. The driver started the engine and the jeep drove off, Miller not bothering to say goodbye to Maddox.

Maddox didn't mind. Colonel Miller was a great man; he didn't need to bother with the usual etiquette if he didn't want to.

Still, he didn't understand what all the fuss about Watson was for. If he wanted the man to disappear all he had to do was take him in the middle of the night. Even if there was an outcry, a few hangings or impalings would settle any protests quickly. Deciding he shouldn't question his commander, as Maddox was a good solider who knew how to follow orders unquestionably, he called a nearby corporal over to him and whispered orders into the man's ear. The man nodded, grabbed two more soldiers to accompany him and moved back into the crowd. They had a mission and they would accomplish it.

More than half the crowd had wandered away from the bleachers and there was now room to move without feeling elbows and shoulders all around. Inside the ring, three older women and one man with a bad leg were already cleaning up the gore from the exploding ghoul and also placing Wagner in a body bag. All the people unfortunate enough to have been hurt from flying shrapnel had left minutes ago, carried away by able bodied civilians, and escorted by rifle-wielding soldiers.

The companions, too, decided it was time to leave, and with Henry leaning on Jimmy for support, they began the long walk back to the barracks. They were halfway through the path, passed the barracks when Jimmy stopped and looked around.

"Hey, where's Cindy?"

All the companions looked around themselves, shocked to see their friend was missing.

"That's weird, she was right next to me a second ago," Mary said, scratching her head in curiosity.

"Maybe she had to go to the bathroom or something," Sue suggested.

"No, Cindy wouldn't just leave like that," Jimmy said and glanced to Henry. Hey, Henry, maybe something's wrong."

Henry was in no mood to think of anything but sleep and he said so. "She's probably fine, Jimmy. Maybe she went on ahead and we didn't hear her tell us she was leaving. She'll probably be waiting for you guys at the barracks when you get back. Now, if you don't mind, I'm in a lot of pain here."

"Oh, Jesus, Henry, yeah, of course, let's get you back to the barracks. Do you need a doctor?"

He shook his head as he walked. If it wasn't for Jimmy to lean on, he truly believed he would have fallen over. The adrenalin rush was gone, leaving him drained and tired.

"No, I think I'll be okay. Maybe we can do that Crazy Glue trick again."

Mary moved close and studied one of the wounds, the freshest one. "If not I think I'm gonna have to give you a few stitches." Then she decided yes, she was. "In fact, yeah, I am. As soon as we get back; and no arguing."

Henry was in no condition to protest and they moved through the bleachers and onto the path that would lead them back to the barracks.

"Christ, this is gonna take forever," Henry said as he studied the buildings in front of him. After winding their way through the streets, they still had to reach the far end where the barracks were located.

"Hey, Mary, maybe Cindy got a ride. That would explain why she's not in sight,"

Jimmy suggested.

"Yeah, possible, but still, I'll be glad when we get back to see if she's there. She's got to be, where else could she have gone?"

The companions moved in silence, no one talking; only Henry grunting every so often when one of his wounds troubled him. When they came upon an unoccupied jeep ten minutes later, Jimmy was the first into the driver's seat. He frowned when there were no keys and punched the steering wheel, sending a few choice imprecations at the hunk of metal.

Mary strolled over to him and pushed him out of the way. She began feeling around under the seat, under the mat and then opened the small opening where a glove box would be on a car. With a triumphant smile she held aloft a set of two keys and tinkled them happily.

"Ta daa!" She said. "Climb aboard; we're riding in style the rest of the way."

"But won't someone miss this jeep if we take it?" Sue asked as she climbed into the back, with Raven next to her. The teenager was quiet as always, but her eyes never stopped moving, watching for trouble.

"Nah, in a place like this, one hand doesn't know what the other hand is doing," she said as she slid into the driver's seat, pushing Jimmy away.

"Hey, that's a great idea. We'll just make sure to park it a little ways from the barracks after we drop Henry off, that way no one can prove it was us"

"That's Jimmy, always with the angle," Henry said, coughing at the same time and wincing in pain. Jesus it hurt to laugh. Wagner may not have broken any ribs but he still did a number on him.

Mary started the jeep and drove off, everyone jerking back and forth from the movement of the vehicle. After a few seconds, Mary had the controls better understood. It wasn't like driving a car. It was stiff. No power steering and no power brakes. Figures, she thought, just like the military to cut corners wherever they could.

With the companions finally riding, they drove through the streets, Mary deftly avoiding the pedestrians as they made their way back to their barracks after the battle.

With the movement of the jeep and exhaustion overwhelming him, Henry leaned back and rested his head on Sue's shoulder. She began rubbing his hair with her hand, telling him he would be all right and before he knew it, he'd drifted off into a restless sleep.

Cindy was furious. She'd been standing next to Mary when, without warning, a hand had gone over her mouth and she was pulled backward by three soldiers. The crowd had been thick, no one noticing the altercation, and in moments Henry and the others were ten feet away and disappearing behind a sea of heads. Though she struggled valiantly, her right arm had been yanked behind her back, and when she tired to fight back, her attacker would press upward on her arm, causing her shoulder to scream in pain.

She felt her weapons stripped from her as she was pulled through the crowd and soon she was at the far end of the bleachers. Henry and the others were lost, swallowed by the crowd and she saw her captors for the first time. Three soldiers in BDU's had grabbed her for some reason. She was about to protest when the hand was removed from her mouth and a gag was wrapped around her lips, the cloth siding between her teeth and stopping any questions or noise she hoped to make. Both her arms were secured behind her back and she was dumped into the back of a blue cargo van with government plates, not that license plates mattered anymore.

The soldiers weren't rough, but they weren't exactly gentle with her either and she bumped her head on the floor of the van, seeing stars for a few minutes. One of the soldiers climbed in back with her while the other two went to the front. There was nothing separating the front from the back, no roll cage or divider.

The engine started and she began to bounce around while the vehicle drove over the grass and uneven landscape. The soldier in the back with her moved closer, then sat down next to her. His eyes roved over her body and he reached out with his left hand, squeezing her right breast gently, caressing her like she was a work of art. His hand slid down her stomach and he began to rub the inside of her thighs, already preparing to slide his hand inside her pants and the warmth he knew was waiting for him. His eyes were wide and he was breathing hard and Cindy could see the front of his pants had grown outward.

She tried to squirm away, but he only smiled wider. He liked the way she squirmed and he'd just begun undoing her belt, ready to have some fun with her, when the soldier in the passenger seat spun around and saw what his buddy was doing.

"You idiot, we're bringing her to the commander. Are you crazy?"

"Aww, come on, why can't we have a little fun with her before we get there? Look at her, man, she's so hot."

"No shit, she's hot, but do you want to explain to the commander how you fucked his prisoner? What do you think he'll do to you if he finds out? And I'm pretty sure she'll tell him."

Images of the impaling poles by the gallows flashed through the soldier's mind and his pants shrunk in size immediately. He quickly redid Cindy's belt and smiled wanly at her.

"Sorry, ma'am, I didn't realize what I was doing. Hopefully, we can forget this ever happened?"

With only her eyes for communication, Cindy tried to look compassionate. The soldier saw her eyes and he relaxed slightly, moving to the side of her some more. Cindy's feet were only a foot from him and she kicked out with her right foot, the sole of her boot connecting with the man's groin. He doubled over in pain, his head striking the floor of the van. Bile slid from his mouth as he sucked in air that wouldn't enter his lungs.

The soldier in the passenger seat turned around again and saw his buddy bent over at an odd angle. He chuckled at his agony.

"I told you to leave her alone," he grinned, then turned around and began chatting with the driver while the van wound its way through the streets of the base.

Behind her gag, Cindy mumbled two words to the suffering soldier.

"Apology accepted," she said though it was highly doubtful the soldier understood her.

Cindy laid back, her head bumping the metal floor every now and then. The soldier she'd kicked in the balls eventually recovered and he now sat far away from her, his back pressed against the van's wall, as he eyed her warily.

The van came to a jolting halt, causing her to roll forward. The driver and the soldier in the passenger seat both climbed out of the van, walked around to the rear double doors and threw them open.

Sunlight blasted her face and Cindy closed her eyes while they adjusted. With the help of the other soldier, the two at the rear door grabbed her feet and pulled her towards them. Cindy debated putting up a fight, but in the end decided it was pointless. All she could do was bide her time and wait for the right moment to act. Though not a soldier herself, she was a battle-hardened soul and was three times the fighter of any of the three men who escorted her to the home of Colonel Miller. She took in her surroundings as best she could, and over the tops of the closest buildings, she could see the bleachers and the chain-link fence where the battle with Henry and Wagner had taken place. She was on a slight incline to the land, all the houses on this block higher than the rest of the base. Knowing where she was gave her a point of reference to follow, and she felt hopeful when she found the opportunity to escape, she now knew which way to run. On the other side of the bleachers, were the barracks and cafeteria, and her friends, who should be wondering what had happened to her. Even now they should be searching for her. She had to hold on to that. If she believed there was no one coming for her, well that was too much to contemplate right now.

She was shoved and dragged up the small walkway and into the one-story house. It was a light yellow with white shutters, flowers planted along the walk and green grass lining the front and sides of the home. It was something out of a magazine and Cindy hated to admit she was slightly curious about what was happening, though she had a good idea.

The door opened as she approached and another soldier greeted her. He was wearing an apron and a t-shirt and had flour on his hands and clothing, a few white smudges on his face.

Entering the home, she smelled something resembling baked goods coming from the kitchen and the sun filtered into the hall, giving everything a bright, airy feeling.

"'Bout time you yahoos got here," the man said brusquely. Cindy knew the man was obviously the cook for the house. Miller's personal chef no doubt.

"Shut up, Portman, we don't work for you," the driver of the van said. "Is the Colonel here yet?"

Portman shook his head no. "He won't be here for another hour or so."

"That's what I thought," the driver said. "So it doesn't really matter when we got here, does it. Just as long as it's before the commander. So shut the hell up and tell me where to put her."

"Yeah, she's a real spitfire. She kneed Tyson in the nads, got him real good, too," the other soldier said, the one who'd rode shotgun.

The wounded soldier called Tyson shot both the others a look that would melt skin if it could. "Shut the fuck up, you guys, I don't need your shit right now."

"Aww, Tyson ain't happy 'cause he got whipped by a girl; is that it?" The driver asked, grinning widely.

"All of you shut the hell up." Portman ordered them. "Go put her in the den for now and make sure you lock the damn door, too."

The driver flashed Portman an aggravated look. "We know, Portman, we're not idiots."

"Not like some of us," the soldier who rode shotgun said, chuckling at Tyson. Tyson flipped him off and shoved Cindy past the foyer and down to the den door. The other two soldiers followed, but let Tyson do the work. At the den, Tyson leaned forward, opened the wooden door and kicked Cindy as had as he could, his boot pushing on her backside. Cindy sprawled to the floor, only the soft carpeting saving her from a bad fall. Tyson had a sneer on his face when he closed the door, the sound of a key turning in the lock filling the den with its finality.

Cindy could hear the three soldiers arguing, at least one of them not happy with how Tyson had kicked her. Then their voices faded away.

Cindy sat up, and looked around herself. She had an hour before Miller arrived. Going to her knees, she tried to undo her bindings, but they were strong. She knew she would have to see if there was something in the den that could be used as a blade to cut her free. The den was sparsely decorated, with a small desk and a wing chair in the right-hand corner. A grandfather clock stood in the left corner, but it wasn't moving, the pendulum hanging like a dead animal, defunct.

There was one window in the room; tan, cotton drapes covering it, and she walked over to it, using her teeth to pull the drapery away from the middle. But if she thought she was going to escape through the window she was vastly mistaken.

The window had vertical bars on them, and she realized for all its décor, she was in a prison.

The desk and wingchair were to her left and she walked over to them, using her knee to push the chair away from the desk, then she plopped down in it, careful not to lean back to far and crush her wrists and hands.

With a weary sigh, she studied the walls; the pictures hung here and there in no apparent order, and wondered what the hell she was going to do next.

It was then that her eyes caught the small, silver letter opener sitting unobtrusively on the desk blotter, its handle just peeking out from under a pile of papers.

Slowly, a smile crossed her lips. She may be a prisoner, but she was a prisoner with a weapon.

CHAPTER THIRTY-NINE

THOUGH EXHAUSTED AND wanting to sleep for a week, Henry stripped and took another shower while his friends waited outside near his bunk, discussing the whereabouts of Cindy. Normally women weren't allowed in the men's barracks, but one look at Jimmy and the women's faces, not to mention their weaponry, and the soldiers on guard duty at the front door let them inside.

Standing under the cascading water, Henry gritted his teeth, the water slicing like daggers into his open wounds. Blood pooled around his feet to be swallowed by the drain and it was only when Jimmy came in to check on him that he realized he'd dozed off under the stream of warm water.

"Hey, you okay, Henry?"

"Yeah, I'll live. You got a towel for me, I'm done here."

Jimmy handed him a towel and Henry began drying off. His arms felt like lead weights and it was all he could do to stand up straight. His torso had some black and blue marks and there was a large red welt on the side of his head where Wagner had scored a direct hit.

"Damn, Henry, you look like shit," Jimmy said, the master of the understatement. Henry merely chuckled, but then stopped when it hurt too much. When he was through drying off, the towel was stained crimson in more than one place. Wrapping the towel around his lower half, he walked out of the shower stall and back to his bunk.

The women were there, waiting for him, and Sue ran over and helped him limp to the bed. Gently, wincing at every muscle movement, he crawled into bed and within seconds was fast asleep.

Sue sat down on the edge of the bed and brushed his damp, graying hair off his forehead and studied the bruises on his face where

Wagner had managed to connect with fists, then she turned to look up at Mary and Jimmy.

"He looks terrible. Will he be okay?"

Mary moved her shoulders slightly, the gesture apparent. "We can only hope so. Hopefully there's no internal injuries."

"Internal injuries? Oh my Lord, maybe we should see about getting him a doctor. Surely they have one on this base somewhere." Sue looked at each of the companions expectantly.

Ralph walked over, deciding the time was right. He'd been hovering just out of earshot and now moved up to Jimmy.

"That was some fight, yes sirree, Bob, that was some fight. That guy is all right in my book."

"Screw that, pal. What have you got in this dump for a doctor?" Jimmy's voice was hard. True, this man had helped them before, but like hundreds of others, he had watched Henry battle for his life, something Jimmy wouldn't be forgiving the man for anytime soon.

"A doctor? Shit, we had one, but he died about a month ago. Got bit when one of the recruits came in with a bite and turned later. Took a chunk right out of his arm. Or was it his ass? Hell, I don't remember, but what I do remember is he changed into one of them soon after and had to be put down with the recruit. We was just lucky he didn't bite anyone else before the soldiers found him."

"That's just great, so what the hell does everyone do around here when they get sick?"

Ralph shrugged. "Die I guess, or get better. The commander doesn't worry about us like that. Figures he can always get more recruits, I guess. He's a tough one, I tell ya. Don't cross him or you'll end up dead. I guess you folks saw those poles when you came in?"

Jimmy nodded, as did the others.

"It was barbaric," Mary said angrily. "Miller is nothing but a monster dressed in an army uniform. Anyone who would condone such torture on other human beings willingly should be shot, or better yet, have the same thing done to them."

"Maybe so," Ralph said, "but after someone winds up on a spit in the yard, there's zero breakouts for a while. No one tries to escape for more than a month after someone gets spiked." He rubbed his butt as he thought about those dead corpses. "Just thinking about it gives me a pain in the ass, though. And if I were you, I'd keep my opinions to myself. The walls have ears, if you know what I mean." The companions looked around the room at the other men sitting on their beds, talking to one another. A few eyes looked their way, but as soon as one of the companions retuned their gaze, those same eyes quickly turned away.

"So what do we do?" Sue asked. Her voice filled with concern.

"There's nothing we can do but wait. I'm sure he's fine. He's a tough old man, am I right or what?" Jimmy asked the others.

Henry rolled over in his sleep, snoring soundly. Sue caressed his face again. Mary looked down on her and for the first time saw how much she seemed to care about Henry. She remembered the way Henry was with her and realized the two were becoming a couple. She smiled at that. Henry deserved someone special. Ever since Gwen had died after the boss of the mall, Barry, had thrown her off the mall roof, Henry had been in a fugue. But it looked like enough time had passed that he could take the chance and open his heart again.

"Come on, guys, let's let him sleep," Mary said. "Jimmy, you're gonna stay with him right?"

"Yes, Mary, I'm gonna stay with him. Sheesh, tell you what, though, how 'bout getting me some grub when the chow line opens up in another hour or so. I gotta eat, ya know, I'm a growing boy. Henry, too, when he wakes up."

"Okay, fine, just don't leave him alone. And take care of those cuts on his shoulders."

With a wide grin, Jimmy produced the Crazy Glue Ralph had given him. "Already on it, babe, you just go find Cindy and tell her to come and see me. I want to talk to her about this going off on her own."

Mary nodded and moved a few feet away from Henry's bed, then glanced to Raven. "You want to say anything, Raven? God, you're so quiet, how come?"

She shrugged, the gesture almost poetic on her lithe frame. "Got nothin' to say, don't worry, I'm cool."

"She's like that, Mary; never says anything unless prodded. But she's been a good friend to me, especially when we got captured by those cannibals."

"Okay, fine with me, besides, after traveling with chuckles over there," she pointed to Jimmy, "The peace and quiet is a welcome change of pace."

"I heard that, Mary, and don't pretend you don't like it when I talk, it passes the time," Jimmy told her.

Mary gazed over her right shoulder, batting her eyes seductively. "Yeah, but sometimes it would be nice if time stopped."

Jimmy stuck out his tongue to her and she laughed, then headed for the front door. Sue and Raven followed her and they passed through the doorway, the two soldiers on guard watching them as they left.

"Thanks, boys, don't work too hard," Mary joked as she slid between the two soldiers.

Neither soldier spoke, but each had eyes only for Mary's backside as it swayed back and forth while she walked away.

The soldier on the right turned to the other one and smiled like a Cheshire cat, nodding his head. The other returned the smile. Both had admired Mary's form and now would have something to talk about to pass the rest of their watch.

$$* \quad * \quad *$$

Cindy sat behind the desk, twiddling her thumbs. Her hands and wrists were now free, but she had a few scrapes from her escape. The letter opener had been sharp and her soft skin had been no match for it. But her freedom was worth the strings of the thin cuts crisscrossing her wrists, making her look like a suicidal teenager.

She was restless, and was almost hoping someone would come for her. Anything would be better than just sitting around waiting for something to happen. Her stomach was rumbling; reminding her it had been a few hours since she'd eaten. She hadn't eaten too much at lunch, the stew unappetizing, and now she regretted it. Rule number one of traveling in the deadlands was to eat what you could, when you could, because there was no way of knowing when the next meal might come.

Footsteps sounded from outside the door and the doorknob began to turn, the clicking of the lock as it was turned sounding loud in the silent room. With letter opener in hand, Cindy jumped over the desk like an acrobat and ran to the door, plastering herself against the wall. She was ready for whoever came in, already imagining how the letter opener would pierce the jugular of her captor, their blood shooting out to paint the room a new color...the color red.

The door swung inward and she prepared for the moment of attack, her breath coming in shallow gasps as adrenalin began pumping.

She waited for three heartbeats but no one entered. Still she didn't move, wondering if this was some sort of trap. Was her captor playing with her?

After a full minute passed, she pushed off from the wall and moved to the open doorway.

Colonel Miller stood there, a smile on his face, his arms crossed in a pompous manner. On each side of him was a grim-faced soldier, each with rifles now aimed directly at her midsection.

"Come now, Miss Jansen, do you really think I'd be so stupid as to walk in there unawares? Drop the weapon please."

The letter opener dropped from her open palm to land on the carpeting without a sound.

"Well, yeah, I kinda hoped so. How do you know my name?"

"Ah, you forget you had to register this morning. I take it then that you gave your real name to the desk sergeant?"

"Sure, why wouldn't I? It doesn't really matter that much anymore anyway. A name is a name. Without the internet and phones, one name is as good as another, so why not keep the one God gave me?"

"Ah, touché, my dear. May I enter now? On the hopes that you won't try anything?"

Cindy nodded slowly, her head moving like it was made of cement.

"Excellent. You two stay out here. If you hear anything out of the ordinary, come in shooting." He then stepped into the den and closed the door. Cindy noticed the door wasn't latched. Miller noticed her downward gaze and frowned deeply like a disappointed father.

"Oh my, I thought we were past all that. I assure you there is no escape. Even if you got past those two guards there are many more between here and the front door."

Cindy flashed him a smile. "Can't blame a girl for trying."

Colonel Miller walked in and sat behind his desk. "No, I suppose I can't. Now, shall we get to know one another better?"

"Why? What am I doing here. Last time I checked, kidnapping is a crime, even in this screwed up world we live in."

Miller slanted his head to the side, considering her words.

"Perhaps, but I am the law now and if I say something is all right, then it is all right." He reached into one of the voluminous drawers of the desk and pulled out a box of cigars. Taking one out, he lit it with a pocket lighter, then began blowing smoke rings into the air. Cindy twitched her nose, the smell making her sick. Miller either didn't notice or care for her discomfort.

"Besides, the old government has a history of making the criminal proper and the amoral legal, just by saying it was so. So why should I be any different?"

"Look, Colonel, why don't you stop with the bullshit and tell me why I'm here."

"I want you to become my partner in life. If you say yes, I will give you everything your heart desires. In fact, when I take back control of this great nation, you will become my first lady. We will rule the new United Unions of America together side by side." Blowing another smoke ring in the air, he smiled like a petulant child. "Well, what is your answer?"

At first her eyes opened wide in surprise and shock, but then they creased slowly, as she realized what she was being asked. That the man in front of her was a stark raving loon was of no doubt, but he was a loon with power and perhaps she could use that to her advantage.

Cindy moved to the desk, sliding around it so that her hip was touching Miller's knee. She rested one buttock on the desk and leaned forward sensually, trying to keep a straight face through the cigar smoke. Miller returned her gaze and as he looked into her eyes she realized she couldn't do it, and she let her temper get the better of her, regretting it as the words escaped her mouth.

"I say you can go fuck yourself. Now free me and let me go back to my friends. They'll be looking for me soon if they haven't already started!"

Miller pushed off the chair, and Cindy jumped backward, thinking he was going to strike her, but he didn't. Instead, he twisted around and stomped to the door. Opening it, he spun around and faced Cindy. His face was a mask of rage and spittle slid down the left side of his mouth, thanks to the cigar keeping his lips parted.

"You're no brighter than Watson, I see. What is it with you strangers? You all seem to think you're somehow better than me, than what I am trying to create. You know the saying you can't make an omelet without breaking some eggs? Well, I plan on breaking every goddamn egg in this great nation of ours if that's what it takes to bring us back from the brink of destruction. And you, my lady, will be there with me. In time you'll come to like me, nay, love me. Until then, you can stay in this room. Oh, and I wouldn't plan on a rescue. By tomorrow morning, Watson will be dead, and the women with him will be in one of my brothels on the east side of the base. With so many soldiers needed to be kept happy, I suspect they'll be kept quite busy. As for the other man in your party, he's going to have an accident during gun training."

"Jimmy? No, you bastard, don't you hurt him!"

Ignoring her, Miller backed out of the doorway and slammed the door, the lock clicking once again.

Cindy stood up and crossed the room, staring at the door, her hands curled into fists of rage. She huffed and puffed, until she became lightheaded, then realizing her fate was sealed for the time being, she walked around to the wingchair behind the desk and plopped down hard, almost falling backwards. Why did she snap at him like that? She could have played the nut job and perhaps even killed him in his sleep or when he tried to make love to her. She had blown it that was for sure, a screw-up worthy of Jimmy.

Her friends were in mortal danger, but what could she do to warn them?

She was right back where she'd started again hours earlier, only now the fetid odor of cigar smoke clung in the air like a small animal carcass was rotting inside the wall. Covering her nose with her shirt, she leaned back and closed her eyes, visions of revenge dancing like stars in a clear night sky.

She had to get free, but how?

CHAPTER FORTY

HENRY ROLLED OVER in bed, the light of the morning cascading through the long windows that lined the upper half of the barracks. Checking the clock on the wall about amidships of the room, he saw it was going on five a.m.

All around him beds were full, men snoring loudly like a symphony with nostrils as the instruments. Across from him, Jimmy lay snoring, as well; his even bass a conflicting tempo to the song around him.

Sitting up, Henry rubbed his sore shoulder. His wounds were bandaged and the white bandage crisscrossed his chest like a warrior's garment, a few small circles of blood seeping through to mar the pristine cloth. All he needed was a large broadsword on his back and he'd resemble a mythical Viking.

He briefly recalled waking up around ten last night and eating from the plate of food Jimmy had saved for him. Jimmy had told him the girls sent their love and would see him in the morning. After Henry had eaten, he'd used the latrine and had immediately gone back to bed, still exhausted from his ordeal.

But after more than twelve hours of sleep, more than he'd had in the past year combined it seemed, he felt slightly refreshed, despite the aches in his bones and twinges where strained muscles had been put to the test.

Standing up, he felt a wave of nausea crest over him like a wave, then recede like the tide from the shore. When he was confident he had his legs under control, he headed for the bathroom once again. After emptying his bladder, he splashed some water on his face, still marveling at how the military base had running water, and got dressed from the pile of freshly laundered uniforms waiting for the men to don them once they awoke to a new day. A cavalcade of women picked up the dirty laundry each day and washed, folded and dried it; then returned it to the shelving unit.

He ignored his multiple days' worth of stubble, not feeling up to a shave. If Maddox or Miller had a problem with it, they could kiss his ass. His weapons were at the foot of his bed and he gladly slid them on, feeling like a million bucks once his panga, Glock, and Steyr were attached to him again. The weapons had been returned after dinner last night, while he was fast asleep. Jimmy had taken them, checking over each one to make sure it was in good working order while he passed the time watching over Henry.

Walking back into the barracks, he stood over Jimmy.

Jimmy lay on his back, his head to his side with his thumb in his mouth. Henry grinned down at his friend, who resembled a five-year-old-tot who'd passed out after a long day of playing. All he needed was a stuffed bunny or favorite teddy bear to complete the picture.

Leaning over with a twinge of pain, Henry shook Jimmy awake. But the young man was sleeping soundly and only rolled onto his side, his thumb sliding out of his mouth. Henry shook him again, stronger this time.

"Aww, come on, Mom. Five more minutes, I don't want to go to school yet," Jimmy mumbled and shoved his head under the pillow.

Frowning down at him, Henry raised his right boot, placed it against Jimmy's hip and pushed him off the bunk. Jimmy rolled over the edge and fell to the floor with a squeak of surprise. No sooner did he land, then he jumped up again, his head swiveling like an owl's. In his hand was his revolver, which had been hidden under his blanket, and the .38 was cocked as he looked for a target. It was only when Henry came into his vision, arms crossed like a strict parent, that Jimmy realized what had happened.

"What the Hell, Henry? Why'd you do that? I was having this dream about this busty brunette who..."

"Better not let Cindy hear about it," he chuckled. "Now, come on, sleepyhead, it's time to get up. I want to grab something to eat before I have to report for duty and I don't want to go alone, especially after last time I went there."

Jimmy nodded, understanding completely. The last time Henry had gone to the cafeteria he'd ended up in a death match.

"Fine, fine, just give me a minute, I need to pee like a racehorse," Jimmy said this while moving his knees up and down like he was ready to run a race.

"So go, just don't take too long, I'm starving. I'll watch your stuff while you're gone."

Jimmy nodded, rubbing his eyes of sleep, and then with nothing but bare feet, tip-toed to the bathroom. A few heads popped up at the two warrior's conversation and some terse words were thrown around. Henry waved to the faces, apologizing for waking them up then sat back down on the bed.

He moved his arms, flexing his shoulders, the pain uncomfortable, but manageable. He'd had worse and no doubt would have worse again. Getting bored with waiting for Jimmy, he stretched out and gazed up at the pockmarked ceiling tiles. Small holes were scattered like small stars, the remnants of long-gone soldiers playing with sharp pencils.

He didn't realize he'd dozed off again until he felt Jimmy shaking his foot.

"Hey you, wake my ass up and then you go back to sleep, nice," Jimmy chastised him as he slid his Remington pump over his shoulder and made sure his knife and revolver were in their holster and sheath, respectively.

"Huh? Oh shit, sorry, Jimmy, guess I'm still tired." Standing up, he stretched, but then thought better of it. He didn't want to open his wounds anytime soon.

"Come on, let's go eat."

Jimmy nodded, his stomach now rumbling, too. Both men exited the barracks and made their way to the cafeteria, while all around them, the base was slowly waking up for a new day in Hell.

*　　*　　*

Cindy woke up suddenly at the sound of a motor vehicle. Climbing to her feet from off the carpeting, she ran to the single, barred window. Outside was a jeep, idling on the lower driveway, only the driver sitting in the driver's seat, smoking a cigarette while he waited for his charge to exit the building.

Three minutes passed and then she saw a figure coming down the walkway leading from the front door. As the figure came into full view, she saw it was Colonel Miller, dressed in casual attire, brown khakis and a brown shirt. His pair of .357 Colt Magnum Pythons rode each hip, seeming out of place on the average-sized man.

He climbed into the passenger seat, never acknowledging the driver, and as the jeep spun around to drive away, Miller glanced up to the window she was peering through.

Cindy jumped back, not wanting to be spotted, and then realized what was the point? Miller already knew she was in here and would be here for the time being. Unless she could figure out a way to escape her prison. Her friends must be worried sick about her, not knowing where she'd disappeared to.

Feeling the need to pee, she crossed the room to the small bathroom connected to the den, but all that was in there was a toilet and sink, the medicine cabinet empty with the exception of some old Q-tips and cotton balls. Using the facilities, she returned to the den.

Now feeling slightly more refreshed after a few hours of sleep, her eyes scanned the room once more. There had to be something she could use as a weapon. The letter opener was gone, taken by one of the soldiers as was every and all sharp objects he could find. The entire time the search had been conducted, another soldier had covered her, his rifle cocked and ready to fire.

No more pens and pencils were in the desk, hell, they even took the paper clips. What was that about? Did they think she was a female MacGyver? Frowning as she walked circles around the room, her hands went to her hips, then to her hair, which she pushed back from her face and tied into a loose bun for easier management. She didn't do it often, liking the feminine way her long hair made her look, but now was not the time for vanity. Her friends were counting on her, even if they didn't know it yet.

Her eyes came to a stop by a framed diploma on the far wall. Walking over to it, she read the inscription. It was for some doctor that most definitely was not Miller. Made sense, this wasn't even his house, probably. He'd just conscripted it like so much of the people and items he needed.

She gently took the picture off the wall, holding it in her hands. She saw her reflection gazing back at her and studied the smudges of dirt on her face and the small wrinkles under eyes. She was growing older every year, the tough life of a warrior taxing on the human body and spirit.

But as she gazed back at herself, the glass came back into focus and a smile crossed her lips. They would be bringing her breakfast soon, as they did dinner last night. She would be ready this time, and not with a pathetic letter opener.

Slowly, a plan was coming into focus.

*   *   *

For a change, breakfast went smoothly and Henry and Jimmy had a good meal. The women joined them halfway through and the news about Cindy's absence was troubling.

"We have to go look for her," Jimmy said anxiously. "Who knows who's got her," he reasoned, wanting to charge out and begin shooting and screaming her name. When he'd found out she hadn't returned to the women's barracks the night before, he became fraught with worry.

"And we will," Henry told him, shoveling more eggs into his mouth. They were powdered, but were still damn good in his opinion. "But first we need to do what's expected of us. After we do our watches or training or whatever, we need to split up and begin searching the base. We can only hope we can get lucky and someone's seen her." He reached for a piece of toast made from homemade bread, the wheat grown only a few miles away. "We'll find her, we have to," he said in a low voice, but the concern was clear to all

Mary nodded. "He's right, Jimmy. 'Sides, we can still ask questions while we work," Mary referred to Raven and Sue, as well as her. Who each nodded in kind.

"Oh yeah, and how are you gonna do that on your back?" Jimmy asked. You're going to the brothel, right?"

Mary made a disgusted face. "Yes, Jimmy, but get your perverted mind out of the gutter because nothing's going to happen. I'll make sure of it."

"I sure hope so, Mary, I don't think I could handle it for very long," Sue said.

Henry reached out, touching her hand. "You'd be surprised what you can handle if it's a means to survival."

She nodded, slightly, understanding, but not wanting to contemplate it.

"No, guys," Mary said. "I figure we'll just be a little late showing up for work. Hopefully we'll find her in time and then try to get out of here. Henry, you have a plan yet?"

Henry shrugged, popping the last of the toast in his mouth. "Sort of, something's coming. But listen, if something bad happens and we need to try and duck and run fast, let's meet by the hangar where we first landed, where the soldiers took our names. There's another hangar there and the motor pool is right behind it. Maybe we can force our way through and grab something like a Humvee or an APC. Then we can run for it."

"But what about the helicopters?" Jimmy asked. "They can blow us to hell before we've gone half a mile."

"Yeah, Jimmy, I know, don't remind me. I still haven't figured that one out yet, just give me time. One thing at a time, all right? For now, we need to find Cindy."

"At least they let us keep our weapons," Mary said. "That still strikes me as strange."

"Oh, I found out last night while I was sitting with Henry," Jimmy said. "A couple of guys were talking nearby. It seems there's not enough soldiers to guard the perimeter fence and so the chance of deaders getting in here is pretty good. So they let anyone who has weapons stay armed in case of trouble. Without weapons, it would be a massacre if the deaders got in here."

Henry nodded. "That explains a lot, and it's not like an uprising can take place with every soldier carrying an assault rifle, plus the choppers for air support. The civilians wouldn't stand a chance."

Finishing their breakfast, the companions all agreed on the priorities for the day and left the cafeteria. Maddox was waiting for Henry and Jimmy with four soldiers and the major eyed the women lazily as they exited the cafeteria.

"Don't you three have to be somewhere?" Maddox asked the women.

"Yeah, Major, we were just going there now," Mary told him. Maddox frowned slightly, but let them go without another word.

The major glared at Jimmy next. "You, Cooper, you're to go with these men for weapons training on the far side of the base."

Though concerned for Cindy, he knew he needed to play the part of the good soldier. He nodded brusquely, moving to the two soldiers who gestured for him to join them.

"Okay, men, move out, dammit, what in holy hell are you waiting for?" Maddox snapped like a drill sergeant. The two soldiers and Jimmy moved off, running at double time. Maddox turned to Henry and his grin widened.

"As for you, you're coming with me. We have two birds going out today to recon the city and you're in the lead one. I want to keep my eye on you at all times."

"Oh, goody, can't wait. I love playing soldier. Do you?" Henry asked with a derisive smirk.

Maddox answered him by shoving him forward, Henry wincing when his shoulder wound was brushed. But he began walking to the jeep waiting for them and climbed inside. The jeep began to move, the worn muffler causing it to rattle loudly, and because of this, Henry never heard Maddox's reply to his question about playing soldier.

"Yes, Watson, I do. More than you want to know."

CHAPTER FORTY-ONE

THE TWO AH-64A Apache attack helicopters rose easily into the air, the rotors nothing but a blur, cycling too fast to see by the human eye.

Maddox's copter banked to the right and the aircraft shot by Henry's window. Henry watched it soar by, seeing only the tinted window of the cockpit. The graceful machine was in perfect running order and responded perfectly to the pilot's touch.

If only Henry's helicopter would do the same.

Inside his Apache, Henry was with three other soldiers. The first man was Private Green. He was an inept man who could barely hold a rifle in his hands, let alone fire it. While they had boarded and waited for take off, he'd shared a story of how he had almost shot Colonel Miller in weapons training. He still didn't know how he'd scored the opportunity to ride in the Apache. Usually, only the skilled soldiers had the opportunity, almost as a reward for excellent service. He had continued to chatter on until Henry had finally told the young man to pipe down and be quiet.

Private Green now sat sulking like a scolded child against the far wall of the aircraft.

The next man to share the helicopter with Henry was a hard-faced soldier with the face only a mother could love, named Slater. His complexion was horrendous, scars everywhere on his forehead and cheeks from a bad bout of acne when he was young. The scars were from him picking the blackheads and never letting them heal properly. He wore a perpetual scowl and Henry only found out about what he'd done to piss off the colonel by accident.

When they were boarding the helicopter, Slater and Henry had a disagreement about who was going to sit where. Slater wanted the copilot's seat, but so did Henry.

Henry needed to see where they were geographically and the best way was to sit up front.

That was when Slater pulled a knife and told Henry he had killed a family that had pissed him off. They had a teenage daughter he liked, and when he'd raped her, she'd told. Not wanting to be discovered, he had slaughtered the entire family in their beds that night. But had been caught leaving the house and had spent more than a month in the stockade waiting for his death sentence. He had many allies with the civilians despite his horrible crime and so Miller hadn't killed him, not wanting to create a stir among his labor force.

And now the man was here, with Henry on the helicopter.

Henry had settled the dispute by sliding his panga out of its sheath. The blade shined like a massive scalpel, the edge honed to razor sharpness now that it was clean once again. Henry had taken excellent care to clean the sheath and blade with love. The long, sixteen inch blade had saved his life more times than he could count and had been with him almost from the first day the world began to crumble. Next to his Glock it was his most cherished possession.

Slater had taken one look at the panga in front of his face and had immediately backed down, knowing when he was out-classed. Despite this, Henry never turned his back on him, knowing his kind had a penchant for betrayal.

Still, even with one misfit and one killer, if Henry didn't think there was something off about the mission he'd been thrown into, he would have come to that realization as soon as he met the pilot.

Corporal Bowen was a twenty something, black man with a southern accent that made his voice a sharp contrast to his looks. He was a nice enough fellow, but he was most definitely not a skilled pilot. The Apache waved like a baby bird learning to fly as the sweating pilot attempted to keep the bird in the air.

Sitting next to him, Henry tried to calm the man down by asking questions about how to fly the helicopter. He was also very interested and this was his first time in the large aircraft. The thing was, he didn't want this to be his last.

"So, Bowen, right?" Henry asked through the mike he wore over his mouth which was attached to the helmet on his head.

Bowen nodded. "Yes, sir, it is."

Henry was about to tell the man not to call him sir and decided against it. Maybe that would be good. If trouble arose the pilot would listen to him, deferring to his authority.

"So, tell me how to fly this thing. What's that stick between your legs do?"

Bowen looked down at the stick, and when he did, he pushed the stick forward. Immediately the nose of the Apache dipped forward.

"Whoa, there, sorry, sir. I keep doing that. My instructor says I can't stay focused."

Nice, Henry thought. I'm with the only pilot in the world with a case of ADD.

"That's okay, Bowen, just try to stay focused now, okay?"

Bowen nodded, his features hidden by the mask and helmet.

"So, you were telling me about that stick?"

"Yes, sir, this is called the Cyclic Control Stick and it makes the bird go backward and forward and from side to side."

"Uh-huh, and how about the pedals? What do they do? I've seen them on an airplane, too; do they do the same thing?"

Bowen shrugged. "I don't know, sir, but on this bird they control the tail rotor, the pitch of the rotor actually. Push the left pedal to make the bird go to the left and push the right pedal and it goes to the right."

"Sounds easy enough," Henry said. "And what about that stick by your left hand that looks like a handbrake, what's that do? I saw you using it before when we took off." A little shakily, he thought, but didn't say. Bowen was fragile enough as it is.

"Yes, sir," Bowen told him. "That's the Collective Control Stick. Moving it up and down changes the pitch on the main rotor blades overhead and causes us to rise. It's the pitch of the rotor that actually move the bird; the chassis really just hangs here. In fact, if the tail rotor wasn't there to stabilize us, we would just spin around un-controllably."

"I see, well we wouldn't want that," Henry said and tried to smile. Behind his goggles, Henry couldn't tell if the pilot saw the gesture.

"Tell me some more, Bowen. I want to learn this stuff. How about the hydraulics? It is hydraulics that controls everything internally, right? So what happens if the engine fails? Do we crash?"

Bowen nodded curtly, the sweat on his forehead beading on his goggles to drip to the sides. Henry thought the man should install tiny windshield wipers like on expensive cars' headlights.

"No, sir, we don't have to crash. Even if the engine fails for some reason the hydraulics still work. You can land this baby by using the collective control stick and by managing the pitch of the blades. It's tricky, but it can be done."

"Cool, so can I have a go at it? Is it safe?" Henry's stomach was filled with butterflies, but if he learned how to actually fly one of these Apaches, perhaps he and the rest of the companions could escape in one. That would solve the problem of being blown away while driving on the ground.

"Well sir, I don't think you shou…"

Henry's voice grew hard as he turned to look at Bowen. "I don't care what you think, Private. I want to fly this helicopter, now!"

Cowering with intimidation, Bowen nodded, his voice cracking. "Well, all right, sir, here, take my seat and I'll take yours. He climbed out of his seat, but held onto the Control stick, the chopper wavering in the air as he moved. Henry sat down and took the stick, his heart beating like a trip-hammer.

"Okay, sir, just be gentle and slowly feel the bird move. It's really not hard. I get the logistics of it, but when it comes to sitting in the seat and just flying her, I just can't get it. I don't even understand why they put me in this bird today. Last I heard, I was going to get grounded, then my instructor told me to suit up."

Henry barely heard him, concentrating on flying. He moved the collective control stick up and down and felt the chopper rise and fall. Bowen taught him how to throttle the engine higher when rising, the Apache needing the extra power to ascend. He used the pedals and turned from left to right, getting the feel for it with ease. Ten minutes after he'd sat down, he was flying the chopper on his own, Bowen only giving him rudimentary instructions.

"Wow, sir, you're a natural. They say some people just get it real easy. Not me, though, I should never have been given this job."

"You what? What did you say? What do you mean? You saying you never should have been a pilot? Is that what you mean?" Henry finally heard the man speak, realizing what he was saying.

"Yes sir, I'm a terrible pilot. On paper I get it no problem, but once I'm in that seat, forget it. I almost crashed into the colonel's house one time. Boy was he pissed."

Henry stared at the man for one brief moment, the reality of what he was telling him finally sinking in. He was with nothing but misfits and malcontents. Any good commander would have eighty-sixed these soldiers immediately, but Miller had kept them around for one reason or another. When you were the master puppetsmith, anyone was fair game for some fun. The colonel was like a cat with a mouse, wanting to play with his food instead of merely killing it outright.

"Jesus Christ, what have I gotten myself into?" Henry mumbled to himself. Below him, the land passed by, the Kentucky bluegrass, though green, looking blue in the morning sunlight, hence its name.

Maddox buzzed him again and Henry jumped, spooked. Now that he was in the pilot's seat, everything felt so much more vivid. He watched the accompanying Apache turn to his right and Henry matched course, following like a pro. He chuckled to himself. He always thought it was so hard, flying a helicopter, but it was no more difficult than driving a car. All one needed was to be taught. He still didn't know how to land, but he wasn't worried about that at the moment. Once they were near their touchdown point, he would give the controls back to Bowen. As for the Private, he seemed relieved not to be flying. His sweating had slowed and his posture seemed less tense. The man was actually a very good instructor, like he said, he understood how to fly, but wasn't any good at it.

From what Henry had gathered from Bowen, their destination was thirty miles south of Fort Knox. They were heading for Louisville, their mission to see if there were any survivors and also to take out any large complements of the undead.

Maddox's Apache flew slightly in the lead, and it was only as they approached the outskirts of Louisville that he began to fall back, letting Henry take point. So far there had been no communication with Maddox. Henry knew they could talk to one another, but the channel had stayed closed. Bowen had said Maddox wasn't much of a talker and not to sweat it.

Below the Apache, the buildings came into view. What was left of them. The fires that had blazed more than a year ago had devastated the city. There had been over 500,000 people living in Louisville before the rains came, infecting anyone unfortunate enough to be outside. Henry could only imagine what it must have been like to watch thousands of people fall over onto the ground or in the street as the first drops of contaminated rain touched their flesh and penetrated their circulatory systems. How for one brief moment the city would have been silent; only the ones under cover still unaffected. But then the bacterium would have jump-started the body, reanimating it, and every undead soul would have risen, turning on the ones that had tried to help those struck down only moments ago. It would have been absolute chaos and carnage on an epic scale no one would have ever have believed possible.

The Apache flew over a school, the playground empty with the exception of a few bleached bones and a murder of crows resting on the long metal pipe that spanned the jungle gym. The swings moved back and forth eerily with the slight breeze, forever empty. Heading deeper into the city, the streets were choked with rusted out hulks that had once been shiny silver Beamers, Toyotas and Hondas. Skeletal remains hung from open car doors, and ivy, kudzu and crabgrass covered almost every open spot of cement. The city had been left unattended for over a year and even now it was hard to remember what it once was. Five years from now the streets would be covered under inches of moss, Mother Nature taking back what was rightfully hers once again. It was a tableau that played all across America in every city and town that had been relinquished to the undead.

And the undead were here. The engine noise of the two Apache helicopters woke the walking dead. They stumbled out of shattered coffee houses, copy shops and boutiques, wearing faded denim pant suits and polo shirts for casual Friday. Some wore business suits; ties still knotted around desiccated necks. Crisp, white shirts were now stained black with dried puss and gore.

They came onto the streets by the thousands, pouring into the streets like roaches, arms uplifted like a massive chorus wanting to sing their praises to the God that had failed humanity or perhaps to the Devil that had created them.

Looking down on the shambling mockery of the remnants of the human race, Henry believed there had to be an evil at work, for what else would allow such a thing to happen? He tried not to focus too much on the grand design of the one and only Creator, because if he did, he wondered if he would just say "to hell with it" and just eat a bullet.

No, better to deal with what was in front of you. If a ghoul got in your way, blow its head off. If a Boss of a town was overflowing with despotic power, slit his throat and let the next asshole take over. And if that one got too big for his britches, then go back and do the same to the second asshole. And if it happened again, repeat steps one and two until someone got the message that life wasn't cheap, that everyone mattered; that all life was precious.

These rules were simple and Henry was able to stay sane by living by them. He had to believe there was someplace the walking dead hadn't tainted, and when he found it, he and his friends would live happily ever after.

Maybe it was a pipe dream, but it was all he had.

Gazing down at the thousands of undead faces glaring up at him, their moaning and wailing filling his heart with dread, he realized what a hellish world it had truly become.

Next to him, Bowen was in awe, and behind him both Green and Slater stared out the small windows with mouths open, eyes wide with fear.

Suddenly, the radio crackled and Bowen looked to Henry.

"Come in, Bowen, answer me goddammit!" Maddox's garbled voice screamed through the small earpieces.

"Here, sir," Bowen said nervously. "I'm right here."

"'Bout damn time, Bowen. Hey, is that you really flying that bird? Looks like you're gettin' better at it. Listen, I want to speak to Watson, put him on the radio for me."

"How 'bout that, sir, you fly better than me and this is your first time," Bowen said to Henry.

"Huh, lucky I guess. I have a good teacher."

Bowen smiled then, a wide smile that penetrated his eyes. Henry realized though Bowen might be a bad pilot, he was a good man.

"Come on, Bowen, put Watson on the damn radio!"

Bowen looked to Henry, who only shrugged, not knowing what the major would want. "I'm here, Maddox, what do you want? And where are we gonna put down? There's no place to land that I can see."

Below them the buildings, twenty to forty stories high, seemed to flow underneath them like small islands in a sea of bodies. Every rooftop was charred and filled with the skeletal remains of desperate survivors who had thought to escape the onslaught of the dead by going to the rooftops. Once there, they had waited for help, praying aircraft would come to lift them to safety. But it had never come and they had died from starvation or by the undead when they'd been found and cornered. Or worse, had stayed on the rooftops too long and had been infected with the deadly rain like their predecessors below in the streets.

"That's because you won't be landing, Watson. Look, I think this is all a little extravagant. If it was up to me, I would have dragged you away in the night and put a bullet in your head. But I'm not in charge, Colonel Miller is. And he's a great man that is going to bring this country back to its greatness once again. But first we need to get rid of the undesirables, Watson, the ones who don't want to get on board. Men like you, Watson and those lowlifes with you." Bowen squeaked like a mouse and the others in back turned, wondering what was going on.

Henry felt his gut tighten, the meaning of Maddox's words coming though like lasers.

"What do you mean, Maddox? What the hell are you talking about?" He knew exactly what the major meant, but was now trying to stall for time, his mind racing for what to do next.

"It's simple, Watson. You need to disappear, and on a mission into the city would be just fine."

"And what about this chopper? You don't really think we'll set down knowing what you want to do to us, do you."

Maddox chuckled then, and Henry knew something was going to happen. It was the way Maddox seemed to know the answer to each question.

"Watson, that Apache is held together with gum and spit. It's a piece of shit. I can't believe Bowen managed to keep it flying for as long as he has. And as for the rest of you..." There was silence on the radio and for a second Henry thought the connection had been severed. Then a streak of a white contrail flew by the right side of the Apache, missing by inches, just as Henry was flying past a massive skyscraper. The fiftieth floor exploded outward, spraying glass and cement shards at the Apache's cockpit.

Henry fought to keep the aircraft stable, while warning lights sounded, the two men in the back screaming bloody hell in their blind panic to know what was happening.

Through it all, as the Apache began to dip toward the earth, Maddox's voice sounded in Henry's ear.

"...As for the rest of you, you can die."

CHAPTER FORTY-TWO

JIMMY WAS HOT and tired and getting real sick of this weapons training. For one thing, he wasn't allowed to use his own weapons, having to practice with an AK-47. He found out Miller had found a stash of them in a storage facility on the base and had started to use them, liking the rapid fires better than the M-16As which had a bad habit of jamming when you need it to work the most.

On top of that, he was firing with blanks, the war games he'd been forced to participate in ridiculous. They had set up near the north edge of the perimeter fence where there were numerous trees, shrubs and foliage to use as cover. There were seven of them in all; six soldiers and Jimmy. Talk about feeling like the odd man out. And to top it off he couldn't concentrate, too worried about the fate of Cindy. He loved her, and he tried to tell her as often as possible. She was a breath of fresh air on a smog filled day, a ray of sunshine on a cloudy afternoon, she was a...well, that was enough, he figured, He loved her and would lay down his life if it would save hers.

And now she was missing.

Movement to his left caused him to focus on reality, sensing someone was nearby. He'd been out here for almost an hour and was already trying to figure out how he could get pretend killed and bow out of this farce. Hell, he'd killed more deaders than all six soldiers combined. And he wasn't talking about using an M-60 to mow the undead down, though he'd done that, too. No, he was talking about close kills, where you saw those dead vacant eyes peering into your soul.

That was a real kill, and if Jimmy had his way, he'd kill every damn deader he could find. Henry knew how compunctious he was and reined him in, his bloodlust liable to get him killed. Jimmy had his reasons, of course. His parents had been killed by the bacterium. His father had turned into one of the undead and had killed his mother. So he had killed his father, crushing him under the den television set. They were probably still lying in the same spot he'd left them over a year ago; rotting in the den of his home in the Midwest.

More sounds of leaves being compressed made him pay attention. Sure, he wanted to get pretend killed so he could leave and look for Cindy, but he knew those damn blanks still hurt if the weapon was discharged close enough to his skin, or worse, his face. He could lose an eye that way and he didn't think an eye patch would make him any more appealing to the opposite sex than he already was.

Watching the branches shake on a nearby tree, he saw one of the soldiers exit through a copse of shrubs about thirty yards away.

The soldier was a short man, no more than five-five with a bald head and long jowls that made him look like a bulldog. His lips were creeping into a sly smile when he spotted Jimmy standing there between two tree trunks, exposed for all to see.

"Looks like you got me," Jimmy told the man. He thought his name was Rudolph, or Randolph or something similar sounding. It didn't matter really, he was Bulldog to Jimmy. "I give up, I'll be going now. Great job, guy."

But the small soldier wasn't accepting his surrender. Instead, the man raised his sniper rifle to his eyes and aimed directly at Jimmy's head.

Jimmy was about to protest, telling the man he gave up already when a round left the sniper rifle and struck the tree to Jimmy's right, about even with his cheek. Wood splinters exploded from the tree, peppering his face with splinters.

"What the fu...?" Jimmy began; about to yell at the soldier for all he was worth, planning on kicking the man's ass when another shot rang out, this one coming from behind him. Spinning around and dropping to the ground, another shot from Bulldog missed him by a hairsbreadth. Reaching up to his hair, he could swear he felt a few strands were missing, shaved off by the passage of the round.

Staying low, he crawled a few feet from his dropped-down point and peered through the holes in the shrubbery, trying to see the Bulldog and the other shooter who was firing at him from behind.

There they were, near a copse of trees, three of them total, all pointing towards his last known opposition. Jimmy brought his AK-47 up and aimed the barrel through one of the spaces between the leaves and was ready to fire, finger on trigger when he realized his rifle was worthless.

He was shooting goddamn blanks!

Slinging the weapon over his shoulder, he pulled his hunting knife from its sheath on his hip. At least he'd been left that. His revolver and Remington were sitting patiently, waiting for his return, in a supply locker near the beginning of the training field. All he had to do was reach them.

But first he needed to distract his would-be killers.

Crawling about fifty feet to his right, away from Bulldog, he unslung his rifle, took off the green uniform shirt they'd made him wear and stuck the barrel of the rifle through the collar.

Then, moving slowly, he crawled across the leafy earth, smelling the wet soil in his nostrils, the shirt he'd once worn dangling over his body like a ghost in a bad movie. He didn't make it more than seven feet before three shots rang out, bullets zipping through the shirt. Stopping for a moment, Jimmy began crawling again; only this time the shirt was slightly lower, as if he'd been wounded. When he reached a suitable hiding spot, he jammed the butt of the rifle between two branches that would serve his purpose, then melted back in to his hiding place. Then he waited and watched.

More bullets zipped through the shirt, one after the other until the material looked like moths had enjoyed a tasty snack for more than a year. Still, he stayed silent, waiting like the patient hunter should. Henry had taught him to let the prey come to him, not the other way around.

Soon, footsteps could be heard crunching through the underbrush and Jimmy held his breath, his tongue just sticking out of his lips like a snake smelling the air. His heart began to pound and he could feel his adrenalin pumping, making him feel like he could fly.

The first of three men appeared, moving towards his location. Their weapons were shouldered, all of them confident their prey had been killed, and Jimmy saw it was Bulldog who was first in line. For some reason, Jimmy was glad he would get it first.

Staying silent, Jimmy watched as Bulldog reached his shirt and blank-filled AK-47. Picking up the shirt, he held it up for the others to see, poking his stubby fingers through a few of the bullet holes in the material. The four soldiers began to talk, arguing about what had happened when Jimmy jumped from his hiding place and landed between the three men. Bulldog got it first, just like Jimmy had planned. When he landed on his right foot, his left was already coming up to connect with Bulldog's testicles. The man's eyes almost popped out of their sockets when Jimmy's combat boots connected. While Jimmy's left boot was crushing Bulldog's testicles, his right hand was arcing out in a horizontal slice, catching the next soldier in line across the throat. The move was executed perfectly and a little luck helped. The man's jugular exploded in a crimson spray and the gushing hot fluid struck the next soldier right in the face. Dropping his weapon, the man raised both hands to his face, protecting them from the warm and sticky plasma. Jimmy ignored him for the moment and spun to face the last soldier. This man was staring at Jimmy like he was a forest demon come to life. Jimmy rolled across the ground, coming up in a pop-jump, his blade already sinking into the man's chest. For added measure, Jimmy twisted the blade, and pulled out, guaranteeing a messy wound. The soldier staggered backwards, clutching his chest in shock, but Jimmy was already spinning again, going back for the blood-blinded soldier. The man's face was bright red; his eyes peeking through like an art project gone terribly wrong. In the sun-shaded trees, the light was similar to twilight, and the blood on his face was a visceral sight, seeming ethereal in its free-form color. The man sputtered, trying to spit the copper-tasting froth from his mouth. Clearing his eyes enough to see, he saw Jimmy's blade come down too late to stop it and felt the tip slice into his clavicle, sinking down and deep into his upper chest cavity. Jimmy used both hands on the handle and forced the blade down, slicing a fifteen inch gash from the man's shoulder to groin. The soldier wobbled for a moment, internal organs spilling from the jagged wound, not believing what was happening to him, then toppled over onto Bulldog, who was still huffing and puffing. Bile slid from his mouth to coat the tips of his black boots, the shine now ruined.

Jimmy held his blade over the back of Bulldog's neck and at the last second stopped his blow. Instead, he spun the wet blade around and used the shaft to slam Bulldog on the base of the skull, sending the small man into oblivion.

"That's my good deed for the day," Jimmy mumbled to himself, picking up his bullet-shredded shirt and wiping blood spray from his face and arms.

When finished, he picked up one of the sniper rifles, and added one of the soldier's sidearms, a .45 if he was right as he gave the handgun a quick glance over. Popping the clip, he checked the load, satisfied the rounds were real, then slammed it back home. After wiping his knife clean on Bulldog's pant leg, he moved off to the supply locker and his weapons.

Halfway there he spotted the other two soldiers, who were waiting casually near some high weeds. Their faces seemed rather surprised to see Jimmy walking towards them, and before they could bring their weapons up, Jimmy shot each man twice in the chest with a quick double-tap from the .45. They tumbled backwards, large gaping holes where their backs should have been. Blood seeped under them and soaked into the ground. Jimmy walked by them, never slowing down, there was no time, though he did admire the wounds the handgun had made.

"Not bad," he mumbled to himself, "I just may have to keep this one."

Reaching the supply locker, he opened it, retrieved his weapons and then double-timed it out of there. It wouldn't be good to hang around when the training sergeant arrived to see how things were going. Jimmy didn't know if the training sergeant was in on his assassination, too, but had to assume he was. Besides, his goal wasn't to try and kill every soldier on the base, the goal was to find Cindy, get to the rendezvous point, and get the hell out of Dodge.

Picking up his pace, Jimmy began to run back to the main part of the base, near the barracks. Once there, he could begin canvassing outward, and hopefully he'd find Cindy.

*   *   *

The cook for Colonel Miller walked down the small hallway on his way to feed Cindy her breakfast. On a small tray he had frozen orange juice fresh from the base galley's voluminous freezers, two pieces of toast, and powdered eggs made with powdered milk.

Behind him walked two soldiers, the woman's guards for the morning shift. They had just come on watch an hour ago and were already bored. Watching a woman was the last thing they would have chosen to do, but rather would have preferred to be on the perimeter fence, shooting zombies down like stray rats in a junkyard.

But the watch commander had assigned them this duty and so they would have to do it. Disobeying wasn't worth contemplating. Where before the world had collapsed you might get court-martialed, now a firing squad or an impaling was more likely.

Neither soldier was battle-trained, no combat experience to think of. They had joined the army only a few months before the rains first came and had just graduated from boot camp as the world began to crumble around them.

But they weren't stupid men, either. When they had been told by their commander to be vigilant while watching the blonde woman, they had taken the advice to heart. So when the cook reached the door leading to the den, both lowered their rifles in expectation of trouble.

The cook turned to look at them, making sure they were ready, and when he was sure they were, he unlocked the door, using his foot to open it. With the exception of the creaking hinges, something the cook would have to attend to later that day, there was no sound inside the room.

Stepping inside, making sure the soldiers had his back; he stopped cold when he saw Cindy sprawled against the front of the desk, unconscious. She was slumped to the side, her left hand lying on her lap while her right was hidden behind her back.

But that wasn't what had halted him in his tracks.

He wouldn't have been stupid enough to fall for a simple ruse like pretending she was unconscious, especially after Colonel Miller had warned him and the guards about what she'd done with the letter opener, but this was more than a ruse.

Cindy's left arm was a bloody mess, the blood dripping off her wrist to pool in her lap and slide down between her legs. It was obvious what had happened the second he set eyes on her.

She had slit her wrists rather than be a captive of the colonel.

The tray of food toppled from his hand to crash onto the carpet, the dishes shattering noisily. Still, Cindy didn't move, not so much as a flinch, which told the cook that was one more reason why they were in real trouble here.

"Guys, get in here, she's killed herself!" The cook screamed at the top of his lungs.

Both soldiers charged in, their weapons ready to fire at the woman if she was stupid enough to try anything, and their eyes went wide when they saw her slumped, bloodied form.

"Oh shit, what the hell happened?" Guard number one yelled.

"How the hell should I know? I'm just the cook, for Christ Sakes!"

"Oh, man, we are so fucked," guard number two said. It was one thing if the woman tried anything and the men had to defend themselves, but if she killed herself while the guards stood oblivious outside the door, well, Miller wasn't going to like that at all.

"Did you take her pulse? Maybe she's not dead yet," guard number one said hopefully to the cook.

The cook stepped away from the body, waving his hands back and forth in front of him. "Whoa, now don't be asking me to do anything, I'm just the cook. You do it; after all, you were supposed to be guarding her."

"Yeah, through a solid wooden door. How were we supposed to know she was gonna off herself?"

The cook shrugged, not caring a bit. "Not my problem."

Number two nudged number one. "Go ahead, you go check, you're closer."

Guard number one glanced at the two men and realized he was outvoted. "Shit," he muttered and knelt down next to Cindy.

He leaned his rifle against the side of the desk, not needing it anymore, and slowly, like he expected her to wake up and try to bite him, he reached for her neck, which was smooth and soft. Touching her skin, he searched for a pulse, and it was then that his mouth curved down in frown. If she had slit her wrists and bled out, then why was her skin so warm? Then he found her pulse and was surprised to feel it chugging along like she was alive and well.

"Hey, wait a second, I think she's…"

That was all he managed to get out when Cindy opened her eyes and bared her teeth, snarling like a wild animal.

"Surprise!" She said, and as she spoke, her right hand came up from around her back, a piece of the glass picture frame gripped firmly in her palm. Before the soldier could do more than stutter a warning, Cindy sliced the blade of glass across his throat. Blood geysered across the room, Cindy catching some of it on her chest, the guard's blood mixing with her own. The man gurgled in shock, then reached up with both hands to try and staunch the flow of precious plasma, but he was already losing consciousness as he slumped to the carpet. Guard number two couldn't see what was happening, guard number one blocking his view, but when his partner fell over like he'd fallen asleep and he saw all the blood, he realized something had gone horribly wrong.

But he wasn't a warrior, and had never been tested on the battlefield. He'd never stared his enemy down and felt the life force recede from another human being as he plunged a knife through their heart.

Cindy had, and would do so again if she acted fast.

Jumping to her feet, faltering as she fought to climb out from under the dying soldier, she slapped a bloody hand on the desktop, leaving a crimson handprint, and heaved herself to her feet. Guard number two was shaking, but he still managed to get his rifle up. Cindy had two seconds or less to do what she had planned or she'd be riddled with bullets.

Standing tall, she lunged through the air at the frantic soldier and raised the glass shard like a dagger over her head. Just as the soldier managed to get his finger on the trigger of his rifle, Cindy plowed into him, ramming the crystal dagger deep into the screaming man's right eye, the shrieks growing louder in pitch as the point of the dagger slid through optic nerve and grated on bone. The orb exploded like a cream egg at Easter, the whitish, pinkish ooze dripping down the shrieking man's cheek to pool in his shirt.

Cindy pushed the man to the floor and rolled to her feet. Picking up the closest rifle, she slid the lever, making sure the weapon had a bullet in the chamber and put the man out of his misery. The gunshot sounded loud inside the den, out of place amid the tan drapes and scholarly desk and chair.

Behind her she heard a gasp and she spun, realizing she had almost forgotten the cook. The scared man raised his hands in the air, his cheeks wet with tears. Cindy looked down at the man's feet to see a small puddle of urine. He was shaking so bad he looked like a cartoon character who'd just come out of the freezing water in the middle of winter, his teeth chattering like a jokester's wet dream.

She stood there; rifle aimed at his chest and weighed the man's life in her hands.

"Please, I was only following orders. If I didn't, I'd have been in here with you, or worse. I was never mean to you, was I?"

Cindy considered his words, rolling them around on the tip of her tongue, and in the end even she couldn't kill this pathetic, frightened man just for trying to survive.

"Over there, by the desk, move it," she spit, hard and fast. The cook did as he was told, sliding his feet across the carpet like he was on ice.

"Good, now sit," she told him, pointing to the chair. He dropped down like a ton of bricks, his hands still in the air.

Cindy nodded. "Good, now stay," she said like she was commanding a dog, then she backed out of he room and slammed the den door closed, trapping the cook inside.

Footsteps sounded from down the hall in the direction of the front of the house so Cindy moved to the rear, charging through the hallways until she found the back door. Flinging it open, she charged into the late-morning sunlight.

She was free, but she was far from safe. Her plan had worked perfectly. She had shattered the glass frame of the picture on the wall and had sliced shallow cuts on her upper forearm with the best shard she could find. The blood from the shallow wounds had dripped down her arm, looking for all purposes like she had slit her wrists, catching the soldiers entirely off guard.

Looking over her shoulder, knowing the alarm would be sounded at any moment; she ran through the backyard and headed in the direction of the barracks. She needed to find the rest of the companions before all hell broke loose.

CHAPTER FORTY-THREE

THE APACHE SHIVERED like a newborn baby from the blast of the Hydra rocket that pulverized two floors of the skyscraper. Rubble and cement plummeted to the earth to crush the hordes of ghouls clustered in the streets below.

For one brief nanosecond, Henry saw them pulverized under tons of debris, squished flat like ants. Others nearby never moved, never wavered, as their brethren were crushed under steel timbers and sliced to ribbons by falling glass.

Henry thought it seemed odd to see human forms merely standing still, instead of running and screaming for their lives so they wouldn't be another casualty. Then he had to focus on controlling the falling Apache as the main rotor cycled down from the shockwave of the explosion.

His stomach felt like he was in an elevator car and the cables had been cut, the plummeting feeling making him want to retch. Panicking, he tried to level the chopper out, the ground coming closer with every passing second.

He pushed down on the collective control stick and Bowen realized what he'd done and screamed for him to stop.

"No, sir, up, pull the stick back to you, we need to go up! Up!"

Henry did as he was told, pulling the lever up; remembering to increase throttle at the same time. The engine roared from stress, the pitch of the rotors increased to maximum.

Just as the ground came into focus, the chopper caught air and slowed, then began to ascend once again.

Breathing hard, sweat pouring down his back, Henry glanced at Bowen. The young black man looked almost white, his hands gripping the metal frame above his head as if his life depended on it.

Machine gun fire took the celebration from Henry's mouth as Maddox fired at him as he angled his chopper down, like in an old war movie. The 30mm bullets shook the aircraft on its foundation, the armor plating holding, but they were still vulnerable. One good shot to the rotors and Henry would find himself falling to the earth like a dead bird.

"Holy shit, why is Major Maddox shooting at us?" Private Green yelped from the rear of the chopper.

"Because we were all brought out here to get shot down, that's why!" Henry yelled back. "It's some kind of sick joke Miller is playing on us. Now hold on because I don't know what I'm doing!" He turned to Bowen. "Maybe you should take the controls; I don't know how to handle this shit."

"Me? I don't either. I told you, I don't fly well. I barely passed my simulation test. Just keep going, you're doing good so far."

More bullets shook the aircraft and Henry pushed on the right pedal, the Apache banking hard to the right. He found himself heading straight for another building and desperately tried to change direction. The building was a Ford plant, the entire structure charred and black. Every window was shattered and the roof had the tattered remains of corpses lying everywhere. Henry pressed the left pedal and he felt the chopper bank left. Pushing down on the cyclic control stick, the bird shot forward. Henry pushed the collective control stick forward as far as it would go, the helicopter reaching peak speed. He was sweating profusely, trying not to crash into the buildings that popped up in his windscreen like he was playing a videogame.

Behind him, Maddox followed, obviously playing with his prey. Maddox fired another Hydra rocket and Slater screamed as he watched the white plume of smoke eject from the chasing Apache.

"He fired at us again! Here comes another rocket! Oh shit, we are so fucked!"

"Bank left or right, Henry, do it now!" Bowen screamed.

Still not believing this was actually happening; Henry pressed the right pedal, the chopper turning hard to the right in response. The Hydra rocket missed by inches, striking another building. An explosion of glass and concrete filled the air, like a sideways volcano, fire and ash following right behind the initial blast. Henry plowed through it, unable to turn in time, holding his breath when they came out the other side. Maddox had to bank around the blast, not wanting to get caught by any flying debris and began falling behind for a few seconds.

Gritting his teeth, Maddox moved his finger over the button for the radio, wanting to talk to Bowen and Watson one last time.

"Not bad, Bowen, I didn't know you had it in you. You might have made a better pilot than I thought if I'd given you half a chance. But playtime's over. Tell Watson goodbye for me, will you?"

"Tell me yourself, you bastard, I can hear you," Henry said as he struggled to fly the Apache in a straight line. He kept dipping and going up, finding it hard to hold the cyclic control stick level.

"Ah, Watson, good. I wanted to talk to you personally. I don't know what you did to piss off the colonel so bad, but this game ends here. See you in Hell, Mr. Watson." He flicked off the mike, so if Henry replied, he couldn't hear him. With an evil grin creeping slowly across his face, he moved his finger to the button for the 30mm cannon. This time he wouldn't miss.

Henry yelled back to Slater and Green, wanting them to tell them what was happening with the following Apache, while he struggled to keep the chopper aloft. It was shaking badly and smoke could be seen coming from just below the main rotor. Bowen said it might be the hydraulics or one of the seals on the main rotor. Either way it was bad news.

"I told you this bird is a piece of crap! It shouldn't even be flying!" Bowen shrieked when Henry swung around a building, the rotors missing the corner by inches.

Henry frowned deeply, wrinkles appearing on his brow. "Yeah I know, you already said that. How 'bout saying something constructive."

Slater was peering out the small window on the cargo door at Maddox's chopper and he spotted the 30mm cannon swiveling towards them. Maddox had closed to less than fifty feet and the man's masked face was visible through the canopy.

"Watson, something's gonna happen, I can feel it," Slater called as he stared at the cannon's muzzle.

The cannon roared; Maddox sending his entire load of ammunition towards them in one last shot. Henry felt the Apache shake and then all side to side movement was gone. He pressed the pedals again and again, but nothing happened. Bowen strained his neck to look behind them and he squeaked in terror.

"He shot out our tail rotor, oh shit, he shot it right off!"

"Okay, so what happens now!" Henry yelled as he tried to keep the bird level. The stentorian cascade filled the inside of the chopper, sounding like hail was pounding it on all sides. Smoke began shooting out from where the tail rotor had been and Henry felt he was losing the battle to stay airborne. Little did he know it was only dumb luck that he was still in the sky at all.

Maddox cursed his bad luck when he saw Watson's Apache wobbling like a baby bird flying for its first time. He'd shot his entire load, and though the back of the chopper looked like a junkyard wreck, it was miraculously still airborne.

Well, he was about to fix that. He had one last Hydra rocket onboard and he would make sure he sent it right down the exhaust of Watson's engine.

Calling up his electronic display, he sighted on his target, his finger hovering over the button that would send Watson and the other losers to hell in a fiery explosion worthy of a blockbuster movie. That made him nostalgic and he decided when he returned to the base he was going to get Blue Thunder from the base library. That would be a nice way to pass the night.

Henry knew he was losing the battle as the Apache dipped and he couldn't get it to go back up.

"The throttle, the throttle, up, we want to go up!" Bowen yelled.

"No shit, don't you think I know that?" Henry snapped back. For God's sake, this was his first time learning to fly a helicopter and he was in a dogfight for his life.

"The pitch, Henry, pitch the rotor forward!"

"I'm doing that, dammit! It's not working!"

Bowen checked a few gauges then tapped the fuel gauge with his finger. "Oh shit, we're losing power. One of those bullets hit the fuel tank or a hose broke loose. Henry, you've got to put this thing down before we crash!"

"What? Are you crazy? I don't know how to land this thing. I can barely fly it. Here, you take the controls." Henry was about to get up when Slater yelled from the back.

"Oh, Christ, no! He's firing another rocket!" He made the sign of the cross on his chest and moved away from the window. Green was curled upon the floor, the mantra; I don't want to die, being repeated from his trembling lips over and over like a skipping vinyl record.

Henry tried to do something, anything, but there was nothing to do. At the last second, which was two seconds after Slater warned him, he jammed both the cyclic control stick and the collective stick down, sending the Apache into a forward dive.

The chopper dropped like it had been plucked from the sky, but not before the Hydra rocket connected with the rear fuselage, blowing it off and sending the chopper spinning out of control.

Everyone screamed, the world spinning like a top, and the rooftop of a building came racing up at them at Mach speed.

"Henry, pull back on the stick, try to catch some air, it's our only chance!" Bowen yelled as his eyes popped out of their sockets with the sight of the approaching rooftop. It was a low roof, only three stories tall. It had once been a paint factory, but now it was one more tomb for the undead to live in.

Doing what Bowen told him, Henry pulled back on the cyclic control stick and amped up the throttle for all he was worth. The engine surged for a brief few seconds and then sputtered and died. Spinning around like a top, the main rotor continued swirling and the chopper came in at an odd angle.

"We gotta jump for it, it's our only chance!" Henry yelled to Bowen, his voice filled with terror. Only an idiot wouldn't be scared, falling from the sky like a rock. But he was still fighting and would continue to do so until he was finally sucking his last breath.

"That's impossible, we'll die!" Bowen yelled back.

"We're gonna die anyway, at least if we jump we might have a fighting chance!"

"No, stay in the chopper, it's safer!" Bowen screamed back. Alarms were sounding, warning lights flashing and it was seconds before the roof would connect with the helicopter. Deciding Bowen had made his decision, Henry unbuckled his seatbelt and flew out of his seat, striking the wall hard .It was like he was in a blender, and it was all he could do to get the cargo door open. The wind buffeted him, and even up in the air, hovering over the city, the stench of a half million zombies assaulted him. Bowen grabbed the controls, now having no choice. Green was still in the corner of the aircraft and Henry reached out a hand for the solider to take.

"Come on, it's our only chance!" Green shook his head no, too terrified to move. Slater tried for the door, but he was thrown to the far wall and was knocked unconscious. Knowing it was now or never, Henry closed his eyes and prepared to jump. But before he could do so, the remaining rear frame of the Apache separated from the main body, jack-knifed in on itself, and struck him as he stood in the open cargo door. Like he'd been hit by a giant fist of a god, he went flying into the sky. Immediately knocked unconscious, he fell threw the air and landed on the rooftop; rolling under the ductwork of an air-conditioning unit, and becoming hidden from view from overhead. The roof was covered in loose gravel, and if it had been anything but that, Henry would have died on the spot. But like a drunk in a car accident, he was limp and his body took a beating, but held together, the gravel helping to cushion his landing.

At the far end of the roof, the doomed Apache helicopter finally came down. It landed on its skids, then rolled onto its side in a spray of gravel. The main rotor snapped off, flying off the roof to slice into the building next door, but not before slicing into the Apache like a lawnmower blade. With no fuel in its tank, the chopper didn't explode, just rolled five times until it came up against the four foot high wall that surrounded the rooftop.

Overhead, Maddox hovered over the scene of impact, watching the smoking rubble and twisted wreckage. He saw an arm and what looked like a leg, the boot still attached to the foot, and he nodded.

Mission accomplished.

Banking to the right, he left the wreckage behind, heading back to Fort Knox to report to Miller on a job well done.

CHAPTER FORTY-FOUR

HENRY HAD NO idea how long he was out, but slowly consciousness came back to him. Trying to move, he immediately stopped when pain flared from every nerve ending at once.

He lay quiet, waiting for his body to tell him it was safe to try again.

When it was time, he shifted position. Twinges of pain filled him, but not as powerful as before. Slowly, a little at a time, like baby steps for a one-year-old, he pulled himself to a sitting position against a large air conditioning unit.

At the far end of the roof, the Apache lay smoking, the twisted, mangled wreckage tinged with spots of what looked like blood. He waited for more than an hour more before he felt he was strong enough to stand on his own. Fighting off a wave of dizziness, he pulled himself to his feet. The first thing he did was check to see what weapons he still had with him. He was relieved to see his panga and Glock were still secured in their holsters and sheath.

But his Steyr was nowhere to be found.

Oh well, it had served its purpose well, and he could always get another rifle. Besides, without the rotary clips the Steyr was more of a nuisance than an asset. Hobbling on battered feet, Henry began his walk across the rooftop towards the Apache. Maybe one of the others had managed to make it out before the chopper crashed. It was possible.

But as he moved closer to the smoking wreckage, he saw that though it was possible, it wasn't probable.

The first body was discovered about halfway to the wreck. The head was missing, sliced clean off and it took a moment for Henry to figure out who it was. It was the slim frame that gave it away. It was Private Green, or what was left of him. He noticed both hands were clenched into fists, almost as if the young private had braced himself before the crash and had held the pose in death.

There was nothing he could do for Green, so he moved on.

The next dismembered corpse was found only a few feet away from the twisted and crushed metal and steel framing. Leaning down, wincing in pain, he turned the body over, or the half that was in front of him. It was Slater all right, cut in half like it had been done by a surgeon. The edges of the wound were perfect, not tearing or ripping. The rotor blade must have sliced through him like a ginsu knife through a tomato.

The eyes were open, staring at nothing and Henry reached down and closed them. The man was a murderer, no question there, but in the end he was still a human being and deserved at least the simple act of having his eyes closed for eternity.

Pushing himself to his feet, Henry walked closer to the wreckage. The metal shifted and Henry stopped, wondering if the roof was still safe. For all he knew, the roof would give out sending him and the Apache onto the floor below. He waited for almost five minutes, staring near the small plumes of smoke, and when the roof remained stable, he decided to check out the rest of the chopper.

It appeared when the rotor had separated from the top of the Apache; the blades had sliced the aircraft multiple times before spinning away. If that unfortunate event hadn't happened, it was very possible Green or Slater might have survived the crash. To bad, too, he could've used the extra manpower to fight his way back to the base.

Climbing into what was left of the rear hold, he moved through the twisted mess of hanging tubes and sparking wires until he was at the controls. Bowen was there, slumped over the cyclic control stick and Henry shook his head. He was turning to leave when he heard coughing, then vomiting. In awe of what he was hearing, he turned around and saw Bowen's head move.

Rushing to his aid, Henry felt sharp pains in his sides and back. Brushing them off, he pushed through the wreckage until he was next to Bowen.

"Hey there, you're alive. Hold on and I'll get you out of there," Henry said, but when he moved the first piece of metal that was covering the man's waist, Henry stopped. The front of the cockpit had pushed in on Bowen, the jagged metal severing his body in twain.

Bowen's lower half was missing, lost in the tumbled wreckage, and Henry knew if he so much as moved the young pilot an inch, his organs would spill out and he would be dead in seconds. Probably very painfully, he assumed.

A dark red froth seeped from Bowen's lips as he turned his head to look at Henry.

"Guess...you...were...right. Should've...jumped," he gasped; each word a chore.

"Yeah, guess so," Henry said softly.

"Is it bad, sir? I...can't feel...my legs," Bowen whispered.

Henry had seen too much in his travels to sugarcoat the man's condition. If he was gonna die, he'd want someone to give it to him straight, too.

"Yeah, it is, sorry."

Bowen tried to smile, but couldn't muster up the energy.

"That...really...sucks. Guess I...shouldn't complain, though, I lived...longer than most...after the rains."

"Yeah, suppose you could look at it like that."

"Sir, do you...believe in God?" The words were forced even more and Henry realized Bowen was slipping away. There was probably some leakage where his lower half had been severed and the man was probably bleeding to death.

"Sure, guess so. Sometimes it's hard to, ya know? I mean, what kind of God would exist that would allow what happened to us? Sometimes I think we're all on our own, and when you're done, you're done. Ya know what I mean? Bowen?"

He stared at Bowen's face and it took him a moment to realize the man was dead. He reached out and closed his eyes, positioning his head so it was more comfortable, even in death.

With nothing more to be done, he turned and exited the craft. It was just as he was stepping onto the roof that he spotted an M-16. There were two actually, Slater's and Green's. The shoulder straps had become tangled and had prevented them from flying too far from the crash zone.

Checking the first rifle, he saw the barrel was bent and the second had a broken stock. But he thought he might be able to take both weapons apart and make one working firearm. He'd learned a lot in his past year of travels, mostly from gunsmiths that were more than happy to pass on their knowledge. Henry now knew how to assemble and disassemble most handguns and rifles and the ones he didn't know how to, he didn't want.

He moved away from the wreckage, walking all the way to the far end of the roof, and with the sun beating down on his head, he got to work disassembling the rifles.

An hour later he was prepared to leave the roof.

On his shoulder was the M-16 salvaged from the two he'd found. He knew he was about thirty miles away from Fort Knox and the only way to get back there quickly would be to find transportation.

That would mean finding a car or motorcycle, both highly difficult after a year of sitting inactive. It was as he was trying to figure out how to get down off the roof that he felt a slight tremor and went to his knees. Was it an earthquake? In Kentucky?

But then he gazed across to the opposite end of the roof to the Apache wreckage and watched as the roof seemed to open up and swallow the wreck hole. Dust and smoke swirled into the air and Henry waited for a full ten minutes before venturing a look-see.

What he saw was the Apache laying on its side on the floor below, and best of all, the floor wasn't that far from the ceiling, the latter being the roof Henry was standing on.

It was a simple task to climb down, using the steel girders for handholds; a rough ladder made just for him. When his boots were planted on the floor again, he turned away from the wreckage and made his way to the stairwell, where below, in the underground parking garage he might be able to catch a ride back to the base.

The building was empty of ghouls. The entire climb down to the parking garage, not one zombie popped its rotting head up. Henry figured the building must be sealed. It made sense. When the state of emergency went into affect, factories and similar business would have closed down until the crisis had passed, sending their workers home. The buildings would have been locked tight and their owners would end up never returning.

On the second floor, Henry found an old vending machine with stale candy, chips and pretzels. Insects had managed to find their way into most of it, but a few had held the battle and Henry had quickly devoured them, wishing he had a Coke to wash it all down with.

There had been a soda machine next to the candy machine, but all the cans had exploded. One of the empty cans was lying near his feet and he saw the can had teeth marks on its bottom. Guess there had been some rats in the building that had a craving for something refreshing.

Feeling a hundred percent better now that he'd eaten something, he finished his journey to the underground garage.

Upon entering the parking garage, he felt the oppressiveness of the site almost immediately. Deep shadows were in the far corners, hinting of monsters waiting for an unwary soul to venture near.

Shrugging off the ominous feelings, he began moving down the middle of the garage, making sure to keep as much distance between himself and any possibility of attack from behind the deserted vehicles.

The variation in automobiles was incredible. Volvos, Cadillacs and Lexus' sat alongside Buicks, Saturns and Toyotas, all waiting for their owners who would never return. A small part of him couldn't help but see the dollar signs and it took all of his willpower to forget about the frivolity of the past and focus on the present. Expensive didn't mean better. He needed something reliable that he could hotwire.

Round circular windows were on the sides of the garage, similar to small skylights placed in residential homes. The cylinder of the skylights had a reflective surface, bouncing the sun's rays through six feet of concrete until it ended up inside the garage. Homes with attics used this technology and whoever had owned the paint factory had invested in the skylights, thereby cutting their lighting costs for the parking garage to almost nothing. Where the underground parking garage would normally have been pitch black, there was more than enough light to see by.

Though his eyes lingered on the BMW's and Cadillacs, eventually he settled on a handsome 1973 Dodge Charger. It had a bright red paintjob and mag wheels and was a labor of love for some dead soul who'd fixed it up with tender-loving care. The rear, side louvered windows made it hard to see out of them and the slanted rear windshield gave it a mean look, but none of that was why Henry picked it as his transportation of choice.

It was the small solar battery charger connected to the driver's side window. The wire leading from the small panel--which was ten inches long and six wide--went straight into the cigarette lighter and would keep the battery charged with its small trickle of power.

The door was locked, of course, so Henry had no choice but to go to the passenger side and break the window with the butt of the M-16. The safety glass shattered, small cubes looking like ice raining across the front seat. Not a problem, he could brush them off later.

Unlocking the door, he slid inside. Now came the ultimate test if he could use this car. Turning on the headlights he breathed a sigh of relief when the cars across the lane were exposed in the artificial light.

Smiling slightly, he turned them off, then got to work on hotwiring the car. One more useful bit of information he'd picked up over the past year. If the car was under 1980, he could usually hotwire it in seconds, newer cars becoming more difficult. A small, wiry Spanish guy, named Pedro, had been kind enough to teach him. Pedro had said almost every American car in Mexico was stolen and that he personally had managed to bring over hundreds before the border patrol began cracking down. Pedro had died a week later after getting caught by a group of ghouls that had managed to slip inside the town's perimeter. Henry was sad to find out the man had been killed, but his memory lives on thanks to his teachings.

The engine turned over, but didn't start. Remembering that old cars needed to be pumped manually, Henry pressed the gas pedal twice, careful not to flood the carburetor. He tried again and the starter whirred. Pumping the pedal yet again, he was rewarded with the engine roaring to life, exhaust smoke spewing out of the back like a fire-breathing dragon as the 318 V-engine settled down to a dull roar. Good old U.S. of A manufacturing. Guzzles gas and single handedly destroys the ozone. What more could you want from an American made car?

Pulling the driver's door closed, he let the car idle for another five minutes, making sure the engine was sure and strong. The gas gauge was low, a lot of the fuel lost to evaporation after more than year of sitting unattended, but if he was lucky, he would have enough to make it back to the base. The garage began filling up with exhaust, the ventilation fans not working and probably never would again. At the end of the five minutes, he put the car in drive and roared out of the car's parking space, driving up the ramp that would lead to the outside world.

There was a metal gate blocking the exit and Henry slowed until the front bumper was almost touching the links. Stepping out, he walked over to the edge of the gate and saw the large steel padlock. Retrieving the M-16 from the passenger seat, he went back to the lock, took a step back in case of ricochets, and shot four rounds at the steel lock, two double-taps sounding like one massive explosion in the underground, man-made cavern.

The padlock broke apart and tinkled to the floor and Henry rolled the gate up. Climbing back into the driver's seat, he placed the car in drive and drove up the ramp that would lead him to freedom.

A few ghouls were on the ramp, attracted to all the noise from the helicopter crash above and possibly from Henry's gunshots. Henry slowed his speed to make sure he had control of the car and knocked the ghouls out of the way or gently nudged them to the side. He had to drive around some wreckage from the Apache and his jaw went taut as he thought about how close he'd come to buying the farm.

Pulling onto the street, he drove onto sidewalks and over medians as he worked his way out of the dead city. He always found a way through road blocks that came his way, bringing creative thinking to entirely new heights. One time, when the entire street was blocked by abandoned cars and ghouls, he turned to the left and drove into a small, open air strip mall. Knocking benches and trash barrels aside, he made it to the next street over and was on his way again.

Once he reached the edge of the city, he detoured off the streets and highways altogether, driving along the sides of the highway and crushing the six foot high grass down to a foot, as he cut his way to freedom.

He found it ironic that though the outbound sides of the highway were jam-packed with abandoned vehicles, their owners trying to escape the city in a mad exodus. But when the highway had become packed and stalled cars had blocked the way, the vehicles had been abandoned.

No one had been bright enough to take the initiative and just pull onto the dirt shoulder, or better yet, had simply driven onto one of the off ramps and headed out of the city by driving on the inbound lanes. Even with their lives in jeopardy, the average citizen hadn't comprehend breaking the law, to go out of the conventional box we all live by; or bending the cohesive rules that keep civilization running smoothly.

It took Henry more than three hours to finally breach the stranglehold of dead vehicles surrounding Louisville, but eventually he did.

With mostly open road ahead of him, he stepped on the gas, the eight cylinder engine thrusting the car forward like a rocket.

He needed to get back to Fort Knox for two reasons. The first was to grab his friends and make a run for it, but the second reason was more selfish.

He was going to find Colonel Miller and Major Maddox of the United States Army and make them pay.

CHAPTER FORTY-FIVE

Upon REACHING THE barracks area, Cindy slowed down, not wanting to be seen. She had found an old jacket hanging outside one of the buildings and had donned it quickly, making sure to tuck her long, blonde hair under the hood. She didn't know who was looking for her yet, and for all she knew it was every soldier on the base or none at all.

She slowed when she reached the building that had housed her, Mary, Sue and Raven last night. Keeping her head low, she stepped inside the building. It was deserted, every single bed empty and the occupants out working in the fields and doing the other chores assigned to them.

Biting her lip in thought, she wondered what she should do and where should she go next. She couldn't just go traipsing around the base; it was too likely she would be seen by someone looking for her. Deciding she might as well stay in the barracks as anywhere else, she went to the far corner and dropped down onto a crouch, her body hidden from view by a cabinet.

Sooner or later the others would return, and hopefully once they did, she could tell them what happened to her and they could all get the hell out off the base before the shit really hit the fan.

*　*　*

Jimmy slowed as he passed a platoon of marching soldiers, making sure to look down, not making eye contact with any of the men.

The man calling cadence glanced at him momentarily, but then looked away. The soldiers marched by him, one or two glancing his way, but none thought anything out of the ordinary about one of their own walking along the road.

With the exception of missing his shirt, Jimmy looked like every other soldier on the base. The blood splatter was barely noticeable unless someone got too close to him.

With the soldiers marching on behind him, Jimmy continued walking down the street, passing by men and women as they went about their daily chores. A few more soldiers walked by him, and when he passed them they glared at him, not understanding why he was out of uniform. But they were all privates and so had no authority to say anything to him.

He realized he needed to find a new shirt and fast, before another person of authority stopped him. Rounding a bend in the road, he saw a jeep, and three soldiers who were working near it. They were digging a hole in the lawn, and when Jimmy moved closer to them, he caught a few words about a new flagpole going up and how the men were just doing it to be kept busy.

Busy work, was what they called it. Keep the men occupied so they didn't get restless.

One of the men had his shirt off and it was lying on the spare tire of the jeep.

Casually, like he most definitely belonged, Jimmy strolled near the jeep and reached out and grabbed the shirt, never slowing down as he moved away.

While he walked away, he was waiting for one of them to call out and stop him from stealing the shirt, but it didn't happen. Sighing with relief, he turned another corner and stopped against a one-story cement structure that was used for storage.

Setting down his Remington, he put on the shirt. He'd just managed to slide the right sleeve on when a master-sergeant turned the corner and spotted him. This man was a soldier through and through, with a small mustache and large bushy eyebrows. His jib was perfect and his shoes were mirror-polished. The instant he saw Jimmy half-in/half-out of his shirt, he turned smartly and almost ran at him.

"You there, soldier, what in the hell do you think you're doing out of uniform in the middle of the day? And is that blood on your t-shirt?"

Jimmy stopped fiddling with the shirt and looked up at the master-sergeant. The man had a few inches on Jimmy; his eyes where Jimmy's forehead was.

"Uh, I, uhm, I don't know. Sorry?" Jimmy stammered each word. The master-sergeant had an air of authority about him and he reminded Jimmy a lot of his father.

"Sorry?" A heartbeat went by. "Sorry? You're sorry? Why you little shit, you'll be digging latrines for a week for this!"

"Latrines? Why the hell would I do that? We're on a base with flushing toilets?"

The master-sergeant was flabbergasted and went white with shock at the way Jimmy was speaking to him.

"Why you no good...Get on the ground and give me fifty right now, goddammit!"

Jimmy bent his head back slightly, at first not getting it, then understanding settled in. Deciding this had gone as far as it was going to go; Jimmy looked around to the left and right, making sure there was no one else on the street. It was quiet for the moment, but anytime someone could come around the corner and see him arguing with the master-sergeant.

"Did you hear me, private?" The master-sergeant screamed, seeing the rank on Jimmy's shirt. "I said give me fifty pushups right fucking now?"

"How 'bout I give you five instead?" Jimmy quipped and punched the master- sergeant in the throat. The man gasped, his larynx crushed by the blow and he began gagging. He tried to talk when another blow caught him in the right eye, knocking his head to the side. Reaching down, Jimmy retrieved the shotgun and used the butt of the weapon to club the master-sergeant on the side of the head. The old warhorse went down like a ton of bricks and began wheezing softly over and over.

Looking around quickly, Jimmy saw the area was still empty. And better yet, the soldiers who were digging the hole for the new flagpole were gone, the jeep gone too, the men taking a break for lunch.

With no time to lose, Jimmy dragged the wheezing man over to the hole and rolled him into it, now gasping for air himself. The man was heavy and Jimmy's back was killing him.

The master-sergeant landed upside down, his ass in the air and Jimmy could see there was a small pool of water in the bottom of the hole. Bubbles were popping on the surface as the drowning man tried to breathe the muddy water.

Jimmy shook his head sadly, staring at the upside-down man's ass. His pants had split and Jimmy had a grand view of the master-sergeant's bare ass. Evidently, wearing underwear wasn't a priority to the drowning man.

With a wide smile creasing his lips, Jimmy shook his head.

"Guess the moon's comin' out early today," he joked, but after looking around to make sure the area was still clear, he remembered there was no one to hear his joke. Sighing wearily, he turned and trotted away, slinging his shotgun over his shoulder. While he jogged, he quickly buttoned up his shirt, frowning when he realized it was a size too small.

He needed to find transportation that no one would miss. It was the only way he could cover the entire base while he searched for Cindy and the others.

Looking up at the sky, he saw it was almost noon. The day was already half gone. Feeling a renewed sense of urgency, he began running instead of jogging, his eyes now on the lookout for some vehicle to steal.

*   *   *

Henry slammed the hood of the Charger and looked up at the sun. It was well past noon with the sun still high in the sky. Perspiration beaded his face and under his arms, not to mention the pool of sweat that was collecting in the small of his back, then seeping down into the crack of his butt.

God he was hot. And thirsty. There was no water to drink for miles and he wouldn't be drinking anything until he made it back to the base.

If he made it back, he thought.

The Charger's engine had begun making clanking noises about five miles back, and the temperature gauge had begun to rise steadily, so he'd finally decided to pull over and check out what was wrong. Popping the hood, he discovered a severed arm had wedged itself between the fan belt and the water pump, causing the fan belt to stop spinning. The Charger had begun to overheat and the loud noise had been the fan belt catching the bone in the arm. He had to unwedge the arm, which had managed to get in there real good and then had to bend the fan blades back to their correct angles. It had taken time, and with no tools to use, it was twice as hard. But he believed he'd finally finished, and with the hood now closed, he wiped his brow clear of sweat and walked back to the driver's door of the Charger.

Just when he was about to open the door, a large zombie popped up below the shoulder of the road. He was a nasty one, with dried skin that gave him a facelift and made him look like he was always smiling. The dead man's stomach was bloated from gases and looked like it would rupture at any moment.

Caught off guard for the slightest second, at first Henry only watched the shambling, weaving dead man stumble up the shoulder and reach out for him. A dry rasp left the mottled lips and Henry could almost imagine a puff of dust seeping out, like when an old book is opened in a dingy attic.

Then he regained his senses and reached inside the Charger, grabbed the rifle and aimed for the dead man's forehead. The ghoul never stopped, only opened his mouth wide, preparing to sink his teeth into whatever choice part of Henry he could reach.

Henry waited perfectly still, a statue alone on the highway, until the ghoul was three feet away. The rifle barked in his hands and the dead man's head exploded, sending bits of bone and black ichor in all directions. Henry turned his face away, knowing to be wary of blowback, and when he turned back, the headless body was still standing. The ghoul hand managed to place one foot forward, the other in the perfect spot to balance the headless corpse.

"Well I'll be, that's one for the books," Henry said to the open road. Turning around, he slid into the Charger and turned over the engine, relieved when it started on the first try. His fuel was almost gone, but he was almost there. The base was ten more miles away and he was confident he would be there soon, barring anymore obstructions.

The Charger roared, and the rear tire spun, the car shooting down the highway like a spear.

Behind him, like an artist's muse, the headless ghoul remained standing until ten minutes later, when a heavy gust of wind caught the billowing clothing and pushed the headless corpse to the pavement.

*　　*　　*

Mary, Sue and Raven slowed their stride when they reached the edge of the base designated for military operations and looked on the housing aspect laid out before them. Neat rows of one-family homes lined the streets. This is where the families of the soldiers once lived.

Some were still occupied, but others were abandoned. The grass was waist high on front lawns until the tall stalks had fallen over from their own weight. Doors and windows of the homes were broken and missing, some front doors hanging open, like yawning mouths hungry for food. Gutters were filled with debris and soil, weeds growing out of them like planters. Shrubs grew wild, some so big they connected to each other, obscuring the walkways of the front porches they once lined like good little soldiers on parade.

"Well, what do you think, should we go check 'em out?" Mary shifted her feet, staring at the empty street. From somewhere nearby the sound of music could be heard, Spanish influence, she thought. And what sounded like a baby screaming from far away floated on the wind.

"Do you think she's in there somewhere?" Sue asked. They had been looking for Cindy for hours and it was well past noon. They were all hungry and tired and knew this was their only chance to find her. When they returned to the barracks that night it would be known none of the women had reported to the brothel.

But their hopes were to find Cindy first, then Jimmy and Henry, and then get the hell off the military base fast by hijacking a vehicle from the motor pool.

Mary glanced down over to Raven, but the teenage girl said nothing. She sensed Mary looking at her and turned her face up to Mary's.

"Well, Raven, you have an opinion on what we should do?"

"Sure, why not? She's got to be somewhere. Let's check it out."

Raven had said more in that sentence than she had all day and Mary nodded, pleased the girl had chosen to speak.

Mary smiled. "Couldn't have said it better myself. Come on, then, let's go."

Walking side by side, the three women moved down the street, hoping Cindy was in one of the homes nearby.

CHAPTER FORTY-SIX

DARKNESS WAS JUST beginning to descend across the land when Henry reached the outskirts to Fort Knox. The base was only a mile away.

He was running on fumes and knew he needed to move fast, not wanting to waste even a drop of the precious gas.

He also knew he couldn't just go through the main gate, which was surrounded by hundreds of ghouls, all wanting into the base. Plus, there were soldiers there, guarding the gate. He needed to find an unguarded entry, so he turned the Charger perpendicular to the road that led to the main gate. He would circle around and come at the base from the side, where there was nothing but empty homes and fields that had once been massive grass lawns and were now used for crops.

Revving the Charger's engine and patting the dashboard, he sent good thoughts for the gas to last just a little bit longer and roared off into the falling darkness. With the last of the setting sun kissing the horizon, the car's headlights sliced through the growing dark like a knife, chasing the shadows away.

Henry slowed the Charger on the hill overlooking the cyclone fence below. All around him were trees, weeds, and wild grass.

It had been a hard drive to get where he was and he thought back to the last hour.

He'd gone over five miles out of his way, circling around the base until he found a small goat trail that led in the right direction. When the goat trail ended, he drove up the slight incline, the rear tires churning sod and spitting it out the back like a dog digging for a bone.

Walking corpses were everywhere, moving about like lost souls in limbo. Before he arrived, they merely wandered aimlessly, but when his headlights cut through the night, they immediately turned and followed. Some wore only stockings on their feet, their footwear long gone, and others wore nothing at all, on either their feet or their bodies. Sagging flesh hung from frail, weather-beaten frames and the pale white of bones could be seen peeking out through mottled torn and ripped flesh. Some were ragged, ghastly creatures, humanoid in shape only, but others were fresher, looking for all purposes like typical people out for a walk. It was only if a person moved closer and inspected their bodies that the torn flesh of bite marks could be discerned.

The Charger left two ruts of muddy earth in the land as it forced its way through the soil. The rear wheel drive worked and pushed, slowly inching the car up and over the hill. With such an easy path to follow, every ghoul in the vicinity moved towards the tire tracks, and slowly began marching after the car.

Oblivious of his followers, Henry continued onward, praying he wasn't lost until he stopped on the top of the hill and was able to gaze down on the cyclone fence below.

He'd made it, only a few more minutes and he'd be inside the base again.

The front bumper and grille of the Charger was bruised and dented, from both striking bodies and trees. Once again he thanked himself for taking an older car. If he had taken a more recent vehicle, he wouldn't have made it twenty feet into the dense brush before the airbag would have gone off when the first tree or body connected with the front of the vehicle. That was why the older ones were better, they could take all the damage you could dish out and keep on ticking.

But he knew it was more than skill that had brought him to the end of his journey. Henry wasn't afraid to admit there had been a lot of luck involved. The engine began to sputter and Henry realized the car was about to die, the gas in the tank finally exhausted.

Realizing there was no time for subtlety, he jammed his foot on the gas pedal and the Charger flew down the hill, bouncing on all four tires. He seemed to fall more than roll down the hill.

The cyclone fence was coming closer; the headlights catching the metal links and making them sparkle. The engine was coughing, and even with the advantage of going downhill, gravity doing its best to pull him earthward, the grass and soft earth seemed to swallow the tires and bog them down.

But Newton's first law of motion is that an object in motion tends to stay in motion, and the law was as true now as before.

The Charger's engine finally choked and died, Henry immediately feeling the steering go numb. The power steering was gone and he could do nothing but hold on while the Charger rolled down the hill like it was nothing more than a boulder with wheels attached.

Inside the car, Henry was bounced around like he was in a spaceship achieving reentry. His head continually struck the roof of the dash and the steering wheel as he struggled to maintain some semblance of control over the vehicle. Then before he knew it, he was staring at the metal fence and he swore to himself later he could have counted each metal rung individually when time seemed to stand still.

For one brief instant the world stopped and he could see a small bug on the windshield, the dust floating in the air around him, and his own face reflecting his terror back to him from the glass of the windshield.

Then time returned to normal and the front bumper of the Charger hit the fence, tearing into it and ripping the moorings from the ground like a child pulling up a strand of grass. Caught in the fence like a shark in a fishing line, the Charger flipped onto its side and rolled over.

Metal twisting into metal in violent copulation filled his ears. And Henry yelled in fright, thinking he was about to die, when the world stopped moving. All sound ceased and there was nothing but a few chirping crickets coming from some nearby trees.

Lying on his head, his neck crooked at an odd angle, he undid the seatbelt and tumbled onto the roof, which was now the floor. Huffing and puffing, he managed to retrieve his rifle and crawl out of the shattered driver's side window.

He crawled away, praying the car wasn't about to explode, then remembered there was no gas left in the tank. When he felt he was far enough away, he turned over, staring at the spinning rear tires and dented frame of the Charger.

"Jesus Christ, I can't believe that just worked," he said into the night, hearing his raspy voice, his throat dry from thirst.

A chorus of moans floated on the wind like wind chimes and he looked up to the hill he'd just slalomed like a snowboarder to see more than a score of bodies moving towards him, their darker forms silhouetted by the contrasting starlight of the night sky.

Rolling to his feet, he winced in pain, feeling his shoulder go numb for a second. He'd opened his shoulder wound again and could already feel a wetness spreading under his shirt. Ignoring the pain, he stood on shaking legs and turned towards the base. It was easy to know where to go; the lights of the base were already on, the soldiers able to see easily as they did their rounds along the winding streets of the military base. That was okay for Henry, too. The same light that allowed the soldiers to see by was also useful to Henry. With the base lit up like a Christmas tree, he would be able to move about freely, not another mysterious shadow in the dark trying to see beyond the next pocket of darkness.

As far as he knew, no one would be looking for him. Maddox had tried to kill him covertly, so it was possible only he, Miller and a few others of command even knew what had happened today.

Henry could use that to his advantage.

Feeling better with every step he took, he adjusted his heading so he was walking to the building that housed the armory. His hands clenched involuntarily into fists as he thought about what he would be doing this night.

Payback was coming for Colonel Miller, Major Maddox and all who stood in his way.

But first he needed to resupply. Then it would be war.

*   *   *

Jimmy stopped walking and leaned against a stone building with an American flag attached to its side. He'd been walking for hours and had slowly been coming to the realization he wouldn't be finding Cindy anytime soon. The military base was huge and he was only one man.

Sliding to his butt, he leaned his head back against the stone, closing his eyes in failure. His woman was lost, and he could only imagine what had happened to her. Was it Miller or Maddox? Probably Miller, that bastard. Henry had said the colonel had eyes for her. He would never know unless he confronted him.

Opening his eyes, he set his jaw firm, his countenance taking on a grim look of determination. That was it. Enough chasing shadows like a child. Either Maddox or Miller would know where she was, and besides, it had to be one of them that had given the order for the training exercise to take a deadly turn. He was sure the dead soldier's bodies had been found by now and wondered if the discoverers had figured out what had happened yet.

Possible, but not a guarantee.

Standing back up, he fixed the shoulder strap on his Remington, then made sure his .38 was secure in its holster. The .45 rode in his belt behind his back. He liked the weapon and would use it until the ammo ran dry.

So he would go find Major Maddox first. Yes, he would find Maddox first and make him tell where Cindy was. Looking around the street, he realized he was lost. Numerous people moved about, passing him without care. Some were soldiers, but most were civilians, moving about on tasks and chores. He debated asking one of them for directions, but in the end chose to hold his own council, not knowing who he could trust. One of his best resources was his animosity.

Turning and walking back up the sidewalk, backtracking the way he'd come, he knew before he could find Maddox he would had to figure out just where in the hell he was.

*   *   *

Colonel Miller walked through the front door of his house after a long day of trying to take back America from the undead scourge. It had been a busy day, filled with decisions that changed many lives for the worse. Well, maybe a few for the better, but most for the worst.

Maddox had just finished briefing him on his mission to kill Watson and it had gone off perfectly. Tomorrow, he would gather most of the base together near the bleachers and tell them the tragic fate of one of their own, the hero named Henry Watson. He would tell them what a terrible tragedy it was and give them a pep talk about how the world would be getting better; all they had to do was work harder toward the same common goal.

And if they didn't, they would be hanged or worse, visit the impaling pole.

As for his soldiers, they were another matter completely. He was slowly weeding out some recruits from the civilians, but not fast enough to recoup his losses. And to top things off he'd heard six of his men had been killed in a training accident and another was missing, the young man who was in Watson's party, Cooper. There was an alert out and he was sure Cooper would be found soon enough. After all, there was nowhere to go. He wondered to himself how much worse it could get when he walked into his home to see no one there to greet him.

Usually the cook was there, as he also pulled double duty as his butler of sorts. Not that Miller needed him for much other than cooking and some small cleaning. He didn't trust the civilians. After all, he'd taken them from their homes kicking and screaming. Only a fool would let those same people into his home where they could get close to him when his guard was down. Besides, he considered himself to be a self-sufficient man, not wanting to be fawned over. But he enjoyed a good, home-cooked meal and so kept the cook on staff.

Hanging up his jacket, the ribbons weighing the hanger down, he moved down the main hall to his den. He was looking forward to seeing Cindy, wanting to finally convince her of the advantages of staying with him willingly. But if she wouldn't give in, then he would just have to force her. He wasn't a man who enjoyed rape for the sake of pain, but as a way to break a woman's spirit it would do nicely.

It was when he turned the corner that led to the den that he began to hear pounding. Was the woman banging on the door? And as he moved closer, he saw the guards were nowhere to be seen.

He'd see them hang for this, leaving their post unattended.

Then a voice could be heard, but instead of the melodic voice of Cindy, it was a man's voice. Opening the door, and drawing one of his Colt Magnums, he stepped back, suspecting some kind of trick, and his eyes went wide when the cook charged out, stopping suddenly at the sight of Colonel Miller.

"What is the meaning of this? Where's the woman?"

"She's gone, sir. She killed the guards and locked me inside. I thought she was going to kill me, too, Then she just left...locked the door and left."

Holstering his weapon, Miller squeezed his hands together, so hard nails dug into his palm, drawing blood.

"Dammit, I'll have someone's head on a spike for this!"

The cook cringed, expecting that head would be his.

Miller gazed at the frightened cook, his eyes burning with intensity. His right hand actually crept down to his right side Colt Magnum again, weighing if swift punishment should be meted out, and the cook readied himself for death.

"No, not yet. I still have need of you. Get out of my sight and get me something to eat, I'm starving."

"Yyyyes, sir," the cook stammered, barely believing he was going to live to see the sunrise tomorrow morning. Turning, the frightened man ran down the hall, his destination the kitchen. Miller watched him leave, then moved through the den door. He gazed down at the two dead soldiers and he lifted his head to the ceiling, furious of being defied, and let out a guttural yell that had the cook cringing in fear as the echoed scream of anguish and frustration filled the house. Then all was silent and Miller turned around, closed the den door behind him, and walked to his small office at the opposite end of the house. That was where he kept a two-way radio. He needed to contact the watch captain and Maddox. Tell them what had happened, and above all else, he wanted them to start searching for Cindy. She wouldn't go far, she couldn't. Like Cooper and the other companions they were trapped inside the base.

There were guards at all the main exits and hundreds of stenches surrounding the perimeter fences. She was trapped, whether she knew it or not. The only safe way in or out of the base, without soldiers fighting off the stenches so the gates could be opened, was on a helicopter, and those were safely ensconced in the hangar under heavy guard.

Crossing the hallway, his right hand raised in a fist while he gritted his teeth. He would have that woman, even if he had to kill her.

CHAPTER FORTY-SEVEN

HENRY SLOWED HIS pace when the armory came into sight. A non-descript building with large steel doors, a loading dock, and stone slabs for walls and ceiling. With the exception of a small plaque near the side door that read Armory, anyone on the base would have missed the importance of the building.

Creeping near a tree-lined structure across the street, Henry realized it was used for a church. He saw a sign with pamphlets tucked under a faded plastic panel, notices of services a year overdue.

Two soldiers stood a lazy watch over the armory. One pacing back and forth while the other leaned against a small half-wall near the loading dock.

These two men needed to be dealt with before Henry could enter the building.

He thought about trying to sneak up on them, but with the street lights all lit, it was more like twilight than actual night on the military base.

Biting his inner cheek as he wracked his brain for an idea, he looked up when three civilians rounded the street corner from whence he'd come and began moving towards the soldiers. Melting into the trees and shrubbery near the church, Henry waited while the three civilians stumbled across the sidewalk, none of them talking to one another.

For where he hid, it looked like all three were drunk. Their jerky movements resembled puppetry; and one walked with his head at an odd angle, like he was already sleeping on his feet. It was only when the three men wandered under a streetlight that Henry realized the men weren't drunk at all, they were dead.

Zombies inside the base? But how?

Then he remembered the rather large hole he had made in the perimeter fence on the southeast corner of the base and had his answer.

Things were about to get a whole lot more interesting in Fort Knox.

At first, the two soldiers by the loading dock didn't notice the three shambling dead men, and why should they? But when the first ghoul made it within ten feet of the pacing soldier, the cracked lips of the ghoul's mouth opened wide and a dull groan issued from withered vocal cords.

The soldier spun around, the other going to his feet. Quick words were exchanged between the guards and the pacing soldier lowered his rifle so it was aimed directly at the first ghoul's chest.

A warning was given, to no results, of course, and the soldier fired, sending three rounds into the zombie's chest. Staggering back from the blow, the dead man quickly regained his balance and began moving forward again. From a distance, Henry thought the ghoul looked like he'd been gently pushed back by a soft hand, before proceeding onward once again.

Now both soldiers were up and one was screaming into a radio, trying to get reinforcements, Henry assumed. Both men sprayed the ghouls with bullets, but neither man went for a head short. Neither guard was battle seasoned and panic was their main emotion. Scratch that, panic and fear would be a better description.

The ghouls charged in, and the two soldiers went down under them, screaming as rotting teeth and dirty fingernails tore into their flesh, ripping and devouring them, turning their bodies into large, bloody gobbets of scarlet meat.

Henry extricated himself from his hiding place and shook his head as he walked over to the three feeding ghouls and two whimpering and dying soldiers.

He stood behind the five bodies and shook his head tightly. This should never have happened. Two well-armed soldiers against three unarmed deaders.

Pathetic.

Walking up behind the three feeding ghouls, he raised his rifle and shot each one in the head. Gazing down at the half eaten remains of the soldiers, he shot each one in the head, as well, not wanting any returning visitors while he was inside the armory. He retrieved one of the soldier's rifles, popping the clip to see it was still half full. He tossed his old one away. The soldier had a spare clip on his belt so Henry grabbed that, too, careful to avoid the spreading pools of blood.

On the ground next to a soldier's limp, severed hand, the two-way radio squawked, the operator wanting a status report.

Picking up the radio and securing it to his belt, Henry stepped over the pools and gobbets of blood-soaked gore on the ground and opened the armory door, ignoring the off-line touch pad near the doorknob. At one time the armory might have been locked with access codes and special combinations to gain entry, but now it had been reduced to a simple large building with shelves and crates full of the remaining weapons of the military base; the touch pads taken off-line in case of emergency. There just wasn't the manpower for complex security anymore, so the pads had been discarded as a relic of the past. Plus, it was obvious the weapons in the new armory were taken from somewhere else, conscripted like the slave labor Miller was now using.

Flicking the light switch on the side of the door, fluorescent lights staggered on, one at a time, bathing the massive open area in a golden glow

Gleaming with happiness, he stared at the crates of brand-new, factory fresh Kalashnikovs, their steel barrels gleaming with oil. In the crates next to them, were thousands of rounds of 7.62mm brass for the weapons, and the crates next to those had the empty, curved magazines for the weapons. The clips had to be loaded when they were ready to be used or else the owner would risk a jam during a critical point in a firefight. There was a spring that pushed up on the loader and if the magazine sat for too long, the spring became weak, causing failure.

There were only a few crates of M-16s and these did not look new. That was why more than half the men used the Russian made Kalashnikovs. Use what you got and be damned the rest.

Walking in a daze around the armory, he stopped at the last crates in the line. Grenades, still in their packing from the factory. Nothing extravagant, no thermite or Willie Peter's, white phosphorous for another name; just simple HE charges. That was fine with him. The small wads of C-4 in the egg-shaped housing would be more than enough for what he had planned.

A box of web belts and harnesses were stacked on a nearby shelf and Henry grabbed one, sliding into it. There was a pile of Kevlar vests next to the web belts and he decided, why not, a little added security on his body wouldn't hurt. The vests weren't that heavy and would help to camouflage him as just another soldier. He began clipping grenades to the web belt as fast as he could and then went to the assault rifles, picking one that looked good to him. Hell, they all looked good to him. He shoved as many loose rounds for the rapid-fire into his pockets and grabbed a few empty clips. When he was out of the armory, he could find someplace safe and load them one at a time, but for now he had the M-16 for firepower.

Only a few minutes had passed since he'd entered the armory and he knew his time would be up soon. Reinforcements would be on the way when the now very dead guard didn't answer the radio. Hefting his brand new Kalashnikov, he slung it over his shoulder for later use, and jogged for the loading dock doors. His body jingled from all the rounds he'd stuffed in his pockets, but it couldn't be helped. He was confident he would need every last bullet before the day was over.

Once at the doors, he rolled them up a few feet, and peeked out just as three jeeps rolled up to his right. He prepared to move to his left, but first he needed a distraction to cover his retreat. Pulling the pin on one of the newly acquired grenades, he threw it at the oncoming jeeps. The grenade bounced like a baseball and went off just as the last jeep was over it. An earsplitting explosion ripped through the night and the jeep jumped up and split in half in a ball of flames. Soldiers went flying, crashing to the ground in rolling heaps of blazing bodies. One hapless man's face was entirely engulfed in flames and his arms jerked in spasms over his head as he beat at the flames. His eyes were melted and his flesh sloughed off the bone like wax as he screamed for help. He sucked in the caustic flames and smoke, mercifully suffocating, his twitching limbs slowing and stopping. But Henry didn't see any of this. As soon as the grenade went off, he was running away from the armory, his boot soles slapping the concrete like a marathon runner. Behind him he heard gunshots and when he reached the edge of the church, he slowed, risking a look behind him. In the glow of the flames he saw other, slower moving bodies surrounding the remaining soldiers and then more gunfire split the night.

More ghouls were arriving from the tear in the perimeter fence.

A low moan came from Henry's right and he saw a middle-aged woman, most definitely undead, shambling toward him. Her face was a mockery of what it once was. Though she still had her nose, ears, hair and cheeks, all of the flesh was hanging by thin tendons, the skin attached in patches over the skull. She reminded Henry of one of those clay sculptures he'd seen on television, where the forensic artist places putty over a bleached skull to build up the features for identification.

Deciding he didn't have time for her, he turned and jogged away. The dead woman moaned at seeing her prey escaping, then turned and headed for the flames and surviving soldiers. Finally, after long months of a diet of small animals and bugs, meat was plentiful. If a zombie could cry in happiness, this woman would have, that is if her tear ducts still worked.

Seeing a lone soldier standing by one of the barracks doorways, Henry slowed, walking casually up to the man. When he was closer, the soldier raised his rifle, but Henry smiled casually and waved slightly. Acting like he belonged, like it was perfectly natural to be strolling in the middle of the night, weighed down by weapons and ammo, Henry greeted the man. On his hip, the two-way was filled with screaming voices as soldiers tried to understand what was happening.

The soldier looked scared, real scared, and Henry could see he couldn't have been older than eighteen.

"Hey, there, pal, how's it going?" Henry asked idly, like he was a member of the man's unit.

"Do you know what's happening? I heard an explosion and then saw the fire. Rudy went to see what's happening, but he hasn't come back yet and no one will answer me on the radio."

Henry turned to see the orange glow where the jeeps were, two streets over. Smoke billowed into the night sky, casting dark clouds over the base.

Henry was able to get right up to the soldier and he playfully placed his hand on the young man's shoulder. "Let's see, number one, yes I do know what's going on, and two I think I'm the cause of most of it, and three, drop that rifle before you end up seeing God, son."

The soldier didn't understand at first, but then he turned his head slightly to see the hand Henry had placed on his shoulder actually held a handgun, aimed directly at his head. The Glock gleamed black and the oil from its last cleaning seeped into the man's nostrils.

Out of his element, the young man dropped his rifle.

"Good, that's real good. Listen to me very carefully, son. If you do what I say to the letter, I promise I won't hurt you. Now, look into my eyes and see if I'm telling you the truth."

The young soldier did and Henry stared back. The man saw no malice there, no evil. A hardness, yes, and something more, a silent grief that he kept inside. But yes, he did believe Henry. The soldier nodded that he understood and believed what Henry said.

"Good, then we need a jeep, and from there I'll tell you where to go, okay?"

The young soldier nodded.

"Good, now get on the ground face down for a second, just in case you're foolish enough to try anything." The soldier did as ordered and Henry placed his foot on the man's back, then unlocked and opened the barracks door. Inside, the lights were out and in the dim gloom he saw faces glaring back at him. Then one solidified from the shadows and Henry saw a man in his fifties with silver hair and wretched wrinkles on his face.

"Who the hell are you? Where's the guard? What's with the explosions?" The man rapid fired the questions, the others behind him nodding and asking their own at the same time.

"Who I am doesn't matter, but what does is things are happening tonight and you can stay here and hide or you can take back what was taken from you." He gestured to the fire light over the next building. "Over there is the armory. The soldiers there are a little occupied right now. Now's your chance if you want to take it."

The silver-haired man's eyes creased for a second as he sized Henry up.

"Why should we, scratch that, I, believe anything you say? How do we know this isn't one of Colonel Miller's sick games?"

"Hey, wait a sec, that's the guy who fought and beat Wagner and the giant stench in the ring yesterday," a voice sounded from behind the silver-haired man. "Yeah, it is; all right, man, you were great yesterday!" Another yelled.

"That was you? You're Henry Watson?" The silver-haired man asked with a look of surprise.

"Yeah, that's me, now I gotta go, do what you want after I'm gone. Oh, and watch it, the zombies have gotten inside the base, they're everywhere." Without waiting for a reply, Henry reached down and grabbed the scruff of the young soldier's collar, dragging him away from the barracks like he was a sack of laundry.

The silver haired man watched him go and then his jaw went taut.

"All right, men, this is it, it's time to take back what that bastard Miller and his goons took from us! For our families!" He yelled this with enthusiasm, pumping his fists in the air.

A roar of agreement sounded from behind him and men began racing out of the barracks, heading directly for the armory, some still in nothing but their underwear and socks. Others took a few seconds to get dressed, and then they too, ran for the armory.

Cheers and screams filled the night, and in minutes the sounds of gunfire filled the base, followed by explosions from multiple grenades.

The revolution had begun.

With the soldier driving the jeep, Henry sat next to him in the passenger seat, the Glock jammed into his side.

All around them the chaos was growing as more and more ghouls found their way into the base. The radio squawked non-stop and Henry heard a voice yell that someone had tried to run the main gate with an APC and it had been breached by the vehicle when it plowed into the gate. The order to fallback was given, and reports of hundreds of zombies pouring through the fractured perimeter filled the airwaves.

If things were getting bad, they were about to get a whole lot worse.

The revolution was spreading through the streets and more and more civilians were hearing the cry to arms as the soldiers guarding the barracks were pulled off to defend the beleaguered military base.

Driving through the running crowds, the young soldier glanced at Henry. "So, where are we going?"

"Major Maddox. Take me to Maddox. With luck he's still around where I can find him."

"He's probably at the main headquarters or at the repository. The commander likes to have meetings there."

"Then take me there, and step on it."

The young soldier did as he was told, flooring the gas pedal. He had to continually weave in and around shambling figures and fighting civilians and it was a harrowing ride. The soldiers left them alone, thinking they were on their side, but more than one bullet chopped the air by Henry's head, the now armed civilians thinking he was the enemy and wanting to take him out.

Ducking low to create a smaller target, Henry held on to the jeep as the young soldier turned a corner on two wheels and headed for the gold repository and Major Maddox.

* * *

Jimmy scratched his head and stopped at the corner of two buildings connected to one another by a small walkway over his head. While sucking in deep lungfuls of air, he began to catch his breath, his eyes taking in the unholy tableaux surrounding him. His heart was beating fast and a headache had crept up on him from out of nowhere, a result of the stress from everything he'd been going through today and probably for the past year. He felt a small sense of relief when the cramp he'd felt in his side began to go away.

What the hell had just happened? One second the base was quiet, with the exception of patrols and civilians going on late night errands, and the next second there were deaders everywhere, fiery explosions filling the night and now the civilians were shooting anything wearing a uniform, and guess what? Jimmy was wearing a uniform.

As if to illustrate his point, bullets ricocheted off the building he was leaning against less than a foot from the top of his head. Ducking instinctively, he slid behind a few decorative shrubs and small trees to weigh his options.

Though he hated to admit it, his search for Cindy was at an end. In the unbelievable madness the base had fallen into, there would be no way to find her, at least not in if he wanted to stay in one piece.

But there was still hope. It was very possible one of his companions had found her and they were even now waiting for him to return. Remembering Henry's words about a rendezvous near the helicopter hangar, he slipped out from behind the shrubs and turned to make his escape, hoping he could get around the corner before any more hicks tried to take him out.

He considered taking off his uniform, so he could blend in better with the civilians, but figured that was a no go, too. Then he'd only have the soldiers shooting at him. Either way, he was a target.

A jeep screamed around the corner, heading in the opposite direction and Jimmy stopped short when he thought he recognized the passenger.

"Henry? Holy shit, it is," he said to himself and ran out into the street after the receding jeep. "Henry, hey, Henry!" He called out, but there was no reaction from the older warrior. There was just too much noise for him to hear Jimmy's voice. The jeep hung a sharp left and headed away from him, but Jimmy wasn't about to let it end like that.

Ripping off his green shirt, in the hopes of a balance of blending in with both sides of the battle, he gave chase, trying to keep the small taillights in sight. He hoped he didn't look as much like a soldier with his dirty t-shirt on, and the green military-issued pants might still slow a soldier's trigger finger.

With arms pumping for all he was worth, he forced his legs to move faster, while the jeep slowly pulled away.

*　　*　　*

The gate for the perimeter fence for the gold repository was abandoned, the soldiers long gone. Bodies could be seen lying at odd angles, some wearing military uniforms, some obviously the destroyed walking dead.

"Where'd everyone go?" The young soldier asked.

Henry shrugged at the question, not answering. He'd put the Glock away, the young man was obeying him without qualms. Henry felt bad for the kid. He was so young and he now was thrust into this world of life and death at every tick of the clock. At least Henry had made it into his forties before the world had imploded. More than half of his life had been lived, and hopefully, he would still have another half left, but every day in the deadlands was a crapshoot and the dice were usually loaded in the Grim Reaper's favor.

The large front lawn was devoid of movement, the large spotlights illuminating the Kentucky bluegrass like it was on display. The lawnmower was sitting to the far side near a copse of saplings. This late in the night it was off and empty, though with the base in chaos, it was highly unlikely the machine would be used again.

"Over to the front exit, Eric, will you please?" Henry was now on a first name basis with the kid. Once Eric realized Henry truly didn't want to hurt him, the young soldier had relaxed.

"Sure, Henry, no problem," he said as he swung the jeep around a few bleeding corpses sprawled in the road. Henry gazed down onto the pavement as the jeep drove past the gate, the glazed and dead eyes of a young woman staring up into the night sky. The jeep rolled over her left arm and a soft crunch floated to his ears. Sheepishly, Eric mumbled an apology.

"Its okay, son, I don't think she minded," Henry said, trying to calm the man down. It was quieter near the gold repository, most of the fighting taking place near the barracks and armory. The staccato of rapid gunfire filled the air, sounding like firecrackers on the Fourth of July.

The second the jeep rolled up the long driveway, shapes began to seep out of the shadows. The entire base was slowly being saturated with the walking dead as more and more flowed through the breaches and gaps in the perimeter. The main gate was like an open wound, a choked throat straining to allow the rotting bodies to force their way in. It was possible some didn't know where they were going, but followed just the same. Most ghouls had a herd mentality, following the one in front of it. But some, called roamers, would break off from the packs in the search for food.

The jeep slowed to a stop at the top of the drive and Henry slid out, watching the wide open doors warily. Those doors should not be open, he thought, but once again it was probably due to soldiers abandoning their posts in need of self preservation. There were three other jeeps parked on the edges of the drive and Henry ran to the first, checking if there were keys in the ignition. As fate would have it, there were. Taking the keys and pocketing them for later, he went back to Eric. This was good, now he didn't have to send the kid away on foot.

"Okay, son, why don't you get out of here? If things don't go as planned, I don't want you getting blamed for bringing me here."

"But where should I go?"

Henry shrugged. "Don't know, don't care," he said bluntly, "but right now anywhere's got to be better than on this base."

Eric looked like a lost puppy, but he nodded curtly. "Good luck, Henry, I hope you find what you need in there," was all he said and drove off, swinging around the first pair of ghouls as he rolled back out of the repository gate and into the base, proper.

Henry watched him go, wondering if he'd made the right call sparing the kid's life. Yes, he knew he did. Sometimes, with all the cruelty and evil he was witness too on a daily basis, he forgot what it was like to show mercy. Eric wasn't a bad kid; he was only following the orders sent down from above. Henry sent the kid a silent good luck, and with one last look at the sprawling blue-green grass around him, stepped inside the repository.

He was going on a hunt, and when he finished, either he or his prey would be dead.

*   *   *

Jimmy slowed when he saw the main gate for the gold repository, breathing heavily from his dash to keep the jeep in sight. He watched from a distance as the jeep with Eric driving pulled around some shambling bodies and drove off into the night.

Looking up the hill, he saw the bright spotlights surrounding the large building and at the main doors he saw a lone figure looking back over the area.

The figure stopped and gazed around him, as if he was taking stock of his situation. Then the figure entered the repository and was gone.

Jimmy couldn't be absolutely sure, but that figure sure as hell looked like Henry.

Taking a risk that it was, he pumped his Remington and made sure the small strap holding his .38 Smith & Wesson was off, the .45 still behind his back.

With an intake of a heavy breath to psych himself up, he began running for the gate. There were more and more shambling corpses moving about, and when Jimmy began running towards them, they all turned like spectators at a parade and began lurching towards him.

Already dodging and weaving around the closest ones, he ran up the driveway towards the main doors of the repository. He didn't know what Henry was doing in there, but he knew, knowing Henry, he'd need his help eventually.

Off in a nearby tree, a cardinal chirped cheerfully, hopping along from branch to branch, ignorant of the actors playing on their world stage below, and the actors, too, ignorant that said stage even existed.

CHAPTER FORTY-EIGHT

UPON ENTERING THE hallway, Henry felt the cool air of the air-conditioning again and felt the sweat on his brow grow cold. With his AK-47 lowered, he painted the entire hallway with the muzzle, prepared to fire at the first sign of movement.

It was dead quiet.

The desk at the end of the hall was empty, the small lamp tipped onto its side and the phone off its hook. After waiting a heartbeat more, Henry decided it was as safe as it was going to get.

His boots made no sound on the red carpeting and he stayed to the right, trying to use the wall and planters for cover. From behind him, a soft moan drifted on the cool air and Henry spun to see two ghouls entering the doorway, one male and one female. He shot four times, twice for each attacker, striking the male ghoul in the neck. The bullet ripped through flesh and tendon and severed the spinal column from his head. The zombie flapped around like a disco dancer, then dropped to the rug. His mouth and eyes still flapped open and closed; the moan now a dry rasp. The female ghoul was ignorant of the fate of her brother's destruction and continued forward until the two bullets earmarked for her connected. Both rounds impacted on the top of her brow and her head blew apart like a melon dropped from the top of a gorge. Brain matter painted the lintel and sides of the doorframe and the body slumped to the ground like she was tired and wanted to rest for a while. The red carpeting absorbed the blood, almost a perfect match.

Distracted by the two ghouls, Henry was taken off guard when he spun around and the elevator doors were open.

Wearing a wide, sinister grin and holding an M-16, Maddox fired two shots directly at Henry's chest. Before the bullets found him, they went through a planter in front of Henry, the ceramic bowl shattering and falling to the carpet.

The double-impacts picked him up and tossed him back like a rag doll and his back slammed against the carpeted floor as hard as gravity would permit. The new AK-47 slung on his shoulder dug deep into his back, despite the vest.

His hands twitched, his M-16 falling from limp fingers as he stared up at the acoustic tiles on the ceiling. Laying there immobile, he sucked in a deep breath, let it out, then sucked in another until the pain in his chest subsided. With each breath inhaled, the pain was lessening and the blackness trying to descend over his vision lifted. A small thought went through his mind of what would have happened if one of the rounds that struck him had hit one of the grenades on his web belt instead.

The Kevlar vest had held, but only because the bullets fired from Maddox's rifle had gone through the planter first. That small amount of resistance was enough to blunt their kinetic energy and allow the Kevlar to absorb the double-impacts sufficiently enough to save Henry from a stopped heart.

Blinking the stars in his eyes, Henry realized he was still alive.

Instinct took over and he knew he needed to move fast, and for the life of him, he didn't understand why he was still allowed to move at all.

It was when a shadow hovered over him and he felt cold fingers bite into his throat that he knew he was far from out of danger. The fingers squeezed like steel traps and cut off his oxygen, the bushy eyebrows and dark eyes of Maddox filling his vision. Henry was lifted off his feet, his boots dangling in the air while Maddox squeezed the life from him. His vision began to go soft and blackness closed in again.

His hands were out to his sides, but he couldn't reach his panga hanging low on his hip. The same went for his Glock. His body was being held aloft by just Maddox's hands around his neck and Henry could swear his spine was being stretched an inch or more by the weight of his hanging body.

Maddox grinned widely, spittle accumulating in the corners of his mouth as he used all his strength and will to hold Henry aloft.

"I'm not as easy to kill as that dumb stench you fought in the ring, Watson, or that idiot Wagner," he snarled. "I don't know how in God's name you survived that chopper crash, but I tell you this, you shouldn't have come back. You should have gone the other way and kept on running."

A fog was overwhelming his consciousness and Henry knew he was about to pass out. His right hand flailed around and suddenly felt something, a handle.

Like a drowning man reaching out for a thrown rope, he wrapped his hand around the hilt of Maddox's Buckmaster knife. He was blacking out, his breathing a hoarse rasp in his throat, but he gritted his teeth and yanked the blade from its sheath on Maddox's upper hip. Barely knowing what he was doing, he raised his arm and slammed the seven and a half inch blade into Maddox's left side.

Immediately, the hands around his throat were gone and he dropped to the floor like a sack of flour. Coughing and gagging, he felt bile sliding from his mouth. His breathing sounded like a bad respirator and he continually had to force the air through his bruised trachea. Next to him on the floor, Maddox lay twisting; his left hand bent back, his palm wrapped around the knife hilt jammed into his side.

"You bastard, Watson. I should have killed you quick, instead of playing games with you." He ripped the blade from his side and stood up, his indomitable will carrying him forward.

Henry was on his knees and he nodded at Maddox's words.

"You're right," he rasped. "No more games." Henry reached down and wrapped his hand around the grip of his Glock.

The Glock barked three times, the first bullet striking the major's stomach, the next to the center of his chest, and finally one to his right eye.

The man stopped moving forward and he wavered like a drunkard after last call. Henry stared at him, the Glock held at arms length in case it was necessary to fire again.

He could see the major's iris dilate in fear in his remaining eye as he realized he was an angel's second away from death. He toppled over onto his left side, the Buckmaster slipping from limp fingers, and his left eye closed for the last time, while oculus fluid and blood seeped from the destroyed right.

Henry didn't move, his body trying to recover from the beating he'd just received and the Glock dropped to the carpeted floor.

Another moan from behind caused him to try and turn around, but he was exhausted. Looking over his shoulder, he saw a fat blob of a ghoul stumble inside the hallway. He was so big the dead man's hips brushed the sides of the doorframe.

Henry could only look up at the behemoth as it waddled toward him.

He reached for the Glock, but his hands were like strings of spaghetti. He chuckled slightly. After everything that he'd gone through, everything he'd suffered, he was about to get eaten by the Blob from the X-men.

When the blubber challenged corpse was almost on top of him, the roar of gunfire filled the hallway, only the carpeting and paintings helping to absorb the noise.

The left side of the Blob's neck disappeared in a red and black spray and Henry had to turn away while liquid flesh rained down on him.

Another shot roared and the other side of the Blob's neck disintegrated, and it was now only its spinal cord holding the head upright. The entire wall of blubber swayed over Henry, and he knew if that pile of rotting flab fell on him, he would probably be killed. A shotgun butt appeared from behind the Blob and whacked the side of the head. The spinal cord snapped and the Blob tilted to the right just enough to miss Henry when the body fell. It seemed the entire complex bounced from the landing, but it was all just imagination.

Henry blinked up at his savior and a wide grin creased his face when he saw who it was. "Well, I'll be, its good to see you, pal."

Jimmy stood there, bloody t-shirt and green army pants, shaking his head while cracking one of his patented shit-eating grins.

"I leave you alone for five minutes and you start World War 3. Just what am I supposed to do with you, old man?"

"You can help me up, that's what, and close that door before more deaders get in."

Jimmy helped Henry to his feet and waited a heartbeat while Henry swayed like he was sea sick and when Henry recovered he let him go.

Henry picked up his Glock and searched for his rifle.

He found it a second later, but it was unreachable. When the fat blob-ghoul had fallen over, he'd landed on the rifle. The M-16 was out of reach for now, unless Henry had a spare crane lying around. Shifting the AK-47 from off his shoulder, he began taking loose rounds from his pockets and loading them into an empty clip. A wave of dizziness overcame him and he had to pause for a second. Jimmy gave him a concerned look, but Henry waved it off telling him he was fine.

Jimmy left him to go close the main door. He returned an instant later with bad news.

"It's stuck in the open position; some kind of magnetic lock or something."

More moans could be heard and the shapes of bodies could be seen outside the doorway, as more and more ghouls wandered into the building in search of prey.

"Forget it. Let's get downstairs. Once we're gone they won't be able to follow us," Henry said, finishing the load on the clip. After slapping it into the weapon, he began filling a backup.

Jimmy nodded and the two men moved to the elevator.

Stepping over Maddox, Jimmy bent over and retried the Buckmaster knife. "Oh, that's sweet," he whispered.

Wiping the blade clean on Maddox's shirt, he slid it through his belt and headed for the elevator.

Jimmy looked for a button to call the elevator, but there wasn't one.

"Over there, on the desk, press the button," Henry said softly, still wasted from his fight with Maddox. Jimmy studied the desk and found the call button, then pressed it. The elevator doors parted and the two men stepped inside, just as more than a dozen ghouls fought their way around the corner of the hallway and charged into the foyer. The elevator doors hissed closed and the car began going down. From above came the distinct sounds of bare fists on metal as the ghouls banged on the elevator doors.

"So why are we here, Henry? What aren't we just grabbing the girls and getting the hell out of Dodge?"

Leaning his head against the smooth, cool wall, with the sound of Muzak playing softly through the hidden speakers, Henry closed his eyes and tightened his jaw.

"We're here for justice, Jimmy. Raw, pure, and no bullshit, justice."

Not understanding what Henry meant, he shook his head and listened to the Muzak, the car dropping deep into the earth.

The elevator doors hissed open and a cacophony of angry bullets entered the car, causing the two warriors to duck down and dive for cover. One ricochet scraped against Henry's calf and he yelped in pain as he rolled out of the elevator car and into the massive gold vault, his back coming up against a crate of 14K gold. Next to him, Jimmy walked like an animal on all fours, and managed to scramble to the side wall and take cover behind a stacked pile of gold bars. Above their heads, bullets flew by, sounding like a hive of angry hornets.

They had walked into a trap.

After the worst of the onslaught subsided, Henry managed to sneak a peek around the sides of the crate. What he saw did not make him very happy.

More than a dozen soldiers were spread out across the repository, hiding behind gold bricks and behind steel stanchions supporting the massive stone ceiling.

"Looks like they were expecting visitors," Jimmy quipped as he, too, snuck a peek. A bullet whined near his head and he squeaked like a girl, pulling his head back. Henry heard his outburst and frowned at his friend.

"What? I was surprised?"

Henry's countenance never broke.

"Oh, come on, you never got caught off guard?"

"Only around you, Jimmy, only around you," he said with a slight shake to his head."

Henry turned back to the problem at hand, namely the soldiers. It was while he was surveying the situation that he saw his real target moving in and around the soldiers, giving orders and ranting like a mad man.

Colonel George T. Miller was doing what he did best; taking charge. He was repositioning his men for maximum vantage points and Henry knew he and Jimmy were in very big trouble. Deciding to stir things up, Henry swung around the side of the crate and rolled to a nearby stack of bars, each stamped with the county's seal. He sprayed the area near Miller with a sweeping fire of steel-jacketed death.

He saw Miller literally jump off his feet and hit the floor, then Henry lost sight of him, the man crawling for cover. Henry, too, had to seek cover as the incoming fusillade peppered the gold bars protecting him, the soft metal becoming dented and marred by the hundreds of rounds striking them.

Jimmy picked up a gold bar that had dislodged from above his head and weighed it in his hand.

"To think this was worth something only a year ago. All it is now is a piece of metal. You can't eat it, drink it, or shoot with it. Nowadays it's worthless."

"Focus, Jimmy, we've got a little more to worry about right now than the nation's economy."

To illustrate his point, he swung around the opposite side of the gold bars he was hiding behind and sprayed the room with hot lead. Soldiers ducked to avoid getting shot and Henry saw one man hit in the chest. The impact punched him backward, a fist size hole appearing on his back and he dropped to the polished floor, his pants discoloring when his bowels released. The man's pain-contorted face was horizontal; his left cheek pushed hard against the floor, the eyes open and staring at nothing.

It was a gruesome scene to witness and any military general or politician who has ever said there is honor in a warrior's death has never been in real combat.

Death was death and how you got to that point in time was irrelevant. Whether you slipped in the bathtub or were shot by an enemy insurgent, at the end of the day you're dead and there's nothing honorable about it.

More bullets rang out and Henry jumped back when the weapon in his hands stopped cycling from a misfire in the ejector port. With his back against the bars of gold, he worked the bolt on the AK-47 to clear the jammed round. It popped free of the ejector port and he reloaded with a new magazine from one of his pockets. Next to him, Jimmy fired a few rounds with the Remington, the room cleaner working quite well in the confines of the crates of gold. The pellets bounced off the gold and ricocheted around, slicing into soldiers left and right.

But when concentrated fire caused him to duck back, he did so reluctantly. Turning to Henry, he frowned.

"We can't win this Henry, there's too many of them."

Henry bit his lower lip while considering his friends words and then nodded curtly, as if he had made up his mind about something. He looked back to Jimmy and his face was grim.

"Well then, I guess we need to up the ante a little more."

"What do you mean?"

Pulling two grenades from his web belt, Henry pulled the pins.

"I mean it's time for more drastic measures, hit the deck, Jimmy!"

Spinning, Henry tossed the grenades out into the open area separating him from the soldiers spread out across the massive room. Three soldiers had been about to try a flanking maneuver to surround the companions when the two grenades landed near them and rolled to a stop at their feet. The first soldier looked down, as if he'd seen something rather interesting. Then his face changed to complete terror and shock and he screamed at the top of his lungs. "Grenade!"

Every soldier caught trying to flank the companions was caught in the initial blast, their bodies sliced into ribbons as the shrapnel cut through them like a blowtorch through ice.

The smell of burnt meat and offal added to the gun smoke already in the air and Henry looked into the blast zone to inspect his handiwork. Nothing but body parts littered the once polished floor near the far wall and Henry ducked back when more than a hundred rounds struck his gold shield. The cascade continued for more than three minutes, the acoustics in the room echoing the gunfire into a crescendo of epic proportions. All Henry and Jimmy could do was tuck in tight and stay under cover as round after round ricocheted around them.

But even with revenge in their hearts for their fallen comrades, sooner or later the men had to reload.

Slowly, the withering gunfire slowed and only a few shots rang out here and there. Henry took a chance, and with his face against the floor, he peeked around the gold.

He was just in time to see Miller slipping out the rear, heading toward the gymnasium-sized room that held the paintings and security monitors.

"Jimmy, Miller's getting away, I need you to distract the soldiers so I can go after him."

"What? Are you crazy? It's a blender out there. No way, man, let the fucker go. There's always another time."

Henry shook his head no. "Not this time, Jimmy. Either he dies or I do. I owe that bastard."

Jimmy stared at his friend, at his piercing eyes, and saw the resolve hidden within. He knew there would be no talking him out of it. Henry and Jimmy had traveled together for more than year. They had become true brothers from the experiences they'd endured together and both men knew the other would give his life to save the other if it came down to the line.

"I think you're crazy for doing this, but all right."

Jimmy ran for the crate of gold and so did Henry, the two meeting at the same time. Bullets ricocheted off the crate, the soldiers keeping the two men pinned down.

"Damn that was close, Henry said, sucking in a breath. "Here, take these." He handed Jimmy three grenades. "I need to travel light anyway. When I tell you, throw two of them to the right and I'll take the left, okay?"

Jimmy lowered his head in a tight nod, signifying he did.

"Good, here take this, too. I need my hands free. My Glock will have to do for now on." Henry handed Jimmy his AK-47. Jimmy would need it to fend of the soldiers that were spared the blast from the grenades.

"Okay, let's do this. One…two," Henry pulled the pins on his two grenades while Jimmy did the same for one of his three. The other two grenades were lying on the floor at Jimmy's feet and one more would be tossed consecutively after the first; he'd be saving the third for later.

"Three!" Henry yelled and threw his grenades overhand, keeping hidden behind the crate. The grenades arced into the air and the screams and yells of the soldiers filled the repository. Then there was a sickening crunch and Henry's ears popped as the multiple explosions ripped through the room. Gold bars were toppled, more than a few crushing soldiers unlucky enough to be standing under them, and others were simply blown into a hundred bloody pieces of red and gory meat chunks.

Henry didn't see any of this, his eyes only for the small hallway that led to the gymnasium. After the initial blast rocked the large room, he jumped to his feet, creasing his eyes to see through the smoke, and charged towards the small hallway at the far end. A few shots rang out from soldiers spared the main brunt of the blast, but it was sporadic and sloppily aimed. He managed to reach the hallway just as a few of the remaining soldiers were able to regroup, and as more bullets rang out near him, he climbed over the wreckage partially blocking the entrance to the hallway and ducked down the side corridor, leaving the massive vault, and Jimmy, behind. As he ran, he heard the sickening thump of another grenade. Jimmy was keeping the soldiers busy.

Jimmy heard a small ding amidst the chaos and noise surrounding him. He turned to see it was the warning for the elevator, signifying the car had returned to the ground floor. The doors hissed opened and he expected to see reinforcements, looking for more soldiers coming to Miller's aid, so his jaw dropped open when the elevator doors spread wide and disgorged a packed car full of zombies.

"Oh, you have got to be kidding me," Jimmy whispered as he began firing at the first bodies in line.

Unknown to Jimmy, when he and Henry had descended into the vault, one of the ghouls had placed his hand on the call button on the desk as it stumbled about the foyer. When the elevator doors opened, the packed hallway forced the ones closest to the opening inside the car. The elevator shot down and once the ghouls had disembarked, the elevator doors slid closed, the car rising back to the upper floor once more to start the process again.

The desk button was the perfect height, and a hand or limb pressed it continually as the packed bodies bounced off the walls and knocked the paintings and planters to the carpeted floor inside the hallway and foyer. Maddox's corpse was nothing but hunks of meat, the ghouls tearing him a part and feeding on his fresh corpse. There would be nothing to revive; the ghouls were starving. Wandering around the countryside searching in vain for food, the pickings had been slim.

Jimmy kept firing, trying to keep the ghouls at bay. When the elevator doors opened yet again and more ghouls piled out, he knew things were really getting bad.

When his Remington clicked on an empty chamber, he dropped it to the floor and pulled the pin on his last grenade, his hand already dropping to the AK-47 Henry had left behind for him.

With the soldiers trying to take his head off and the zombies wanting to eat it, Jimmy hunkered down for the siege, hoping Henry wouldn't take too long, because they were both running out of time.

*   *   *

Henry dashed down the hallway, expecting to see Colonel Miller at any second with a gun in his hand, but the man was nowhere to be seen. Reaching the end of the hall, he entered the gymnasium-sized room, the door yawning wide.

He stopped at the doorway, his eyes scanning the room once again, remembering the last time he'd been there.

Miller was across the room, watching the monitors. On the security screens, the military base was in ruins. Soldiers ran around like green gerbils in a maze and zombies and civilians were mixed together; attacking each other and then separating. More than a dozen buildings were on fire with more blazes sprouting up with each passing minute. An explosion filled one of the screens, silent with no sound from the monitors, and Henry thought it was the armory. Miller stared at the screens like a despotic ruler who realized his people had overthrown him and at any moment would be knocking down the ornate doors to storm the castle and kill him.

As if he sensed there was someone behind him, he spun around quickly, his eyes wide with anger and frustration. He didn't seem to even care why Henry was standing in the room with him when he should have been dead, as was reported by Maddox.

Miller's right arm shot out accusingly to Henry. His face was manic, spittle frying from his lips to land on his once crisp uniform.

"You! You did this to me! You took my dream from me!" His frantic voice echoed off the walls, bouncing around again and again.

With his Glock in his hand, Henry crossed the distance until he was halfway into the room, his eyes scanning the corners for enemies. Henry spotted a soldier rounding the corner from the hallway, and before the soldier could step three feet into the room, Henry shot him twice, the rounds decimating his heart and throwing him back to the wall. He slid to the floor, dead, leaving a crimson stain on the wall behind his slumped form.

"You did this to yourself! You were the one that tried to take back this nation with the barrel of a gun instead of trying to work with the people who live in it! What the hell did you expect? Sooner or later this was gonna happen. It always does with assholes like you. If not now, then a year from now. And if it hadn't been me, than someone else would have done it."

"Perhaps, but either way, you won't be around to enjoy your victory," Miller said in a cold voice. At first Henry didn't understand what the man was talking about, but the change in Miller's demeanor gave Henry the heads up he needed to avoid death.

From behind him, two soldiers stepped out from behind a small alcove near the door. Henry had been at the wrong angle upon entering the room and had missed the hidden cubby entirely. Both soldiers had AK-47's aimed at his chest and Henry rolled to his right, just as the first shots rang out.

"Kill, him, men, kill that bastard!" Miller screamed, raising his hands in the air like a spectator at a hockey game.

Henry rolled to his right and came up shooting.

With bullets stalking him across the floor, he fired four rounds, double-tapping twice for each soldier.

The first soldier went down with two shots to his sternum, his finger spasming on his rifle's trigger; he sprayed bullets wildly into the air. Million dollar paintings were chewed to confetti, the rounds peppering them with metal multiple times. In the middle of the room, Miller screamed with loss.

The second two rounds Henry fired went wide, missing the second soldier completely and the soldier fired directly at him, only his Kevlar vest saving him from death yet again. Just as the bullets struck his chest, Henry was firing again, sending one last 9mm round in the soldier's direction. A black flower blossomed on the man's forehead and he slumped to the floor, his rifle clattering away.

Henry went flying across the room, his Glock falling away to bounce twice and stop at Miller's feet. Miller ignored it and crossed the distance spanning him from Henry's supine body. Miller's eyes were filled with hate and the tightrope of insanity he'd been walking for more than a year finally snapped.

Henry was barely conscious; his chest feeling like a lead weight was sitting on it. After the blows and beating received from Maddox, his ribs had finally succumbed to the abuse heaped upon them. Searing pain filled his chest each time he breathed and in a fog of half-consciousness surrounding him, he knew at least a few of his ribs were cracked.

He rolled over, trying to get up, when he felt cold fingers on his neck and Miller's legs straddling him. With an animal grunt, Miller began to squeeze.

"Not again," Henry croaked while Miller's fingers contracted, cutting off his air supply.

Henry's face began to turn blue and white spots danced in front of his eyes, like small supernovas dancing back and forth in a galaxy of agony.

He was dying.

The light cleared after a few heartbeats and he was stunned to see his wife, Emily, standing before him, her white nightgown seeming to billow around her like it was a living being.

Her face was perfect, her hair shining in the light and her eyes were glowing with happiness.

"Emily," he croaked, actually reaching out to the ephemeral form while Miller squeezed harder.

"Emily?" Miller said. "Who the hell are you talking to, Watson?"

But Henry didn't hear the colonel and he strived to reach his late wife.

"Emily, is it really you?"

She smiled, her perfect teeth reflecting the golden glow surrounding her.

"Yes, my love, it is. I miss you so much."

"Emily, I'm so sorry for what I did to you. I'm so goddamn sorry. I miss you so much I can't stand it sometimes." Tears formed in his eyes as he reached for her with outstretched arms, but she continually stayed out of reach, frustratingly so.

"I know, dear heart, I know and it's all right. When you killed me that wasn't me. I was already gone."

"But where are you? Are you in...?" He hesitated to actually say it.

"Yes, my love, I am, and you will be, too. One day."

At that moment in time, with his body suffocating under Miller's ministrations, he didn't want to wait for one day.

"I want to be with you now. I can. It would be so easy to just let go. We could be together...forever."

She smiled again, her lips curving up sweetly. He longed to kiss those lips again. Just one more time.

"And we will, my love, but Henry, now is not your time. There are people counting on you. People who need you. You have to stay...for them."

Emily began moving away from him, the white void she was in receding, pulling her back like a retracting wire.

"No! Emily, don't leave me, I want to come with you!"

"Remember me, my love, and be happy," Emily said and then, like a light switch was flicked off, she was gone, leaving Henry staring blankly. He blinked twice and Miller's face came into view, his snarling, psychotic face glaring down on him.

"Die, you bastard, die! I want to watch the light go out of those damn eyes of yours!" His arms were taut, his fingers white as they circled Henry's throat.

Henry gazed up at Miller's face and his own jaw went tight and he felt a surge of adrenalin flood through him, pushing the pain in his chest down and overriding his need for oxygen.

Colonel Miller, staring down into Henry's eyes, saw something change in there, saw a fire, a spark appear that wasn't there an instant ago.

And it chilled him to the bone.

Bucking his hips, Henry tossed Miller off him, the colonel rolled onto his side hard, letting out a snarl of anger. Henry came to his feet like a man possessed, almost jumping straight up from his prone position. His limbs were on fire, and he felt like he was immortal. Miller was just coming to a sitting position on the floor and Henry ran at him, his right boot coming up and kicking Miller under the chin. The crack of bone filled the room and Miller was slammed back to the floor.

High on insanity, Miller rolled to his side and then rose to his knees. Wiping blood from his chin, and spiting out teeth, he glared at Watson. Henry looked down on the colonel, his eyes gleaming with anger.

Miller smiled up at him, two of his front teeth missing, and faster than Henry would have expected, Miller drew his Colt Magnums, firing from the hip.

Seeing the large hand cannons rising at him, Henry jumped away, rolled across the floor, and scooped up his Glock at the same time. The boom of the Colt Magnums filled the room, echoing off the stone walls. Three security monitors exploded in a shower of sparks as the rounds missed Henry. Just before one of the monitors was destroyed, however, Henry caught a glimpse of the aircraft hangar and the distinct figures of Mary and the rest of the companions. They were hiding behind a stack of crates and firing at soldiers and ghouls. The camera angle was from behind them and even in the black and white monitor; he recognized Cindy's blonde hair and Mary's long brown tresses. Sue and Raven were there also, shooting rifles by the look of it.

Miller continued firing his guns, laughing like a kid at a carnival. Henry ran around the room, ducking and weaving while all around him bullets ricocheted. One bullet singed his ankle and he felt a small burning sensation. Only a flesh wound, the bullet had missed his Achilles heel by less than an inch, which would have hobbled Henry for life.

Running and weaving back and forth, at first Henry didn't realize the shooting had stopped. Smoke filled the room, a low haze resembling Los Angeles. during a smog alert.

Slowing his running and hiding, he saw Miller trying to reload his Colt Magnums, but Henry charged the man, kicking both weapons from Miller's hands. Loose bullets tinkled like spare change across the floor and the large weapons slid to the opposite end of the room. Miller let out a yell and was about to charge Henry, when he realized the barrel of Henry's Glock was aimed directly at his forehead.

"Go ahead and do it, kill me. It doesn't matter in the end. You'll never escape this base, Watson, and even if you do, my men will hunt you and your friends down and kill you all like dogs!"

The colonel spit at him, the dark red saliva leaving a large glob in the middle of Henry's chest. Henry ignored it, the Glock never wavering.

"No, Colonel, they're all dead or have deserted you, in case you haven't been outside in the past hour or so. The people you enslaved have taken back their freedom. It's over and so are you," he said quietly. His finger tensed on the trigger of the Glock when the sound of footsteps and voices could be heard coming from down the hallway leading from the main repository.

"Ha, that's my men coming to save me. Shoot me now and they'll be on you before you take two steps out of this building. Spare me and I give you my word you and your friends can leave unharmed."

Henry gave Miller's proposal careful consideration, weighing his options, and then with a shake of his head, he calmly looked Miller straight in the eyes.

"Pass," he said coldly and squeezed the trigger of the Glock.

But instead of watching Miller's head snap back from the impact of the 9mm round, the gun clicked on a dry chamber. The gun was empty!

"Ha, you're out of ammo, you fool. You should have kept better track!" He screamed triumphantly, the fear he felt fading away.

The footsteps were getting closer and Henry knew he had seconds before he was overwhelmed by soldiers. He sent a silent prayer to Jimmy. If the soldiers had managed to turn the tide and come to

Miller's rescue, that could only mean one thing. Jimmy hadn't made it.

Henry's mind raced with his options, but none of them ended in Miller's death, unless he wanted to sacrifice his own life in the process. The dead soldier's rifles were scattered across the room, but they were out of reach and the time it would take to try and reload the Glock wasn't there. All Henry had was loose rounds in his pant's pockets, and there was no time to pop the spent clip and feed even one round into it and slap it home again. If he went for his panga, Miller would react and try to run away, and Henry would never be able to kill the man in time before his men arrived.

All this went through Henry's mind in a microsecond and the grim warrior decided survival was better.

Even if he didn't want to live, he would do it for Emily.

Raising the Glock in the air, Henry brought it down hard on the top of Miller's forehead. Miller's eyes rolled up in his head and he slumped to the floor, unconscious. Turning, Henry dashed to the rear of the room where he'd seen that first soldier appear. There was another passageway, hidden from casual view, and he took it, leaving the room with its Van Gogh's and security monitors behind. He sent a silent wish to the void that answered wishes that perhaps the blow Miller had sustained might have killed him. It was possible.

Dashing down the hallway, Henry pulled the spent clip out of his Glock and quickly fed in as many rounds as he could in the time it took to reach the far end of the hallway. Counting eight rounds total, he slapped the clip home and charged the chamber.

Upon reaching a fire door, he pushed it open, the stench of death and explosives assaulting him hard.

He was back in the repository and it was full of the walking dead. Everywhere he looked, zombies were feeding on the dead soldiers, some tearing into body cavities to reach in for the good stuff. Livers, spleens and hearts were sucked, chewed and devoured as the menagerie of undead humanity fed till their unbeating heart's desire. Arms were ripped from torsos, the undead gnawing on them like large turkey legs. Intestines were everywhere, some wrapped around feet and legs as the ghouls stumbled around, dragging the hundreds of coils along behind them. Blood was everywhere, covering the gold bars and blunting their once golden brilliance. It was a charnel house of horrors and Henry was trapped in the middle of it. A ghoul noticed him and he shot it in the head, the body slumping to the floor silently.

Looking for a way out, Henry saw the elevator was packed with bodies. There would be no escaping that way. Then a familiar voice sounded over the moans and wails of the dead.

"Henry, over here! Hey, Henry!" Jimmy called out and waved to get his attention. He was holding open a fire door, and whenever a ghoul came close to him, he sprayed it with the AK-47 in his hands. His Remington hung on his back, empty and useless for the time being.

Henry ran for the door, dodging ghouls and punching, kicking and shooting any who blocked his path. His only saving grace was that almost every ghoul was already occupied, feeding on the massacred soldiers.

Upon reaching Jimmy, Henry slapped him on the back, and both men entered the stairway, Jimmy slamming the door behind them. Ripping his shirt, he wrapped the cloth around the horizontal metal bar along the middle of the door, preventing it from being opened from the opposite side.

"That should hold for the time being, come on, I already checked. It looks like these stairs go all the way to the top. Must be here for emergencies, you know, like if the power goes out or something."

"Good, let's get moving. I saw the girls on one of the security monitors, they're at the rendezvous. Looked like they were holding their own, but anything can happen from now to when we get there." Jimmy's eyes lit up at that. "Was Cindy with them?" He asked hopefully, his heart beating fast.

He nodded. "Yeah, she was; looks like she's okay."

"Okay then, what are we waiting for?" Jimmy said this with excitement and began charging up the stairs, taking them two at a time. Henry watched him go, shaking his head at the man's resilience. Henry would not be going that fast. His ribs were killing him and his sock was wet with blood from the graze on his heel.

Taking one step at a time, he began the long trudge up the concrete stairs to the ground floor high above.

The road back to the aircraft hangar was difficult, but far from impossible. After clearing the repository's main gate, it had been easy for Henry and Jimmy to acquire a jeep and drive back to the hangar. The roads were mostly clear of soldiers and civilians, but the undead were everywhere. Abandoned weapons lay in the jeep, the owners probably long dead and while Jimmy drove, Henry sprayed the walking dead from side to side, making them dance the jig. The jeep shot past them and continued onward. Destroying ghouls wasn't a priority; their goal was to get back to Mary and the others. Twenty minutes later, the jeep pulled up near the hangar, the motor pool just beyond.

The area around the hangar was a mess of dead bodies and scattered fires. Multiple corpses were spread over the pavement, more than half wearing the uniform of soldiers.

The women were nowhere to be seen and at first both men began to panic.

"Where'd they go?" Jimmy asked nervously. "You said they were here."

Shaking his head, Henry studied the area. Turning around. He saw the security camera mounted on a high pole, and then followed the line of sight to the crates he'd seen the women behind. Spent shell casings littered the ground, testifying that some group of individuals had made a stand here. Picking up one of the spent brass, he rolled it between his fingers, feeling any residual warmth.

"Slightly warm; they were here recently."

Suddenly, from out of the shadows, the roar of an engine sounded from their right and both men turned to see an APC rolling out of the hangar. Its twin mounted machine guns swiveled in their general direction and both men stood stock still. Whoever was in that vehicle could cut them down with the slightest pressure on the firing button.

The APC rolled to a stop six feet in front of them. Both Henry and Jimmy held their weapons to the side, careful not to so much as twitch a finger.

"Okay, guys, we surrender," Henry said to the blank faced grille of the APC. "It's over; you got us fair and square."

At first the vehicle was immobile, only the diesel engine rumbling softly, the vibration felt through Henry's boots, but then the machine guns swiveled up and both Henry and Jimmy realized they were about to die.

Without realizing it, Henry closed his eyes, thinking of Emily one last time when the machine guns began spitting fire, 600 rounds a second pounding the pavement. The guns roared for three seconds, all three of those seconds feeling like hours, and when the guns went silent, Henry opened his left eyelid, and upon seeing he was still in one piece, opened his other one.

Jimmy was standing next to him, eyes squeezed tight, mumbling prayers to every deity he could think of. Henry punched him in the arm.

"Hey, stupid, we're still alive."

Jimmy opened his eyes and his mouth fell open. "No shit?" He felt his body, relieved to see he was still whole. "Hey, I'm not complaining, but how come?"

Looking behind him, Henry saw ten ghouls no more than twenty feet away who had been coming for Jimmy and Henry out of the shadows. The bodies were now chopped into mincemeat, the mighty guns chewing the bodies into bits and pieces that still glistened in the night air. Whoever was in that war machine had just saved their lives.

The sound of sliding bolts could be heard, and the top hatch of the APC opened, the hatch slamming down hard on the roof. Henry and Jimmy tensed, wondering if the soldiers inside the APC had saved them only to serve them up to Miller once order had been restored to the base. But then the tense moment passed and a familiar face popped out of the hatch.

Mary was smiling from ear to ear as she waved down at the two warriors.

"Hey, guys, need a lift?"

Henry felt his heart begin to beat again and he let out the lungful of air he'd been holding.

"What the? Mary? Oh my God, what are you? I mean, how did you?" Henry stammered each question, relief filling him up to the top of his head.

"Forget about all that now, Henry, let's get out of here. The deaders are everywhere and the soldiers stationed here are either dead or running for it. The people Miller enslaved have taken back their freedom and most have already evacuated in other vehicles." She smiled proudly. "But we managed to keep this one for ourselves."

More moaning sounded from the shadows nearby and Henry and Jimmy decided they could talk inside the APC.

"Is Cindy in there? Is she okay?" Jimmy asked as he climbed up the front of the APC.

Mary nodded. "Yes, Jimmy, she's fine. She's been busy, though, wait to you hear what happened to her. Raven and Sue are in here, too."

"Oh, man that's great," he said and Mary moved out of the way so Jimmy could climb down inside.

Just before his head disappeared, Jimmy stopped. Henry wasn't moving; he was just staring into the aircraft hangar.

"Hey, Henry, what's up? It's time to go."

"Yeah, in a minute, Henry said. Tell whoever's driving to back up to the hangar door, there's something I need to do before we head out." He walked away then, picking up his pace as he moved towards the aircraft hangar. He paused as he passed a prone body of a solider and Jimmy saw him grab a couple of small objects from the dead soldier's web belt, then he continued onward.

The APC bucked and began rolling backward, stopping just shy of the hangar doors. A few bodies were crushed by the large wheels, the torsos popping like balloons full of meat. The doors to the hangar were wide open, but the inside was dark, nothing but shadows to fill the voids where the helicopters sat, still waiting for their pilots. But in all the chaos, no pilots had made it to the choppers and taken to the air.

Suddenly, an explosion rocked the night, a bright light filling the hangar. One of the empty Apaches inside the hangar were on fire, the cockpit a raging inferno of yellow and orange flames. No sooner was the first blast seen and felt, then two more rocked the hangar, smoke and fumes bellowing out of the open doors as the other Apache and the Chinook were blown into scrap metal.

Mary was in the hatch again, Jimmy now inside with the others. He was hugging and kissing Cindy, relieved to be with her once again after fearing the worst. Mary watched the inside of the hangar and began to become worried. Where was Henry? He should be in there somewhere. It must have been him who blew up the helicopters.

She watched carefully, the fumes of the burning aircraft stinging her eyes, and then, out of the smoke, a shadow slowly began to solidify. Out walked Henry Watson, his gait slow and steady. Behind him one of the Apache tanks blew, sending shrapnel in all directions. Mary ducked low in the hatch, not wanting to be hit by flying debris, but Henry never flinched, never quickened his pace. He was like a demon walking out of the flames of Hell, defiant to stay in the nether realm. A shambling form crept up behind him, and before Mary could shout a warning, Henry spun, fired his Glock and put the ghoul down with a shot between the eyes. The entire time he never slowed his pace.

Walking up to the APC, he reached for the handholds and climbed up until he was looking down on Mary.

"Now we can go," he said calmly.

She moved to the side with a slight smile, not fully understanding what just happened, and he climbed down into the APC.

The hatch slammed shut and the motor revved. Swinging around to the main road that would lead out of Fort Knox, the APC began rolling, leaving the burning wreckage of the helicopters behind.

EPILOGUE

COLONEL GEORGE T. Miller pulled himself from the brink of unconsciousness only seconds after Henry disappeared down the rear hallway.

The footsteps from the front hallway leading to the repository were growing louder and Miller pulled himself to a sitting position, holding his aching, throbbing skull in his hands.

"Hurry up, you idiots, I need help in here!" Miller yelled to his men who were taking their goddamn time getting to him. He could feel blood dripping down the side of his head and he gingerly touched the gash on the top of his skull. That bastard Watson had conked him on the head like a steer ready for the slaughter, but he had failed to kill him and that would be a mistake he would pay for dearly.

With a mighty groan, he pushed himself up, standing on wobbly legs.

His vision swam in front of his eyes, but after a few quick breaths he felt slightly better. Christ, he needed an aspirin.

He looked up just as the first soldier entered the room. It took Miller a second to realize the man wasn't right. Half his neck was gone and his stomach was a gaping wound, his intestines swinging back and forth like a pendulum with each step the man took forward; splattering the floor with blood and excrement. Behind him, other men, and then some women, which was odd as there were almost no women in his army. Didn't like them, women were good for one thing, and that thing only required them to lie on their backs and be quiet.

He blinked twice, only his rattled brain the reason he didn't understand what was happening.

Then focus clicked and his jaw dropped open and his heart began to beat fast, his breathing quickening as his body prepared for the fight or flight response to the stimulus before it.

Miller chose to fight as he had never run away from anything in his life.

There was an AK-47 lying on the floor about three feet from him and he ran for it, scooping it up, racking the bolt and firing the weapon on full-auto

He sprayed the first dozen ghouls that entered the room, yelling in pleasure as their bodies danced and twitched. But he was unused to battling the undead himself and not one round found a head. Instead, torsos were shot up, shredded to the consistency of Sloppy Joe, but still the ghouls continued towards him undaunted. Miller began backing up, firing the rapid-fire until the clip was spent.

"Shit!" He screamed loudly while dropping the weapon and moving away as the first bloody hand reached out for him. Pulling his SOG Desert dagger, he swiped at the first ghoul to come for him. The knife sliced through the dead man's jugular and blood seeped out of the wound, but the man kept coming. Miller continued backing up, his back stopping when he was against the wall displaying his paintings. Portraits of Van Gogh and Picasso, among others, gazed down on his misfortune; all ignorant and uncaring of his plight.

Another ghoul, an old woman, came at him and she bit into his arm, tearing a chunk of flesh from him as he screamed and pushed her away. Another, a revived soldier, came at his left and he stabbed the dead soldier with his dagger. The blade caught on bone and he couldn't retrieve it, so he kicked the man away.

There were more coming, dozens and dozens who had found there way to the elevator and had been transported down into the nation's largest gold repository.

All wanted him, his warm flesh to stuff into their waiting maws. Miller fought bravely, never giving in, even when a hundred teeth and nails sunk into his skin and began ripping and tearing. One zombie came at him, and sank its teeth into Miller's nose, tearing off the cartilage and swallowing it in one gulp.

Miller screamed to the Heaven's, his throat filing with blood as he watched himself literally be ripped to pieces.

The zombie who had taken off his nose went in for more and Miller stared at the bright red hair and freckles on the dead, pale face. Terrance Jorgenson, or Rusty to his friends, had wanted to reach

Miller alive, but that wasn't to be. But he had made the journey nonetheless, and as he went in for more of Colonel George T. Miller, scooping out the colonel's left eye and popping it into his mouth with a squirting of pinkish and white ooze, he savored his revenge, chewing merrily.

Rusty was pushed to the side as the other ghouls dove in and finished the job, ripping Miller apart and pulling his intestines out of his abdomen like magicians at a magic show. Blood fountained into the air and splashed onto the bullet-riddled paintings on the wall. Miller's plasma mixed with the colors on the paintings and blended into the artwork, the canvas absorbing some, while on other parts it only dripped to the floor. Though Miller would never know it, he had joined his works of art forever, his crimson life now on display for the dead to enjoy as they fed on his carcass in the underground golden tomb of the dead.

*   *   *

About one mile from Interstate 24 was a crossroads. In the middle of this crossroad stood six souls; all looking at one another while they studied the road signs in front of them. Behind them, about a half mile, was the APC, now out of diesel fuel and abandoned. The night was fading and the first rays of light were beginning to appear, chasing the darkness away.

"So tell me again how does one steal an armored personnel carrier and not check if it has enough fuel?" Jimmy was asking Cindy and Mary.

Mary was angry and she speared him with her eyes. "Well, excuse me if we didn't have time to try and find the gas pump. I didn't see you arguing when we rolled up!"

Henry waved his hands in the air trying to keep the peace "Okay, okay, now cut it out, you two. It doesn't matter anyway. Even if you managed to get a vehicle with a full tank, sooner or later we would have run out, and diesel would've been pretty hard to find anywhere nowadays."

He was filled with antibiotics, his ankle was wrapped and cleaned, his shoulder wounds stitched shut and his ribs were taped from bandages from the well-stocked first aid kit from the APC. He was still feeling sore, but getting better with each passing hour. They all had weapons with full loads. The APC had been well-stocked with ammo and extra rifles, and now the companions had most of it with them. They carried a few extra guns in hopes of using them in trade at the next town they came across. Weapons and ammo were the currency of the day, money only good for wiping your ass.

As for food, the APC had been a horn of plenty, the large stash of MRE's found under a bench enough to keep the companions fed for weeks if they were careful. The Mylar sealed envelopes were military rations. Meals Ready to Eat, all preserved and as fresh and delicious as the day they were made.

Cindy cocked her head as she stared at the road signs and read their options out to the others for the fifth time.

"Well, we could go north to Ohio, which is thirty-five miles or we could go south to Tennessee, which is fifty miles. So which way do we go?"

They began to argue again, each giving their opinion on which way they should go, when Henry finally stepped in and held up a shiny quarter. Though he didn't need it for anything special, he still liked to carry it, feeling like he used to with change in his pocket. He would always jingle the change when he was happy and Emily would always know when he was home as he would jingle the change while he stepped through the door. He would walk over to her then, where she would be at the sink or stove and give her a big kiss on the cheek.

Thinking of Emily made him pause and he took on a wistful look as sweeping images of what he'd seen while Miller strangled him touched his consciousness. Only now they were ethereal feelings, like he'd experienced something important and didn't remember what it was.

None of the others said anything, each staring at him until Mary reached out and touched his arm.

"You okay, Henry, you look like you just saw a ghost?"

He shook himself back to reality and he smiled at her. "Yeah, Mary I'm fine, I was just thinking of something, that's all."

"Oh yeah, old man, what? Spill it, we want to know."

He shook his head slightly, a shrug of shoulders to say he wasn't talking. Then he tossed the quarter into the air.

"Okay, heads is north and tails is south."

It fell to the dusty ground and began to roll. He stepped on it to stop it from getting away from him. Picking it up, he blew the dust off it and studied the coin, then slipped it back into his pocket.

"So, what did it say? Heads or tails?" Jimmy asked with baited breath.

He shook his head again. He reached out, took Sue's hand in his, the woman smiling sheepishly at the gesture, and began walking.

"Doesn't matter, now come on, let's get going, the sun'll be up soon and it looks like a hot one."

The rest of the companions fell in line and began walking behind Henry and Sue. Raven and Cindy chatted, the teenager interested in how Cindy had managed to escape from Miller's clutches. She was opening up more with every passing hour, and there was no doubt now she had joined the team, as well as the companions accepting her as one of their own.

With a long road of walking ahead of them, Jimmy continued to chastise Mary for stealing a vehicle with almost no fuel, doing it for the fun of teasing her, if for no other reason. As for Mary, she walked with her arms crossed and pretended she wasn't listening.

The six figures moved down the dusty road and were soon lost from sight as the rising sun, filled with hope and promise, spread its life-giving rays on another day in Hell.

BOOK 7

DEAD VALLEY

by Anthony Giangregorio

Untouched Majesty

After nearly drowning in the icy waters of the Colorado River, the six weary companions come upon a beautiful valley nestled in the mountains of Colorado, where the undead plague appears to have never happened.

With the mountains protecting the valley, the deadly rain never fell, and the valley is as untouched as the day it was created.

But the group is soon captured by a secret, military research base now run by a few remaining scientists and soldiers.

On this base, unholy experiments are being carried out, and the group soon finds themselves caught in the middle of it.

Mary, Sue, Raven and Cindy are taken away to be used as breeders, the scientists wanting to create a new utopia, which the living dead can't reach, but the side effect of this is the women will lose their lives.

Henry and Jimmy, now separated and captured themselves, must find a way to save them before it's too late; the scientists unleashing every conceivable mutation at their disposal to stop them.

In the world of the living dead, the past is gone and the future is non-existent.

DEAD RECKONING: DAWNING OF THE DEAD

By Anthony Giangregorio

THE DEAD HAVE RISEN!

In the dead city of Pittsburgh, two small enclaves struggle to survive, eking out existence of hand to mouth.

But instead of working together, both groups battle for the last remaining fuel and supplies of a city filled with the living dead.

Six months after the initial outbreak, a lone helicopter arrives bearing two more survivors and a newborn baby. One enclave welcomes them, while the other schemes to steal their helicopter and escape the decaying city.

With no police, fire, or social services existing, the two will battle for dominance in the steel city of the walking dead. But when the dust settles, the question is: will remaining humans be the winners, or the losers?

When the dead walk, the line between Heaven and Hell is so twisted and bent there's no line at all.

RISE OF THE DEAD

by Anthony Giangregorio

DEATH IS ONLY THE BEGINNING!

In less than forty-eight hours, more than half the globe was infected.

In another forty-eight, the rest would be enveloped.

The reason?

A science experiment gone horribly wrong which enabled the dead to walk, their flesh rotting on their bones even as they seek human prey.

Jeremy was an ordinary nineteen year old slacker. He partied too much and had done poorly in high school. After a night of drinking and drugs, he awoke to find the world a very different place from the one he'd left the night before.

The dead were walking and feeding on the living, and as Jeremy stepped out into a world gone mad, the dead spotting him alone and unarmed in the middle of the street, he had to wonder if he would live long enough to see his twentieth birthday.

THE DARK
By Anthony Giangregorio

DARKNESS FALLS

The darkness came without warning.

irst New York, then the rest of United States, and then the world became veloped in a perpetual night without end. /ith no sunlight, eventually the planet will wither and die, bringing on a new e Age. But that isn't problem for the human race, for humanity will be dead ng before that happens. here is something in the dark, creatures only seen in nightmares, and they e on the prowl. volution has changed and man is no longer the dominant species. hen we are children, we are told not to fear the dark, that what we believe exist in the shadows is false. nfortunately, that is no longer true.

DEADFREEZE
By Anthony Giangregorio

THIS IS WHAT HELL WOULD BE LIKE IF IT FROZE OVER!

When an experimental serum for hypothermia goes horribly wrong, a all research station in the middle of Antarctica becomes overrun with an my of the frozen dead. Now a small group of survivors must battle the arctic weather and a rde of frozen zombies as they make their way across the frozen plains of tarctica to a neighboring research station. What they don't realize is that they are being hunted by an entity whose e reason for existing is vengeance; and it will find them wherever they run.

DEADFALL
By Anthony Giangregorio

It's Halloween in the small suburban town of Wakefield, Mass. While parents take their children trick or treating and others throw stume parties, a swarm of meteorites enter the earth's atmosphere and sh to earth. Inside are small parasitic worms, no larger than maggots. The worms quickly infect the corpses at a local cemetery and so begins e rise of the undead. The walking dead soon get the upper hand, with no one believing the th. That the dead now walk. Will a small group of survivors live through the zombie apocalypse? Or will they, too, succumb to the Deadfall.

DEADWATER: EXPANDED EDITION
By Anthony Giangregorio

Through a series of tragic mishaps, a small town's water supply contaminated with a deadly bacterium that transforms the town's populatio into flesh eating ghouls.

Without warning, Henry Watson finds himself thrown into a living hell whe the living dead walk and want nothing more than to feed on the living.

Now Henry's trying to escape the undead town before he becomes the ne victim.

With the military on one side, shooting civilians on sight, and a horde bloodthirsty zombies on the other, Henry must try to battle his way freedom.

With a small group of survivors, including a beautiful secretary and a wis cracking janitor to aid him, the ragtag group will do their best to stay ali and escape the city codenamed: **Deadwater.**

DEAD END: A ZOMBIE NOVEL
By Anthony Giangregorio

THE DEAD WALK!

Newspapers everywhere proclaim the dead have returned to feast on the living!

A small group of survivors hole up in a cellar, afraid to brave the masses of animated corpses, but when food runs out, they have no choice but to ventu out into a world gone mad.

What they will discover, however, is that the fall of civilization has brought out the worst in their fellow man.

Cannibals, psychotic preachers and rapists are just some of the atrocities th must face.

In a world turned upside down, it is life that has hit a Dead End.

DEAD RAGE
By Anthony Giangregorio

An unknown virus spreads across the globe, turning ordinary people into bloodthirsty, ravenous killers.

Only a small percentage of the population is immune and soon become pre to the infected.

Amongst the infected comes a man, stricken by the virus, yet still retaining his grasp on reality. His need to destroy the *normals* becomes an obsession and he raises an army of killers to seek out and kill all who aren't *changed* like himself.

A few survivors gather together on the outskirts of Chicago and find themselves running for their lives as the specter of death looms over all.

The Dead Rage virus will find you, no matter where you hide.

Also available as The Rage Plague by Permuted Press.

LIVING DEAD PRESS
Where the Dead Walk

www.livingdeadpress.com